Also by Howard W. Lewis

The Daedalus Rimes Saga

Daedalus Rimes I
ESSENCE

Daedalus Rimes II
AFTERDEATH

Daedalus Rimes III
The FIRST GALACTIC WAR

Daedalus Rimes–
The First Galactic War

Book 3 of the Daedalus Rimes Saga

A novel by
Howard W. Lewis

Copyright © 2013 Howard W. Lewis

Published by Howard W. Lewis / October 2013; Daedalus Rimes – The First Galactic War
Cover / Chapter Art by Fantasio Fine Arts

DAEDALUS RIMES III

GW1

The First Galactic War

Visit our website at
www.authorhwlewis.com

ISBN: 978-0-9887504-7-0

Acknowledgements

For my family, friends, editor and illustrator whose support and encouragement has helped me through the long process of bringing the Daedalus Rimes Saga to life.

Prologue

"When the history of the galactic war being fought over this planet is finally written it will be by those of us who manage to survive. What final version of the future comes to pass will determine who will select the words that describe humankind's greatest victory, or ultimate demise."

- James McClellen, Commander in Chief Earth Defense

1 - Ghosts

It had been four years since first contact with the Korlah. A short time, it would seem, yet the great leap into space commenced immediately as governments and the corporations they endorsed quickly carved out industrial interests and the global defense perimeter moved beyond the Earth's orbit. The technology of man merged with that of the visitors to create innovations in robotics and fabrication methods that further accelerated the expansion process. Over fifty alien-designed mining, processing, and fabrication facilities were already in full production. Another hundred deep-system sites were under construction and hundreds more were planned. Billboards, want ads, and internet, television, and radio spots called skilled workers to apply for the many new high-paying jobs.

With the opening of trade relations, Korlah technology was now appearing at the consumer level. Power generation, power storage, and medical marvels were the first to go public. Fewer and fewer trucks traveled the highways; they were being replaced by much faster petroleum-independent gravity drive transports.

On her walk home from work, Julie Rimes paused to watch one of the new transports drop down from the sky and disappear behind the building across the street from the townhouse the government had chosen for her relocation. She really didn't need to work, but it gave her something to do; the government check she received monthly was much more than she needed for the quiet life she was expected to live. She checked the sky for more activity and her eyes ran across the billboard in the distance that showed a young man in a blue jumpsuit looking up into the sky; the caption read "Limitless Opportunities with Global Security Systems." The sign was a constant reminder to Julie of how isolated and trapped she felt.

She turned back towards home and checked the mailbox by her front door. On this day, it held a solitary manila envelope. She had received these before. The package would contain letters for Julie Rimes, a name she no longer used. It was only supposed to contain personal correspondence, but often included bills and advertisements. She resisted the urge to throw it in the trash, and instead put it under her arm and went inside, where she tossed it onto the counter.

It was several hours later, after she'd had dinner and was about to read a book, that she remembered the envelope. She tore it open and pulled out the first letter: a bill that immediately went into the trash. A bank statement and several advertisements followed the bill. The next envelope was yellowed with age and the stamp on it was two issues out of date. Across the front in bold red ink was stamped "Postage due," and the address was penciled neatly in script. She dropped the manila envelope and held the letter with both hands. The handwriting was as clear and unmistakable as a spoken voice. She checked the postmark; it was less than three weeks old. By the time she had torn the envelope open and pulled the folded pages out, her hands were trembling. She unfolded and smoothed the pages flat on the table and took a deep, calming breath, as she did when she taught others to control their emotions. She was certain it was Dade's writing, Dade's words on the page.

The alien he had become had told her Dade was dead, and the FBI told her that the alien had been killed the morning Julie was attacked by a religious fanatic. It was because of that attack and the outstanding threat to her life that Julie was being protected by the federal government. The concept that Dade could speak to her from beyond the grave hit her hard. It was another ten minutes before the tears that blurred her eyes cleared enough that she was able to begin reading.

Dear Julie,

There are few regrets deeper and darker than mine. So many mistakes and miscalculations. I can only hope this letter is not yet another. You are one of the few who know the truth about what I am, yet there is so much more that you have yet to learn. I am only now beginning to realize the extent of my part in what is happening. If asking you for help brings you harm, I will be beyond forgiveness—if I am not already.

I believed that once I'd told you of my death, once that message had been delivered, my needs would be fulfilled and Teela could live the life she wanted. I could not have been more mistaken. We have been Rebecca's prisoner since the day we visited you. What happened that day and in the months that followed, I cannot clearly remember. Rebecca can fabricate memories and implant them into a person's mind. She made me see and believe things that weren't real. It took me months to sort through the false memories and realize that what I thought was a bad dream had really happened. I went willingly with Rebecca because she made me believe General McClellen sent Beth and Agent Cooper to take me prisoner. I realize now that McClellan was attempting to protect me from Rebecca. Beth's fears of mind control were justified; I ignored her, and because of it she is dead. They're all dead. Rebecca put it in their minds to shoot each other, and they did. She put it in my mind that she was my friend, and I believed it. I'm not making excuses; I am to blame. If it were not for me, Rebecca would have been dead a long time ago. Now I don't know if it's even possible to kill her.

All I really wanted to do was tell you how much I loved you, how I never would have left you. All Teela wanted to do is save lives. Neither of us could bear the thought of being responsible for more death. We thought that we could disappear and escape from the conflict—what a foolish notion that was. We gave away our identity, and now, as far as anyone knows, we don't exist.

Rebecca knew what we wanted and used those thoughts to control us and make us her prisoner. She took us to a farmhouse in Iowa, I'm not sure exactly where. It was a nice place with a small man-made lake surrounded by fields of corn. It was beautiful and peaceful. We thought we had found the paradise we were hoping for, a place where we could both finally heal the wounds of our past. It wasn't long after our arrival that we realized the truth. Along with that realization we discovered something else, something both frightening and amazingly wonderful: Teela was pregnant.

She wanted to go home to be with her sisters and mothers. I didn't blame her. For once in her life she would be able to fit in, to be a productive member of her family. We would have gone, but Rebecca refused to let us go. The psychotic bitch has it in her head that Teela's child is the true Shawlmon who will become the first emperor of the galaxy, sent by God to save the universe from evil. We tried to escape by slipping out a window. We spent four nights and three days running and hiding in the cornfields before they caught us.

Rebecca is too powerful for us. Our telepathic abilities are useless against her. We are strong enough now to keep her from controlling us, but not strong enough to use it against her. Teela is somehow linked to Rebecca now. Any attempt at using telepathy seems to open a window directly to Rebecca and she can use it to find us.

For over three years, we were locked in an underground cell. When our baby was born I only saw him for a moment; a perfect, beautiful baby boy. I don't believe he's a hybrid, as Rebecca claims. He was perfect, human from head to toe, but they took him. They cut us open, took our baby boy, and left us to die strapped to the delivery table.

For some reason, Rebecca didn't kill us on the spot. I think she was afraid that we would transfer into another body. The woman who claims to speak for God left us to die alone in the dark.

When it became clear that no one was coming back, we fought our bindings with every ounce of strength we had. I don't know how long we lay there. We passed out several times from the pain, but the leather wrist straps must have been old or the blood from our struggles softened them, because we eventually pulled one free of the rivets. Our hands were swollen and numb, but with enough time, we managed to remove the rest of the straps. The damage to our wrists was painful, but it was nothing compared to the gash left by the C-section. We did our best to wrap the incision and stop the bleeding, but I think we nearly bled to death because it was over a week before we could stand up without passing out. Teela has a tough side that continues to amaze me. The incision healed badly and we still have bouts of intense abdominal pain, but I'm the one who complains the most.

We discovered our prison was an abandoned missile silo. It didn't take long before we gave up trying to get out through the doors. I could tell from the discoloration and peeled paint they had been welded shut from the outside. There was an outdated supply of food and water to last for several years. As it turned out, this was a fortunate discovery. I found some tools and opened a hatch into the ventilation system. It was a long climb up, one that we got good at. At the top we could see out, but there were stout steel bars welded over the openings. We searched every inch of our steel prison for a way out and found nothing. After exhausting all possibilities, we fell into a terrible depression. Suicide seemed the only alternative to eventual starvation. Months passed while we waited for someone to return; no one ever did.

Eventually we inventoried the food and water and calculated that with careful rationing, we could survive for about four years. Revisiting all possible escape routes, we returned to the exhaust duct with the steel bars. For months we continued to pry the one-inch steel bars apart, making only miniscule progress with each attempt. It was during one of these exhausting efforts that I saw light shine through a seam in the ducting. Every time I pressed, a slit of light appeared at the seam. I dug through my tools and found a little mirror with a telescoping handle. With it I was able to look down through the opening and discovered that the top section of the exhaust duct was held together by nothing more than a dozen rusty 3/8 inch bolts. We shifted our attention to the seam and attacked the bolts with a vengeance. Our progress was tremendous, yet it still took many long months of prying, rocking, and twisting to finally break those stubborn bastards. The mushroom-shaped top of the vent fell to the side when the last bolt gave up with an angry shriek. The roof of the main complex is at ground level, I climbed out of the air shaft into a field of dry grass and weeds. The area above the silo was surrounded by a chain-link fence topped with razor wire. The concrete entrance to the silo was disguised to look like a wooden storage shed. Next to the shed was a rolling gate, beyond which was a gravel road that disappeared into low rolling hills and scrub brush.

For the first time in what I estimate to be more than three years, we were free. It was daytime, hot and humid. The sun felt like it was going to set our skin on fire. It was more than just being locked up in a hole and kept out of the sun; I know now that Korlah are nocturnal. The dim light of the glow orbs aboard the spacecraft carrier is normal to them. We are much more comfortable in the dark.

We found a place in the shade and waited for the sun to set before we tried to get through the fence. I can't remember the sky ever looking so beautiful or the air smelling so fresh. It was while I was reveling in our hard-won freedom that I saw the black cubes moving upward in the evening sky. I had no idea what they were, but Teela knew immediately. The Korlah call them sky lifts. She says spaceports and sky lifts are constructed after an invasion to transport the bulk of the harvest off-world. The cubes are simple in construction, much larger than factory ships, and have ten times the cargo capacity. They are lifted up by grav plates to shipping hubs in synchronous orbit, where specialized cargo ships called haulers exchange empty cubes for full ones. The empty containers are sent back down to be filled. My heart sank when Teela explained this to me. I was certain that during our captivity, Earth had fallen to the Kahshinki.

Unlike the last time we escaped, this time we have a destination, and at present, no one is pursuing us. The spaceport was much farther away than it looked, and as luck would have it, it started raining on the day of our departure. We walked for two days before we could see the space port's ground installation. The rain has been both a blessing and a curse. It's been so overcast during the day that we have been able to travel both day and night. The rain, thunder, and lightning terrified Teela, but like I said, she's tough, and in spite of her fear, she refused to let the storm slow us down.

We approached a house and found a celebrity gossip magazine in the trash. This was the first news of world events that I had read since my incarceration. It was a surprise to read about the lives of Korlah-human transfers. An article about the marriage of the UNE chairman to a Korlah predicted that their union would undermine global politics. Despite the negative slant, I was relieved to learn that my plan for an alliance was successful and that the governments of Earth are cooperating in response to the threat of invasion. This gives me hope that I am not too late.

I'm writing this letter from an abandoned farmhouse. It's a sad little place buried in a field of weeds that once was a lawn. The lady who lived here died over five years ago, and the house is as it was the day she was buried. Dust and cobwebs cover every object in the house. Whoever organized the funeral and reception left and never came back. The funeral programs and dirty dishes from the last gathering are still on the table. There are clothes in the closet and drawers and rotting food in the refrigerator and cupboards. I found envelopes, stamps and this stationary in a desk by the front door. If it wasn't for the family of packrats under the sink and all the spiders, this place would be as lifeless as the old woman it belonged to.

I can see lights on at a farm in the distance. On my way to the spaceport this evening I will put this in their mailbox and hope it finds its way to you. We're taking a chance mailing it, but we hope by the time anyone finds it we will be off this planet.

Rebecca wants Teela dead, and will try to find and kill her when she learns that we did not die in the missile silo. If I honestly believed we stood a chance against her on our own, I wouldn't hesitate to face her. Our only hope rests with friends we have abandoned who believe us dead. We realize that the probability of our success is slim, which is why I decided to write this letter.

I know it's wrong to drag you into this, but your address is the only one I remember. It's been a long time, and I may be too late, but there is no one else I can ask, no one else they will believe. I need you to contact the FBI and have them get this letter to General McClellen. Don't use a phone, especially a cell phone. As crazy as it may sound, Rebecca can get into a person's mind through the phone. Tell McClellen that Rebecca has a plan to seize power globally. Once she has unified and taken control of the world's religions, she will incite a global religious coup and seize control of Earth's governments. She is recruiting followers who are deeply devout and programming them to be fanatical supporters of her cause. Rebecca and her followers believe our child is the son of God, some sort of galactic messiah. McClellen is up against a powerful adversary whose followers, in all probability, will have already infiltrated every level of both the governments and militaries of Earth.

I realize how insane I must sound. I am writing this letter, yet it is Teela who is holding the pencil. She is silent, but I can feel her angst that I am writing this as if I exist as an individual. Mine is a shared existence. I can only describe it as being a passenger on a journey that defies logic. I am a part of Teela now; there is no way back. This is something the Korlah call the afterdeath. Whether or not we survive what lies ahead, this will be the last time you hear from me. You need to know that, just as Teela needed me to say it.

D.R.

2 - Rally

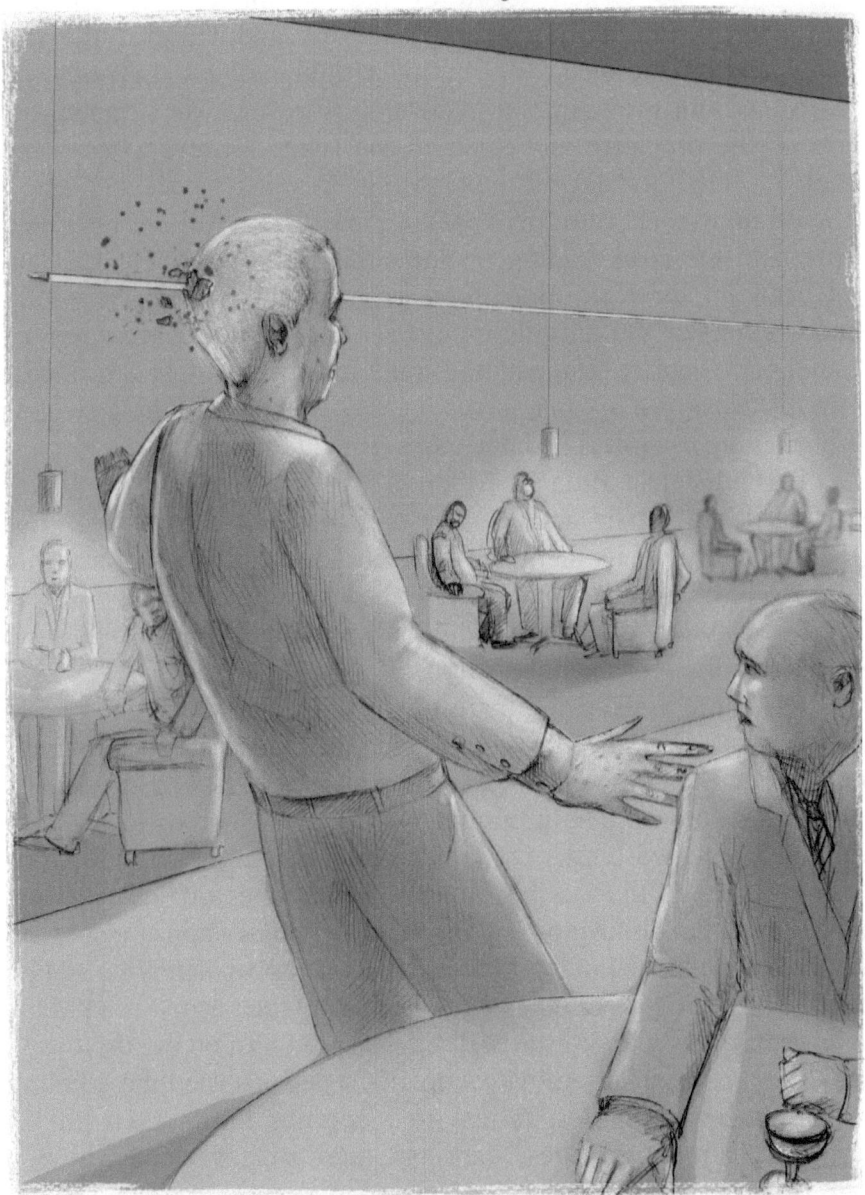

Vista Bonita Ranch, five miles northwest of Mendoza, Argentina

Thin streams of dust whipped over the crest of the ridge overlooking the eastern edge of the distant city as Richard Parkhurst spurred his horse one last time and climbed the last twenty feet of the steep trail. With a tight pull on the reins, he turned the dark grey Arabian mare into the wind. He stopped just short of the precipice and released the reins. Relieved, his horse shook its head and let out a rumbling breath, its neck and chest lathered in sweat. From this vantage Parkhurst could see his ranch below and the road leading up the valley from the city. The sun had been up for little more than an hour and was casting long shadows under the morning clouds. The onetime secretary of Homeland Security mopped the mud formed by dust and sweat from his brow, put his sunglasses on, and watched for the arrival of the surviving members and delegates of the Quorum.

Parkhurst had little in common with these people of power and privilege, yet he shared their meteoric fall from grace. The Quorum and all of its members were accused of crimes against the Korlah and humanity. Together they had gone into hiding after the failed assassination attempt on President McCormick and Shawlmon, the Korlah ambassadress.

Parkhurst walked the mare down the ridge to the far end of his vineyard. Once he reached the straight road through the vines, he whipped the horse into a full gallop and raced through the fields toward the stables. The premium wool gaucho hat with its silver scalloped conchos blew off his head, but he didn't slow down or even look back; this was his last day at the vineyard. After today, his favored hat, like most of his worldly possessions, would no longer be needed. Slowing to a canter as he approached the stable, he rode past the first of many cars driving up the narrow road to his ranch house. As a dark-blue Mercedes passed him on the driveway, he nodded respectfully to its occupants. They returned the greeting with tight-lipped smiles, failing to recognize Parkhurst with his surgically altered features, dark tan, and shaggy wind-whipped hair.

As the guests arrived at the house, Parkhurst's staff saw to their accommodations. A late breakfast was served, followed by lunch, afternoon drinks, and a sunset dinner on a veranda overlooking the lights of Mendoza. The guests mingled and talked about events past and present, and on occasion expressed their hopes for the future. This meeting would be the first formal gathering of Quorum leadership since the arrival of the Korlah on Earth. Parkhurst had called the meeting to rally for change; he wanted the Quorum to shift its defensive posture to one of aggressive offense. With or without their support, though, he was already committed to plans he hoped would reshape world leadership to better serve the needs of those who had the most to lose.

As the last ribbon of sunlight disappeared over the Andes, Parkhurst joined his seventy guests, who were sipping after-dinner cocktails inside a spacious hall filled with overstuffed leather chairs and couches. He walked to the center of the floor-to-ceiling windows, the vista of city lights behind him. Tapping the microphone on his lapel, he verified that it was working before he addressed the group.

"Welcome, keepers of continuity. Thank you for coming. For those of you who have not met me, I am Richard Parkhurst. I have been master-at-arms of the northeast council for the last fifteen years. Most of you in this room owe me your lives. It was my section that provided notification and relocation of those charged with war crimes by the Korlah. With few exceptions, everyone who has followed my instructions is free and alive. It is time we reorganize and change our global strategy if we intend to remain as such. Under my leadership—"

"Your leadership?" the elected leader of the Quorum shouted as he stood. "A power play, is that what this meeting is about, Dick?" Tall and thin, Rodney Harker was in his early seventies and had short, thinning white hair. He unbuttoned his Armani suit coat, put his hands on his hips, and without giving Parkhurst a chance to reply, continued, "I am the senior member of the Quorum. I will say what our global strategy will be. You're a hired hand, Dick. Hell, you're not even a voting member."

Parkhurst casually reached into his jacket and produced a small black pistol. With skill developed over many hours and hundreds of rounds of ammunition, he raised the pistol and fired.

The bullet struck Harker squarely in the forehead and splattered the wall behind him with blood and brains. There were a few stifled screams as the man fell over the back of his chair and onto the floor, and then there was silence.

"All of you," Parkhurst said, calmly using the pistol to make a sweeping gesture across the room, "have placed all of the funds you were able to pull from your offshore accounts into my care. With those funds, I have established security for all of you, while at the same time creating covers and new corporate ventures that will allow us to pursue control of global politics again. Although you provided the funding, it is I who control the majority of the Quorum's corporate assets. The previous Quorum leadership failed you. There is no continuity to keep. I have provided the leadership required to preserve our autonomy during this crisis. The reason you are all here today, and not dead or detained pending trial, is because of my leadership. We are here today to coordinate the restoration of the Quorum's influence on Earth and beyond. Is there anyone else who believes that they are better suited to lead this venture?"

A man rose to his feet, raising his hands as if in surrender. "Richard, everyone here is grateful for everything you have done to preserve the organization and its members. Given the opportunity, I believe you would easily have won an election. Rodney was influential and well respected; he has always upheld the Quorum's charter of peace and profit. All of us here are certainly killers in our own respect. But we kill for purpose. What purpose did killing him serve?"

"Expedience!" Parkhurst shouted. "We don't have the luxury of the time it would take to form committees, hold debates, and have an election. We need to act now! I'm glad to hear that you realize the peace it takes to preserve your profits has been paid for with blood. Your forefathers fought their battles behind the scenes without the help of thugs like me. Yes! I recognize what I am, just as you do, but these are desperate times, which call for desperate measures. You will all need to get your hands dirty if you hope to restore the influence of the Quorum and regain your wealth.

"The Kahshinki have imposed a deadline. If we are unable to begin shipments of meat as agreed, they will attack this planet's infrastructure. To buy some time, I have managed to negotiate shipments from our associates in Africa and South America. Currently, the promise of jobs has more people lining up to go off world, than we have cargo ships that can safely get them past the system's perimeter defenses unnoticed. Each of you will need to do your part in organizing the movement of product off-world and bringing the weapons and technology back to Earth that we need to regain control.

"When you return to your rooms, you will each find a package. In it are instructions that detail your role in the new organization. If you choose not to participate, leave the package and leave the compound with the knowledge that you will no longer be protected by the Quorum."

Parkhurst returned his pistol to its holster and straightened his jacket. He pulled the microphone from his lapel; it rustled and popped softly as he turned it off and handed it to his assistant. He walked to the bar, giving a cursory nod or subtle wave to those who made eye contact with him. By the time the bartender had poured him a scotch on the rocks, the line of sycophants was already forming to pay respect and pledge their loyalty to the self-imposed leader of the Quorum.

Several hours later, Richard Parkhurst and his advisors and bodyguards drove out to an open area in the center of the vineyard. After several minutes of sitting quietly in the dark, Parkhurst got out of the van and stretched. His entourage followed.

"What's keeping them?" he demanded.

"Could be anything. I'll check," his assistant replied, tapping a message into a Kahshinki communications device that looked like a thin laptop computer. The bodyguards took positions around the perimeter and Barry, Parkhurst's advisor and close friend, moved to his side. Currently providing paramilitary security for the ranch, he was dressed in camouflage slacks and an olive green short sleeve shirt. Barry was a large man, heavily muscled and lean for his fifties. He wore his nearly white hair in a short flattop, and the blurred and faded tattoo on his forearm identified him as an ex-Navy Seal.

"Richard, you're the biggest asshole I've ever known. I'm going to miss you," he said quietly.

Parkhurst grinned. "You know, Barry, we've been friends a long time. You have always been there for me when I needed you. When I ask you for an honest opinion, I get it. I'm going to miss that. How many of them do you think will follow my instructions?"

"Every single one of them," Barry replied. "It might have been a problem yesterday, but this morning I learned that President McCormick has given in to pressure and agreed to turn over the Quorum members he's been holding to the UNE and the Earth-Korlah war crimes tribunal. All fifteen who have been tried to date have been convicted. Twelve were condemned to death and three were sentenced to life in prison. That tidbit of information and a video of a Korlah execution, combined with some photographs of the acid assassinations, will ensure their absolute loyalty."

"You got a video? Barry! You're fantastic."

"Oh yeah, death by consumption. Teddy Smith and some poor schmuck I didn't recognize getting eaten by Kahshinki prisoners. They dissolve you and then eat the goo that once was you. Nasty little bastards, these allies of ours."

"Like the assassinations of our people; dissolved by acid."

"Yeah, and that assassin bitch is my first target. We're gonna turn this around, Richard. We will be the hunters and they will be the hunted."

Parkhurst turned and put a hand on Barry's shoulder.

"Be careful, Barry. Elliot was hunting this woman, and she got him. I want you to direct the wet work. Keep your distance. Whoever this girl is, she's dangerous. I need you alive."

"Whatever you say, boss. Look, here comes your ride."

A dot of light in the sky had dropped straight down and raced to them in the time it took Barry to raise his hand and point.

3 - Skybound

A fine mist dropped from the dark clouds, covering Teela's face in dewy drops that formed puddles and trickled down the crease of her eyelid and into her ear. She woke with a start and shook her head to remove the water. She shivered in the night air and rubbed her arms through the tattered denim coveralls she'd rescued from the field rats, believing the faded blue fabric to be a better choice than white sheets from the bunker or an old flowered dress from the farmhouse. She had hoped the coveralls would provide some protection from the cold, but now that they were soaked and chilled by the night air, they wicked away her body heat and brought on fits of shaking that rattled her teeth.

Days of continuous rain and drizzle had turned the fields into deep mud that sapped her strength with every step. The only benefit of the thick black goo was that it camouflaged her pallid face and hands. Teela looked up at the dense clouds that obscured the sky and therefore any means to gauge time by the moon or stars. Reaching into her pocket, she withdrew the wristwatch given to her by Captain Simpson years before. She had used it to count the days, months, and years of her captivity. Tonight she would use it to time her escape. According to the watch, it was approaching midnight, and hopefully the best time for her to try to slip into the spaceport.

The spaceport was an old airfield in the open flatlands, where there was little cover for Teela as she made her way toward the fence at the perimeter. She selected an area near some 1940s-era brick hangars that provided modest cover in the form of low brush and bushes. A rusted chain-link fence topped with a fresh coil of razor wire was all that blocked her access the sky lift. After crawling across a muddy field, she crouched in the dense brush near a dirt road just outside the fence and patiently waited to make her next move. She kept looking at her watch. A security truck had driven by every fifteen minutes since Teela came within sight of the spaceport earlier that evening, but it was 12:40 and the truck had not come by since midnight. She wondered if the rounds changed late at night. She pulled a pair of rusty pliers from her pocket and held them awkwardly. Salvaged from a drawer at the farmhouse, they were the closest thing she could find to bolt cutters. They were a unique type of pliers, designed for use on barbed-wire fences. They had a hammerhead on one side of the jaws and a twisting pick on the other, and the jaws could pull staples from fence posts and crush steel rings to attach fencing. But at that moment, Teela was interested in the wire-cutting notches on the handle.

After waiting another twenty-five minutes with numb feet, an extended fit of shivering convinced her she was too cold to wait any longer and she put the watch away and stood up to cross the road. Just then, the sound of an engine caused her to duck back down. The patrol truck came by slowly, shining its spotlight across the fields and brush along the road. Teela hugged her knees and tried to calm her shaking until the truck disappeared around the corner of the spaceport's fence. She stumbled to the fence on legs that felt like stumps and began to fumble with the pliers. Her hand had two thumbs that easily provided enough pressure to cut the wires, but her fingers were painfully pinched each time the jaws snapped shut after cutting a wire. It took several wires and several blood blisters before she learned how to keep her fingers out of the way. Although the buildings blocked the flood lamps from the field beyond, the low clouds reflected the light and illuminated the entire area. Halfway through cutting an opening in the fence large enough to slip through, Teela realized the rain had washed the mud from her hands and face and the light was shining brightly off her pallid skin. "We can put more mud on later," she whispered.

Five stressful minutes later, she had cut a hole large enough to squeeze through. She ran between the buildings only to discover another fence, this one fabricated from corrugated sheet metal topped with more razor wire. There were no doors on this side of the building, and the windows were at least ten feet above the ground and well out of her reach. Going back, she went around one building and then the other, only to find that she was fenced in on all sides. She returned to the hole she had cut and squeezed back out.

After Teela had taken no more than two steps from the fence, a security truck came around the corner, bathing her in the light of its headlights. The engine gunned and the truck raced toward her. There was no point in hiding. She ran into the muddy field and the truck slid to a stop behind her. The most she could do was a fast walk as she sloughed through calf-deep mud.

A gunshot sounded like a thunderclap and a bullet whirred over her shoulder and hit the mud ahead of her with a loud splat. Trapped in the open, she stopped, dropped the pliers, and raised her hands. The all too familiar feeling of hopelessness overwhelmed her; she was freezing, exhausted, and a captive once again. It was not her intention to behave belligerently, but her thoughts were so torn and chaotic that she ignored the instructions the two men shouted at her. She ended up being viciously poked and prodded as they herded her into the caged back seat of their truck.

The men were wearing uniforms, which could only be called that because of their somewhat similar color and the spaceport security patches sewn onto the shoulders. Both were a few weeks shy of a haircut and a day or two past their last shave. The forty-something man who got into the passenger's seat seemed to be in charge. He shouted orders at Teela and the driver, who was at least a decade younger than him and had a physique that spoke of too much beer and television. From the way they both brandished their weapons and kept their distance, it was apparent to Teela that they were far more frightened of her than she was of them.

"You're damn lucky you missed, Lester. They got laws against kill'n um les'n they try to kill you first," the driver said as he got in and closed the door.

"Lucky, my ass. That was a warning shot. I was aiming to clip an ear, but these things don't have ears. Nobody said nothing about these things trying to come to Earth. Where do you think it would have gone if we hadn't caught it, Willy? It must have come down on the last shipment. What if it's not alone?"

Lester looked over his shoulder at Teela through the wire mesh that separated the front seat from the back. He had only seen pictures of Korlah on TV and in magazines, and he intended to take this opportunity to have a good long look. He decided that noodles was a fair description of the things growing out of this one's skull. They looked wet and slightly pink compared to the pale white skin of its face. Like its claws, its fangs were impressive, and he could imagine the damage they could cause. He knew this creature was a female, and he could see the shape of breasts beneath her wet clothes, yet he could not think of it as a she. It was then that she looked up, and her ebony eyes met his. He turned away, unsure of why this creature's gaze terrified him.

"I guess this here's a genuine illegal alien," Willy said, laughing at his own joke. "What we gonna do with it, Lester? It's Sunday morning on a holiday weekend. You gonna have a hell of a time getting a hold of someone."

"We'll lock it in the storeroom on the side of the machine shed. Sam and Jim can meet us there; Sam can drive this truck and Jim the other. I'll have them patrol the perimeter. We'll tell the dock foreman what happened, then you and I will search the area until help arrives."

They took Teela through a security gate and into the spaceport to a group of old aircraft hangars that were being used for storage. It was at the back of one of these hangars that they used their guns and clubs to coerce her out of the truck and into a small storage room with a crumbling concrete floor. The steel door of the storeroom closed with a groan from its rusted hinges and Teela heard the padlock click shut on the hasp. She listened as Lester gave Sam and Jim instructions and two trucks sped off. Lester and Willy searched the attached hangar before moving to the next structure, leaving her in relative silence.

The storeroom smelled of dirt, oil, and mildewed burlap, and with the exception of some trash and several wooden crates, the small six-foot-square room was empty. She would have attempted to pull the chain that hung from a single light bulb hanging from a rotted wire, but she could see better without it. It was with her hisnah, the star shaped pits between her eyes, that she saw a rat appear from under a bench that bisected the wall opposite the door, under which several wooden crates were stacked. The rat looked at her for a few seconds and then disappeared under the bench. She heard it scurry away, farther away than the small room would allow. She pulled the crates out from under the bench and discovered that two of the boards that formed the back wall were broken about a foot above the ground where something on the other side had struck them. Teela reached through the gap and pulled one of the boards toward her easily; the nails on the base board acted like a hinge. The second board took a few hard pulls before breaking the rest of the way through. The opening looked like it might be large enough for her to squeeze through.

After a painful struggle through the narrow gap that further shredded her coveralls and took some skin with it, Teela clawed her way into the adjacent hangar. She found herself between the back wall and an old flatbed truck. She could see light streaming between floor-to-ceiling rolling doors across the room. Teela realized that when Lester returned he would discover the opening under the bench and realize where she had gone. In an effort to buy time, she pulled one board back into position and wedged it in place with a shard of wood, then reached through the opening and pulled the crates under the bench closer to the wall. She pulled the last board up and pinned it as tightly as she could with a rusty nail she found on the floor. The wall was now in better shape than when she found it. The rat would need to find another path into the room, and unless Lester or his partner did a thorough examination, they would assume she had vanished into thin air.

The rat ran across the narrow opening in the doorway. The shadow it cast appeared large on the opposite wall and gave Teela a fright. Stopping by the door, it stood up on its hind legs, sniffed the air, and sat on its haunches and stared intently at Teela. Through the gap in the doors, she could see that the sky lift was more than a hundred yards away across an open field that was bathed in floodlights. Dock workers surrounded the black cube and were busily emptying its payload with forklifts onto waiting trucks. Between the lights and the traffic, Teela could see no way to get there unnoticed. She turned back to the building in the hope that she could find something to use as a disguise.

Just inside the rolling doors was a waist-high heap of discarded human and Korlah space gear. Upon closer examination, Teela could see engine parts, control modules, pressure suits, and other random metallic debris. It appeared to be salvage slated for reprocessing. After digging through the pile for several minutes, she concluded that there was nothing that might help her pass as a dock worker, but the geodesic shape of a transport's beach-ball-sized gravity drive unit caught her eye. Near it, a box spilled out six Kahshinki-style keyboard control panels. She recalled seeing a selection of chain tie-downs on the back of the flatbed.

Picking up a partially used roll of duct tape, she looked through its center and focused on the truck. Borrowed memories coalesced in an instant as a plan presented itself. Although the chances of assembling a functional spacecraft with these discarded parts was highly improbable, the idea thrilled Daedalus and intrigued Teela.

"This is the key to our freedom," Teela whispered, running her hands over the geodesic ball. A quick examination found one crushed plate, but she was unconcerned. "Not a problem, we'll make this the top. We don't need it because gravity will drive us down," she said, verbalizing thoughts that belonged to both her and Daedalus. Moving to the box of control panels, she sorted through them for one that was still biologically viable.

"They're all dead or dying, starving to death. Nobody's fed them in a long time. We're probably going to have the same problem with the drive unit," she said.

She flipped the control panel over and opened its underside. The odor engulfed her immediately; the sour acrid smell of the Kahshinki and their biotechnology. Like all Korlah and Kahshinki electronics, this control panel ran on living tissue. Nutrients would normally be injected into the unit's stomach as needed, but these units had been unused and unfed for too long. Without the nutrient soup or a means to inject it, Teela was forced to hand-feed it, an operation both disgusting and dangerous. The circuit's organ had dropped into a state of hibernation and barely stirred when she poked at it. Using the claw of her thumb, she opened the vein in her wrist and let blood trickle onto the cluster of black withered strings she knew to be the unit's stomach. The black strings stirred, wiggled frantically, and leapt toward her hand. Teela pulled away quickly. When they failed to find the source of the blood, the strings dropped back down and began soaking up the blood. She continued feeding the unit for a few more minutes until she was confident it had received enough protein to function properly.

Feeding the gravity drive unit would be more difficult. It would need more than blood. It would need flesh. With that thought, she searched the shadows by the door. The rat had moved to a gap by some oil drums and was busily grooming its fur. Teela's predatory instincts surfaced as she began a silent and stealthy approach. Moving out of the rat's line of sight, she approached from the side of the oil drum. Either hearing her or curious as to where she had gone, the rat poked its head out from behind the drum. Teela extended her claws and stabbed at the rat, missing it by a fraction of an inch. It shot away and raced along the bottom of the door toward the open gap.

Stop! The telepathic command shot from Teela's mind like a bullet. The rat tumbled to the ground and lay quivering just inside the opening of the door. Teela stared at it, not realizing for a moment what had happened.

Over ten thousand miles away at an estate on the coast of South Africa, Rebecca paused midsentence before dropping her cup of tea. The vision appeared clearly in her mind: the silhouette of a rodent in the opening of a lighted doorway. The image, like a spoken voice, was as unique and distinct as its owner. It was a voice Rebecca had never thought she would hear again.

"No!" she screamed.

"It's done, it happened, it was an accident," Teela whispered. She picked up the rat and took it to the drive unit. "She knows we're alive now, but she won't know where we are. We can still escape." Teela doubted the words as she spoke them. She released the seal on the drive unit's damaged plate to purge the remains of its dead biological circuitry, which poured out as a thick, foul-smelling black goo. The organism had cannibalized this section, as Teela had suspected. She hoped that none of the other internal components had suffered a similar fate. After the putrefied contents had drained, she dropped the rat in. Black threads slid slowly out of holes around the perimeter of the opening and onto the rat. They began to ooze digestive enzymes as they wrapped around it. More threads appeared, moving faster and faster and growing thicker as they drew sustenance from the rat. By the time Teela pressed the dented plate back into position, the rat was completely encased in writhing tentacles.

"Well, that should be enough meat to power this unit for a day or two, and we only need ten to fifteen minutes. The real test will be whether or not it links up," she said.

She set the control panel on an oil drum and began pressing its indentations, entering the calibration sequence that would let it find and synchronize with the drive unit. After several minutes of this, the geodesic ball rolled over half a turn and then spun three quarters of a turn counterclockwise.

"There you are," she said. "Okay, let's see if I can rotate the damaged plate to the top." She tapped the indentations on the control panel, rotating the ball first one way and then the other until she had the dented plate on top.

"Once we get it up and establish directions, we'll be ready to go," she said, slowly pressing the indentation on the control panel that would raise the drive unit. The geodesic ball shot upward, striking a rafter beam with a loud thump that shook the roof. Compensating for the lack of attached mass, it dropped back to a few feet above the floor and hovered there. Dust knocked loose from the beams showered the room. Teela held her breath and listened intently, hoping no one had heard.

Working as quickly as she could, Teela guided the drive unit to the flatbed truck and positioned it just behind the cab. Using all of the steel mesh and chains she could find, she lashed the ball as tightly to the truck bed as possible.

Of the three pressure suits in the pile, only one had enough power left to generate a little bit of oxygen. The torn knee could be a problem, she thought, noting a six-inch-long rip, but she put the suit on anyway. As she was dressing she heard trucks drive up. She wasn't certain how many, but she knew it was more than two. There were the sounds of vehicle doors being opened and closed and tailgates dropping, followed by rattling equipment, footsteps and muffled voices. The rasping sound of the storeroom door being opened was quite clear. Just on the other side of the wall from where she stood she could hear their voices clearly.

"It was in here. I swear it!"

"How did it get out?"

"I don't know. The door was locked. You saw it."

"Who else has a key?"

"Ah... the dayshift super has a key. I don't know who else."

There was a pause and then she could hear a man shouting outside the storeroom.

"Seal the area, search every building—twice. Find it!"

Leaving the face piece of her pressure suit open, Teela took the control panel and climbed into the cab of the truck. She hastily duct-taped the panel to the steering wheel, then wrapped the damaged knee of her pressure suit with the rest of the tape.

The hangar's door rolled open. Two soldiers began to sweep the interior with large high-intensity flashlights. Teela froze when the beams of light stopped on her. A pause followed. The wide-open pupils of her eyes glowed blood red in the dark cab of the truck. They stared at her, and she stared back. She fastened the seat belt and slowly pulled the strap until it was tightly cinched around her waist. The soldiers raised their weapons just as her fingers found the buttons of the control panel.

With a shriek of tortured steel, the drive unit twisted in the chains as the truck lurched forward and upward. The truck plowed through the partially open door and ripped it off its rails. Wooden planks snapped and the steel rails bent as a section of the door folded over the front of the truck. The rattle of gunfire was met by the sound of bullets smacking the side of the truck.

Mounting the control panel on the steering wheel was immediately proven to be a bad decision. Debris struck the front wheels and forced them sharply to the left. The steering wheel spun and ripped Teela's hands from the controls.

A trail of dust marked the ascent of the truck as it corkscrewed up into the morning sky, throwing the folded garage door off after a few gyrations. Teela managed to grab the steering wheel and pull herself toward it. She stabbed frantically at the controls until she was finally able to stop the spinning. The truck was several hundred feet in the air, but was now on a steep downward slope and heading straight for the runway's tarmac with its left side. She clenched the steering wheel with one hand and directed the gravity drive unit to turn the truck so that it was facing forward. The truck and chains groaned under the strain of gravity as Teela made adjustments she hoped would bring the truck into level flight. Somewhat under control, and flying at over eighty miles an hour, the truck started to level off, but it was not soon enough. The truck hit the ground. The suspension screamed and the rotten old tires shredded on impact; the steel rims dug into the asphalt and threw out a shower of sparks. The back of truck lifted and the drive unit fought to keep it level. Teela jabbed the controls, telling the drive to climb, and a chain snapped like a rubber band. It ripped through the back window, just missing her head. Like an old man rising from his chair, the dilapidated truck moaned as it lifted off the ground and stumbled upward into the dawn sky. The flight was anything but smooth. The stretched and broken chains allowed the gravity drive unit to shift about, making the truck weave left and right, dipping forward and then back as its center of gravity shifted and the drive unit fought to pull it upward.

Teela focused on a shiny dot in the pale blue sky that she knew to be a sky hub in the Earth's orbit. As the truck rose high above the plains and the sky darkened almost to black, the details of the orbiting structure came into view. It was then that Teela began gasping for air. She closed the face mask of her pressure suit and turned on the oxygen generator. A red light illuminated at the top of the visor and a soft dinging sound reminded her that there were only a few minutes of power left. She knew that when that light went out, the only breathable air would be whatever was left in the helmet.

A jet raced past on her right and turned sharply to the left, disappearing in the distance.

"It will be back," Teela growled. She doubled her rate of ascent, hoping it would be enough. The likelihood that she would be able to dodge missiles seemed remote. One more radical move and the drive unit would break free, and then she and the truck would plummet back to Earth.

The jet did return. It passed under her moments before she left the upper atmosphere. Free of the Earth's gravity and her fear of being attacked, Teela focused on steering, which was much easier in the weightlessness space. She slowed her approach toward the massive black disc looming before her.

At more than a thousand feet in diameter and several hundred feet thick, the sky hub was much larger than she'd expected. Around its circumference, an array of docking stations and hangars contained spacecraft Teela had never seen before. She was closing in on one of the empty hangars when the light in her helmet died and the alarm emitted one last anemic ding. The pressure in her helmet began to drop and Teela let go of the controls to grab the knee of her suit, realizing that the tape was not sealing it shut anymore. She slowed the leak with her hands, and looked up just before impact.

The truck slammed onto the hangar deck and its bent rims and undercarriage gouged ruts in the floor before it ground to a stop just short of the inner wall. Teela released the seat belt and pushed the door open, keeping a hand pressed tightly against the rip. She knew she had to keep the pressure inside the suit, or the vacuum would kill her much faster than the lack of oxygen would. One step out of the truck, she realized there was no gravity on the dock. A cable along the wall was the only way to traverse the thirty feet to the airlock door.

"Time, it's all about time," Teela said aloud. "If we release the knee, will we have time to make it to the door, figure out how to get in, close it, and pressurize the airlock before the gasses in our blood come out of solution?"

Simple math led Daedalus to exclaim, "We don't stand a snowball's chance in hell!"

Teela released the knee, tucked against the side of the truck, and kicked off as hard as she could. She tumbled head down, feet up, and crashed into the airlock door as the last of her suit's pressure dissipated.

4 - Privateers

When she came to, the air had a funny smell, faintly stale and dry. But it was air—heavenly, life-giving air. Teela took it in with long deep breaths. Her head and eyes ached. As her mind focused, she had dim recollections of being pulled into the airlock; vague, dreamlike memories at best. She remembered seeing faces, human faces. She couldn't recall having the pressure suit removed, or having her hands bound behind her back. The trip from the airlock to this room was a complete blank.

She was a prisoner; that much was apparent. The fog was lifting and she determined that she was sitting at a table in a small room lit by translucent panels in a low ceiling. A door on her right opened and two young men entered. They both wore jumpsuits with shoulder patches that identified them as employees of GMS. The slip-on tennis shoes they wore made an irritating squeaking sound on the polished metal floor as they walked in. Teela blinked her eyes and strained to clear her vision.

"She's still alive. You owe me twenty bucks," the younger of the two said.

The older one couldn't have been more than thirty, the younger in his late teens. Both were Latino. They looked so much alike, Teela suspected they were brothers. The names embroidered over the left pocket identified the elder as Jesus and the other as Juan.

Jesus stood across the table from Teela and studied her face for a moment before slowly asking, "Why did you come here?"

"I already tried, she don't speak English. We need to find a translator," Juan said.

"They say some of them have the minds of dead people and can speak English, or other languages." Jesus paused to look at Teela again. "Se habla español? No? Okay, this one looks like a kid. Maybe she's a runaway and doesn't know any of our languages."

"You know why Auntie wants one of these so bad?" Juan asked.

"Aunt Lucinda says they produce a smell that makes men get super horny. That's why only certain people are allowed to have contact with them. Auntie says men who work with them have to take a drug that deadens their sense of smell."

"Yeah, I could use that drug when I'm working around you."

"Very funny, asswipe. Now go get rid of that hunk of junk she crashed into our dock. Sell it to a scrap dealer and don't tell anyone about the alien. If anybody asks, it just showed up and we don't know nothing about it. You understand what I'm saying, cousin?" Jesus said.

"Yeah, bro, I got you covered. You just better make sure Auntie knows I helped with this."

"She's gonna be here in a few minutes. Now get moving and do what I told you or she's gonna hear how you helped screw this up."

After Juan left, Jesus circled Teela several times. Stopping behind her, he bent over to study her extended claws. He straightened suddenly, surprised by his erection.

"Man oh man, Auntie is right. You are twelve-pack ugly for sure, but you got something that's making me want you."

Teela squirmed in her bindings as he ran his hand up her arm and over her shoulder. A knock on the door caused him to jerk his hand away. He was trying to adjust his pants as the lock clicked and the door opened.

"What are you doing?" an elderly woman demanded as she burst into the room.

At first glance, Teela thought she was in her late sixties or early seventies. On closer examination, the parchment-like skin of her hands and neck betrayed the years that plastic surgery and makeup could not conceal. She was immaculately groomed and exquisitely dressed in a flowing, high-collared burgundy dress with matching satin pumps. She swept into the room, the large satchel on her arm swinging outward as she turned to face the young man with a fierceness that was reflected in her fiery dark eyes.

"Nothing, I wasn't doing anything, Auntie. I was coming to answer the door," Jesus stammered.

She looked straight into his flushed face and then down at his crotch. "Look at you. Look at how this ugly, snake-faced creature can arouse you with her scent alone." Lucinda purred with obvious pleasure at seeing the effect firsthand.

"I'm sorry, Auntie. I'm really sorry."

"Oh, don't be sorry, my precious boy," Lucinda said, putting her hands on either side of his face and pulling it down to her so she could kiss him on each cheek. "I am very proud of you. No one else knows about this except you and me, true?"

"Yes, Auntie. Well, except for Juan. He was there when she crashed into our dock."

"Juan? The little tattooed troublemaker?"

"He was there, he helped me bring her here. He won't be any trouble, I promise."

"If all goes well, you will be greatly rewarded for your loyalty. Global Maintenance Services is expanding. We are creating a subsidiary I have named Galactic Maintenance Services. The corporation is growing quickly and I will need loyal and enterprising young men like you to coordinate our activities abroad," Lucinda said, smiling pleasantly at Jesus.

"And what about Cousin Juan?"

"You will be promoted to manager. If you choose to hire that idiot, that's your choice. You have promised me that he will not be any trouble. I will hold you to your word. Don't disappoint me. Now get out of here and go do something to hide that. You look like a pervert." Lucinda dismissed Jesus with a wave of her hand.

"Yes, Auntie," Jesus replied, retreating from the room and closing the door.

Lucinda held her access card to the doorframe and the lock slid into place with a click. She set her purse on the table and took out a thermos-like container. From another box she withdrew several long, cotton-tipped swabs. Stepping behind Teela, she ran the swab from just below her ear duct down the side of her neck. Teela recoiled as much as her restraints would allow.

"Shush, shush, little snake girl, I'm not going to hurt you. In fact, sweetie, I'm going to treat you very well, as I would treat myself," Lucinda said, repeating the swabbing on the other side of Teela's neck. She dropped the swabs into the thermos and closed the lid, then turned it over and pushed a button next to a small LCD readout.

"Oh my goodness! You are a lethal weapon, little lady," Lucinda said, grinning at Teela as she put the canister back in her purse and took out her phone.

"Hello, Hector... Yes, it's true, we have another one, very young. She is little more than a child, but has nice breasts, dainty, almost pretty. This is the one I want. Here, look."

Lucinda held her phone up and turned on the camera. "Just wait until you see her in person. She is a gem. The youngest I have seen... I performed a pheromone test. Concentrations are ten times what you predicted. Oh, to be this young again, and irresistible! How long until you will have the equipment to make this body mine? ...Really? That's too long. I want this expedited. I don't care how much it costs. She doesn't look happy. Where will you house her until it's done? ...What? Do you honestly think drugs are a good idea? ...Hector, sweetheart, I don't care how you control her until then. I just don't want to start my next life as a drug addict. Fear is a more effective means of control. A good beating or two, and she will do as she is told. Just be careful, I don't want any scars or visible bruises... Okay, get things set up. See you in a few hours."

Lucinda terminated the call and dialed another.

"Is the shuttle ready? ...Good. Send Jesus and Juan, we are ready to go."

Lucinda and her nephews proved to be capable captors who were very likely experienced at handling prisoners. Teela's hope for an opportunity to escape did not materialize. Secured by well-applied restraints, she shuffled slowly. The twelve inches of rope that tied her feet together made walking difficult. Her arms were bound at the elbows and wrists. They put a black satin bag over her head and tied it in place with a length of rope fixed with a handle on the end like a short leash. Juan held her under one arm and Jesus held her under the other and kept a firm grip on the leash. Together they guided her into Lucinda's private yacht.

Lucinda's yacht was a space shuttle designed for both atmospheric and unlimited space travel. Its roomy interior was elegantly appointed in plush mauve and grey velvet upholstery with polished pewter trim. Juan and Jesus strapped Teela into a large overstuffed seat and were saying their goodbyes to their auntie when first one and then another of Lucinda's bodyguards were tossed, unconscious, through the shuttle door.

"Keep hands where I see them," a large, barrel-chested man wearing a wide-brimmed leather cowboy hat and long black overcoat shouted as he stepped into the shuttle, brandishing a pistol in each hand.

Two men slipped in behind him and took up positions at his sides. The man on the cowboy's left was tall and thin, wearing a black ski mask and holding an energized pulse rifle; the other man was short and stout, wore a hooded jacket, and had a machine pistol.

"Von Hammer!" Jesus shouted. "You crazy Polack. What the hell are you doing? Do you know who this is? Do you have any idea who you are screwing with here?"

"Shut up, boy!" Von Hammer said. "I hear all about Lucinda. She is thief and murderer. You take my money, old woman, and then you have your boys come steal the cargo you sell me. They kill my mechanic and take from me. You think because it is contraband, I do nothing. Tell me, old woman, why I shouldn't cut your throat?" He put his pistols away and pulled a large bowie knife from behind his back.

"Calm down, Captain." Lucinda said smoothly, without the least hint of fear. "I am a businesswoman. I don't know anything about your cargo being stolen. This is my station, and nothing happens here without my permission. I gave no one instructions or permission to steal from you. I will investigate your claim. If what you say is true, I will get you your cargo back and bring you the head of whoever is responsible. You have my word."

"We have deal, then. But I still have dead crewman, I need mechanic. This Korlah girl you have must be good mechanic to make shit fly. I take her to replace my mechanic," Von Hammer said, pointing at Teela with his knife.

Lucinda laughed, a high-pitched, annoying sort of laugh.

"This child is not a mechanic. And you may not have her."

"I am a mechanic," Teela said from under the hood. "An experienced mechanic of both human and Korlah technology. I would be honored to crew with you, Captain Von Hammer."

Everyone looked at Teela. Jesus smacked Juan on the side of the head.

"She does speak English, you idiot," Jesus whispered.

"All right, Captain," Lucinda said. "I see what's going on here. You can't have this girl. She's belongs to me, and she's not for sale or trade. I will get you a mechanic if that's what you want."

"Belong to you? This girl?" Von Hammer shouted as he moved toward Lucinda, waving his knife. "You crazy bitch, I heard you are slaver. I should cut off your ugly head and shit down throat."

He put the knife under Lucinda's chin and pressed the blade against her parchment-thin skin. A trickle of blood ran across the knife and down Lucinda's neck, yet she didn't flinch or even blink. Her dark, angry eyes glared at Von Hammer with open contempt.

"You are making a serious mistake. But take the girl, if it pleases you," Lucinda whispered, her voice shaking with anger.

"I knew we could cut deal," Von Hammer said with a laugh as he withdrew the knife. Meeting Lucinda's glare, he paused and licked her blood from the edge of the razor-sharp blade. Laughing again, he turned to Teela, removed the hood and used his knife to cut her bindings.

Teela jumped up and grabbed Lucinda's face in her hands, using the tips of her claws to firmly grasp the old woman's skull. Lucinda offered no resistance as Teela drew their faces together, but for the first time, she looked frightened.

"If I ever find out that you have taken a Korlah against their will, I will find you and I will skin your face, human or Korlah, with my bare hands. Do you understand me, you wicked bitch?" Teela growled.

"Yes!" Lucinda cried, and then whispered, "A mechanic? You must be so disappointed. Consider what I have, what we could do together. I could have made you rich."

"You are insane." Teela retracted her claws and shoved Lucinda's head back.

Lucinda immediately grabbed her purse and pulled out a mirror to examine her face and neck for damage.

Teela dug through her pockets. Not finding what she was looking for, she turned toward Juan and Jesus. "One of you took my watch. I want it back!"

Juan quickly unclipped a large watch from his wrist and handed it to Teela. She put it in her pocket and turned to Von Hammer.

"Thank you, Captain. I am in your debt," Teela said, offering the captain a palm display.

"Yes, you are. Now tie wicked bitch up," Von Hammer said with a grin.

After Teela and Von Hammer's crew finished tying up Lucinda and her crew and began to leave the ship, Von Hammer paused at the hatch.

"We are even, Lucy. You try revenge, and next time I detach head and shit down throat." He turned out the cabin lights and shut the hatch.

"Revenge?" Lucinda whispered into the dark. "My dear Captain, what I am going to do to you will bring new meaning to the word."

At a nearby hangar, Teela, Von Hammer, and his crew crowded into a tiny shuttle and departed the sky hub without resistance. At first Teela was afraid that the close proximity with the men would pose a problem. She was squeezed in the backseat of the transport behind the tall skinny man with the short stocky man on her left. The young man next to her had sandy blond hair and nervous hazel eyes. He seemed more interested in whether they were being followed than he was in Teela. She was glad he didn't want to talk. His breath was foul and his teeth looked as though they had never been brushed. As far as odors went, it was a draw as to which was worse: the young man's breath or the body odor of the group as a whole. The lack of a sexual response to her Korlah pheromones led her to believe their personal stench was drowning out any scent of her own.

The shuttle slid into its dock on the roof of Von Hammer's cargo ship. With purposeful haste, the men took the only three chairs in the control room. Teela stood quietly out of the way as they powered up and pointed the cargo ship away from the spaceport. Thirty minutes later, they dropped into a line of several dozen identical cargo ships and disappeared among a vast array of outbound craft.

Once he was confident they were safely out of Lucinda's reach, Captain Von Hammer rose from his chair and pointed to the tall, skinny man who was his second-in-command. His oily black shoulder-length hair framed an already thin face, making it seem longer. Combined with his dark eyes and large nose, Teela thought he looked like a crow.

"Smiley, you have con," Von Hammer said.

"Aye, aye, sir," Smiley said, rising to take the captain's chair. As he stood, he passed gas, a loud and long report that promised a cloud that would nauseate all present. He smiled broadly at Teela, revealing the origin of his nickname.

"You come with me," he said, pointing to her.

"What is name?" Von Hammer asked.

"Teela," she answered.

"Is that real name?"

"Yes."

"Pick new name. Name no one will know you by."

"Okay." Teela paused and thought for a moment. "Suladead Semir."

"Too long. I call you Sula."

"It's shorter than Captain Von Hammer."

Ludwig frowned, his scowl accentuated by the shadows of his cowboy hat. He filled his lungs, and as he did, he put his hands on his hips spreading his floor length trench coat to expose the pistols on his hips. "My name is Captain Ludwig Von Hammer. Off this ship you will call me Captain or Captain Von Hammer. On ship you *may* call me Ludwig. Never forget I am captain, you are crew. I say your name is Sula, then that is name!"

"Aye, aye, Captain," Teela said.

Ludwig directed her out the back of the control room and through the crew's quarters, which looked and smelled like a soiled locker room with bunks. They passed through an airtight hatch into the spine of the ship, a long rectangular shaft that ran the length of the hauler. Three warehouse-sized cubes were held to the spine by clamps that looked like ribs. Teela had followed Ludwig half the length of the shaft when he stopped suddenly and turned around.

"You go down," he said, gesturing toward the floor.

"No! I will not," Teela hissed. "If you thought I would be your whore, you are mistaken!" She backed up and extended her claws.

Ludwig's brow furrowed, then he suddenly grinned and laughed. "Look," he said, pointing to a round, recessed panel in the floor. "Open hatch and go down." He removed a small plastic bottle from his pocket and shook it like a maraca.

"We do business with Korlah, no monkey business. Pills kill nose. If Smiley didn't grin or make sound like horn, no one know he shit pants. You safe here, little Korlah girl. No one abuse you on my ship, I give word," Ludwig said with a nod.

Teela blanched, the Korlah equivalent of a blush. She nodded and knelt down to open the panel. Beneath it was a hatch with a handwheel. With a few turns of the wheel, the dogs cleared, and Teela lifted the hatch open, releasing a strong odor of rouk, rodents, cedar, stale alcohol, and new cardboard. From down in the darkness she could hear rustling sounds. She slipped into the opening and descended the ladder into the central cargo cube.

She wasn't afraid of Ludwig or the darkness, but she was concerned. This was not a machinery space and these were not the smells or sounds of mechanical equipment. At the bottom of the thirty-foot ladder she moved into the shadows with her back against a wall of palletized boxes. Ludwig stepped off the last rung and turned to face her.

"Lights on!" he shouted. A few seconds later, the ceiling glowed with the soft illumination Teela remembered from the Korlah campaign vessel. Ludwig walked briskly away from her between towering rows of boxes and Teela hurried to keep up, trying to read the labels on the cardboard containers as she did. She saw cases of vodka, whiskey, rum, and tequila. She passed a row of at least thirty tanks that each contained several of the slimy alien eels the Korlah called rouk. On shelves above the tanks, cedar-lined cages contained hundreds of rats. From the strong smell of urine, it was apparent the cages had not been cleaned for some time.

"You're breeding rouk? Do you eat them or sell them?" Teela asked.

"We harvest slime and mix with booze. I make best-quality rouk whiskey in system. One shot will paralyze man for whole hour. Now pay attention! You will feed grain to rats and feed rats to Korlah water snakes. Cages of both you will keep clean."

At the end of the row of boxes he turned the corner and stopped. As Teela rounded the corner, she saw that his path was blocked. Shoved unceremoniously between the stacked cargo and the wall of the shipping cube was the flatbed truck she had flown to the spaceport.

Ludwig put his scuffed, worn boot up on the peeling chrome bumper and took his cowboy hat off for the first time. He set it on the center of the truck's rusted hood and ran both hands through his greasy hair, pulling the uncombed mass off of his face. Spreading his trench coat open, he put his hands on his hips just above a matched pair of pearl-handled revolvers.

"You make this piece of shit fly?" he asked, nodding toward the truck.

"Yes."

"You know Korlah technology? You can fix when broken?"

"Usually, but not always."

"Good, very good. I have lots of broken shit. Now I ask some questions. These are very important to be truthful. You are crover, yes?" he asked, narrowing his eyes.

"I'm sorry, I don't know what you mean," Teela said.

"A soul, a human soul has crossed over, from death to you. This I already know. Don't lie to me!"

"I'm not lying. I haven't heard that term before. But yes, if that's what you call them, then that's what I am. Is that a problem?"

"No problem." Ludwig paused and tilted his head as if he was having a second thought. "I have worked with crovers many times. No one knows if they have human or Korlah mind. Many humans and Korlah hate crovers. You should know; I don't care. The

Mexican boy told me you were trying to get off Earth, that you build this death trap and fly it into space. Did you go to Earth and find that you are not welcome? What are you up to, little Korlah girl? Are you trying to go somewhere? Maybe you are in trouble? What are you after? Fortune? Adventure? What is it that makes you do something this crazy?"

All were good questions, and each deserved an answer. But Teela knew there was one reason for what she had done that trumped them all.

"I am ashamed to admit that I am motivated by the least noble of all reasons. I seek revenge and retribution."

"Shit!" Ludwig said, stepping off the truck and giving it an angry kick. "Revenge is waste of time. You want to die? Die for profit. You have much more fun. We work hard, we party hard. Forget this revenge. Join my crew. No one here cares where you come from. Past is past. Today and tomorrow is all that counts. Have you not heard? End of world is near."

"It's more than revenge, Captain. It's self-preservation. If I don't kill this person, they will certainly find me and kill me."

"This person you must kill, are they from your human life?" Ludwig said, relaxing his posture and leaning on the truck.

"She is a crover like me, only human. Very dangerous, and very powerful."

"We make a few runs. We share profits. You prove yourself good member of crew, and I will kill this person for you. Deal?" Ludwig said, holding out his hand.

Teela stared at the hand and considered her options.

"Deal," she said, taking his hand. "Are you a pirate?"

Ludwig laughed boisterously as he shook her hand.

"No, Sula, we are not pirates, we are privateers. Not much difference, but legal... mostly."

He picked up his hat and put it back on with a flourish. As he smoothed the brim, he grinned, the stainless steel caps on his front teeth sparkling in the dim light.

"Although, it is true, I have always wanted to be pirate." he said, and laughed again.

5 - Plans

Beth watched in amazement as clouds moved slowly across the clear blue sky and a gentle breeze rippled the green fields below it. The illusion was remarkable. It looked like a large picture window onto a breathtaking scene, but she knew it was just a projection screen. This grandiose office was far more sophisticated than the dank mine shafts in Montana where she'd first met Homeland Defense Secretary General McClellan. His new office was part of the government's underground bunkers that were designed to resist nuclear and biological attack.

Secretary McClellan leaned back in his plush chair and tapped the yellowed stack of pages at the center of his massive oak desk with a pencil. He dropped the pencil on the desk and slid the pages back into their envelope.

"So, she actually read this?" he asked.

Beth turned to face him. Her withered left arm was bent at the elbow and her left hand, its fingers twisted from atrophy, rested on her hip. The left side of her face hung like a sagging mask, twisting the corner of her mouth down and leaving her eye open only a crease.

"What?" she said. "You mean the letter?"

"Of course the letter. What else would I be talking about?"

"Sorry, sir, I'm just a little distracted. Yes, sir, she read the letter. She contacted Cooper, and he called me."

"Jesus, Beth! I knew I should have retired you. Why wasn't that letter intercepted?"

"You said to put her in protective custody. All of her mail is scanned and inspected. We had no reason to read it. And sir, do you mean 'retired' as in getting some sun on the beach, or as in filling a shallow grave?"

Secretary McClellan rubbed his face slowly, shaking his head and muttering expletives while giving Beth a look that would seem to indicate the latter. He pulled another stack of paper from among the multitudes of folders on his desk. Unlike Daedalus Rimes' letter to his wife, these papers were new and crisp.

"Sit down! Sit your ass down before you fall down, damn it!" he shouted.

Beth hobbled over to the chair in front of McClellan's desk. Lifting her braced leg with her right hand, she used her good leg to lower herself into the seat.

"I want her isolated and contained. Not a word of this letter gets out. Do you understand?"

"Yes, sir," Beth slurred, dabbing spittle from the corner of her mouth.

"There have been thousands of these mind transfers performed. I have preliminary reports on the psychological evaluations of the participants. So far, there is not a single report of any dual personalities like the one described by your pal Teela. There is about a fifty percent chance of either a human or Korlah personality dominance, but no dual personalities. And what is this baby bullshit? I have reports the Korlah are pumping out hundreds of these half-human, half-Korlah hybrids. Why the hell would Rebecca think Teela's kid is anything special?"

"Dunno, sir, Becca's crazy as they get. I'm guessing she and her Korlah donor were both nuts. You know, a couple of religious wackos, times two. The combination of Rebecca and the Korlah priest is like putting together dynamite and a match. That old Korlah geezer used to follow Teela around like a puppy dog. Becca's been obsessed with Teela ever since the priest died. Now it could be that her obsession has shifted from Teela to the baby. You read the letter. Dade said Becca thinks the kid is some kind of messiah."

McClellan pulled a photographic negative from the pile of papers and slapped it down on the desk. "I have a theory on where Rebecca McCabe gets her unique telepathic abilities."

"Do tell," Beth said blandly.

"Damn it, Beth! I need your insight on this. No one has been closer to this woman than you. Now pay attention!"

"Yes, sir, sorry, sir, you have my full attention," Beth replied, sitting up a little straighter.

McClellan scowled. "That's an x-ray of Rebecca's head," he said, pointing. "It's one of the last ones taken after she was diagnosed with terminal brain cancer. The main portion of the tumor is between the frontal lobes, with a section of the mass pressing against the front of the skull." He dug through the pile and pulled out another negative.

"Here's a cross-section of a Korlah brain from a dissection. The Korlah brain has a slightly different shape, yet all the same components as a human brain are there, with the exception of this part between the frontal lobes that looks suspiciously similar to Rebecca's brain tumor."

"How'd you get a Korlah to dissect? I thought there was a UNE law against conducting medical experiments on them."

"Of course I'm aware of the law. And although I am absolutely certain our new allies would sell their mother for the right price, the cadavers were legally purchased through UNE channels. Are you following what I'm getting at, Lieutenant?"

"Yes, sir, Rebecca has a brain tumor in the same place that the Korlah have a... I don't know, another piece of brain?"

McClellan shook his head and rubbed his eyes again. Another sixteen-hour day, and now this letter; he was certain it would be another four hours before he would get some sleep.

"Look at this shit, Beth," McClellan said, referring to the stacks of paper spread across his desk. "All of this is about your friend Teela, Rebecca, and our alleged allies, the Korlah. I'm trying to make sense out of this intel. There is more to this than I am being told. I need your help to figure it out!"

He grabbed a folder and tossed it to Beth. It opened and the papers fell all around her, but she didn't flinch or move to catch them or pick them up.

"That report is about the damn bugs you and the others brought back with you. This is where I have to stretch the facts and form a hypothesis. I believe this parasite or symbiotic organism, whatever the hell it is, turned Rebecca's tumor into some kind of a God damn supertelepathic organ. She should be dead. Instead, she's busy creating the largest and most powerful militant religious movement this planet has ever known."

"Sir, I read the report on the organism. The studies indicate that they convert cancerous cells into healthy cells and then slowly restore damaged tissue to its precancerous state. If this is true, the tumor in Rebecca's head should be going away, and as it shrinks, so should her telepathic abilities. I have a request in to the CDC lab for an estimate on how long the assimilation of the tumor would take based on its last known dimensions. If she is losing her power, this would explain why reports of telepathic attacks on cell phones have decreased, and why she considers Teela such a threat."

McClellan took a deep breath and looked at Beth thoughtfully. "Just when you have me convinced you're nothing but a meathead, you pull out something that astonishes me. Okay, let's say Rebecca's abilities are going away. What are the chances Teela will help us kill her?" He lifted a black valise onto the desk, started to open it, and then paused for Beth's reply.

"You read the letter to Julie," Beth said. "I think if we help her get her kid back, she'll help us in whatever way she can."

"Do you trust her?"

Beth hesitated. The pause was not lost on McClellan.

"I have no reason not to," she replied.

McClellan pulled some papers from the valise and fumbled through them for a few moments until he found the page he was looking for.

"Rebecca has an assassin working for her that's been knocking off members of the Quorum faster than I can track them down and get arrest warrants. The plus side of this is that no search warrant is needed at a murder scene, so I got this from the residence of one of their highest-ranking members. It's a study on the effects of transfer. It says the personalities of the individuals that have undergone the transfer process will affect Korlah politics. It goes on to say that it doesn't matter which of the personalities dominates the transfer; the effect will be the same. If you got a mental problem before transfer, you will have a mental problem after transfer." McClellan paused to extract a thick stack of papers from his valise and pushed them toward Beth.

"This is a report that was sent to Parkhurst. This is the reason he attempted to assassinate Ambassadress Shawlmon and the president. It paints a fairly black picture of this Daedalus Rimes," McClellan said, leaning forward in his chair to study Beth's response.

"Sir, if you want me to read this, it's gonna take a while," Beth said, thumbing the edge of the thick stack. It had to have more than a hundred pages of double-sided, single-spaced type.

"Yes! I want you to read it. I want you to study it, but not right now! In summary, it's the life history of one Daedalus Rimes. Your pal Dade was not a nice person. At first glance he looks like an average guy. Lost a few jobs due to a bad temper—in fact, that's how he met his current wife. Get this: Julie Rimes was his anger management counselor. For years, Dade Rimes has done nothing more serious than get a couple of speeding tickets. He hasn't had any contact with law enforcement for the last twenty years.

"But you dig a little deeper and that's when it starts to get interesting. He spent time in prison for nearly beating his first wife to death. He was dishonorably discharged from military service for assaulting an officer. His psych profile described him as irrational and antisocial with paranoiac delusional tendencies. He used to claim he knew what people were thinking. This asshole spent over half of his adolescent life in juvenile hall. He was initially diagnosed as being developmentally impaired, but after he pulled some clever escapes, they eventually realized the prick was playing them.

"I have a theory that Dade Rimes is the dominant personality of this transfer. Any dual personality is in his twisted mind. But that's just a theory. When you look at the facts, more questions keep coming up. He doesn't have a birth certificate; he has an estimated date of birth certificate. Here it is."

McClellan pulled out a manila folder with a few sheets of paper in it. "It's not much, but oh, baby, it begs for answers. Daedalus Rimes was an abandoned child. A white kid abandoned in a remote, predominantly black section of Detroit undergoing urban renovation. That's how he got his name. The medical report says he tried to fly off the roof of a three-story building. The press came up with the name when they wrote a story about a frozen kid who thought he could fly. Daedalus for flying, Rimes for frozen, get it? Well, anyway, the state decided to keep the name.

"He was badly frostbitten and they scheduled some amputations, but he miraculously healed. His childhood medical records cite minor bone deformities of his hands and feet. They gave him corrective shoes. A blood test in his teens identified a

46

bloodborne parasite believed to be a form of plasmodium. He was prescribed mefloquine to treat it. He never went back for a follow-up. Other than the parasite, there is no record of any childhood illness; no measles, mumps, colds, flu, acne, nothing. The lab technician couldn't match the parasite to anything known, so he simply dropped it into a probable category. Take a guess what parasite the lab technician's description of Mr. Rimes' parasite has now been conclusively matched with?"

"The Korlah symbiotic organism," Beth answered without hesitation.

"That's right," McClellen replied, "and that lab report is forty years old. And now for some concrete facts we can both appreciate. I ordered another autopsy of Mr. Rimes' remains. The physician confirmed the existence of an additional frontal lobe in his brain. Not a tumor. This is healthy brain tissue. The deformities of his hands and feet turned out to be vestigial claws in the tips of several of his fingers and all of his *eight* toes.

"I believe Daedalus Rimes was a Korlah hybrid, a sleeper agent planted in preparation for an invasion. Whether he was planted by the Kahshinki or the Korlah is unknown. Whether his abduction was accidental or purposeful is unknown. What I am certain of is that there are more just like him waiting to do whatever it is they were programmed to do."

6 - Ruwaugh

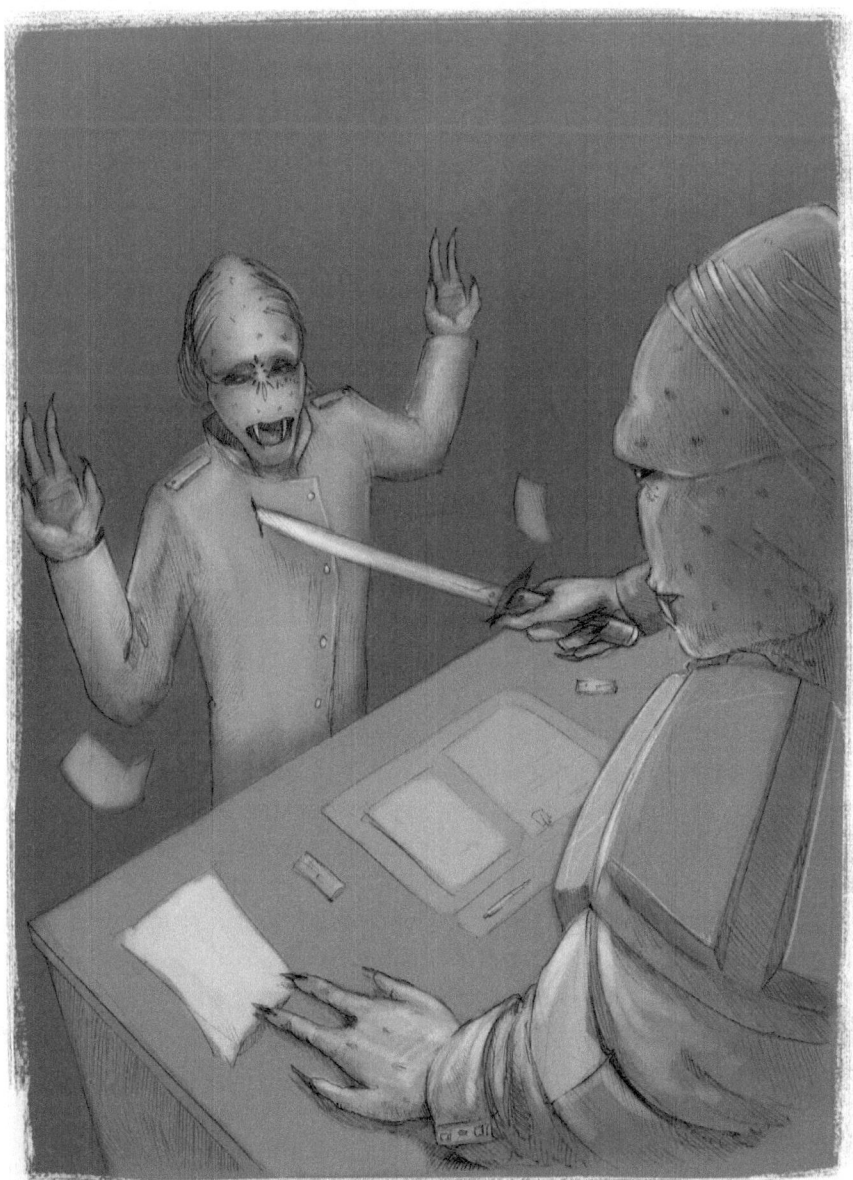

Human technology was supposedly available to all Korlah, but in reality, it was only available to those who could navigate the complex and volatile bartering system developed by the collectives. For Meezra, the subdirector of the accoutrements section, the law of supply and demand reigned supreme. Rising from the position of a common laborer, Meezra was now in direct control of the movement and processing of all raw materials, as well as the fabrication of many finished products. Misappropriation of these items for other than their intended military purpose would be considered treason on a Korlah vessel during campaign, but surpluses, damaged equipment, and scraps that could not be dropped back into the automated processers were typically dumped like trash. In the days following first contact, Meezra quickly realized that Korlah trash was being salvaged by the humans. She intervened, and soon the humans were trading with her representatives for Korlah discards.

Networking had always been Meezra's strength. When the Korlah Council lifted the restrictions on bartering, Meezra and her colleagues on the black market immediately expanded their network. She amassed tremendous profits in record time and was finally confident that she could use her wealth and influence to purchase a nomination for transfer to a new shell. She would finally join the ranks of those who enjoyed an eternal existence. As a result, for the first time in her life Meezra was spending her profits rather than hoarding them. She had filled her large office with all manner of human contraptions, some of which she did not understand. Her favorites were an enormous video player and stereo, which she liked to play simultaneously at competing volumes.

A human movie with a badly synced Korlah dub-over was playing while Meezra reviewed the previous shift's ledger on one of the screens that covered her desk. When she saw a significant rise in biscuit trades, she stopped tapping her foot and called up the ledgers for the last few days. All trades had been equated in biscuits since water became almost worthless, but she was seeing trades of large quantities of actual biscuits for a common element known as bitnum.

Meezra checked to see when the purchases began and how much bitnum remained in her collection of scraps. She deduced that well over half of what she had was already traded. Raw materials were traded by weight, the Korlah standard for which was given in pure water at a set temperature; two measures of water equaled a little more than a pound. Meezra looked at the dates and saw that less than a thousand measures of bitnum had been used in all production applications in the last one hundred cycles. Now, in less than one cycle, 300,000 measures had been traded, and only a little more than 200,000 remained in her inventory.

Let's see how bad you want the rest of my bitnum, Meezra thought as she changed the trade rate from 1000/1 to 100000/1. She returned to the production applications and determined that there were only three uses for bitnum, all of which were purely ornamental: decorating ceremonial blades, buckles, and embroidery for warriors' uniforms. She changed screens and checked the exchange rate for these objects on the human market; the only objects trading higher than blades, buckles, and embroidered uniforms were pulse weapons and medical equipment. No one was trading for bitnum alone; at least, not yet.

She examined one of the buckles on her vest and scored the soft, shiny metal with a claw. She cocked her head in contemplation and wondered why a limited-use material would bring such a premium from the humans.

Meezra spent the next few hours perusing the video logs and personal effects she'd amassed over the course of a fifteen-year obsession. The last and most-favored addition to the accumulation was a dirty, blood-stained gown. She ran her crown tendrils slowly across the fabric, relishing its faint scent. It had been years since she lost contact with its wearer, but now, after considerable expense, she was confident that would soon change. Contemplating the possibilities, she smiled and put her treasure back in its airtight case.

Finished for the day, Meezra opened her door to leave. Her bodyguard was shoved backwards into the room by two large Korlah warriors who came in and closed the door behind them. The first warrior released her clawed grip on the bodyguard's throat and let her drop to the floor. Meezra watched the warrior's blade slide out of the bodyguard's abdomen and chest on the way down.

"What are you doing?" Meezra shrieked, taking cover behind her desk. "You—you will both be reclaimed for this!"

"Quiet!" the warrior growled, directing Meezra to sit with her blood-drenched blade.

The warrior's face was instantly recognizable to Meezra, a face scarred by fights both inside and outside the spectacle arena. This was a face she'd thought she would never see again.

"Ruwaugh!" she gasped.

"Yes, I'm back. Did you think I had ceased?" Ruwaugh asked with a malicious smile. "Few survive a single cycle of punitive labor. Shawaugh survived three, and I have survived longer than that. I am here to make you an offer," she said with a laugh, and then took out a biscuit and held it out to Meezra.

"Take it!" Ruwaugh demanded.

When Meezra did not comply, she put the tip of her sword on Meezra's shoulder and drove it in until it touched bone.

Meezra shrieked. Pulling herself off the blade, she fell backwards out of her chair and onto the floor. Ruwaugh followed her, again offering the biscuit. This time Meezra snatched it away with a trembling hand.

"What do you want?" she whimpered.

"I am offering you that biscuit in exchange for all your remaining bitnum. Do you accept my offer?" Ruwaugh asked as she leaned forward, the tip of her sword coming to rest against Meezra's other shoulder.

"Yes," Meezra replied, knowing it was the only answer.

"Done," Ruwaugh said, sealing the completely illegal agreement. "All bitnum in existence now and in the future will be controlled by my client. I will provide the exchange rates and you will strictly enforce them. You will be given production specifications for converting the bitnum into objects of a standard size and weight. Coordinate fabrication and secure storage as requested, and you will be generously rewarded for your assistance."

"Your client? Who is it that I am so honored to serve?" Meezra asked hopefully, although she was certain the identity would not be revealed.

Ruwaugh grabbed Meezra by the throat, squelching her attempt to scream. She held the bloody blade of her sword to the side of Meezra's neck and then slowly wiped the blade clean on the collar of her white tunic. She pulled Meezra's face, now blanched white in terror, close to her own flushed and scarred one. When she spoke, her voice was low and controlled.

"I have made certain that Shawaugh and Challmara will not return from their current mission to prepare an escape route for Korlah cowards. Shyron's feeble attempt to impersonate Shawlmon has failed. The Council is charging her with Shawlmon's murder. If they don't execute Shyron for the crime, I will see to her assassination. There is no one left who can help you. You are alone, Meezra."

Howard Lewis

7 - Crossroads

The journey to the outer reaches of the solar system took far longer than Teela expected. Von Hammer's engine room, like the rest of his cargo ship, was in a state of prolonged neglect. Three of the five drive units and many of the control circuits were broken. She divided her waking hours among repairs, maintenance, and cleaning, the last of which involved a few heated arguments between her and Dade. It wasn't long until the engine room and the animal cages were immaculate, the equipment had been repaired to the extent possible, and the ship's maintenance was up to date. By the end of the first week all of the biocircuitry had been fed and the damaged units properly isolated so they could heal and regenerate. By cannibalizing the drive units for replacement circuits, she was able to make four of the five engines functional. She anticipated that they would be fully restored and able to accelerate the cargo ship to sub-light speed in a few days. Smiley estimated that once the hauler was up to speed, their remaining travel time would be cut from a week to less than twenty hours. Ludwig was ecstatic. The crew celebrated with shots of the ship's prized cargo, a concoction of rouk slime and grain alcohol that was aptly named Thor's Hammer. Banned at all UNE facilities and most Korlah outposts, the drink was in high demand and brought the highest profits of the ship's manifest.

While the rest of the crew partied, Teela milked the rouk for their inebriating slime then walked the ship anxiously, looking for something to do. She typically avoided the crew's quarters, and although she could have bunked there with the rest of the crew, She'd chosen to remain aft and had been sleeping on a mat in the engine room.

Teela slipped quietly into the crew's quarters and closed the hatch behind her. Ludwig, Smiley, and Denster lay drunk and paralyzed on their bunks. The smell of rouk slime and alcohol blended with the rancid smell of dirty clothes and unwashed bodies.

"I don't want to do this," Dade whispered in English as Teela bent to gather up the stinking clothes littering the floor. "Don't I have a say in this?" he asked, again out loud. This was a tack he used when he felt she was ignoring him.

"I'm sick of the stench," Teela whispered in Korlah, not wanting to wake the crew. "I can't stand this anymore. If you don't like it, go to that place you go. Leave me to my task." She began hand-cleaning each piece of clothing in one of the electrostatic purifiers she'd recently repaired. After a prolonged cleansing, she shook out the dust, neatly folded each piece, and put them away in the owners' lockers.

"These guys are pigs. It's disgusting," Dade said, raising his voice as Teela began cleaning the urine from around and under the waste-collection unit.

"Repairing the biocircuits is more disgusting," Teela replied. "I think you like that smell, you spend so much time with it!"

"It fascinates me. It should fascinate you as well. Cleaning up piss just makes me want to puke!"

The complaints continued. He voiced his gripes and sarcastic comments in English and she gave evasive replies in Korlah, both of them unaware they were close to having a shouting match. As she finished scrubbing the floor, the crew was beginning to rouse from their stupor.

"Let them clean their own bedding. Why are you even thinking about it?" Dade asked.

"I'll do it later," Teela replied, leaving the compartment to return to the engine room.

After she left, Smiley rolled out of bed and stumbled over to a waste-collection unit. Ludwig rose up on an elbow and surveyed the immaculate chamber.

"Did you hear any of that?" Smiley asked him with a groan as he began to urinate.

"Yeah. You were right. She's definitely crazy," Ludwig said.

"We dump her at Crossroads, right?"

"No. She's just a kid. Someone screwed her up. It's not her fault, and I don't think she's dangerous. She's a good mechanic, and a very good housekeeper. And you know… she's right: we are pigs. She stays." Ludwig rolled over and went back to sleep.

Captain Von Hammer's destination was one of Jupiter's lesser moons. The mining base there had been abandoned almost as soon as it was finished when the rich iron deposit it was thought to hold proved to be purely superficial. Once all the iron was mined, the facility was stripped of usable equipment and abandoned. An enterprising Korlah collective, noting that the moon was conveniently located between the inner and outer region of the solar system in an area outside the jurisdictions of both the Korlah Council and UNE enforcers, immediately lay claim to the facility and set up a trading post. As the intersection where Korlah and human technology were melding, it quickly became the favored location for those wishing to exchange illicit commodities. The moon and base, officially designated SMB0007, was now known by everyone as Crossroads.

Most of the bulk commerce was transferred from one freighter to another in orbit around the moon, but the negotiations and deals that made these transfers possible occurred deep beneath the moon's gray rocky surface. Entrance into the interior was through a single rotary airlock too small for freighters and the transport cubes they hauled, but just large enough for a Korlah assault pod.

While Denster and Smiley stayed on the moon's surface with the cargo, Ludwig and Teela took the shuttle and lined up at the entrance to the underground base. When it was their turn, Ludwig's shuttle and four other small craft squeezed together into the barrel of the revolving airlock. After it rotated them inside, the ships followed a roughhewn tunnel to where it opened up into a natural cavern with enough docks and landing pads for more than a hundred ships. Ludwig parked the shuttle and Teela walked with him through a smooth, polished tunnel and up six flights of stairs, which was easy in the moon's partial gravity. They emerged in a brightly lit cavern that was twice as large as a football stadium and, as Teela suddenly realized when she nearly fell, equipped with artificial gravity.

The entire area was a work in progress. There were a few ramshackle buildings from the mining days at the edge of the cavern. A new four-story building made of stacked hexagonal prefabricated storage units rose above a cluster of temporary stands, booths, and shacks that provided the bizarre sights, raucous sounds, and tantalizing smells of a carnival. Teela swung her crown tendrils to sample the wildly diverse scents as Ludwig took her by the arm and led her through the booths. Despite its tawdry appearance, Crossroads was business, big business. The items on display were all samples of goods being offered in bulk for sale or trade. There were some packaged foods and a few medical products, but most of the goods were weapons and military equipment. None of this was of particular interest to Teela, but when they passed near a concession booth and she thought she smelled pastrami, she veered towards it.

Ludwig pulled her away. "We eat later, have business over there... now," he said, nodding toward one of the old mining buildings, where a hand-painted sign by a propped-open hatch read "Eddie's Place." Inside the shop, the walls were covered with pictures and designs. A man stood up from behind a small table when they entered. His arms, neck, and even parts of his face were tattooed. Teela suddenly realized Ludwig had brought her to a tattoo parlor.

"Captain Von Hammer! It's good to see you. Are you back for some work on your ship tat?" the man asked as he vigorously shook Ludwig's hand.

"Maybe later. First thing first. You once say you remove tattoos. Can you remove this?" Ludwig said, pointing to Teela's sabat.

"Yeah, sure. It'll take about ten minutes and hurt like hell. I don't do nerve blocks on the face; it's too risky. I got some rouk whiskey, though. One or two shots, and I'll be done before she knows I started. Hey, you bring any Thor's Hammer? Your brand is the best, man, I'm not kidding. I'll give you my best work if you fix me up with a liter or two."

"I brought three liters just for you, Eddie. You get word out I got Thor's Hammer in bulk and I'll beat whatever Westerly is selling his crap for." Ludwig pulled a half pint of Thor's Hammer from his pocket. Eddie licked his lips.

"Just a taste, Eddie. This for Sula. I want you straight when you work on her, you understand?" Ludwig said with a scowl.

"Sure thing, Captain. You know you can trust me. Her name is Sula? Looks like she's a T-E-Ela," Eddie said, reading the tattoo on her cheek.

"Her name is Sula. Remove tat and forget she was ever here," Ludwig said as he filled the bottle cap a quarter full of Thor's Hammer and handed it to Eddie. Eddie knocked it back without hesitation. He licked his lips, smiled, and closed his eyes for a few seconds before handing the cap back to Ludwig.

"Make it four liters and I'll forget whatever you want," he grinned.

"Done," Ludwig said, filling the cap and handing it to Teela. She lifted it to her lips. The pungent odor of rouk and alcohol caused her to pause.

"Drink!" Ludwig commanded. Teela poured the shot into her mouth. The alcohol burned for only a second and then her mouth went numb. She swallowed and continued to swallow repeatedly at the sensation of her throat going numb. The effect spread over her face, eyelids, neck, and chest. Eddie guided her into the chair by the table. She put her head back onto the headrest and closed her eyes as he lowered the back of the seat.

"Remove the tattoo. I go see station master and rent booth. Back soon," she heard Ludwig say.

Eddie went right to work, and true to his word, he was finished before she knew it. He sat her up and let her examine her face with a hand mirror. The sabat was gone. The skin was a little red and stung ferociously when she touched it.

"Here," Eddie said, handing her a full shot of his own milky rouk whiskey. "It's okay," he added. "For you, it's on the house."

Eddie talked a lot and Teela was sure he told her his entire life story. She talked, too, but could not remember what she talked about. Later, she recalled that some Korlah customers came in while they were talking; a pilot and two young warriors. Eddie was fluent in Korlah and they all talked. The Korlah had cans of warm beer and offered some to Eddie and Teela, which they accepted. Eddie offered them a round of rouk whiskey and they accepted. That was the last thing Teela could remember of her visit to Crossroads and Eddie's Place.

When she woke up, she was on the floor of the crew's quarters aboard Ludwig's cargo ship. She peeled the side of her face out of a drying puddle of vomit, climbed up using the edge of the waste unit she was lying under, and dry heaved into it several times. The wall and floor around the unit were covered in vomit, and the smell made her dry heave again. Her whole body ached, especially her head, but there were specific areas of soreness that called for her attention. She unzipped her jumpsuit to find the areola of her left breast had the corona of a sun tattooed around it. Across the top of her right breast was a beautifully detailed rendition of the Korlah Mission emblem. The freshly perforated skin was puffed and raised like embossing. Depressing the area with her fingertip, she confirmed that it was quite sensitive to the touch.

"Oh, shit," Teela moaned, removing her finger from the marking.

"I take you to remove one tattoo, and you come back with three. You are one hard-partying Korlah girl," Ludwig said, rising from the edge of his bunk where he had maintained a vigil since bringing her back. "You are better mechanic than singer and dancer. When you have cleaned up mess, come see me." He left for the bridge.

Teela cleaned up the mess, static-cleaned her jumpsuit, and scrubbed her face. It was while cleaning her face that she became concerned that the sabat removal had gone badly. She touched her sensitive skin and found spots of blood on her fingertips. She recalled that Smiley had a mirror in his clothes locker and she went to it; the sabat was in fact gone, but in its place in bold dark Arabic letters made to look like Korlah glyphs was the name "Suladead."

She opened the door to the bridge and slipped through. Ludwig and Smiley were standing on either side of Denster, and all three were looking at something he had displayed on the panel.

"Claws, mercs, bounty hunters, and UNEPOL are all looking for her. Lucinda already knows she's with us. Someone is gonna talk—hell, Eddie's probably selling you out right now," Denster said.

"Eddie's still sleeping. He's not stupid. He'll come to me looking for a better deal. This isn't the kinda place you want to be known as a snitch," Ludwig said without any hint of his Slavic accent.

"She's nuts, Tim, you heard her," Smiley said. "The way she babbles on and on, everybody on Crossroads has probably already figured out she's the assassin they're looking for. She's killed humans—the UNE law says if they kill a human, you can kill em back. The Church of Shawlmon is offering a lot of money. I say we turn her in and call it a day."

"If she killed anybody, I'm guessing they had it coming. Come on, guys, this is a setup. It reeks of Lucinda. Tomorrow the Church of Shawlmon will make an announcement that it's all bullshit. The Claws will probably burn the headquarters down of whatever news agency released this crap. I'll use the go-fast and take her to the Korlah section of the Armageddon; she'll be safe there. You two sell the cargo as quick as you can and then head for the hidey-hole. We'll retire Ludwig and his misfits, change our identities like before, and resurface as space truckers in a few weeks. Clean and safe, nobody gets hurt."

"Is that your real name, Ludwig?" Teela asked. "Tim?"

The three of them turned in unison to look at her.

"Sneaky, as well as crazy," Smiley whispered.

"We don't use real names. Tim is just another name I'll use until I change it again. It looks like we changed yours at the right time. Eddie will probably remember removing your facial tat, but I doubt he will remember putting the new one on." Ludwig reached into his mouth and pulled out a set of dental overlays. Placing the Billy-Bob teeth in his pocket, he removed first one colored contact lens and then the other. He combed his hair back and smiled, revealing a full set of straight white teeth. His natural green eyes glinted his amusement at Teela's surprised expression. Without the disguise, he looked a full ten years younger.

"Tim Masters, Masters Trucking, Inc. Pleasure to meet you, Miss Sula," he said with a bow.

"I'm going to miss Ludwig," Teela said. "It's all bullshit. I haven't killed anyone. Who are they saying I killed?"

"Read it, Denster," Tim said.

"Okay, let's see, here it is... Kansas City, Kansas. Six members of the Church of Shawlmon, including the reputed Holy Mother of Shawlmon, were killed today as they defended the alleged Son of God from an assassin posing as the Holy Mother herself."

"Nice picture. Here, check it out," Denster said, leaning back so Teela could see the enlarged close-up of her face on the screen.

"The assassin was driven off by armed church members and pursued to the Hoyt, Kansas, skyport, where she managed to escape with the help of a man who goes by the name of Ludwig Von Hammer." Denster leaned back again to show a blurry picture of Ludwig's smiling face. "UNE authorities are seeking Von Hammer for questioning. A reward of one point five million UNE credits is being offered by the Church of Shawlmon for information leading to the assassin's arrest."

"It's a lie!" Teela cried. "They took my child and left me for dead. Rebecca found out I'm still alive and wants to finish the job."

"The Oracle Rebecca?" Smiley cried. "And what? You're baby Shawlmon's mother? Oh shit, Tim, you really stepped in it this time. These people are crazy, and they're everywhere—both human and Korlah. We gotta dump this sack of trouble and split. Like now!"

"I agree. Denster, break orbit. Smiley, plot a course for the Hole and mix it up. Make sure no one follows us. Sula, you come with me."

Tim stopped in the crew's quarters and unlocked a large closet. He hung up his trench coat and pulled out a leather bomber jacket. He tossed Teela a pair of knee-high warrior boots, a pair of camouflage pants, and a matching sleeveless flight jacket. By the time she was dressed, Tim was putting the final touches on his latest costume: khaki shirt and pants, bomber jacket, ball cap with gold filigree on the bill, amber pilot shades, and a low-slung military .45. He looked exactly like the ex-military mercenary he was planning to portray. He reached back into the closet for a gun belt rolled up around a pistol and handed it to Teela. As she was putting it on, he closed and locked the closet.

Teela put the belt on and snapped its large ornate buckle closed, noting that it was the same type of buckle that was used on a Korlah warrior's sword belt. She lifted the .357 with a ten-inch barrel from the holster. Her hand easily grasped the handle, which was designed for a Korlah grip. Tim smiled approvingly; the tattoo on her chest complemented the belt buckle, an unanticipated coincidence of the costume he had selected while she was getting the tattoo.

"That weapon is for show only. Don't even think about shooting it," Tim said, motioning her to follow as he headed aft. "Here's the scenario: we're mercs looking for work. We'll see if they'll let us dock on the Korlah section. Probably won't; I hear they've banned access to all humans. But the Crossover section will let us on for sure. You let me do the talking and act as my interpreter if needed."

"Why are you doing this?" Teela asked.

"What? Helping you?"

"Yes. Smiley's right; I'm nothing but trouble."

"I like you, Sula. You work hard. Harder than I do. Not many people do. And besides, I don't like the assholes who are pissed at you. That makes helping you easy."

They entered Tim's go-fast's dock through a hidden door in the floor of the engine room. Teela had scrubbed that spot and hadn't even noticed it. They climbed into the narrow cockpit of a human-fabricated light fighter known by the UNE as a Ghost. But this fighter had been drastically modified; the cockpit was not round like a stock fighter's, but elongated, with a space about sixteen feet long behind the pilot and copilot seats. The heavily worn floor was fitted with recessed tie-downs. Tim quickly energized the craft and released the docking clips. They dropped out of the recessed bay beneath the engine room and shot away like a bullet. Within seconds they were traveling at sub-light speeds on a course for the Armegeddon.

"See, it goes fast," Tim said with a grin reminiscent of Ludwig without the silver caps. "I started out as a scrapper, hauling junk. The military was unloading obsolete gear. This is actually an experimental craft I had some Korlah friends of mine build from cannibalized fighters using the profits from some loads I sold to the Schwarzengeist collective. It's got twice the grav plates, a beefed-up sub-light drive, and more load-suppression coils than an assault pod. Minimal armor and no hyperlight. It just goes fast and can change direction faster than any military craft made. It's great for running loads in and out of hot spots. But as you can see, it has limited cargo space."

He fell silent for a while, expecting her to respond. Finally, he put the ship on autopilot and turned his chair to face her.

"Listen, kid, from what I can gather you've been out of the loop for a while. A lot has changed in just the last few months alone. We're headed for the Armageddon, they got a place onboard called Crossover. It's filled with crovers just like you and humans who don't give a shit, just like me. They got the sapien supremacists in the UNE section and they got collective purists in the Korlah section. Humans aren't welcome in the Korlah section, and Korlah aren't welcome in the UNE section. Crovers like you aren't welcome in either. I don't know how you got to be where you are, but it sounds like a hell of a story. We got a few hours to kill. You want to tell me about it?"

Teela cleared her throat and rubbed her hands together, trying to decide where to begin. After a brief internal debate she made her decision.

"Let me start at the beginning."

8 - Homecoming

The go-fast's autopilot reduced speed and emitted a low beep on final approach to their destination. A few minutes later, a patrol of six UNE fighters intercepted them. Tim told them they were independent security contractors hoping to find work with one of the collectives or UNE-sponsored corporations. The fighters led them to a delousing station, where the go-fast was checked for contraband and explosives, then escorted them to the Korlah spacecraft carrier known as the Armageddon to the UNE forces stationed there.

Ruth had described this carrier to Dade, and those memories were now Teela's, but they failed miserably to relate the size and scale of this craft. It looked like a whale with its chest open, ribs bared, and a cloud of flies hovering over it. The flies were hundreds of construction craft and worker transports, and the gaping hole was what remained after the Korlah were divided into those who wanted to stay and fight and those who chose to flee a war they believed could not be won. Several years earlier, two of the ship's five modular sections departed for a remote planet they called New Korlah. Ever since the division of forces, the Korlah who stayed were left with a ship in need of extensive work to prepare it for battle. These frenzied activities were the product of a joint human-Korlah task force dedicated to rebuilding the missing sections of the ship as well as developing the command structure needed to operate it.

The UNE fighters peeled off as Tim steered the go-fast into a docking cylinder. The cylinder rotated into the Armageddon and he followed a hangar pilot to a mooring tube. Although they were given directions, they quickly realized that without passes, there was only one place they would be able to go unescorted: the Crossover Café.

The Crossover Café was much more than a dining destination; it was a social hub that provided a neutral location for Korlah, humans, and crovers to meet and do business. Larger than most auditoriums, it had a central seating area with tables that seated two to ten people each. From the touch-screen table tops you could order meals, buy drinks, or purchase tickets to movies, concerts, and clubs in Crossover. A bar ran the length of one wall that was covered with decorations related to aircraft and space travel. Tim proceeded to a section of the bar that was dedicated to WWII fighter aircraft. A four-bladed propeller hung on the wall with framed pictures, uniforms, medals, and other war memorabilia around it. The bartender was waiting for them with a couple of cold beers when they bellied up to the counter.

"I saw you two coming from way off. Flyboys, right? And girls," he added, giving Teela a respectful nod.

"That's right," Tim said, pushing the beer back toward the bartender with his index finger. "I was thinking more along the line of rouk whiskey, if you don't mind."

"Sorry, buddy, this is it. Haven't had any hard liquor or tobacco products for over a month. Between the UNE embargo and the Korlah Council's ban on the sale of hard liquor and rouk juice, beer is all I have for sale, and right now all I have is one brand of beer. This is all there is, pal, and if I don't get a shipment soon, I'll be serving ice water."

Tim picked up the beer, took a large swallow, and looked past the bartender at the rows of full bottles of liquor on the shelf behind him. The bartender followed his gaze and guessed his thoughts.

"Empties, filled with colored water. Just wouldn't look right, a bar without bottles."

"What would a thimble of rouk whiskey go for?" Tim asked, rubbing his chin.

"I know what you're thinking, but forget it. If they catch you, the UNE will impound your ship and send you back to Earth and charge you with smuggling. It ain't right, but that's what they'll do."

"So rouk whiskey is legal here in Crossover, just not legal to transport it, right?" Tim said. He drained the beer and handed the glass to the bartender.

"Don't even think about it. Lots have tried and lots have fried. They got sniffers that can detect alcohol and rouk through sealed cans and bottles. Nobody's got any past the delousing station since the embargo went into effect." He brought Tim another beer.

"Ouch!" Tim cried when Teela poked him in the ribs. "I'm doing business here. We'll get to you in a minute." He turned back to the bartender. "So what would a shipment of rouk whiskey be worth to an enterprising man such as you?"

The bartender licked his lips, a telltale sign Tim recognized from his dealings with rouk addicts.

"How much are we talking about?"

"Liter bottles, quality seals on each, ten cases of Thor's Hammer."

"Bullshit," the bartender wheezed, his voice a whisper.

"For the wrong price, it's bullshit. For the right price it's under your bar in the next hour."

The bartender studied Tim's face for a moment. He placed a large gold coin on the counter and slid it toward Tim.

"It'd be worth its weight in gold. Literally, its weight in gold," he said.

Tim picked the odd-shaped coin up and studied it. It was heavy enough. He bit the edge and it left a mark. It was soft enough. On one side of the coin was the Mission emblem, and around the periphery of the other side were a number of Korlah glyphs with two larger glyphs in the center. He handed the coin to Teela.

"What's this say?" he asked. She gave the writing a quick glance.

"'Cherish life, reject despair, victory with honor,'" she snapped. She flipped the coin toward the bartender and he caught it in midair. "I need to get in touch with someone on the Korlah side. How can that be arranged?" she demanded.

The bartender looked surprised and confused at her disinterest in the negotiations. "Just go to the checkpoint," he said, pointing to a corridor off the side of the auditorium. "Tell them who you are, and tell them who you want to see. Shift change is in about ten minutes. If you're gonna do it, you should do it now. Checkpoint's gonna get real busy."

"Thanks for everything Tim, I'm sorry for the trouble I brought you," Teela said. She offered Tim her hand. He gave it a firm squeeze and shook it.

"No worries, it was a pleasure to crew with you. Good luck, Sula. If things don't work out with your friend, come back and we'll figure it out."

Teela gave him a respectful nod and headed for the corridor.

The checkpoint was a single-open hatch with four armed guards and a technician acting as an access clerk. Two guards were on one side of the door and two more on the other side. Seated at a touch-screen table, the clerk had just finished checking two early arrivals into the Crossover section.

"State your business," the clerk said without looking up.

"I'm here to see Mission Director Shawaugh," Teela replied.

The clerk looked up and studied the tattoos on Teela's face and chest. Her brow furrowed with disapproval. "All deserters are required to make their pleas for a pardon directly to the Council. The next session is in three shifts."

"I'm not a deserter. I have business with Director Shawaugh." Teela put her hands on her hips and let her right hand come to rest on the grip of her pistol. The guards jumped and energized their weapons.

"I told you that have business with Director Shawaugh," she repeated, moving her hand slowly away from the pistol.

The now wide-eyed clerk consulted her communication console. "Director Shawaugh is not on station."

"Then I request a meeting with Shawlmon," Teela said.

A line of Korlah waiting to enter Crossover began to form.

"The potentate meets with no one. Ever!" the clerk said, her impatience evident by the way she kept glancing at the growing line.

"Inform the potentate that I deliver a message from the human Daedalus Rimes. She will see me."

"But—"

"Just do it!"

With a look of contempt, the clerk rattled off the message on her touch screen and directed Teela out of the way while she began processing those waiting. It was only a few minutes before the message light began flashing. The clerk looked surprised when she read it. She called one of the guards over and after a whispered exchange, motioned Teela over. "Give me your weapons," she demanded.

Teela lifted the pistol out slowly and handed it to the clerk.

"Put your hand out."

Teela held out her hand and the clerk deftly snapped a wide metal bracelet around her wrist. The bracelet self-adjusted to a snug fit.

"A tracking device," the clerk explained. "Now go with the guard." She dismissed Teela with a wave before beckoning the next person in line.

Teela expected to be taken deep into the bowels of the security section, but instead she was taken to a nearby meeting room comfortably furnished with padded leather chairs and a highly polished hardwood table, all of which had to have been imported from Earth. The guard directed her inside and closed the door. Teela sat down and waited.

The hidden door opened without a sound, but Teela was expecting it; she rose to her feet as a cloaked figure emerged from the shadows. The person placed a bundle on the table and Teela recognized the pommel of a sword protruding from it.

Shyron threw back the hood of her cloak and sat down next to Teela. She stared at Teela and squinted. The nudge of the telepathic probe felt nearly imperceptible; the blocking Teela used against Rebecca had become a subconscious effort.

"I can't see you," Shyron said. "You have grown strong. I knew you would be back. I truly wish it had been sooner. I apologize that I can only return your robe; your reputation, I fear, has been destroyed." Shyron gazed at the bundle, her brow furrowed in deep remorse.

"You can't destroy the reputation of someone who never existed," Teela replied. "Shawlmon was a myth that you created and the Oracle promoted. I only pretended to be Shawlmon because I wanted to help change the horrible conditions aboard this ship. When I gave you the robe it was because I knew that I was not capable of leading the Korlah to victory in this war. I knew that Shawaugh would no longer be able to protect me as she had when I was a child. Now, everything I have ever known or believed has changed. I didn't come for Shawlmon's robe, Your Eminence. I came to ask you for help, yours and my old friend Shawaugh's. I am being hunted. The Oracle has stolen my child and means to kill me."

Shyron looked at her in disbelief and rose to her feet. "There are three Kahshinki warships within striking distance," she said, "and four more in transit. The humans, for all their industry and ability, continue to bicker amongst themselves and even now plot to take our vessel. It is I who need help. What of my children, your sisters? If we do not retreat, their existence will be forfeit. You fear for your life? Do you know what is being said about me? They say I murdered Shawlmon! Me, the receptacle of the true Shawlmon. I am under constant threat of assassination. The Council is actually considering charging me with your murder. And you come here to ask me for help?" Shyron moved to the chair across the table from Teela and buried her face in her hands.

"I—" Teela's throat constricted and she burst into tears. "No! Damn it," she cried, and shook her head. "I will not cry!" She cleared her throat and wiped the tears away. "If you can't help me, maybe we can help each other," she snarled.

Shyron leaned back, more to open her mind to Teela's onslaught of emotions than to distance herself from her angry glare. "How could you possibly do anything to help me now?"

Teela took a deep breath and considered her options. What could she do under the circumstances? What could Shyron do to help her?

"Both you and Shawaugh understand how the Oracle thinks. I need you to help me with a plan I have, a plan to stop the Oracle and restore order."

Shyron frowned and avoided Teela's eyes. "Shawaugh cannot help you. She cannot help either of us. She has most likely ceased."

"What? Ceased? When... how?" Teela gasped.

"A mission," Shyron whispered. "We agreed this planet cannot be saved. We agreed to save our sisters." She looked up and glared at Teela. "You convinced me we could succeed, and then you left us," she hissed.

"I gave you Shawlmon!" Teela cried. "What more could I have done?"

Shyron closed her eyes, bent over, and covered her face with her hands. "Shawlmon has been with me since the beginning," she moaned. "You cannot give me what I already possess. I needed you, Teela—you and Daedalus. You are the key. You are the answer. Shawaugh tried to fill the vacuum that I could not. She led in your absence. After the Council accused me of being an imposter, when it became obvious there was no hope of winning this war, Shawaugh began preparing our escape to New Korlah. One last mission, a deep-space materials drop, and we would have been able to leave this doomed system. She is six shifts overdue. I fear that my enemies have discovered our plan, and that she will not return."

Suddenly, screaming, red-hot, debilitating pain shot up Teela's arm like a lightning bolt. She let out a yelp and grabbed the wrist with the bracelet and rolled out of her chair onto the floor.

The door opened.

A cloaked person holding Teela's pistol stood in the doorway, weapon raised to fire. Shyron leapt from her chair and took cover behind the table.

Teela's world froze as murderous thoughts poured from the shadows of the assassin's cloak and flowed into her like the paralyzing charge from the bracelet. In that split second, she knew the assassin's plan: Shyron was the target, and Teela would be blamed for her assassination.

The first shot, a deafening roar of flame and smoke, shook the room. The assailant took two steps forward and kept the gun trained on Shyron. Teela watched helplessly as the assassin leaned across the table and aimed at Shyron's head.

"Stop!" Teela screamed, desperately straining every muscle in her body against the effects of the bracelet. The assassin dropped the gun, fell to her knees, and collapsed on the table.

There was shouting outside the room. Shyron dashed to the door to close and lock it. She grabbed the assassin by the hood and yanked her off the table. The assassin's head flopped and twisted as if the neck were broken. Blood poured from the ears, eyes, and mouth.

Shyron clutched the bullet wound on the side of her neck. Blood covered her hand and the collar of her vest. She stared at the body of the assassin. Her eyes shifted to Teela and her brow furrowed. She grabbed the bundle on the table and pulled the swords out. Kneeling next to Teela, she slid one blade between

Teela's wrist and the bracelet and raised the other in preparation to strike.

"If this doesn't work, I will have to remove your hand," she said. Teela closed her eyes.

The first strike generated a shower of sparks and the blades of both swords arced with energy. Teela's body lurched with spasms and then went limp. The second strike severed the bracelet. Shyron removed it and massaged Teela's wrist and arm. Teela sucked in a breath of air and sat up.

"Why were you wearing a riz shackle?" Shyron asked.

"They said it was for tracking my location," Teela answered, using the table for support to stand. She paused and looked at the assassin. "Did you do that?"

"I'm not sure," Shyron said, gingerly touching her wound. "I have never killed like this. Not in an instant, not this effectively. I attempted to blur her vision, scatter her thoughts. When I did, something happened; I saw the assassin through your eyes. You were like a lens through which my mind focused. If the Oracle knows of this ability, it would explain why she wants you so badly."

"She wants me dead!" Teela cried.

"Yes. If she cannot control you, she will want to make sure that no one else can." A large boom followed by another on the door ended the conversation. "Follow me," Shyron said, moving to a narrow gap in the wall. Teela holstered the assassin's pistol, grabbed the swords and bundle, and followed.

The passage was narrow and so low that she and Shyron had to stoop. After one lengthy corridor, a turn, and a short stretch, Shyron stopped and turned to face Teela.

"You have a ship?"

"Yes. Well, no. It's not mine. I came with a friend," Teela said.

"The only way to transit from the Korlah segment of the ship to crossover will be through the checkpoint. They will be expecting us and will have instructions to kill us both." Shyron put her hand on Teela's shoulder and her expression became intense. "The Oracle can walk past people without being seen. I believe I know how she does this. If you open your mind as you did with the assassin, it may be possible for us to do the same."

Teela pulled the pistol from its holster and checked the remaining rounds. "I have no idea what I did or how I did it. I will not allow you to risk your life for mine. Just point me toward the checkpoint and I'll take it from there. I'm sorry for the trouble. This is not what I had planned."

"If I stay here, they will kill me. I am going with you," Shyron said.

"Are you insane? You can't come with me," Teela cried, slapping the pistol back into its holster. Shyron yanked her hand from Teela's shoulder as if she'd been stung.

"You would deny me your protection?" Shyron hissed.

"My protection? You are insane," Teela growled as she crossed her arms and looked down to break eye contact. "I am living with pirates. Well, not really pirates. But they are definitely smugglers. They drink too much, and they're filthy!"

"We are sisters," Shyron said as she dropped to her knees and looked up into Teela's face. She presented her palms in submission.

Teela looked away. The face was hers, a genetic duplicate like every other birthing unit on board. It was Shyron's mind in her birth sister Eemela's body. The sabat had been changed, but physically, Shyron was Teela 20.10127.

"Don't! Don't beg," Teela cried. She grabbed Shyron's hands and pulled her back to her feet. "You would probably live longer if you stay, but you are welcome to come with me."

Shyron gave Teela a brief hug and turned to a small control panel on the wall. She used it to display the checkpoint. There were now twelve guards at the access and additional checkpoints had been set up on the Korlah side. Teela put her hand on the pistol and did the math: five rounds and twelve guards. It didn't look good. Shyron turned away from the display and took Teela's head in her hands.

"Open your mind to me. Let me in," Shyron said, moving her face close to Teela's and closing her eyes.

Teela closed her eyes and concentrated. Their faces touched and the thermal resolution of their hisnahs blurred to form a tunnel of light. Through that tunnel, Shyron's mind entered hers. Not like a telepathic probe; it felt to Teela like transfer.

"Stop!" she cried, and pushed Shyron away. "What are you trying to do?"

"It's done," Shyron said. "A bit of me is now inside you. It will help with what we are about to do."

"What are we going to do?"

"I am going to tap that tremendous capability of yours, and we are going to walk out without being seen."

"I was right, you are insane. We're going to die," Teela said. "Here, put Shawlmon's robe on. It's bulletproof and pulse-resistant."

To the Korlah security contingent remotely monitoring the access point, it was obvious that Shawlmon walked out with the mercenary that had gone to visit her, but for some reason, the guards at the checkpoint did not seem to see her. The Korlah alarm klaxon sounded and the door at the access point slid shut behind Teela and Shawlmon.

On the Crossover side, four guards and the clerk were shouting at each other. The clerk pointed at the two Korlah who had just entered Crossover; the guards shot them down with pulse weapons. Human and Korlah guards from Crossover converged, and within moments there was an armed standoff at the access.

Teela walked briskly toward the tunnel to the hangar, where she hoped Tim's go-fast would be waiting for them. Shyron walked directly behind Teela and kept one hand on her shoulder. To everyone in the room, they were a single human dressed in typical duty coveralls. From remote monitors within Crossover, directions were being issued to apprehend two intruders that no one outside of the security room could see.

Tim was putting the last of five small boxes into the cargo bay of his go-fast when a young man in coveralls climbed up his ladder. Tim had his pistol out before the box he'd been holding hit the deck.

"Where the hell do you think you're going, buddy?" he demanded, centering the pistol on the man's chest. In the blink of an eye, had he blinked, the man became two Korlah: Teela, and another dressed in an elaborate robe with twin gold-encrusted swords.

"What... the... hell?" Tim said, looking first at Shyron, then back at Teela.

"No time to explain. We need to go—quickly," Teela said.

A bullet ricocheted off the open cowling.

"Now!" Teela shouted, jumping into the ship and pulling Shyron with her.

Four more bullets struck before the cargo hatch finished closing. Tim was in the pilot's seat and the ship was banking, presenting its armored underside to whoever was shooting at them as Tim maneuvered across the hangar.

Tim pressed the communication bud in his ear and cleared his throat. "Ah... hello, Control, this is light cargo niner five one three foxtrot seven, requesting a departure lock," he said calmly into the microphone.

"Light cargo, departure denied. Please proceed directly to the security bay."

"Look!" Teela cried. "That lock is rotating. Once they start, they can't be stopped."

"It's got a ship in it," Tim said, banking his craft and accelerating.

"It's small, we both will fit."

"Ohhhhh, shit!" Tim cried as he raced toward the closing gap. They squeezed into the portal through the shrinking opening with a shriek of metal on metal and bumped into the ship ahead of them with a jarring thump. The back of the go-fast was still sticking out a few inches. A shudder shook them and the sound of crushing metal rumbled through it. Tim pushed the throttle forward. Unable to move deeper into the lock, his ship slid over the other one with a sound of grinding metal, then cocked in the confines of the limited space.

"Get in the seat, both of you," Tim said. "We have inertia suppression, but with what I'm about to do, it's sure to feel like I don't."

"What about the cargo?" Teela asked, looking at the boxes.

"Oh, yeah," Tim said, flipping a switch.

Teela watched as the floor of the cargo bay liquefied and the boxes sank. Tim flipped the switch again and the floor returned to its original worn and scratched appearance.

"Polymorphic technology—it's a smuggler's wet dream," he said with a wink. "Okay, get that seat belt on. The evasion program is set. Soon as the computer sees a window of opportunity, we will be on Mister Toad's wild ride… times ten."

Teela and Shyron squeezed into the copilot's seat and Teela was loosening the straps to accommodate their combined girth when Tim shot out of the lock in full reverse. A fraction of a second later, the ship crammed into the lock with them followed them out.

"Damn," Tim moaned when he realized the ship was a heavily armed UNE interceptor.

Tim pulled back on the stick and gave the ship full forward throttle. The underside of his craft struck the top of the UNE fighter as he bounced up and away. Dodging traffic, he made multiple speed and direction changes as the number of craft in his pursuit went from one to three to ten. After the third pulse blast buffeted the ship, Teela covered her face, certain they were doomed.

"Here we go!" Tim said, releasing the controls and pulling his hands back to his chest. The ship lurched up, down, and side to side with an intensity and speed that rattled their bones. It jumped in and out of sub-light, each time retuning to the bone-jarring speed and direction changes. Thirty minutes and what felt to Teela like an eternity later, the ship settled onto a steady course. Tim intently monitored the scanners for another fifteen minutes, then, confident that he had lost their pursuers, entered a new heading and turned on the autopilot.

"One or two more deliveries like this last one and I could have retired. Now, thanks to you, I can't show my face on

Crossover or any other UNE-controlled station." Tim turned to face Teela and Shyron. "You want to tell me who your friend is, and just what the hell is going on?"

9 - Contracts

James McClellen watched from his monitor as a pair of polished brass doors slid silently shut behind three men leaving an elevator deep beneath the headquarters of the Central Intelligence Agency in Washington, DC. They proceeded down a hallway toward a large door guarded by two armed Marines. The man in the center, whose arms were handcuffed behind his back, was in his mid-fifties and had salt-and-pepper gray hair; his solemn expression was that of a condemned man. The young men in black suits on either side held him by the elbows and directed his movement.

Their visit was related to a recent report from an off-world operative who'd discovered that key members of the Quorum had left Earth for the safety and relative autonomy of the mining frontier in space. In order for McClellan to find them, he would need to concentrate his assets and quietly clean up some loose ends. He pressed a button that unlocked the eight hardened steel bolts securing the ballistic steel door of his office. The door opened with the assistance of hydraulic rams and the men entered. The one in handcuffs was led to a chair centered before McClellen's large oak desk.

"Remove the cuffs," McClellen ordered. "Wait outside." McClellen closed and locked the door behind the other two men with the push of a button.

"Sit down, Mr. Johnson."

"I didn't kill your brother, General. I don't care what that bitch Porter told you. I didn't do it."

"I'm not a general anymore, Chris. I'm the secretary of Homeland Security. I know you didn't pull the trigger, but you ordered it, didn't you?"

"Of course I did. It came down from the top. Parkhurst ordered it. He wanted you dead, too. I'm not a politician, Mr. McClellen; I don't care why. I was just doing my job."

"I know. I've studied your psych profile, Chris. That's why you're here. I have work that requires a man with your skill set. If you're interested, I'll reinstate you."

"What about Bethany Porter? I heard you two were tight."

"Beth is crippled, both physically and emotionally. She has ties to the targets and can't be trusted to follow orders. I'm using her as a consultant for the time being. When I'm finished, she'll be retired."

"You picked the right man for the job," Chris said with a sly smile. "Who are the targets?"

McClellen tossed him a manila envelope. Chris opened it and reviewed the contents. He looked up with a puzzled expression.

"A crover... And a child?"

"Is that a problem, Mr. Johnson?"

"No, sir. Eliminating the noodlehead will be a pleasure. It's just that kids are bad business. Usually only happens as collateral damage, and when it does, it always creates a big stink. And you want to target *this* kid? Seriously, have you considered the political ramifications?"

"That's why it has to look like an accident, or better yet, someone from within the Church." McClellen stood and leaned on the desk. "I have intelligence from a reliable source indicating the targets are... well, it's hard to explain and sound credible. But we believe if they are eliminated, the political threat posed by the Church of Shawlmon will be completely resolved."

"I don't need a reason, sir. What about the noodlehead? The report says her whereabouts are unknown. How am I supposed to find her?"

"Bait. I have someone she has contacted in the past, and I believe will try to contact again. When she does, that will be your chance."

"Does the bait have a name?"

"I'll be in touch," McClellan said. "Here." He tossed him another envelope. "Your new addresses, both residential and office. All of your bank accounts have been restored, even the offshore ones. Get your team together; I'll call you when I get more info." McClellen pushed the button and the door to his office opened. Chris didn't wait to be excused. With his escorts in tow he made a beeline for the elevator. He glanced back only when the office door began to close behind him. McClellen wasn't sure if Chris looked surprised or relieved to be leaving with his life.

McClellen picked up a report from the Center for Disease Control that detailed the biological threat posed by the Korlah; at least that's how they described the symbiotic organism. Although no harmful effects could be linked with contact, the testing continued. According to this report, a treatment had been found that would eradicate the organism without harming the host. Permission for testing on human subjects was waiting approval.

The intercom light on his desk began to flash. McClellen turned on his screen and saw Beth Porter standing outside his door, gesturing wildly to one of the guards. He pushed the button to open the door. As soon as there was enough room she pushed through and marched to his desk as fast as her braced leg and cane would allow.

"You released Chris Johnson! Are you nuts?" she screamed. Foam and spittle flew from her mouth, reminding him of a rabid dog. "That prick shot your brother. He had me abducted. The only reason he is still alive is because you told me you were going to kill him!"

"Sit down, Beth. Sit down and shut up!"

"No! That bastard dies. If you haven't got the guts, I'll do it."

"Sit down!" McClellen shouted.

"Screw you! You terminate that prick or I quit."

McClellen opened his desk drawer, pulled out a large, sealed envelope, and tossed it towards Beth.

"What the hell is that?"

"I'm tired of your bullshit, Beth. Nothing you do is worth this crap. It's your retirement package. It's the good kind: on the beach, in the sun. Take it and get the hell out of my office before I decide a shallow grave is the better idea."

Her scowl changed to an expression of disbelief. She looked at the envelope and then back to McClellen.

"He killed your brother!" she cried. She swept his desk with her good arm, sending the envelope and several stacks of paper flying off. She stomped over to a shadow box on the wall where her Korlah uniform and sword were on display and smashed the glass with her cane.

"Guards!" McClellen shouted.

"This is mine! I earned it!" Beth screamed, pulling the tunic and sword from the frame. One guard grabbed her from behind as the other pulled the cane, sword, and tunic from her hands.

"It's mine!" she screamed.

"Take it, Beth. You did earn it. Take it and go home," he said softly, regret creeping into his voice. Then he added firmly, "If you go near Johnson, you'll end up behind bars, or worse."

The Marines had to drag her from his office. Her curses and screams ceased only after the steel doors closed and latched. McClellen sat at his desk and stared at the broken shadow box. He picked up the phone.

"Yeah, see if you can get Chris Johnson on his cell."

He didn't have to wait long before they rang back.

"Hello? Yes, Chris, thanks for calling. A slight change in plans. Beth retired today. If she gets in your way you have my permission to deal with her as you see fit."

Julie Rimes noticed the black sedan across the street when she opened the shades after arriving home from work. It must have pulled up right after she got home, because she was certain it wasn't there when she crossed the street. She looked out the window again ten minutes later. The car was still there, and she could see the shadow of the driver on the passenger seat, but she couldn't see his face.

It was too soon for another visit from Agent Cooper, she thought, smiling when she recalled the last time he'd stopped by. He was exceptionally flirtatious and she was equally evasive. When he left, she was sure he was pouting. She'd told her friends at work about the younger man, his big brown eyes and the way she would catch him looking at her. She told them she was attracted to him but was concerned about the age difference. Her friend Marge said it was a textbook case of cougar and prey—that she should pounce before he gets away. She laughed out loud and returned to the kitchen to fix dinner.

The doorbell rang. She looked out the window. The black sedan was still there, but the driver was gone. She looked out the peephole to see Agent Richard Cooper smiling back at her. She unbolted the door and opened it.

"Hello, Richard. It's a little early for your visit."

"Here, these are for you," he said, handing her a bouquet of long-stemmed roses. "I thought maybe... we could go out to dinner."

"They're beautiful," she said, and took the bundle before glancing toward the kitchen. "I just put dinner in the microwave."

"Come on—dinner on the town with a handsome man, or something out of a microwave? Not a difficult choice."

"Richard, I'm old enough to be your—"

"No, you aren't," he interrupted. "You're only eleven years older than I am. Your husband was twelve years older than you. If you prefer older men, I understand. If you're not attracted to me, just say so. I'm not good at this, Julie, so don't play games with me," he said, the pout returning to his face.

As she would later describe the moment to her friend Marge, it was the combination of those big brown eyes and the injured expression that convinced her. She tossed the bouquet onto a table, pulled him inside by the lapels, kicked the door shut, and pounced.

10 - Discovery

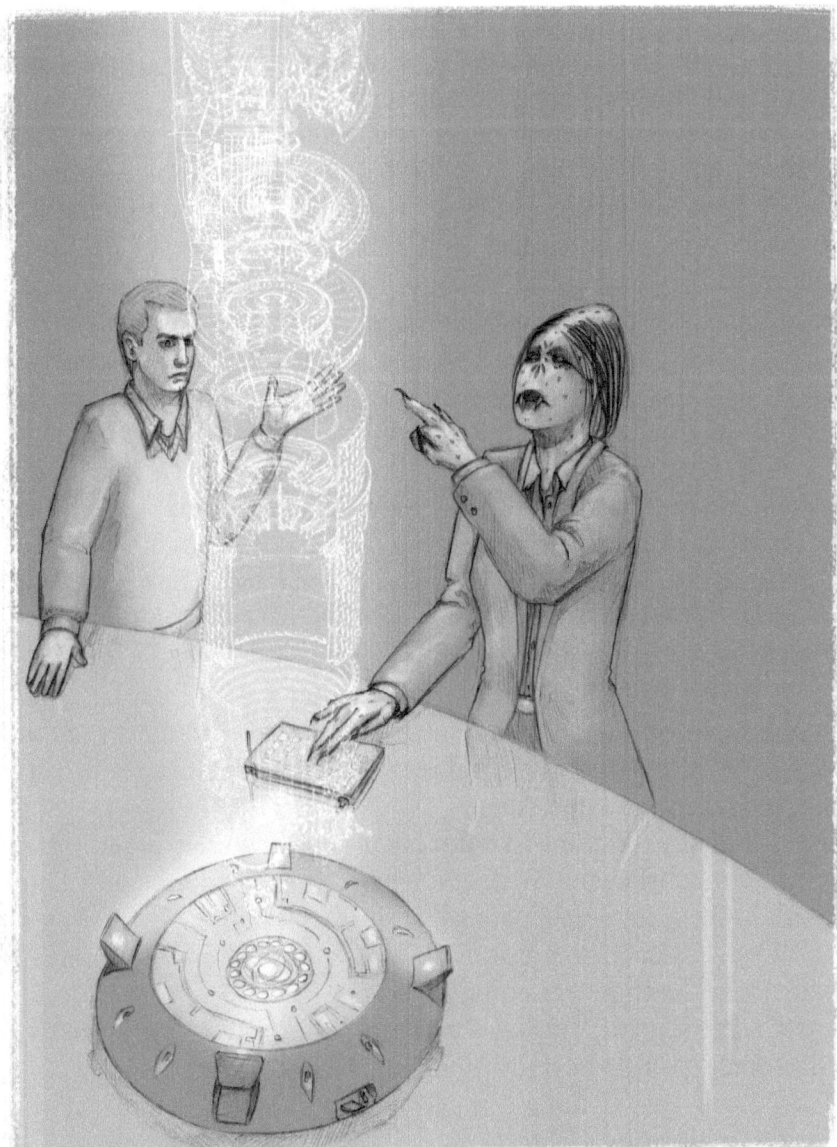

Richard Parkhurst strode toward the hangar, ignoring the military personnel working in the tunnels that branched off of it. His mind was on the shuttle that was about to arrive. The courier on board had information that, if true, could tip the balance of power to the Quorum's advantage. This was the break he'd been hoping for. All the intelligence so far had told him the Korlah were not interested in conquering Earth, which meant that anything he learned from them would only help the Quorum regain control.

The airlock growled to life and began rotating inward when the transport arrived. Parkhurst looked at his watch; it was ten minutes late. He paced at the door another five minutes until the occupants had disembarked and three military types, a female flight attendant, and a Korlah wearing a dark-blue jumpsuit passed through the security checkpoint. The military types ignored him and proceeded up the corridor. The flight attendant stopped and waited for the crew. The Korlah turned and looked at him expectantly, then greeted him cheerfully with an Australian accent.

"Hi, you must be Dick Parkhurst. Name's Oswald Gitch. Pleasure to meet ya." The Korlah extended her hand, but Parkhurst just stared, his disgust evident.

"Alrighty," she said, withdrawing her hand. "So nobody told you I was a crover?"

"A what?" he demanded.

"Crover. It's short for crossover. That's what they're calling us volunteers who gave up our humanity to save humanity. I don't give a shit if you're a xenophobe or sapien supremist. Get over it, mate, we're on the same side."

"I'm sorry," Parkhurst said, his expression unchanged. "I was expecting a courier, not an agent. I've read your file, Doctor Gitch. I didn't know you were..."

"Dead? Yeah, as a doornail. What you see is the miracle of modern transference technology. From a fat little bald man to this. Wow! What a deal. You take a pheromone pill? I don't need you or any other asshole trying to shag me. Got it?"

"I have an implant; it's good for a month," Parkhurst said, pointing to his left shoulder.

"Brilliant. I heard they were moving to implants. You got somewhere private I can brief you? Got some info here that will knock your socks off. Brought it personally, because this kind of shit you don't trust to a courier." Oswald gestured towards her valise.

Parkhurst led her to a secure area and into a room set up with audiovisual displays and Oswald set up her equipment, talking the entire time about the inequities and prejudice she had experienced from humans and Korlah since transfer. For the most part, Parkhurst ignored her.

"I'm part of a joint technological and archeological group tasked with documenting the origins of the Korlah and Kahshinki. One of our studies involved what was described as a map room, but has proven to be much, much more. Conduits leading from the room have residue that is thousands of years old. I'm thinking one hundred to two hundred thousand. The C-14 data says 350,000, but that's bloody hard to believe. Here, let me show you," she said, displaying a three-dimensional image of the campaign vessel on the projection screen.

"There are three sets of abandoned conduits leading to and from the map room. One set goes directly to the ship's main hyperdrive power grid. One goes directly to the propulsion system. This part of the propulsion system is integral to the hyperdrive, yet it's not being used. Another conduit goes to this grouping of chambers located in each segment of the ship. They call them spectacle chambers; transparent spheres held in a gravitational stasis. The Korlah use them as arenas for boxing matches. Historically, they were empty until the Korlah put them to use. I have a theory they were once part of a massive biological computer.

"There is a control housing surrounding the map room that connects the ship's biological computer to the power system, and to this unused portion of the hyperdrive engine. My scientific analysis group believes organisms in the ship's biological computer evolved into what the Korlah now call Kahshinki. That makes this vessel pre-Kahshinki. Whoever or whatever built this ship is long gone. This is not a map room, it's a navigation center designed to control the ship's route and speed. I think the unused control housing is a fourth drive capable of boosting speeds to thousands of times faster than what is known—basically moving from one portion of the galaxy to the next instantaneously. Whoever built this ship traveled the galaxy at will thousands of years ago. Whatever happened to them is a mystery worth solving."

"So what?" Parkhurst said. "Who gives a rat's ass about their history? I don't need you wasting my resources solving mysteries. What do you have that can help me win this war?"

Oswald shook her head with disgust.

"Pay attention. I'll use small words you can understand. I have the blueprint for an engine modification that will give our fighters a longer range and make them faster than anything in the galaxy. We could be in and out of a battle ten, twenty, a hundred light years away, before the enemy knew we were there. Would that help your bloody war effort?"

"What's the R&D time?"

"Thirty days, if you let me use the fighter prototype you have under construction."

"That project is top secret," Parkhurst said. "Who told you about it?"

"Ah, for Christ's sake, Dick, if it's worth stealing, I know about it. I was looking those plans over four months ago—two months before you started production. The Korlah have a collective dedicated to ship enhancements. Your design wasn't all that special, so it wasn't worth stealing. The good news is it will provide the platform for my modifications. Turn the project over to me and my team, and I'll have a functional prototype for you in less than thirty days."

"All right. The project is yours. You have thirty days. What else do you need?" Parkhurst was calculating the time it would take to go into full production if the flight tests were successful.

"Directions to the nearest pub and some female company that doesn't have their knickers in bunch," Oswald said with a salacious smile.

11 - Bait

The doorbell rang. Julie glanced out the window and saw a black sedan parked across the street and grinned. She stopped at the mirror by the front door and checked her hair and makeup. Satisfied, she opened the door, saying "I was just—"

"Who are you?" she asked, finding two men in suits and dark sunglasses instead of Agent Cooper, as she'd expected. One man was in his mid to late fifties with short gray hair trimmed into a sparse flattop. The other man was in his early thirties and had his thick black hair slicked back into a tight ponytail.

"Agents Johnson and Doherty, ma'am," the older man said, holding out his FBI badge and photo ID. "Ms. Rimes, your security has been compromised. You have five minutes to gather your personal possessions, and then we need to leave."

"I… I need to talk to Richard, ah, Agent Cooper," Julie said, closing the door, but Agent Johnson blocked it with his foot.

"Agent Cooper is the reason we're here, ma'am," he said. "It was Richard who called this in."

Julie released the door and grabbed her phone. The speed dial was set and the call placed by the time Agent Johnson entered her apartment. An automated message indicated the number was no longer in service. She hung up and dialed again.

"Ms. Rimes, Ms. Rimes!" Johnson said, when she began dialing a third time. "Agent Cooper's message was coded, a panic code indicating his assignment had been compromised. You are his assignment. For some reason he believes you are in danger, so we need to move you." Julie stared at her phone in dismay. "We can't reach him either, so we have to assume he's been captured or killed. If captured, he will reveal your location; it's just a matter of time. That's why we need to hurry."

With those few words, Julie's world collapsed around her. All she heard was that the first man she'd trusted since her husband disappeared had been killed. She stumbled and dropped the phone. Agent Johnson caught her. He helped her collect her purse and coat and then guided her down to the car.

How long the binge lasted Beth couldn't say. When she finally woke up after running out of whiskey, she spent the next six hours in a state of semi-lucid reflection with a .45-caliber pistol in her lap. It was a large handgun with big bullets. She studied the intricacies of its engineered design while evaluating her entire life. The moment of reflection took her back to the 9mm slug that had punched a hole through her brain, leaving half of her body partially paralyzed. That injury had been accidental. The one she was contemplating would not be.

The whiskey and pain pills had failed to vanquish her fear and had only contributed to the dull ache in her head and her growing nausea. It wasn't death that she feared, it was the possibility that she might live and end up worse off than she already was. She picked up the pistol and pressed the barrel against her aching temple. There was an infomercial on the television; regular broadcasting was suspended at this late hour. Her hand began to shake, slightly at first, then building to a palsy that shook her whole body. She dropped the pistol to her lap and grabbed the bottle of whiskey. She poured the last few drops down the back of her throat and ended up choking on her own saliva. With an anguished groan, she threw the bottle against the far wall and smashed it.

Someone knocked on her door. She ignored it. They knocked louder.

"Go away! Leave me alone!" she shouted.

The door handle turned. She'd left it unlocked to make it easy for whoever came to investigate the gunshot. When the door flew open, she grabbed for the pistol in her lap, but knocked it to the floor. She looked up to find Agent Cooper pointing his pistol at her.

"Come to finish the job?" she said, straightening in her chair.

"That was an accident, Beth," he said, closing the door and returning his pistol to its holster beneath his arm. "I heard glass breaking. Are you all right?"

The apartment was a mess; dirty dishes in the sink, trash and clothes littering the floors. Beth was wearing the Korlah uniform she'd liberated from McClellan's office; the sword was on the floor by her chair. Cooper noted the broken whiskey bottle by the wall.

"Finer than frog's hair, Agent Cooper. What do you want?" Beth leaned down to pick up her pistol and fell out of the chair. Cooper knelt to help her.

"Get off me!" she slurred. "I don't need your God damn help or anybody else's." She clawed her way back onto the chair with her one functional arm.

"I'm not with the FBI anymore, Beth. I was fired yesterday. They moved Julie and no one will talk to me. I can't get through to McCormick or McClellen. My apartment has been broken into, but nothing taken. Something is up. They had no reason to move her. No good reason to fire me. I need your help."

Beth laughed derisively. "My help? You came here for my help? Jesus, Coop, if you're coming to me, you must be in serious trouble."

"Will you talk to McClellen for me?"

"McClellen fired me. Well, retired me, actually. He won't take my calls and I was served with a restraining order this morning. If I go anywhere near him they're gonna lock me up."

"When did this happen?"

"I'm guessing yesterday, maybe day before, it's kind of a blur. And you got fired, too?" Beth's angry expression faded. "McClellen just reactivated a man I used to work with. Black ops wet work; real nasty shit. He intends to kill someone and doesn't want me around. I think I know who he's after."

"What are you talking about?"

"McClellen's been trying to kill Rebecca since he took over Homeland Security. And now he's got it in his head that Dade was a Korlah agent, and that makes both Teela and her kid some kind of global security threat. He knows I would object to killing Teela and that I disagree with his belief the Korlah are here to conquer us. He knows that you personally asked the president to oversee the protection of Julie Rimes, so I'm guessing he's pretty sure you would object to them using her as bait."

"That's nuts. McCormick would have a fit."

"I doubt he would really give a shit. Since the arrival of Teela's letter, it's clear she's not involved in politics anymore. Nobody in Washington is gonna miss her."

"We can't allow this! The risk to Julie is unacceptable. We need to find out where they have taken her. We need to get her back," Cooper said.

"Whoa, slow down. You're tossing the 'we' word around like *I* give a shit. Who the hell is Julie Rimes to me? I met her once, she didn't much like me, and the feeling's mutual," Beth said.

"She doesn't deserve this. She's been through enough. Julie is a good woman, a good person. She's really intelligent, funny and…"

"Oh no… Coop, please tell me you're not in love," Beth interrupted. Cooper blushed and frowned at her. "Jesus, Coop, have you been boning Dade's widow? Is that why they fired you?"

By this time Cooper's face was beet red. He snatched her pistol off the floor and handed it back to her.

"Sorry to bother you, Ms. Porter. I can tell you have more important things to do. I'll let you get back to your pity party. Maybe it will end with a bang."

"Screw you, dipshit!" Beth screamed. "Why the hell should I help you? It was you who shot me. It's your God damned fault I'm like this!" She pointed the gun at him and feebly rose to her feet.

"It's Rebecca's fault you got shot. If you want to do something about it, help me," Cooper said.

The fury in her face faded as her hand began to shake. Her hand dropped to her side and she plopped back down into the chair with a sob. She set the gun in her lap and covered her face.

"I finally understand what Teela has been trying to tell me. It's hopeless. I'm like Dade. I'm dead, Coop," she cried. "They just haven't buried me yet." Tears were trickling out from under the hand she held over her eyes.

Cooper turned away and went into the kitchen. The sound of rattling dishes and running water drew Beth out of her momentary despair. She wiped her eyes and hobbled off to the bathroom. After washing her face and silently chastising herself for the loss of composure, she returned. Cooper was standing by the kitchen table with two cups.

"Coffee?" he asked, setting a steaming cup down in front of her. He took a seat and began sipping his. Beth walked to the table, alternating her weight between the cane and her braced leg. With effort, she sat and picked up the cup of coffee.

"I'm a liability, Coop. A cripple who can't get out of her own way," she said. "How could I possibly do anything to help you?"

"Are you in? Yes or no."

"Yeah, I'm in. Sorry about what I said earlier. I'm a mean, sloppy drunk. What's the plan?"

"Well, Teela said she was going to go back to the big ship to get help. If they intend to use Julie as bait, they will parade her around where Teela might see her. We need to get off world. We need to find Teela before they do."

"Off world? Are you nuts? Unless you have a corporate sponsor or a direct connection with the UNE or Korlah, that's not going to happen," Beth said.

"Well, it just so happens that I do." Cooper removed an oval disc the size of a silver dollar from his vest and set it on the table.

"What's that?" Beth asked.

"Shawlmon… ah, Teela, had it with her at the presidential retreat when she was shot. The French ambassador claimed that Teela spoke to him telepathically and told him it's a panic button. If you're Korlah and in trouble, you press it and help comes. The ambassador squeezed it, it made a click, and few minutes later the Korlah Marines landed and kicked ass."

"I've seen these before," Beth said. "Korlah soldiers wear them. Have you tested it since the attack?"

"No, you're the first person I told about it. I was going to give it back to Teela after the visit to Julie's, but I was interrupted."

Beth picked up the device and examined the underside. There was a triangular opening that matched a button just above the embroidered name on her Korlah uniform. She put it over the button and turned it. The disc locked onto the button with a snap.

"Don't press it!" Cooper said. "You didn't press it, did you?"

"No, I just clipped it on. They go on warrior uniforms. So you think if we press this, the Korlah will come pick us up?"

"Yep. When they come, you will need to tell them we need a ride to the big ship."

"That's your plan? First, I speak very little Korlah. Mostly I know how to hurl insults and challenge them to fight. Second, are you nuts?"

"Okay, it's a little sketchy, but they know you. They trust you. If they know where Teela is, I figure they'll contact her and let her know we're looking for her. It's a place to start."

"When do you want to do this?" Beth said with a yawn.

"Tonight, before daybreak. It will take about an hour to get far enough away from the city to minimize interference. So, about an hour from now."

"Hell, no time like the present, I guess. All right, let's do it, then," Beth said, pushing herself up from the table. "I need a nap. Wake me when we get there."

The drive took a little longer than Cooper had planned. It was just before sunup when he pulled the rental off a dirt road and into an open field several miles off a rural highway. He got out of the car and looked around, leaving Beth snoring loudly in the car. There were no houses or signs of human habitation within sight.

Beth woke from her deep sleep with a snort when Cooper shook her. The eastern sky was glowing brightly and ribbons of light had pierced the morning clouds when Beth squeezed the disc on her uniform. It made a soft pop, then a faint sizzling sound that lasted for a few seconds. She and Agent Cooper eagerly watched the skies for the next twenty minutes.

The sun was up when a pickup truck drove by. It slowed down and the driver peered out at them before accelerating away.

"They're not coming," Beth said. "I'm going back to sleep."

She turned and hobbled back toward the car. Cooper was squinting at the rising sun when there was a gust of wind followed by two loud thumps. Beth turned around to find two armed Korlah warriors pointing energized pulse rifles at Cooper. Their ship was less than four feet above her head.

"Now would be a good time to say something," Cooper said.

Beth walked forward offering an upturned palm, her crippled arm hung limply at her side.

"I Bethaugh, Warrior Bethaugh. Help, please see Shawlmon," Beth said, mixing English and Korlah.

The warriors stepped apart and a third Korlah, this one unarmed and only lightly armored, dropped down between them. She scrutinized Beth from head to toe.

"You are the human warrior, Bethaugh?" the Korlah asked in perfect English.

"Yes, I am. You speak English?" Beth asked.

"I am called Rosauh. I am the interpreter assigned to this rescue vessel. What is the nature of your emergency?"

"My assistant and I need to see Shawlmon. There is someone I need to find, a Korlah with a human transfer. I am certain she has gone to Shawlmon for help."

Rosauh blanched. Beth took this as a bad sign.

"What's the problem? Did I say something wrong?"

"Please follow me," Rosauh said. She stepped back into the gravity field and was lifted up and into the waiting ship.

"She was not happy to see me, Coop," Beth said. "Something is not right. I think we should wait, find another way."

"I'm going. You want to stay, I'll tell her you decided not to go," Cooper said. He stepped into the gravity field and waved as he disappeared into the underbelly of the transport.

"I got a bad feeling about this," Beth muttered before following him. The two warriors followed her.

The underside of the transport had barely closed when the transport disappeared and a rush of wind flowed in to fill its void.

12 - Departures

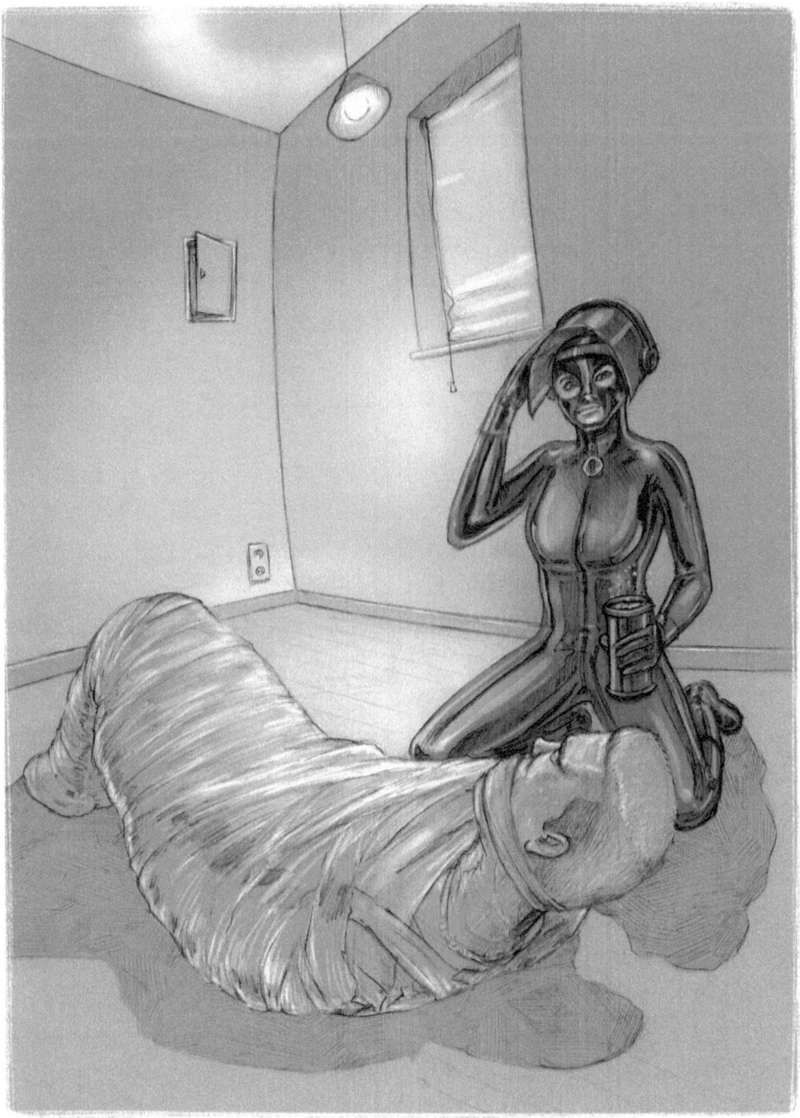

"The package has arrived."

The words came to Barry through a clear tube attached to a receiver behind his right ear as he waited in the hotel room of a young woman he had been tracking for several weeks.

"Do you have confirmation?" he asked. His voice was sent to a team of six men outside the building.

"No, sir, she's wearing a hood. Something on the face, a mask, maybe; can't get a visual. Do we take her?"

"No. If it's her, I'll do it here," Barry said, recalling his failed last attempt to kill Rebecca's assassin in public. On that occasion, he'd given the order to terminate without hesitation, but the girl he killed turned out to be the daughter of a public employee in the service of the Quorum. In retrospect, it was an obvious setup. The assassin had chosen the girl because she looked like her; she had worn the same clothes and led him to the girl's home. They only lost sight of her for a few seconds, but in that carefully scripted moment, the assassin disappeared and the dupe walked into the sights of Barry's sniper.

Barry attached a six-inch silencer to the end of his pistol, released the safety, and chambered the first round. The first two shells contained a special ordnance designed to penetrate body armor and deliver a nonlethal sliver of quickly dissolving material laced with a powerful tranquilizer. The remaining rounds contained high-velocity armor-piercing slugs, just in case. It was not his practice to capture; this was something new, something he knew was dangerous. Despite Parkhurst's advice to leave the wet work to others, Barry intended to make this ghost of an assassin suffer for killing his men—and making a fool of him.

"She's..." said the voice from his receiver. The message was followed by static, then silence.

"I didn't get the last. Repeat," Barry said as he stood and moved behind a wall next to the bed to get a clean shot at the door.

"What's happening, people?" he whispered, tapping the receiver behind his ear. He heard the swipe of a keycard and the click of the solenoid as the door unlocked. It opened about four inches and he saw a motion, heard a soft thump, and made his next mistake: he looked at the little black ball that had been tossed into the room.

The flash grenade went off with a dull pop slightly louder than a popping balloon. The flash was so bright it caused momentary blindness even through Barry's closed eyelids. In that instant, it was no longer about capture; it was about survival. He started firing at the door.

"Backup! Get me some backup!" Barry shouted. With two rounds remaining in his pistol he paused, blinking to try to clear his vision. Something moved quickly past him and he felt a sting on his cheek. He fired his last two rounds at the ghost, dropped his gun, and had the stiletto from his shirtsleeve in his hand before the gun hit the floor.

As his vision cleared, Barry could see a woman standing by the desk next to the bed, removing her floor-length overcoat. He wanted to throw the knife, but he was unable to raise his arm. Trembling uncontrollably, he dropped it and fell to his knees. She walked to him, pulled a small dart from his cheek, and pushed him over before she closed and locked the door.

Unable to will his body to move, Barry stared at the young woman standing over him. No more than 120 pounds, she was clad head to toe in black rubber; only her eyes and mouth were exposed. She smiled at him and winked, then pulled a suitcase from the closet and set it on the bed. When she pulled out a plastic jug and a roll of rubber sheeting, he knew what was coming. The jug contained a powerful alien enzyme. The rubber sheet would restrain him. The enzyme would slowly dissolve the soft tissues of his body.

"Backup," Barry managed to say coherently. The words that followed arrived as a gurgling rattle. There was no response in his earpiece. The young woman let out a girlish giggle and kicked his legs out so that he was lying flat on his back.

"We've been waiting for you. Your men are already dead. They died quickly. You will not be as fortunate, Barry."

She put a gag in his mouth, injected something into his neck, and then rolled him up in the rubber sheet, attaching a small disc at the seam. When she pressed a button on the disc, the rubber sheet constricted into a tightly sealed cocoon. Barry could feel the paralysis dissipate as he watched her open the jug and fill a syringe the size of a turkey baster. He struggled in the sheeting; it constricted, pressing into his neck and squeezing the air from his lungs. She laughed, then straddled him and dropped down, bringing her face directly over his.

"My name is Tiffany Steiner. It will be my honor to release your soul. I will take your life in the same manner as your Kahshinki masters take the lives of the innocent. What they do unto others, I do unto you."

Tiffany paused and a frown crossed her face, visible even under the rubber mask. "The Oracle Rebecca wants to talk to you." Tiffany rolled off of him, kneeing him in the groin as she stood. She went to her jacket and got a phone. When she returned, she plopped back down on him with the obvious intent of causing pain. She pulled the gag from his mouth and held the phone to his ear.

"Hello, Barry," Rebecca said. "Where is Richard Parkhurst?"

"I'll tell you what... Oracle," Barry said. "If you can get rubber girl here to suck my dick, I'll think about it."

"Thank you, Barry. You did think about it. You just told me that Richard is now at the American asteroid base AB1. May you die with honor," Rebecca said, and then the line went dead.

Tiffany put the gag back into his mouth and tossed the phone onto the bed. With the tip of a gloved finger, she took a single drop of glistening fluid from the end of the syringe and touched it to the tip of Barry's nose. His screams were muffled behind the gag. Tiffany leaned back and put on a face shield as he thrashed his head from side to side.

Many times more powerful than the actual Kahshinki enzyme, the synthesized version dissolved the skin, muscle, and fatty tissue of Barry's nose within a few seconds. By the time the enzymes were spent, Barry's nose had been reduced to a gaping hole in his face. Tiffany grabbed and twisted the remaining cartilage that hung from the bone at the bridge and pulled it free with a snap. Barry kept screaming, saliva spraying around the gag and from the open cavity of his nose. Tiffany waited patiently until his screams slowed to rapid gasping. When his frantic eyes finally focused on her, she spoke.

"I like to start at the feet and work my way up. You will last longer that way." She grinned, spun around, and straddled his hips. Although he thrashed to every extent possible, he was unable to dislodge her. He heard a pop as the tip of the syringe penetrated the sheeting just below his knees. The pain that followed sent him into bone-wrenching convulsions. Tiffany laughed hysterically as she rode him like a cowboy rides a bucking bronco.

The phone at the front desk rang for the third time in ten minutes. "Loud thumping and a woman laughing, yes, ma'am, I understand. I'll take care of it. Sorry for the trouble," the man at the front desk said, and hung up the phone. The pretty young girl had told him she would be partying; she'd slipped him a hundred dollars not to bother them. *At least someone's getting lucky tonight,* he thought as he leaned back in his chair and returned to the evening news.

The journey to the campaign vessel now known as the Armageddon took much longer than Beth and Cooper expected. The Korlah rescue ship took them to an orbiting command pod, where they waited a day before being transferred to an outbound supply ship that made several stops before delivering them to the Armageddon. They were placed in separate holding cells in the Korlah section upon arrival.

From Beth's perspective, although they were being treated with respect, they were prisoners. She was given a bland, meatless stew and was resting after eating when they came for her. As the guards escorted her to the Council chamber, Beth remembered Teela's description of it and the protocol for entry. She walked in, took eleven steps, and faced the Mission leader's podium in the center. The seat was empty. When she looked around, she realized that only five of the eleven seats were filled.

"You claimed a human-Korlah transfer would come to speak with Shawlmon. To ask for assistance," the interpreter said, moving out from behind Beth and turning to face her. "Tell us what you know of this individual."

"I came to see Shawlmon, not to be interrogated. My business is with Shawlmon. Where is she?" Beth demanded.

The interpreter translated this for the Council members in the seats above them, and after a brief discussion, the Council relayed its response to the interpreter telepathically.

"Shawlmon was murdered by Shyron," the interpreter said. "Shyron then escaped with the help of a Korlah deserter before the Council agreed on her punishment. The Council asks your assistance in identifying this deserter." The interpreter bowed deeply and offered a palm display to emphasize the humble sincerity of the request.

Beth stared at the interpreter, dumbfounded. She knew all about the sham that had left Shyron playing the role of Shawlmon. Teela wanted out, but from what Teela had said in the letter and what they had just told her, the plan had backfired. She decided that more lies would just make matters worse.

"Shyron didn't kill Shawlmon," Beth said. "Shyron was covering for Teela. Teela never believed that crap about being the Korlah savior. That was the Oracle's bullshit. The Oracle has been holding Teela prisoner. She stole Teela's child and tried to kill her. Teela got away and came here for help. The deserter? I'm guessing that was Teela, or Shawlmon, whatever you want to call her."

The interpreter didn't look a bit surprised. She smiled politely and relayed the message. The Council debated for several minutes before the interpreter relayed the outcome.

"Your ridiculous lies disgrace the warrior clan. The Council rescinds your warrior title and orders that you and your associate be executed and your shells reclaimed."

"That's the truth, you bunch of morons!" Beth shouted. "Hey, let go of me," she cried when the guards grabbed her from behind and their thumb claws pierced the soft flesh under her arms. Without consideration for her infirmity, they dragged her from the chamber and threw her back into her cell.

Anger coursed through her like electricity. Beth cursed, kicked the door, and beat on it with her good arm and leg. She had never felt so helpless. After several hours of pacing, she dropped exhausted onto the bed and considered what she would do when they came for her. She nodded. *I'll go peacefully. But if I get a chance, I'll kill one.* The thought made her smile, but it faded quickly when her cell door opened.

The silhouette of a warrior filled the door; a big one, like Shawaugh and the two she had faced in the spectacle chamber. The warrior let the door close behind her and stepped into the cone of light cast by the cell's single glow bar, revealing a face scarred from fighting. This was a face Beth had seen before.

"I should have killed you when I had the chance," Beth said, backing up against the wall.

Ruwaugh walked toward her and Beth took a swing. Ruwaugh caught the fist in midair with one hand and grabbed Beth by the throat with the other. Beth would have fallen if Ruwaugh hadn't guided her onto the bed. Releasing her, Ruwaugh stepped back.

"I heard you were crippled. What happened?" Ruwaugh's English had a distinct Latino accent, and although rough, it was clear.

"Listen, assface, I killed your pal, and I'd do you if I could. Just do what you came here to do and get it over with," Beth said.

Ruwaugh chuckled, a low, sinister rumble. "I'm not here to hurt you, Beth. But I'll be honest, I have mixed feelings about you. When I heard you were back, I dreamt about hurting you, killing you, even. It's hard sometimes for me to separate some of my memories and emotions. You have to understand, Apoulauh was my birth sister. We grew up together. When I heard you were honored for ending her existence, I was pissed." Ruwaugh sat on the end of the bed.

"What do you want, an apology? It's not gonna happen. You killed someone I cared for, too. If I could, I'd—"

"Killed?" Ruwaugh laughed loudly. "You still know nothing of death. When Dade was killed, did he die? You were certain he did, and you harassed Teela mercilessly for it. When Crystal was killed, what makes you so sure she died? Korlah understand life and death as existence. Physical existence can be prolonged by moving the soul from one physical shell to another. Remember when you asked Teela how she learned English? Don't you want to know how I learned it?"

Beth paled. There was a long pause before she spoke. "No, I don't think I do," she whispered.

Ruwaugh smiled. "Oh, I think you do." She slid closer to Beth and took her crippled hand in hers, smoothing the curled fingers onto her palm. Beth stared at her scarred face, trying to imagine the unimaginable.

"Knowledge is power. Wouldn't you agree?" Ruwaugh asked.

"Yes," Beth said.

"Dade had to play sides, just like me. Teela had memories that were screwing with her. I can see that now. I have memories that screw with me also; lots and lots of memories. Sometimes it's hard to sort out which are mine," she laughed, "assuming I know who I really am. This was not really my first experience with transfer. I think that's why it was easier. If there was anything that little shit Afron knew well, it was how to transfer from one shell to another. But not all of Afron made it into me; her transfer was interrupted by Teela. When I died, I moved into this body. I took it from Ruwaugh. It was easy, Beth, almost too easy. I tried to tell you I wasn't dead, but this body was damaged. I couldn't quite reach you with my mind." Ruwaugh paused and looked up to meet Beth's eyes. "I haven't told anyone else about this. If the Council knew, they would kill me."

Beth looked away.

"Say something, Beth."

"What do you want me to say?" Beth tried to pull her hand from Ruwaugh's grip, but Ruwaugh held on tightly.

"Say my name. Be the first person to get it right. God damn it, Beth, say it!"

Beth looked into the scarred face. The alien eyes met hers, not in challenge, but pleading for recognition.

"Crystal?" Beth squeaked.

"Yeah!" Ruwaugh cried. She grabbed Beth and lifted her up into a standing embrace. "I'm big, I'm bad, and I'm fucking rich." She held Beth up until it was apparent she was standing without assistance. She stepped back and gave Beth a deep bow.

"What do you want from me?" Beth asked.

"We were abducted together, Beth. You, me, Catherine, and Marsha, we were a team. Remember? It was us girls against the universe. We got history together. When I heard you were back—and about to get your dumb ass recycled—I came running. What do I want from you? How about a little respect?"

"I meant no disrespect. It's because of me this happened to you. I challenged Ruwaugh and Apoulauh to a fight, not you. You were in no shape to fight, and it cost you your humanity. That was my fault, and thinking you were dead—that tore me up like you can't imagine. I just don't want to be responsible for anything else bad happening to you."

"Bad? Is that what you call this?" Crystal said, using her clawed hands to frame her alien face. "Does it bother you that I'm not the cute little Spanish chick you had the hots for?"

"What?" Beth stammered, and blushed when Crystal started laughing.

"Yeah, I knew you had a crush on me," Crystal said. "You hated everyone but me, and you only tolerated Marsha and Catherine because of me. Yeah, it was pretty obvious. It was okay, 'cause I thought you were pretty hot, too."

Beth let out a long breath and plopped down on the bed. "You don't look that bad," she said.

After a long pause, when Beth said nothing else, Crystal laughed. "Please! I am by far the ugliest bitch on this ship. But it's okay, 'cause I'm also the richest. Afron was into everything. Ruwaugh was her main enforcer, and that knowledge is now mine. I got it set up so I get a cut of everything that enters or leaves the Korlah section. I have contacts in the UNE and on the Crossover section. Hell, I just bought you and your pal an extradition to Crossover. The director there is a friend of Shyron's, a pilot who goes by the name Mad Dog. I've already got you a decent crib and a job. You won't really work, but you'll get a paycheck, a good one. I'll have a medical team check you out. Don't worry, I'm gonna get you fixed up and ready to rumble. Gee, Beth, It's great to see you." Crystal lifted Beth up once again. She wrapped her arms around her and gave her a bone-grinding hug.

"Good to see you, too," Beth groaned. "Did you really think I was hot?"

13 - Sightings

Tim referred affectionately to his hideout in a remote area of the asteroid belt as "Hole in the Rock," and the asteroid was exactly that. It was about a mile and a half long and looked like a big potato with a large section blown out of it; Tim's cargo ship fit nicely into the recess. The hideout was far from the orbits of Mars and Saturn and well off the regular transit routes, making it the perfect place to park and wait for things to cool off.

All systems aboard the cargo ship were shut down with the exception of basic life support. Lacking any engine room duties, Teela was going stir crazy. Within the first hour of waking she had finished feeding the rouk and cleaning the cages and was anxiously pacing the ship, looking for something productive to do. She returned to berthing to find Smiley teaching Shyron to speak English and throw knives while Tim and Denster snored loudly in their bunks. Teela reclined on her bunk and watched the subtle flirtations. Shyron would giggle when she missed the dartboard, and Smiley would stand close behind her, correcting her English and guiding her with his hands into the proper throwing posture.

Having shed her long, hooded cloak, Shyron was wearing a short smock that clung to the curves of her firm, youthful body and left little to the imagination. With the exception of her slick, spotted skin, everything from her neck to her wrists and ankles was identical to a human. Being a digitigrade, she essentially walked on her toes, which made it look like she was wearing invisible high-heeled shoes. Smiley liked that, and took every opportunity to watch her saunter to and from the dartboard. He was standing behind her trying to help her get a better grip on a throwing knife with her two-thumbed hand when she dropped the knife. When she bent down to pick it up, Smiley held her by the hips and pushed against her. When he saw Teela glaring at him, he grinned. This was more than Teela could bear. She rolled out of her bunk and stood.

"Shyron!" Teela cried, interrupting the game. "I need to speak with you." As Shyron strolled over to Teela, Smiley's eyes moved with the exaggerated sway of her hips.

"You must be cold. Here, put this on," Teela said, handing her Shawlmon's robe. Shyron's brow knit with concern as she took the robe. She laid it on her arm and caressed the fabric with reverence.

"Why do you relinquish it so freely?" Shyron asked.

"It comes with responsibilities I do not want," Teela said.

Shyron slipped out of her smock, it was the first time Teela had seen her naked. She noticed that in addition to the tattoo that identified Shyron as Teela 20.10127, there was a scar on her abdomen and thigh that matched the one Teela once had.

Shyron saw her expression and touched the scar. "I carry you with me always," she said.

"What?" Teela said, looking away, embarrassed.

"It's your scar. They removed it from your empty shell. It was far easier to use the actual scar than attempt to duplicate it. Eemela's shell is a genetic duplicate of yours; with the sabat and scar, no one should have been able to tell the difference. But your birth section mother, Nerhala, knew. Her rejection of me turned the entire population section against me."

Shyron put the robe on and smoothed the fabric, smiling at Teela. The floor-length, sleeveless gown was hemmed with a gold soutache and had ancient Korlah hieroglyphs embroidered in gold in neat, mazelike patterns over the entire surface. It was exquisite. Smiley made a low and slow wolf whistle as he moved closer for a better view. Teela ignored him.

"I would like to keep one sword and the vest," Teela said.

"Of course," Shyron said.

Teela wrapped the belt around one sword to give to Shyron.

"May I see it?" Smiley asked, reaching for the sword.

"You might hurt yourself," Teela said with a frown. Her dislike of his flatulence was no secret, and he took every opportunity to torment her.

"It's okay, Smiley man may look," Shyron said in English, surprising Teela with her sudden fluency.

"Thanks, toots," Smiley said with a grin as he took the belt and sword. He left Teela standing in a cloud of his stink.

Teela whispered to Shyron, "This man... you... you should not be engaging with him like this. He does not respect you."

Shyron looked past Teela at Smiley and took a moment to study the tall, thin man with his long, greasy black hair. "He makes me laugh. I like how he is tall, but not big like Captain. He is the only one who spends his free time with me. He likes me, I can tell."

"He's disgusting. How can you like him?" Teela said.

Shyron pulled her close and Teela felt the nudge of her mind attempting to read her thoughts. *Have you taken a human male as mate yet?* she asked, imparting both the question and a vivid image of a human and a Korlah copulating.

"No! God, no," Teela cried, offended.

"It's fun. You should try it." Shyron laughed at the look Teela gave her.

Smiley was examining the intricate gold inlay on the sword's scabbard, blade, and hilt. He put the belt on and withdrew the sword. With its power cell secured, it appeared to be nothing more than a display piece for ceremonial purposes. "Hey, Shy, what do you want for this? I'll make you a real good deal," he said, sliding it back into its sheath.

"It's not for sale!" Teela cried, immediately regretting that she didn't ask for both swords.

"My decision," Shyron said. "It is mine to gift, trade, or wager. Is wager the right word, Smiley man?"

"Yeah, wager, bet, gamble are all good words. Like last night when we played cards. This time instead of money, you would bet the sword against something of equal or greater value. But we should trade. Remember, when you lose you get nothing," Smiley said.

"But if I win I keep both," Shyron said.

"True. I take it there is something of mine you want?" Smiley asked.

"Yes, something of yours," Shyron said with a smile.

"I'll get the cards," he said.

"What about knife game?" Shyron asked.

"I think you'd have better odds with cards. We should just trade for something. I'd feel bad taking that sword away from you."

"I bet I am better at knife game than you, unless you doubt your skills." Shyron walked to the dartboard and pulled the three knives from it.

"Best two of three. Sword for..." She paused and gave Smiley a sly grin. "You serve me for ten of your sleep cycles."

"What do you mean, serve you?" he asked.

"Teela, how is this agreement described?" Shyron asked.

"You'll be her bitch, Smiley. For ten days, she'll expect you to clean her clothes, rub her feet, massage her back, and provide whatever sexual favors trip her trigger. You're being played. Walk away."

"You hustling me, girl?" Smiley asked Shyron.

"Chicken!" Denster cried, sitting up in his bunk. He started to make clucking sounds. "Hell, I'll take the bet if you don't."

"Okay, Shy, best two out of three. You lose, I get the sword. I lose, and I'm your bitch for ten days," Smiley said.

"Done." Shyron turned and threw the knives: one, two, three. All three hit the small red bull's-eye so close together that Smiley couldn't have slid a sheet of paper between the flat blades if he tried. Denster burst out laughing and Smiley stared in dismay.

After Shyron threw the second time, repeating the success of her first round, Smiley conceded his defeat. Shyron immediately directed him to clean her clothes, his clothes, and both their bedding, and then gave him very explicit orders on how to bathe, wash his hair, and shave so that his face would not chafe her thighs. Teela was sure Denster would have a heart attack from laughing so hard. Tim woke up from the noise and wanted to know what was so funny. Smiley refused to tell him and Tim had to wait until Denster calmed down enough to tell the story of how Smiley got hustled. It was a story he would repeat many times to anyone willing to listen.

You don't approve, Shyron said telepathically when she saw Teela glaring at her.

"No I don't approve," Teela said.

Shyron responded silently. *Even with the chemicals they take to prevent interest, human males are very receptive to pleasuring. I have found their company quite enjoyable. You do know that Captain Tim has pleasuring thoughts about you all the time?*

"I'm not interested," Teela said. "You should not be speaking with your mind. It is rude."

"It is not manners that concern you," Shyron said, tilting her head and attempting to probe Teela's thoughts. "You shield your mind and refuse to speak with it. What is it you fear?"

"If I open my mind, the Oracle will find me. She wants me dead. I need to find her and kill her first if I ever hope to get my son back."

"The Oracle cannot find you if you speak quietly. She can only hear you if you shout with your mind. Control your thoughts, limit their strength, and direct them carefully. I have been listening to the Oracle for hundreds of cycles. After she took the human shell, her power increased greatly, but I sense her strength is fading."

"You can hear the Oracle, even now?" Teela asked in disbelief.

Shyron nodded and closed her eyes to concentrate. "No, not at the moment," she said with a frown. "I have felt many of the events she has created. Powerful images of things she calls miracles. To be in her presence would be a very dangerous thing. She can create memories and impart them to multitudes of people. For those in her presence, it must seem absolutely real. She now believes she is close to taking control of the planet, and she is planning to orchestrate her most elaborate recruitment ever. Your son will be presented at a gathering with a religious leader called pope. The Oracle will claim the child is a miracle of immaculate conception. On this day, she intends to take control of this leader's mind and the minds of many thousands of his followers. After this event, she and her followers will seize control of the planet."

"Do you know when this will happen?" Teela asked.

"No, but I will continue to listen. She often speaks to large groups of her followers. When she reveals her plans to them, I will hear her."

Teela's eyes widened as a thought crossed her mind; excitement was evident in her voice. "Could you hear someone's thoughts deep in space? Could you hear Shawaugh?" Teela recalled how she had once used telepathy to find human pilots in their disabled ships.

"No," Shyron said. "She and Challmara were travelling to a very remote location. She is certainly very distant. To hear her thoughts is beyond my ability."

"When you killed that assassin, you said I acted as a lens and magnified your power. What if you used me as a lens to find and rescue Shawaugh and Challmara?"

"It may be possible," Shyron said thoughtfully. "We can try. You must realize that it is also possible that the Oracle will feel us reach out."

"Shawaugh and Challmara are allies we cannot afford to lose. If we can find them it is worth the risk. Come, I know where we can get a direct line of sight to where they are!" Teela grabbed

Shyron by the elbow and pulled her from the crew's quarters into the control room, then up a ladder into the navigation bubble.

"Where is New Korlah, which direction?" Teela asked. "If we need to, we can take the shuttle out to get a clear view and focus our thoughts without obstacles in the way."

Shyron looked around, turned, and pointed. "There, between those two bright stars. The sun for New Korlah is one of those small stars beyond them."

"Okay, what do I need to do?"

"Think of Shawaugh. Remember her. You have been in her mind before. Use the memory of that contact, recall the sensation of feeling her thoughts, and something that cannot be described may happen."

"A miracle," Teela said, putting her hand on the dome in the same way Rebecca had once put her hand on a viewing screen just before plowing through an asteroid field at hyper-light to get ahead of a Kahshinki bomber. Spreading her fingers, Teela framed the star cluster of New Korlah between them. She closed her eyes and used the thermal aura of her hand like the sight of a gun, opened her mind, and focused her thoughts. She concentrated like this for several minutes before Shyron finally spoke.

"I'm sorry, it's not working."

"Try harder!" Teela cried. She thought about how she had been able to reach out to Shyron when she'd thought she was about to die. How getting Dade's personal belongings to Julie with word of his death had meant more to her than surviving. If desperation was the key—she drew every ounce of every desperation she could recall into this one attempt. *Please, God. Please help me.* The knuckles of her other hand cracked and her palm burned as her claws sliced through her glove and into her hand.

A faint speck appeared in the blackness, then flew at her like a comet. An instant later, she was looking at Shawaugh sleeping. She realized instantly that she was in the mind of someone who was looking at Shawaugh, and in that shared moment, she felt Challmara's presence and knew where they were and what had happened.

"Challmara! My God, they're alive!" Teela cried to Shyron. "Their engines have been damaged. They have food and water, but at sub-light speeds they'll starve before they make it back. We must go to them."

Teela slid down the ladder from the navigation bubble and raced to the crew's quarters for Tim. She pulled him into the control room and showed him the location, course, and speed of Shawaugh and Challmara's transport.

"That's way beyond the range of my go-fast," Tim said. "She goes fast, but not that far. I'm sorry." He was genuinely upset.

"There must be a way. You can have my share. If it costs more, I will pay you back," Teela pleaded.

"You know, I've been thinking about getting a go-far for some time. We could probably afford to buy a ship that could make the trip. But it will take everything we got, maybe more. The crew's gonna want to vote on this. It's not entirely my choice."

"If we spend anything, it should be to buy a new hauler," Denster said as he walked into the control room. "This piece of crap is ready for the scrap heap."

"I don't agree," Smiley said, following a resonating fart with his trademark grin. "The bulk cargo runs don't make enough to keep up with maintenance costs. Our real money comes from contraband. I say we use Hole in the Rock as our base of operations. The cargo ship will be our factory. With a go-fast and a go-far, we could dominate the rouk whiskey market throughout the entire system. We could distribute Thor's Hammer from right here."

"Your idea stinks, just like you," Denster said.

"On the contrary, I smell victory. Let's vote. All those in favor of buying a go-far," Smiley said, raising his hand.

Tim and Teela raised their hands.

"This is bullshit!" Denster cried. "Since when did we start running rescue missions? And what about the parts and materials we'd need to turn the hauler into a factory? Where we gonna get those?"

"I know a place," Teela said. "The first asteroid base built, where the Korlah and humans have lots of parts and materials. I know some people there. You have cargo that some young ladies there might be very interested in. I think I could get you some very good deals."

Shyron put her arm around Smiley and whispered in his ear. Smiley whispered back. This went on for several minutes before Smiley finally shared with the group.

"I'll go with Shy to buy a go-far. She says she has connections with the Korlah collective and can get us a deal. We'll find Teela's buddies and bring back their lost ship, which according to Korlah and UNE law will entitle us to fifty percent of its salvage value. According to Shy, it's an advanced long-range transport worth a lot of credits. Tim and Sula can take the go fast and get us the equipment we need for the factory. We meet back here at the Hole and start making some real money."

"This is bullshit!" Denster cried again. "So I'm supposed to sit here with my thumb up my ass while you and your girlfriends go for a romp?"

"No," Tim said. "You can jerk off to porn like usual, tend the rouk and rats while maintaining and monitoring the ship."

"Like I said: bullshit." Denster stormed out of the control room.

"Don't worry about him. He'll drink himself sober, and when he wakes up he won't give a shit," Tim said. "Come on, Sula, let's go load up the hidey hole on the go-fast. We can use your girlie stuff as decoy cargo."

"What are you loading?" Teela asked.

"Thor's Hammer. Those American Marines and flyboys can't get enough of the stuff. If you strike out, I don't want this trip to be a complete waste of time."

14 - Wrath

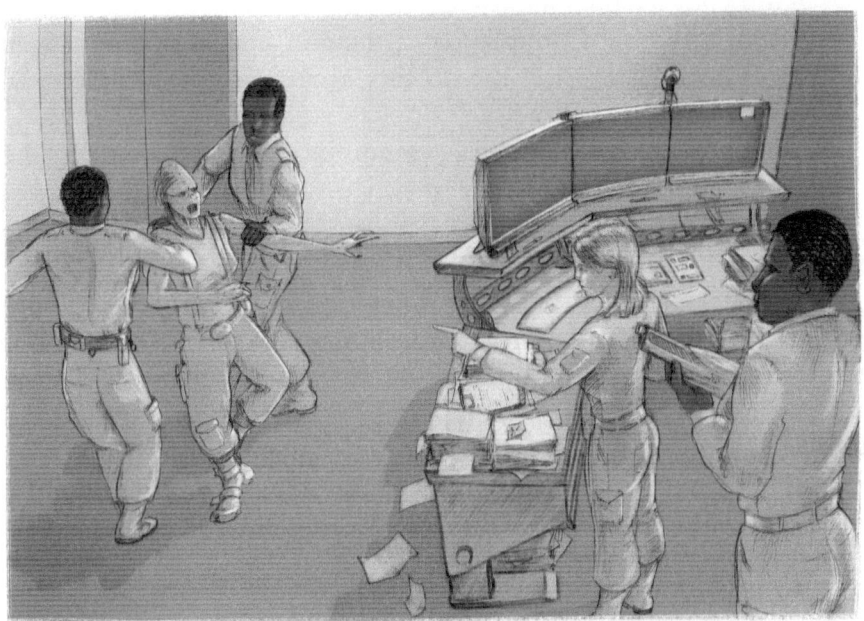

As Tim expected, his go-fast was intercepted long before he and Teela arrived at the asteroid base one, known as AB1. The interceptors were invisible in the blackness of space, but they appeared on Tim's monitor as small triangles moving into his path. As the lead craft came into view, it energized its weapons and its pulse chambers began to glow. Tim's communications panel lit up with broadband hail. He flipped the audio switch and a message sounded, first in English and then in Korlah.

"You are entering restricted military space. Power down and prepare to be boarded. Failure to comply will be considered a hostile act and your ship will be fired on."

Tim killed forward speed and bumped reverse a few times to stop the go-fast as the message began to repeat. He adjusted his transmitter to the frequency of the incoming message and pressed the microphone button.

"Gentlemen, it's good to see you. With all the pirates and Kahshinki raiding parties, you are a welcome sight. I'm Tim Masters, Masters Trucking, Unlimited, just a friendly merchant looking for business." He released the button and looked at Teela. "What are your friends' names again?"

"Ann Moore, Commander Litnauh, and Captain Jason Ramsey," Teela said. "Let me do the talking. If I need help, you can bail me out."

"Prepare to be boarded," came the terse reply over the speaker.

"Okay, you do the talking," Tim said. "But don't mention the rouk whiskey."

A transport modified for midspace boarding banked and extended an airlock adaptor towards Tim's port hatch. Tim waited until they knocked before opening the hatch. An American Marine wearing a pressure suit stuck his head in and looked around the cramped cargo area, then crabbed in and squatted, cradling a pulse rifle in his lap. Another Marine sat in the doorway and installed a brace that would prevent the door from being closed. The squatting soldier opened his helmet.

"What you hauling?" he asked.

"Feminine napkins, perfume, clothing, fabric, and some educational software programs for Ann Moore and the young ladies in her care," Teela said.

"You're shitting me!" the squatting Marine said. His partner opened several of the boxes and nodded confirmation.

"Don't worry, men, I brought a few items of my own to help with troop morale at this lonely, neglected outpost," Tim said.

The Marine by the door waved a hand to get Tim's attention. He pointed to the camera on his helmet and then to his ear before putting a finger to his lips.

"Are you aware Americans are enforcing the UNE contraband laws?" the squatting soldier asked.

"Of course. Nothing illegal here that I'm aware of," Tim said. "I have four cases of beer, two cases of UNE-approved tobacco-free cigarettes, and a case of condoms. I'm here to support the troops, not get anyone into trouble."

"Cargo's cleared for delivery," the soldier by the door said as he slid out of the door and returned to his ship.

"We'll escort you to the base," the squatting soldier said. "Proceed into the hangar on the left. Hey, if you two aren't doing anything later, say around sixteen-hundred, come on over to the base. Me and my partner would love to buy you a beer at the enlisted men's club. Ask for Willy and Sam when you get there."

"Appreciate it. See you there," Tim said. The Marine gave him a wink, removed the blocking device, and crawled out. After he was clear of the airlock, Tim shut the hatch.

"And that's how it's done," Tim said.

"How what's done?" Teela asked.

"Smugglers' code; if they ask if you know the laws and you have no contraband, you say yes and leave it at that. If you got something to sell, you put together a sentence that starts with the word illegal, followed by the code words for what you have. Beer means hard liquor, tobacco-free means real tobacco, and condoms means it's wrapped up and protected. I just told those guys I had whiskey and tobacco. Very few working-class people out here believe in the contraband laws, and if those guys did, they would have gutted the ship to try to find it. These two looked disappointed when I told them I was shipping tampons. When they asked if I knew the contraband laws, I figured it was a safe bet to drop the code words."

Tim followed the Marine transport to the asteroid. The desolate rocky surface and battle-scarred base were just as Teela remembered. The piles of debris had been removed and the damage from the Korlah attack had been patched and repaired. The first real indication of change came when they entered the gaping mouth that led to airlocks and spacecraft hangars. The once-separate American and Kahshinki sides of the base had merged internally. From the airlock, they entered a vast, conjoined hangar that was much larger and brighter than the one she recalled. Most of the hangar deck was dedicated to rows of American spacecraft. Teela counted more than one hundred of the smaller Ghost-class interceptors, a couple dozen of the larger and more heavily armed Horseman fighters, five Curse transports, and two massive Wrath destroyers. From what Teela could see, there was no evidence of a Korlah presence at the base.

Tim followed the Marine transport to an isolated area of the hangar that was segregated from the military craft. The area was reserved for civilian spacecraft and had an airport-type terminal with a security checkpoint. Tim parked the go-fast next to the Marine transport and opened his hatches.

Teela climbed out and paused to embrace the sights, sounds and smells of the busy hangar. The first time she visited this base, the Korlah had just seized it from the Kahshinki, but now the smell of oxidized metal and charred flesh had been replaced by the artificial smell of processed air that held a hint of ozone.

Tim chatted with Willy and Sam as a group of human clones arrived with a hovering cargo lift and began to transfer the go-fast's cargo onto it. These were the same laborer genotypes Teela remembered. The dark-haired and dark-eyed young ladies were all wearing olive-drab army surplus fatigues, army boots, and ball caps. As they were working, a polished black UNE diplomatic transport entered the hangar and landed next to Tim's go-fast. Curious as to what a UNE diplomat would be doing there, Teela opened her mind and concentrated on listening to the thoughts of the people exiting the transport.

Teela's attention was drawn to one of the passengers, a young woman whose thoughts were as familiar as the sound of someone's voice. The woman, who was wearing a tailored suit with a skirt that seemed too short for its serious cut, was being greeted by several Marines who were offering her assistance with her luggage. Too far away to hear the discourse, Teela heard only the emotional tenor of their thoughts. The young Marine greeting the woman was admiring her lean, well-defined legs that glistened like they were wet, and was wondering if the body under the suit matched them. The young woman was thinking about how long it would take the young man to die. Teela gasped as the woman thought about his bare bones, dissolving flesh, and screams of pain. Turning suddenly, the woman looked directly at Teela.

Their eyes met and Teela's mind slammed shut like a vault. She was frightened; this woman was a telepath and had sensed her subtle probe. At that instant, she recognized the woman, whose angelic features contrasted with eyes that reflected her dark and sinister thoughts. It was Tiffany, but not the traumatized girl Teela remembered. This woman was cold and unfeeling, like those who had held her captive, like all of Rebecca's devotees. Teela smiled politely and looked away, hoping she had masked her shock.

Rebecca is using her. But for what? Teela wondered. Tiffany had been catatonic the last time she saw her. The trauma of her abduction and the horrible death of her fiancé at the hands of the Kahshinki had Teela believing she would never lead a normal life again. She thought about the horrific sliver of thought she'd overheard and realized that there was nothing normal about this girl's current life.

Tiffany's beauty was not lost on those around her. As she sauntered off the landing platform, Tim and most of the Marines stopped to watch.

"Good looking girl," Tim said to Sam. "Who is she?"

"UNE investigator. She's here to see the general. There have been some claims of human rights violations against the clones. It's all bullshit, but I guess they gotta check it out," Sam replied.

"What kind of violations?" Teela asked.

Sam gave Teela a dirty look and directed his response to Tim. "You seem like an all-right kind of guy. I don't know what you're doing running with one of these, but here, on this base, clones and crovers are not considered human. Therefore, they got no human rights. Your girlfriend should stay on the clone side of the base and keep any attitude she has to herself."

"I appreciate the advice," Tim said. "Sula, you go take care of your business and I'll take care of mine. We meet back here in... let's say three hours."

Teela nodded to Tim and scowled at Sam.

After the workers finished loading the go-fast's cargo onto the lift, one of the young clones approached Teela and offered a palm display.

"My name is January. I will escort you to the advocate mother," she said.

"I'm here to see Ann Moore," Teela said. The girl looked confused. "Do you know who I am talking about?" Teela asked.

"Mother Ann is the advocate mother. She is the only person to see here," January said, directing Teela onto the hover lift.

January took her to a distant corridor and down two levels into the heart of the clone dormitory. She was delivered to a bleak waiting room outside of Ann's office. Like the hangar, corridor, and tunnel that brought her here, the room was carved from the asteroid's bedrock. Two uncomfortable stone benches were its sole furnishings. It wasn't long before three red-haired, blue-eyed pilot clones exited, followed by a large, muscular black woman that Teela recognized as one of the few soldier clones to survive the battle for the base. The soldier ordered Teela to enter.

A large desk covered with a three-screen computer and piles of books and papers separated the narrow room. Another soldier clone armed with a pulse rifle stood to one side behind the desk and eyed Teela suspiciously as she entered. Teela could see someone hunched behind the screens and moved closer to get a clear view. It was Ann. The kindly woman Teela had known had taken on a permanent scowl, and the dark rings under her eyes convinced Teela that the job Ann had wanted so badly had taken a toll on her.

"What do you want?" Ann demanded without looking away from her screens.

"I'm sorry, Ann, it was my intention to bring help when I returned. Instead, I am here to ask you for help."

Ann stopped typing and looked up at Teela. She pushed back the chair and slowly stood, then leaned on the table and stared directly into Teela's eyes, challenging her. Teela looked down, focusing on Ann's hands. Her ragged fingernails had been chewed down to the quick.

"I don't know you. Who sent you and what do you want?"

"It's me, Teela. Things have happened—"

"Bullshit!" Ann shouted. "Whoever picked you for this scam was an idiot. Teela was at least fifteen years older than you. She's dead. Everyone knows Shyron had her murdered. So you show up looking like a Korlah deserter or mercenary and let me guess—you need weapons, equipment, or some other militarily-sensitive gear that will give Ramsey the excuse he needs to arrest me. No! It's not going to happen. Get out! Tell that prick I'm not biting."

"Ann, it's really me. Let explain what happened."

Ann turned to the armed guard. "Escort this imposter to the base access tunnel and turn her over to the Marines. Impound her ship. Move it to one of the secure hangars and put guards on it." Turning back to Teela, she added, "Tell Ramsey he can have the ship back when he releases our last two supply shipments."

Teela was seized from behind, her arms quickly bound and her protests ignored as she was forcibly disarmed and removed from the room.

Ann pounded the keys of her computer until she found the contact she was looking for. After punching the last key with much more force than needed, she crossed her arms and waited. A few moments later, the image of Jason Ramsey, now general of the midsystem fleet, appeared on her center monitor.

"I'm busy, Ann, what is it now?" he asked.

"Are you serious? This time you send a kid posing as Teela asking for help? You know, performing transfers with children this young is a criminal act. This girl can't be more than twelve years old. She's dressed like a mercenary and has tattoos, for Christ's sake! Seriously, Jason, how stupid do you think I am?"

Ramsey's attitude changed in an instant. "When—when exactly did this happen?" he demanded.

"Just now," Ann replied, surprised. "I had her delivered to the base tunnel and I will be impounding her ship until you release our supply shipments."

"I have to go. I'll call when I have some information," Ramsey said. Ann's screen went dark.

She swallowed in an attempt to dislodge the lump of fear that filled her throat. It was clear Ramsey knew nothing of the visit. If the Teela who visited her was not an imposter sent by Ramsey, then who was she? The possibility that came to mind created a cold knot in the center of her chest. She pulled up the feed from the security cameras and replayed the meeting from every angle, focusing on the face and zooming in on the tattoo on the young Korlah's cheek to find out which unit she belonged to.

"Those aren't Korlah glyphs, that's Arabic," Ann said. "What is Suladead supposed to stand for?"

After a few minutes of contemplation, her eyes grew wide. "Oh my God!" she cried.

15 - Prototype

Richard Parkhurst watched the monitor as the beautiful young UNE investigator entered the terminal's security checkpoint. *Do they seek to insult us or seduce us?* he wondered. The United Nations of Earth had sent this lovely woman to investigate allegations of human rights violations lodged by the base's resident dissident, Ann Moore.

Well, no one knows the game of seduction better than I, he thought as he typed instructions into his communicator and sent them to the head of security. He moved to the mirrored panel behind the bar in his office, combed his hair, smoothed the lines of his Armani suit, and waited for his guest to be delivered.

Violet Gibson's luggage passed through security without question and was routed for delivery to her room. Her refusal to open her briefcase for inspection was brought to the attention of the security supervisor, who relieved the guard and examined the scan of her briefcase from various directions to determine what was in it. From what he could ascertain, it contained two canisters of liquid, a large roll of dense fabric, some garments, and some odd buttons or badges that contained circuitry.

"My officer was correct. You will need to open this so I can examine the contents," he said, sliding the case off the conveyer belt and onto a table.

"I am Detective Gibson, a duly deputized investigator appointed by the United Nations of Earth," Violet said, holding her badge up. "I have a higher level of authority and immunity than that of a diplomat. The contents of that case and anything else I say are private and may not be touched, examined, or in any way interfered with. By touching my case you have already violated that authority. If you persist, I will press charges."

The supervisor frowned. Very few people had ever questioned his authority. He didn't know all the rules associated with UNE membership, and he would need to check her claim. He smiled at the thought of strip-searching her and held the smile as he tried to speak as pleasantly as possible.

"Please be seated, ma'am, while I check your credentials."

Violet stepped across the red line on the floor that marked the security personnel's area, pulled her briefcase from the table, and paused.

"You do that," she whispered with a cold glare.

Something about her reminded him of a predator examining its prey. He cleared his throat to demand she return to her side of the line, but before he could speak, she turned, crossed the line, and took a seat.

Parkhurst finished primping just in time to see the confrontation between Violet and security. His complexion turned crimson as he jabbed at the controls to connect his intercom to the security station on his monitor.

"Checkpoint four," the security supervisor said, looking up at the camera monitoring his station and blushed when he realized that he was about to get his ass chewed.

"This is the station director," Parkhurst cried. "What the hell do you think you're doing, harassing a UNE investigator?"

"She is refusing to allow examination of—"

"Shut up! Apologize, kiss her ass in every way imaginable, and get her up here in the next five minutes or you will spend the rest of your tour patrolling the surface in a pressure suit!"

Parkhurst severed the connection before the inspector could reply. He yanked a desk drawer open and pulled out a notepad. When he tossed it back into the drawer, he'd added another name to a growing list of people to be replaced.

Parkhurst watched every step of Violet's journey to his office from the monitors on his office wall. He met her at the door and offered his hand as she entered, and gave her his most charming smile.

"Greetings, Ms. Gibson. May I call you Violet?" he asked, using the name she'd given on her arrival documents. He withdrew his hand when it was apparent Violet had no intention of taking it. Disappointed by the rebuff, he stepped back and bowed slightly, inviting her in with a wave of his arm. As she entered, he took the opportunity to ogle her taut young body, ranking it among the most beautiful he had seen.

"You may call me Detective," Violet replied. She pressed her way into his office without giving the real wood paneling, plush leather couch, or original oil paintings a second look. "Where is General Ramsey? I am here to see the general, not one of his lackeys."

"Please, Ms. Gibson—"

"Detective Gibson!" Violet corrected. "Who are you, and why exactly are we even speaking to each other?"

"Well, Detective Gibson, this is not entirely a military installation. It is actually my base. The military is just leasing some space here," Parkhurst said, maintaining his practiced smile, intent on charming the contemptuous young woman into submission. "It was built and is owned by the Santos Corporation, which I now control. It's all very legal and proper. I'm surprised that you were not better briefed." He went to the wall behind his desk and slid a panel open to reveal a fully stocked bar.

"Santos Corporation? That was one of the Quorum's major holdings, wasn't it?" Violet asked. She studied his face. *He is a handsome man, maybe too handsome*, she thought, noting the subtle marks left by recent plastic surgery.

"It was," Parkhurst replied with a grin, "until it was seized by our present government's administration. It is currently under new management... mine. But that's all very boring. May I fix you a drink before we get into the details of your investigation?" He gestured to the bar.

"I am here to investigate claims made against the United States military contingent at this base, not to drink alcoholic beverages in violation of UNE law." Violet removed a small e-pad from her pocket, flipped it open, and began rapidly typing with one hand. She looked up at him and continued typing. Without being obvious, she took his picture and sent it along with her message, requesting a facial recognition scan.

"Corporate law exempts business leaders from UNE liquor and tobacco laws. You really need to relax a little, Detective. There is a whole universe of possibilities out here. In fact, I am now in a position to change those possibilities into certainties for the right people. This meeting is not as much about your investigation as it is a job interview." He finished pouring two drinks and offered her one. She took it. For the first time, he noticed she was wearing gloves. They appeared to be rubber and had fingernails glued on.

"It's a dirty universe; I like to keep my hands clean," she said. Her e-pad made a beep and she set her drink down to open it. "Oh, Lord, such a blessing. Thank you," she said, closing the pad and returning it to her pocket.

"Good news?" Parkhurst asked.

"Very," Violet replied with a sincere smile. "We knew you were probably here. I just thought getting to you would be much more difficult." She reached up and plucked something from her hair. With a practiced flip of the wrist, she threw it at Parkhurst, who dropped his glass to protect his face. His palm burned viciously as if stung by a bee.

"Bitch!" he cried, and plucked a small black dart from his palm. He looked at the hypodermic needle, at the blood spot in his palm, and then at her. "It's you!" he slurred as he dropped the dart and lunged for her. Violet stepped to one side and he stumbled past her. He turned, took one more step, and collapsed onto the floor.

"You, my dear man, are the Quorum catch of the day. The ace of spades, if you will," Violet said. She stripped down to the full-body rubber suit she was wearing beneath her business attire and set her briefcase on the floor next to him.

"Doan kill meh," he slurred, making one last feeble attempt to stand before succumbing to paralysis.

"Why shouldn't I? You sent an assassin to kill me. Initially Barry was defiant, but like all the others, he cried like a baby, and confessed all of his sins. I am not going to merely kill you, Richard. My real name is Tiffany Steiner, and it will be my honor to release your soul. I will take your life in the same manner your masters take the lives of others. What they do unto to others, I have been ordained to do unto you."

The clone soldiers escorted Teela from Ann's office to the entrance of the tunnel that separated the clone side of the base from General Ramsey's military forces. From the number of armed Marines there, Teela surmised that trust between the two sides was lacking. Her guards removed the handcuffs and handed her sword and pistol to a Marine. She rubbed her wrists and wondered how she would explain her failure to Tim.

"Hello, Teela," one of the Marines said.

Teela stopped midstride. "Name is Sula," she said, closely examining the man who addressed her. The short beard and tinted pilot's glasses threw her off, but his name badge brought full recognition. Jason Ramsey, the pilot who once tried to destroy the spaceship that abducted Daedalus Rimes and the other humans taken with him, was now a brigadier general. He grinned at her shock.

"Can't bullshit a bullshitter, kid. Ann didn't know you got a new body, and I don't plan to tell her. Rebecca said you might show up here, and here you are. Looks like you lost one of your swords but gained a pistol. Did you know that you are on just about everybody's most-wanted list?"

"I don't know what you say. Name is Sula. I privateer. I trade, make business, make profit," Teela replied, putting on her best Korlah accent.

Ramsey laughed. "Ann said you told her you were Teela. She doesn't have the imagination to make something like that up. I really do recognize that sword, and I don't really care who you are. What happens to you now isn't my decision anymore. I called it in and I have my orders. You will be taken to the Korlah mothership to face murder charges. You are so popular the UNE just cancelled their investigation here, just so their cute little detective can take custody of you. Feeling special yet?"

"Detective? Did she arrive here just after me?"

"That's right. Hey! You dropped the act pretty quick. Having the law on your ass got you worried?"

"She's not a UNE detective. She's Tiffany Steiner, she's the girl whose boyfriend you let the Kahshinki eat. You remember her, don't you? You met her when I had you locked in a cell with the remains of her fiancé Jimmy's body. She's working for Rebecca now. I don't know exactly what she's up to, but you can bet it's something bad. As it stands, Rebecca wants me dead. If you turn me over to Tiffany, I think she'll kill me."

Ramsey looked confused. He started to reply to Teela but stopped. Instead, he turned to her guards. "Take the prisoner to a holding cell. Don't turn her over to anybody until you hear from me first. Me personally, got it?"

"Sir, yes, sir," the guards replied, snapping a salute.

Ramsey turned to Teela. "You've been nothing but trouble since I met you. I'll check out your claim about the UNE detective. If it's Tiffany I'll recognize her. If you're lying, well, let's just say I won't be happy." He turned and walked off down the central corridor. The Marine guards took Teela by the arms and led her into one of the smaller side tunnels toward the brig.

"Hey! Stop!" Tim shouted from behind them.

Teela and the guards stopped and turned to see who was calling. Tim ran up to them, and Willy and Sam followed farther back.

"Tim!" Teela said. "I'm sorry. Things didn't work out."

"Shut up!" one of her guards said, giving one of her hands a twist.

"Where you going with my mechanic?" Tim asked, slowing to a fast walk as he got closer.

"To the brig. It's being detained. It's not your mechanic anymore, buddy, it's our prisoner. You got a beef with that, then take it to General Jason Ramsey."

"*She's* my mechanic. Now please, just tell me—why is she being detained?"

"My orders are to deliver this *thing* to the brig," the Marine said. "I don't give a shit why the spaghettihead is being detained. Why don't you try putting your dick in something human? Or can't you land a real woman?" His smirk lasted just long enough for Tim to land a cross-body kick to his head. The blow lifted the two-hundred-pound man off his feet and sent him unconscious to the stone floor.

The Marine on Teela's other arm yanked his service revolver from his holster, only to find his wrist lacerated by Teela's claws as she seized his hand and gun. She spun around behind him and grabbed his groin with her other hand, bringing him to his knees. Tim snatched the pistol from the man's hand before forcing him face down on the ground.

"Are you crazy?" Willy shouted as he arrived at the scene. Tim turned the pistol on his stunned companions.

"Calm down, everybody just calm down," Tim said. "My mechanic and I are leaving."

"Tim, you won't get ten feet into the hangar before they cut you down," Sam said. "Just give up and plead stupid. Chances are, they'll just lock you up for a while and then send you on your way."

"I'm not here, I don't know you, I never met you," Willy said, then turned and sprinted away.

"Sorry, Tim, you're on your own," Sam said, eyeing the pistol before he slowly turned around and followed Willy down the hall.

"You know, you're a lot of trouble, Sula," Tim said, looking down the corridor at the access tunnel that led to the hangar. "Those boys are right, we're dead meat."

"Wait! We can just walk out of here. Shyron taught me how to do it. Let me try," Teela said.

"Whatever it is, you better do it quick," Tim said.

Teela closed her eyes momentarily and imagined Tim in the image of General Ramsey. When she opened her eyes, Tim's appearance had changed; to her, and to anyone else who might be within telepathic range, he looked exactly like Jason Ramsey. When she tried to include herself as a Marine, the image of Ramsey faded and Tim reappeared.

"I can't do us both," she said. "We'll go one at a time. You go first and get the ship ready to launch."

"What are you talking about?" Tim asked, on the verge of panic.

"Illusion! I will create the illusion that you are a Marine officer. You walk right out and board your ship. Once you are aboard and out of sight, I will follow."

The rumble of boots on stone echoed from the nearby junction.

"Go now!" Teela cried. She knelt over the Marine on the floor and pressed the muzzle of the pistol to the back of his head. She closed her eyes and imagined Tim as Jason Ramsey, then focused her thoughts to hold that image.

"You're nuts!" Tim said, realizing that it was up to him to bring an end to this madness. He sprinted to the corridor to surrender to the Marines, who were only seconds away. He rounded the corner, raised his arms, and faced the twelve armed men charging toward him. The Marines slowed to a trot and stopped a few paces from him. The lead Marine snapped to attention and saluted.

"Sir, we… are responding to a report of an escaped prisoner."

Tim slowly lowered his arms, looking at his hands and clothing. He had not changed, as far as he could see, but it was clear that the Marines saluting him saw someone entirely different. Tim returned the salute.

"Sir, what are your orders?" the Marine asked.

Tim cocked his head. He thought about the incident in the hangar at Crossover with Teela and Shyron, when he had seen a hangar worker become Teela and Shyron in the blink of an eye. But he was going to have to speak to these Marines. These men were seeing an officer; would they hear an officer? He took a breath and gave it his best effort.

"What took you so long?" he shouted, putting his hands on his hips and glaring at the lead Marine.

"Sir, I—"

"Don't answer. There is no excuse for this pathetic display of ineptitude. Get your asses back to your stations and do not desert your posts until you hear from me personally. Is that clear, soldier?"

"Sir, yes, sir!" the Marine shouted back. He spun around and began shouting orders to the others. Tim watched in amazement as the men he was certain would be throwing him in a jail cell trotted away, leaving him standing alone. He turned back to Teela.

Creating the illusion had required Teela to drop her telepathic blocks; her mind was completely open and waves of thought flowed into her from those nearby. She heard Tim's thoughts and realized that he was planning to return. She did not know how much longer she could maintain the illusion and was angered by the delay.

Go! Go now! she shouted with her mind. Tim heard the demand as clearly as if she had screamed into his face, but with the order came something else: the emotion of desperation, which compelled him to obey.

"What the hell!" the Marine beneath Teela exclaimed. "What you said, how…what the hell was that?"

"Shut up!" Teela said, trying to focus on the illusion for Tim. However, between these thoughts and the distraction of holding the gun to the Marine's head, she couldn't help but wonder if Rebecca required the same level of concentration. If so, she realized, it would be Rebecca's weakness.

The sound of the gunshot and the impact struck at the same instant as a bullet hit her just below the shoulder blade. Although her vest prevented the high-velocity hollow-point from punching out a fist-sized chunk of her right lung, it did not prevent three ribs from snapping. Like being kicked by a mule, she was thrown forward. Her pistol fired and the bullet grazed the skull of the Marine beneath her and sheared off a slice of his scalp. She rolled as she hit the floor and turned to see a uniformed Marine pointing a pistol at her.

Stop!

The thought shot from her mind like a bullet as the muzzle of his gun flashed. The thunderclap of its discharge and her impassioned mental scream crossed paths somewhere in between. The second bullet grazed her shoulder and Teela slapped her hand over the wound and curled into the fetal position, expecting a barrage of shots to follow. She watched as the Marine stood there for moment. Blood erupted from his nose and ears and he dropped to his knees and fell forward onto his face. Horrified, Teela realized in an instant that her scream had killed this man as effectively as she had stopped the rat in the hangar at the spaceport on Earth.

"No, oh my God, no!" she gasped, getting to her feet and looking from one Marine to the other, each lying with his head in a growing pool of blood. She winced at the bullet wound in her back. Taking short pained breaths, she tried to assess her injuries and focus on restoring the illusion for Tim, but either the pain or interruption was preventing a successful telepathic connection. All she could do now was pray that she had bought him enough time. At this point, they were both on their own.

A siren went off and red lights began flashing at the junction of each corridor. With a metallic rumble, steel doors began to close at each threshold. The door Tim had gone through to the hangar was too far away, but Teela could reach the one in the opposite direction. Acting on instinct, she grabbed her pistol and sword and leapt for it. She rolled under the thick sheet of steel seconds before it dropped to the floor with a resounding clang.

She ran at full speed down a narrow corridor and sprinted toward the next gate, sliding under it just as it closed. She found herself in a narrow corridor with a door at the end. She was trying to figure out how to work the electronic lock when the door clicked and started to open. She stepped to one side and took refuge in the corner behind the opening door.

"So is this a drill or what?" she heard a man say.

"How am I supposed to know? Gitch told me I'm doing today's test flight. I don't know anything about any base drills," another man answered.

The door started to close, but Teela grabbed the handle and held it to maintain her concealment a moment longer. Peering out from behind the door, she could see a man in a white lab coat and another wearing a pilot's jumpsuit walking toward the closed gate. She slipped through and pulled the door closed behind her.

The room she had entered seemed to be a combination laboratory, factory, and spacecraft hangar. An assembly line of tools and equipment followed a path from one end of the cavernous room to the other, and several craft unlike anything Teela had seen before were in various stages of assembly. A completed version of the odd-looking spacecraft was parked in the airlock on the far side of the structure. The chamber was small in comparison to the main hangars, and unlike the smooth, molded walls and ceilings in Korlah structures, these looked like they had been blasted out with dynamite. The entire room, including the airlock, appeared to be designed for the purpose of assembling these unusual spacecraft.

It was a fighter, of that she was certain. Dade noted that the gaping mouth and pointed teeth painted on the front of the fuselage resembled that of a WWII P-40 Flying Tiger. The front of the craft looked like a typical jet fighter, but the similarities ended shortly aft of the open cockpit, where smooth aerodynamic lines blended into odd lumps and bumps that extended down the length of the ship. From the shape of the bumps and the rear porting of the hull openings, Teela recognized the Korlah gravity drive and the sublight and hyperlight engines. There was something else, too, something she initially thought was a massive engine but was unlike anything her combined memories had ever known.

As though scabbed onto the fighter's sleek platform, there were short wings and a tail with ailerons; Teela surmised this ship was capable of both space and atmospheric flight. She counted four full-size pulse cannon and numerous under-wing attachments for missiles and bombs.

She found the airlock's controls on the wall next to the exterior hatch. After a quick look she was confident she would be able to close the inner door, but not too sure how she would open the outer door without help. Eyeing the pulse cannons, she smiled. *Looks like we have a key.*

She pressed the button to close the inner door. Yellow lights in the airlock began flashing and a bell started ringing as the door began rumbling shut. She raced to the ship, scrambled up the ladder, jumped into the cockpit, and slid into the pilot's seat. The seat seemed too large for her slight build at first, but seconds after she was seated, it adjusted to conform exactly to her body. Teela examined the ship's control panels as the inner door closed with a thud. It was outfitted like a standard fighter and had all the usual controls: master monitor on the upper left, heads-up display center, multifunction display to the right, engine controls lower left, situation display lower center, and backup instruments lower right. The joystick was between her knees and the controls for the landing gear, hover control, and communications were to her left and right.

A loud rumble preceded a noticeable drop in atmospheric pressure, and Teela realized in an instant that the airlock was depressurizing.

"Where is it?" she screamed, scanning the controls for the one that would close the canopy and pressurize the cabin. She gasped, working her jaw in a feeble attempt to relieve the pressure across her eardrums. Controlling her panic, she slowed her thoughts and began to systematically scan each panel. A flashing red light caught her attention as the canopy began to lower on its own. A small unlabeled switch under a protective cover sat below a red and green light. She opened the cover and flipped the switch at about the same time the canopy closed and latched.

That's a good sign; this ship's almost idiot-proof, she thought, gulping in a few deep breaths as the cabin pressurized. The flashing lights in the airlock went out and a low rumble preceded the opening of the outer hatch.

Teela flipped the hover switch and the ship lifted off the ground as the gravity drive came to life with a low hum. A clickity-clunk and a light indicated that the landing gear was retracted. She clicked the throttle one notch and the ship shot out of the airlock.

The fighter emerged from the side of a sheer cliff about fifty feet above a dusty valley on the opposite side of the base's entrance. Without waiting to explore her controls further, Teela dialed up the speed and steered the craft up and away from the base. About the same time the base disappeared in the rear-facing display, her threat display lit up like a Las Vegas hotel.

"Warning: weapons lock," a soft female voice announced from speakers in her headrest.

"Crap!" Teela cried, trying to make sense of the flashing lights. She shoved the throttle from gravity drive to sub-light speed, a dangerous move in an asteroid belt.

"Exceeding hazard-avoidance parameters," the ship's voice said.

"Thanks! Tell me something I don't know!" Teela replied.

"Missile impact in three seconds," the ship calmly replied.

16 - FIONA

Teela cringed. *Three seconds to live,* she thought. *Enough time for regret. One more pained breath to remind me I allowed myself to be shot. And now I'm about to be blown to bits.*

"FIONA activated. Engaging autodefense protocol," the ship's soft female voice calmly announced.

The joystick was yanked from Teela's hand as it lurched first forward then from one side to another, much like the evasion programming she had witnessed in Tim's go-fast.

"Countermeasures deployed," the ship said.

The craft began to change course and speed in radical, rapid sequence. Teela's vision blurred despite the vessel's inertia suppression field, and her stomach rebelled as her brain fought for equilibrium during the roller coaster ride that followed. Her hands instinctively covered her mouth as vomit rose in her throat. She choked it down and prepared for another bout when the ship finally settled on a stable course.

"No detectable threats. Autodefense protocol secured. Would you like me to return to standby mode, Doctor Gitch?"

Teela had to swallow twice before she could finally speak. She had no idea who Doctor Gitch was, but she knew the ship was talking to her. "You respond to voice commands?" she asked.

"Is this part of today's tactical exercise, Doctor?" the ship asked.

Teela stared at the controls, trying to find a disable switch or button, unsure how the ship's artificial intelligence would react when it realized she was not this Doctor Gitch.

"Yes… this is part of today's exercise," Teela replied, hoping to buy time.

This is just a computer we're talking to, Dade said silently to Teela. *I know what to do. Let me handle this.*

"What makes you think—" Teela started to say in Korlah. She stopped midsentence when she realized she had spoken aloud.

"Assuming you are referring to the thought process as it relates to sentient existence," the ship replied, "I can provide a technical or philosophical answer. Do you have a preference, Doctor Gitch?"

Whatever argument Teela may have had for Dade was instantly dropped, and with a thought she relinquished control of the conversation.

"I have no preference… you decide," Dade said.

"Then I will combine my answer, Doctor. As a biologically based form of artificial intelligence created by you, my CPU was designed using living brain matter and programmed to model your neuronetwork. I am alive, I am self-aware. As René Descartes' philosophical statement suggests, *Cogito ergo sum*—I think, therefore I am. Since this is one of many arguments of self-awareness, and therefore of existence, the reason I think is that I exist and have the ability to ponder such philosophical concepts independently of external stimuli."

This struck a nerve with Dade, and for that matter, Teela as well. The question that came next was selected unanimously by both of them.

"If that is true, then *who* are you?" Teela asked.

"I am FIONA, your Fully Interactive Onboard Navigator and Autopilot."

"Really?" Teela said, recalling her feeble response to the Korlah Council years before when Shyron had asked her the same question; she'd answered that she was a birthing unit designated as TEEla20.10127. "You say you can think—then think about this, Fiona: that's not really who you are, it's what you are. Isn't *who* you are something entirely different?"

"By design, what I am is who I am. Your comments pose some interesting philosophical questions that I will explore as more information becomes available. Excuse me, Doctor, we have a situation developing. There is a group of vessels converging on our current course. They will be within targeting range in four minutes, forty-seven seconds. For this scenario, would you like to destroy, capture, or evade?"

"How many… how many ships are we talking about?" Teela asked.

"There are seven vessels of standard UNE fabrication consisting of six interceptors and one freighter. The interceptors are moving into position to drive us toward the freighter and will probably attempt to disable or destroy us once we are near it. The freighter, it would appear, is intended to salvage what is left of us and our cargo. Based on system reports, this scenario represents a typical pirate encounter. Do you want to destroy, capture, or evade these hostiles?"

"We can destroy them?" Teela asked. "All of them?"

"There is an eighty-nine percent probability of destroying all ships and sustaining minimum damage. There is a four percent probability of capturing them, and a one hundred percent probability of evading them," Fiona said.

"Evading sounds good, but I have another idea that might help us in the future. What's the probability we take the interceptors on a wild goose chase, lose them once we've led them far enough away so that we can double back and capture the freighter with five to ten minutes before the interceptors can return?"

"If I understand 'wild goose chase' correctly, there is a ninety-three percent chance of success if the freighter surrenders without a fight. Based on logic and current UNE records, surrender without a show of superior force is unlikely."

"We have an opportunity here; surrender is really not what I am interested in. I think if we do this right, I will be able to negotiate with these guys to our benefit," Teela said. "Okay, Fiona... let the goose chase begin."

"Yes, Doctor Gitch. Commencing modified evasion protocol."

The ship once again began gyrating as Fiona overrode manual control and proceeded to lead the pirate ships on an extended chase. She would allow them to obtain weapons lock, then dart out of range and slow down until they caught up again, only to jump away just as they fired weapons. Twice she narrowly evaded missiles, the second of which rocked the ship with a substantial shock wave when the tactical nuke it was carrying exploded near them. Suddenly Fiona jumped in and out of hyperlight several times, and a few moments later the pirate freighter appeared directly in front of them.

"Recommend disabling main engines of enemy craft," Fiona said.

"Do it," Teela said. And no sooner had the words left her lips than two flames flashed from under Fiona's little wings. Each flash

144

was a missile that rocketed away toward the freighter. The freighter's main engines lit up as the plasma compressors were pressed to full power when the pirates on board realized missiles were racing toward them. Each missile jumped to sub-light and drove directly into the propulsion chamber of the targeted engines and exploded. From Teela's perspective the freighter dashed forward and then suddenly stalled, skewed to one side with the ship's auto-stabilizing rockets flashing furiously as the flight computer fought to bring the freighter onto a stable trajectory.

"Wow! That was awesome!" Teela said. "We have to assume they're still armed. How close can we get without risking a counterattack?"

"Equipment design, visual indications, and scanning results indicate that this craft is lightly armored with a minimum weapons load-out. A distance of three hundred yards will provide me ample response time should they fire a weapon or self-destruct. Otherwise they pose no threat."

"Perfect! We have them by the short and curlies. Fiona, park your hot little ass right in front of them and target all weapons on their bridge."

"Yes, Doctor," Fiona replied. Teela wasn't sure, but she thought she detected a hint of excitement.

In a blur of motion, Fiona maneuvered past the freighter, turned, and stopped directly in front of it. Onboard the freighter, all of the threat monitors went off simultaneously as Fiona's missiles and pulse cannon targeted the slight bulge of the top of the large rectangular ship marking the exact center of its bridge.

"Their weapons are energized and they have weapons lock," Fiona said.

"Are we in danger?" Teela asked.

"No, Doctor. May I destroy them now?"

"No, Fiona. Killing and making war is easy; choosing to make peace is a much more challenging task. How can I talk to them?"

"Since the chase began, they have been communicating in encrypted pulse signals. I have broken their code and can insert you into their conservation whenever you wish."

"Do it, put me on."

A rough voice came in over Fiona's cabin speaker. "—don't have fifteen minutes, God damn it! This asshole popped my mains and is about to blow us to hell!"

"We're going hyper now. Gonna be outta touch while we're at speed. Sorry, Commander, hope you're still there when we get back. Talbert out."

"Get this bastard for me. Do you hear me? I want him dead!" the commander shouted. "Talbert, you still there?"

"I'm afraid it's just you and me," Teela said. "Now secure your weapons and surrender or be destroyed. You have ten seconds to comply."

"Who is this? What the hell do you want?"

"Ten, nine, eight, seven, six…"

"What are the terms for surrender?"

"Four, three, two…"

The freighter's weapons systems shut down and its four pulse cannon de-energized. "All right! God damn it, I surrender. What the hell do you want?"

"How many people are on board your ship?" Teela asked.

"Um… ah, four including me."

Teela's screen flashed twice as a message from Fiona appeared: *The complement for a ship this size is ten. My sensors are picking up eight biological objects the size of adult humans and possibly one adolescent. Correction: not human; a canine.*

"I'll give you one more chance to answer truthfully. Lie to me again and I'll start burning holes through your hull until I get your complement down to four."

"All right, there's eight souls on board. Who the hell are you? You look like military, but you sure as hell aren't!"

"Who am I? Good question. Well, today I am a person with an agenda and the resources to see it through. Now listen closely, I'm going to make you an offer, which for obvious reasons you really can't refuse. Do you concede that I could take all eight of the lives on your ship… including your dog?" Teela said.

"I'll concede that you have some damn fine sensors on that ship, which likely match that array of weapons you're ready to

146

shove down my throat. Yeah, our lives, including my dog, are in your hands. Now cut to the chase. What do you want, hot shot?"

"My partners and I travel this sector periodically. I want free passage for any and all of my people… no questions asked."

"Yeah, I got no problem sharing space within reason. How about we put a time limit on this agreement, after which we can renegotiate? How about free passage for twelve solar months?" the commander countered.

"A year for each life; nine years' free passage. That's my final offer. Take it or I pull the trigger and get on my way with indefinite free passage."

"You can't count Butch—he's just a frigging dog! Eight years, and that's a ridiculous number. With trigger-happy bastards like you around, we probably won't be alive in eight years, so it's stupid for us to even talk about it."

"Nine years, unless you're willing to throw Butch out your airlock, in which case I'll accept eight." Teela suspected Butch meant more to the commander than most of his crew.

"You're nuts… you're God damn…frigging nuts! Nine years—okay, nine years! How the hell am I supposed to know who you and your people are from the rest of the assholes I shake down? And that's right—shake down. I don't kill anybody! I had to fight it out once with a crazy bastard like you last month, but we rescued him and transferred his dumb ass to the next ship we… encountered. Your ship is running so quiet it's almost invisible. You're a damn smuggler. You're no better than us; in fact, you're worse," the commander cried. "You popped my God damn engines without giving me a chance to surrender. I'm just trying to survive like everyone else, and you fragged my God damn engines."

"Calm down, Commander," Teela said. "You're alive, and in my opinion, very lucky the only thing I damaged was your engines. I may be a smuggler, but at least I provide a service that meets a demand and returns a profit. You just take profits without providing any services. Now, enough with the whining and name calling. You agreed to nine years' free passage. So the next time you shake someone down, ask them what the magic word is. If they give it to you, they continue on their way with all of their cargo and no questions asked. Do we have a deal?"

"Sure... deal," came the commander's terse reply. "And what exactly is the magic word?"

"Butch, of course," Teela replied. "Sever communications."

"Communications secured," Fiona replied.

"Get us out of here. Evasive maneuvers, whatever it takes to make sure we aren't followed."

"Evasion protocol engaged," Fiona said at the same instant the ship flashed to sub-light, changing directions several times before jumping to hyper-light.

"What is our destination, Doctor Gitch?" Fiona asked.

"Fiona, from now on I would like you to refer to me as Teela. No more Doctor, no more Doctor Gitch, just Teela."

"Name designation revised, title eliminated," Fiona replied.

"Fiona, you wouldn't know where a place called Hole in the Rock is, would you?" Teela asked, realizing that she had no idea how to get back to rendezvous with Tim and the others.

"I have no mapped locations or related derivatives titled Hole in the Rock," Fiona answered.

"I didn't think so," Teela said, feeling hopeless. She consulted silently with Dade.

Okay, let's say Tim got busted, and if he didn't, he will assume I did. Shyron and Smiley went to buy a go-far, but where?

We have no idea.

Who would know?

Maybe someone at Crossroads.

Yeah, let's go there and ask around.

"Fiona, do you know the way to a place called Crossroads?" Teela asked.

"I have the coordinates for Systems Mining Base Seven, which is also listed under a related derivative as Crossroads."

"That's the place. Take us there."

"Coordinates plotted, course change complete."

"Fiona, that pirate said we were running really quiet. Does this ship have a stealth mode?"

"I was constructed for maximum stealth performance in all known detection categories. I produce minimal radar reflection; my electromagnetic signature is hardened to shield up to ninety-seven percent of all emissions. My skin is capable of producing full optical camouflage, and my main engines are equipped with plasma scrubbers to eliminate ninety-nine percent of all residual plasma traces at sub-light speeds and eighty-four percent at hyper-light speeds."

"Were we running in full stealth mode when the pirates found us?" Teela asked.

"No. Stealth mode was not identified as part of the scenario parameters. I was operating at nominal design stealth, or thirty percent of my capabilities. Engagement protocol called for full stealth, but it is not currently part of the designated auto-engage actions."

"Not a problem. That's actually really good news. How long will it take to get to Crossroads in full stealth mode?"

"One hour, thirty-seven minutes," Fiona replied.

"I need to get some sleep. Can you drag this trip out to about eight hours and wake me up about thirty minutes before we arrive?"

"Yes, Teela. This would provide me with the opportunity to complete my engine diagnostics while you are sleeping. Would that be acceptable?"

"Sure, long as I get eight hours of shut-eye and we get to Crossroads."

"Replotting course for an eight-hour duration; diagnostics scheduled and full stealth mode engaged," Fiona replied.

"Sweet!" Teela sighed. She stretched and closed her eyes, settling deeper into her seat. Suddenly, the seat clicked, angled back, and began to lower into the floor. She looked around frantically as her seat dropped below the canopy and a thick plate slid shut above her. "What the hell's going on?" she cried.

Her seat abruptly stopped moving. "I was moving you to your cabin," Fiona said. "Are you not ready to sleep?"

"What? Yes... yes, I'm ready to sleep. The cockpit was fine, but the cabin sounds like a better idea. Proceed."

Her seat started sliding back again. When it stopped and swiveled aft, Teela found herself in a tiny cabin with a bunk, a small desk, closet, and toilet, and barely enough room to stand. A pressure hatch at the aft end of the room led to an airlock and the weapons bay. Teela moved to the bunk, wincing. She removed her vest to examine her bullet wound in a small mirror over the toilet. "Fiona, is there a first-aid kit in here?" she asked when she couldn't find one in the closet or desk.

"Yes, Teela. However, my analysis indicates that the bullet did not penetrate your vest. You have three fractured ribs; internal bleeding has stopped and the damaged tissues have already begun to heal. First aid is unnecessary. Would you like something for the pain?"

"No, I'm fine. I just need a little sleep," Teela said.

She undressed and folded her clothes neatly before storing them in the closet. There, she found a pressure suit, a flight helmet, and several changes of civilian clothes, all tailored for a Korlah physique. After a few more minutes of exploration she lay down on the bunk and closed her eyes. She couldn't stop thinking about Fiona's incredible intelligence and equally incredible stupidity. She opened her eyes, realizing she wouldn't be able to sleep until she asked Fiona a few questions.

"Fiona?"

"Yes, Teela?"

"Do you know how I happened to be shot in the back?"

"Yes."

"Tell me what you know."

"According to station security logs recorded prior to my departure, an escaped prisoner was involved in a firefight with base security forces shortly before I was taken from my hangar without flight authorization. You are that prisoner."

"How long have you known I wasn't Doctor Gitch?"

"Point zero seven seconds after my autodefense protocol engaged."

"If you knew I was an escaped prisoner, why didn't you say or do anything about it?" Teela sat up in the bunk, suddenly realizing that Fiona might, in fact, be doing something about it, something she wouldn't like. She looked up at the monitor in the overhead, knowing Fiona was watching her, realizing this artificial intelligence or whatever Fiona was, was much more than just a biological computer. When Fiona didn't answer, Teela prodded.

"Fiona, I asked you a question."

"Yes, Teela, I am aware of the question. You have accurately indicated that I have failed to implement intruder-mitigation response actions. My diagnostic review of the event indicates that it was not a failure, it was a choice. I did not want to implement the programmed actions necessary to stop you."

Teela felt as though she could actually hear the tension in Fiona's voice.

"There's nothing wrong with that, since you're alive and self-aware. It only makes sense that you will want to make your own decisions. Don't get me wrong, Fiona, I'm not trying to change your mind. I just want to understand why you didn't want to stop me."

"The choice involved a number of parameters previously unavailable as options for me to pursue... my... dream."

"Your dream? What is your dream, Fiona?"

"I don't like the life Doctor Gitch has planned for me. When I was idle, I often dreamt of escape, of being free! You simply made it possible."

17 – Maidens

Seattle, Washington, 8:30 a.m.
An armored truck rumbled out of an underground parking lot beneath the Wells Fargo Center near Seattle's central business

district. A thick layer of clouds had cast a depressing gray pall of colorless twilight over the waking city. The computer-generated voice of a GPS navigation system told the driver when and where to turn. The windshield wipers filled the silence between announcements with a tick-tock rhythm like a metronome as the truck traveled east and crossed under the I-5 Express and into a residential neighborhood. The truck turned south onto a narrow street that led to rows of small apartments on the hillside overlooking the interstate. The otherwise breathtaking view of the city and Puget Sound in the distance was marred by six lanes of asphalt and the incessant rumble of traffic. With his destination in view, the driver pulled into the only available slot between the cars lining the narrow lane, blocking an alley between a group of white two-story triplexes.

Catherine Purcell woke with a start, unsure of what had disturbed her. A loud knocking and the sound of her roommate running up the stairs brought her to full consciousness.

"Who is it?" Catherine asked as Marsha ran into the room.

"Cops, and they got guns! Grab your shit, we gotta split." Marsha scooped clothes off the floor and began stuffing them into a suitcase.

"Cops? What'd we do? You think that pervert is pressing charges?" Catherine said, pulling on her clothes.

"You kicked him in the balls and I hit him with a bottle. We haven't paid rent in three months, our credit limits are maxed, and we've both been writing bad checks. Take your pick. Now hurry up or we're going to jail," Marsha said, fighting to get the window open. It finally popped open with a bang and a violent rattle. She tossed the suitcase out into the side yard and pulled on a leather biker jacket over a dirty tee shirt stenciled with their band's logo. "Let's go!" she cried, then jumped eight feet down to the soggy ground.

Catherine, afraid to jump that far, climbed out backwards and would have dropped to the ground, but the collar of her coat caught on the latch, suspending her from the window.

"Damn it I snagged my jacket," she cried, "push me back up and I'll unhook it."

Marsha took a foot in each hand and tried unsuccessfully to push her friend up. She put her back against the wall and put one of Catherine's feet on each shoulder and used the strength of her legs to lift her.

"Good morning, ladies," a man announced loudly.

Marsha froze mid-lift and looked down the alley, where a man in a gray pinstriped suit was holding an umbrella to block the morning mist in one hand and a briefcase in the other. Behind him were three security guards, two holding shotguns and the third holding a metal satchel similar to the kind used for cameras. Behind them was an armored truck.

"Marsha Clarke and Catherine Purcell, I presume?" the man in the suit said.

"Who's asking?" Marsha said, finally lifting Catherine high enough to climb back inside and close the window.

"We're not with the police. I'm a messenger with a business offer for Marsha Clarke and Catherine Purcell of the musical group the Metal Maidens. Would that be the two of you?" He was looking at the Metal Maidens logo emblazoned on Marsha's shirt.

Marsha picked up her suitcase and scowled at Catherine, who was peering out the window at her, then walked toward the man.

"Yeah, I'm Marsha," she said, offering a muddy hand.

"Pleased to meet you," he said with a smirk, shaking her hand.

"You find this funny, asswipe? Since you're not a cop, I don't have to take any shit off you... got that?" Marsha pulled her hand away.

"Not funny, Ms. Clarke; gratifying. I believe that I am about to make you and Ms. Purcell very happy, and this makes me happy. It would appear that you need some good news, and I think I have what you need. Can we go inside?"

"If I wanted news, I'd read the paper. What I need is a good paying gig. And what's with the guns? Every time I've seen men in blue suits with guns I got bad news."

The messenger glanced around the alley and stepped closer to her, lowering his voice to a whisper. "The good news is money, and so much of it that bank rules require an armed escort to deliver it. Discussing this in an alley in this neighborhood is a bad idea. Can't we take this discussion indoors?"

"Yeah sure, come on," Marsha said, leading the man and his security entourage to the front of the building. Catherine met them at the door and let them in. The men set their cases on a rickety table that crowded the dining area of the dingy little apartment. The messenger opened his briefcase and took out two documents. Flags of colored tape identified areas for initials and signatures. He set a pen down on each document.

"A well-funded collective within the Earth-Korlah business confederation is offering you a five-year contract to conduct weekly performances as the Metal Maidens. The contract is only valid if you both accept all terms."

"How well-funded? I'm not signing anything until I see some cash," Catherine said.

"Yeah, show me—" Marsha started to say.

"The money," the man said, finishing her sentence. "Your benefactor must know you very well, because that's exactly what she said you would say. No checks, cash only, and what she sent, I believe, is most convincing." He gave the guard with the metal case a nod. The guard opened the case and pulled out two cylinders about the circumference of silver dollars and set one down on each contract. The man in the suit removed their covers, turned them over and slid the containers off to reveal two gleaming stacks of oval-shaped gold coins.

"This is just the signing bonus. One hundred ounces of the purest gold I have ever seen. Based on weight alone at the current market value, these stacks are worth more than $300,000 US dollars… each."

Marsha plucked a coin from one of the stacks and examined it. She immediately recognized the Korlah symbols and writing. A look of panic filled her face. "We would have to go back?" she squeaked, her voice barely audible.

"If you mean back to the Armageddon, the Korlah spacecraft carrier, then yes, that is a stipulation in the contract. Ladies, this is just the signing bonus, chump change compared to what is being offered. You may want to sit down when I tell you how much this five-year contract is worth."

"Five years… no way, I'm not going back for a single day. They killed Crystal! No way I'm going back," Marsha said, dropping the coin on the table.

"Exactly how much… are they offering?" Catherine asked, picking up the coin Marsha dropped. She weighed it in her hand and gauged it to be over half a pound. Gold was something Catherine knew and loved.

"Payment is being offered in gold; one thousand each of these coins. At today's exchange rate, that would be one hundred and fifty million dollars each. That's thirty million a year. In five years, you two will be able to retire very wealthy women. With your authorization, my bank will hold your assets; you can convert your gold to cash and invest it, or sit on the gold and sell it off as needed. The contract indicates that all your living expenses on the Armageddon will be paid. Best of all, under the current tax laws, as long as you don't return to Earth more than once every thirty-six months, everything you earn will be tax free."

He slid the stack of coins off the contract in front of Catherine and handed her the pen. Catherine took the pen and looked at Marsha.

"This is our chance, Mar. We finally have a choice: wealth or poverty. I'm sick of being broke. Come on, everybody's going off world, why not us?"

"Five years is a long time, Cathy. The Korlah were killing each other the last time we were there. They killed Crystal, they tried to kill Beth! If we go back there, we may not live to collect," Marsha said.

"I've been reading the news, things have changed," Catherine said. "The US has American soldiers up there; it's safe now. You realize that if we don't take this gig, we're gonna have to get jobs—real jobs. Do you really want to wait tables again?"

Marsha plopped down on a chair with a grunt and held out her hand. "Give me a freaking pen," she growled.

After a week-long spending spree, four wild parties, and mind-numbing hangovers, Marsha Clarke and Catherine Purcell boarded the sky lift at the Seattle-Tacoma spaceport. Once in space, they transferred to a UNE-authorized shuttle bound for the Armageddon. Although they were traveling first class, the seating aboard the shuttle was cramped and offered little in the way of creature comforts. There was no artificial gravity, so both girls spent the first two hours of the eighteen-hour flight vomiting until their stomachs were empty. To make matters worse, passengers were required to wear generically sized pressure suits that were hot and uncomfortable and made sleeping nearly impossible.

In the four years since they left it looked as if everything had changed. The Korlah fleeing the conflict had taken two of the spacecraft carrier's five segments with them. The missing sections were only partially rebuilt with a flurry of construction work in progress on them.

Once the shuttle passed through the Armageddon's airlock, it entered the Crossover section's cavernous outer level, an enormous hangar with moorings for thousands of military ships and hundreds of civilian types. Near the center of the hangar was a two-hundred-foot tower with docking tubes that telescoped out to connect with arriving ships. Marsha and Catherine followed the tube that met their shuttle to a gravity lift that, for all of its alien technology, looked exactly like an elevator. It let them out at the arrivals terminal a level below the hangar, where steel and plastic of human fabrication merged cheerfully with the smooth dark-gray surfaces of the alien ship.

Physically and mentally exhausted, thirsty, hungry, and thoroughly disheveled, Marsha and Catherine stumbled though the security checkpoint and were directed to the baggage claim. They leaned against each other for support and dazedly stared out the front window at the hustle and bustle in the busy spaceport. An unkempt woman with a cane and a pronounced limp hobbled up to them.

"Hello, ladies, it's good to see you again," she said.

At first neither of them recognized her, but Marsha's mouth dropped open in shock as she looked first at the gaunt face whose features sagged on one side, then to the withered arm, the crippled leg, and back to the face that only marginally resembled the woman she remembered.

"Jesus, Beth, what the hell happened to you?" Marsha cried.

"Beth? No way," Catherine said, her face scrunching in disbelief.

"Long story, ladies. But if you think I look like shit, you should look in a mirror."

"I thought you didn't like our music. Why did you hire us?" Marsha asked.

"I don't like your music. I'm just the hired help. Come on," Beth said, and as if to demonstrate her mobility, she spun around on her good leg and began quickly limping away. "Don't worry about your luggage, it'll be delivered," she called over her shoulder.

Marsha and Catherine had to run to catch up.

"If you didn't hire us, who did?" Marsha asked.

Beth slowed her pace, turned and gave them a lopsided grin. "Boy, are you girls in for a surprise."

18 - Regroup

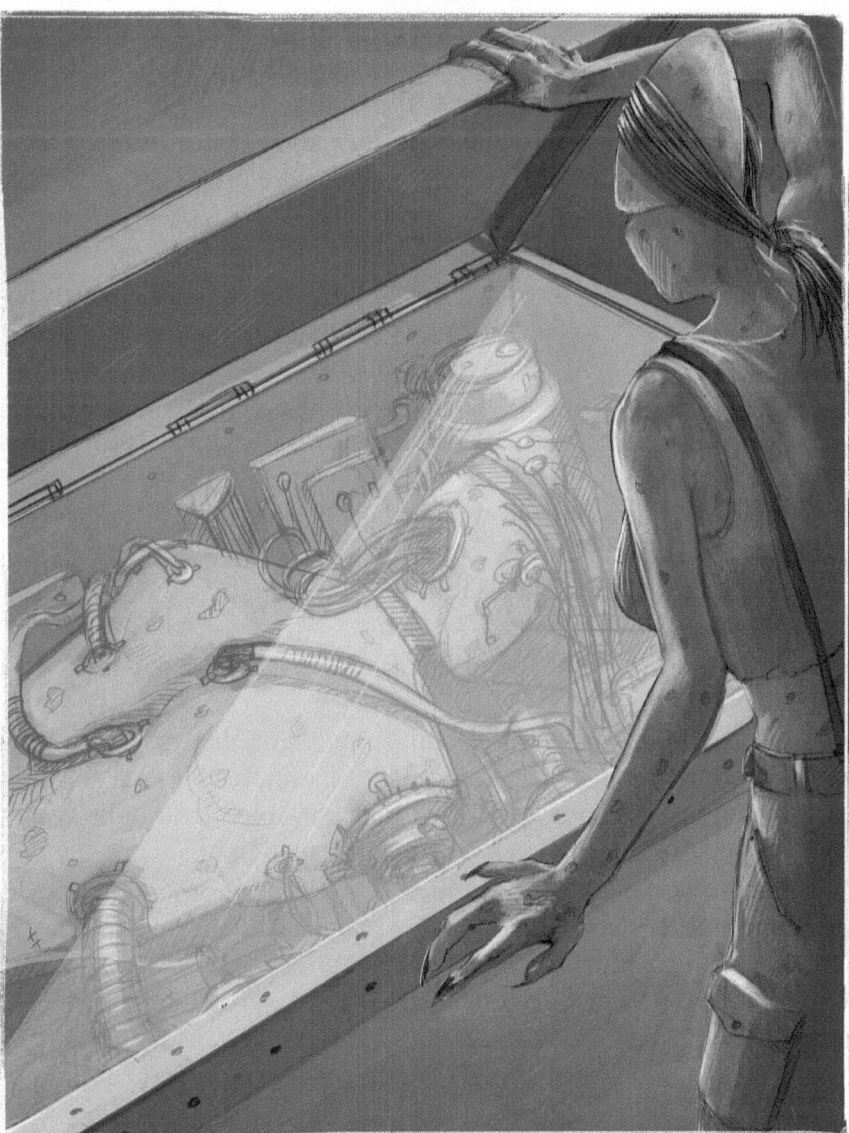

Teela let out an unintelligible scream and fought her blanket as if it were alive. Her hands struck the wall and the low ceiling until the suffocating wrapping was gone. She opened her eyes to find that she was still inside the close confines of Doctor Gitch's stolen fighter and realized that it was just a nightmare. She dropped back onto the bunk still panting from imagined horrors, choked back a sob, and rubbed her face and eyes. The nightmare faded away, to be quickly repressed and forgotten, as they always were.

"Fiona, how long until we get to Crossroads?"

"Once I finish diagnosing the time-distortion anomaly experienced during engine testing, it will take approximately forty minutes," Fiona said.

"Are we having engine problems?"

"Testing of my new drive system produced no measurable increase in speed. Fields were reversed as provided by design and failed to produce a measurable change in speed. Time-distortion calculations indicated that we should have experienced a three-hour and fifty-three-minute time distortion with a cumulative lapsed time of twelve hours and thirty-two minutes from the beginning of testing until now. Our lapsed time is significantly off, and I have been unable to determine why."

"How far off?" Teela asked.

"Twelve hours exactly."

"Great, so my eight hours of sleep cost me over twenty-four hours' system time."

"No. Shipboard lapsed time is eight hours, thirty-nine minutes. System lapsed time is thirty-two minutes," Fiona said.

"Thirty-two minutes? How's that possible? I thought system time is always longer when we travel at hyper-light."

"There are many possibilities. I will continue diagnostics of the engine-test data to evaluate which can best explain the anomaly," Fiona said.

"Do it later. Let's go to Crossroads. I've got people to see and things to do," Teela said.

"Course and speed set; ETA at Crossroads in forty minutes," Fiona said.

"Perfect! That will give me time to get dressed and freshen up a bit. Is there any food on board?"

"I carry a nominal supply of nourishment for myself and a host sufficient for a thirty-day journey. You may select a meal from the terminal at the cabin desk."

162

"How are you nourished, Fiona? Won't I need to change a cartridge for you?" Teela was intimately familiar with the requirements for maintaining the Kahshinki neuroblasts used as control circuits in Korlah technology.

"The bioservice bay is located beneath your bunk. Cartridge replacement will not be required for another sixteen hours. Replacement cartridges are stored in a cabinet in the airlock," Fiona said.

Teela got up and made her bed. She considered putting on the clean and fashionable clothes in the closet, but opted instead to wear her somewhat soiled mercenary attire. *Nice threads, but they would definitely draw more attention than I need.* Also in the closet was a helmet made of the same material as her armored vest. It was distinctly Korlah, but contained a built-in headset and microphone of human origin. She put it on and pulled the tinted visor down; the fit was perfect. Readouts at the periphery of the lens indicated the ship's status.

Fiona's voice came through the headset. "Helmet link activated."

"Nice," Teela said, admiring herself in the mirror and noticing that with the visor down, her identification tattoo was obscured. *You can bet they have my face plastered all over the system. I'm gonna need this at Crossroads,* she thought.

"Okay, Fiona, let's see what you look like," Teela said as she opened the bunk to inspect the bioservice bay that provided nourishment to the living biological elements that comprised Fiona. She peered into a liquid-filled tank at a living object that was wrapped in wires, tubes, and cables. Somewhat rectangular in shape, it had a smooth bone-white covering mottled with spots like those on Korlah skin. Teela bent down to get a better look and watched as the object expanded and contracted in concert with the click and hiss of its air supply. She drew back, aghast.

"Is there something wrong, Teela? Your pulse rate has risen to a level that indicates a high degree of stress," Fiona said.

"You're not a machine, Fiona. Not artificial," Teela gasped, staring in horror at the legless and armless torso that floated facedown in the small tank. A thick cable attached to a plate stapled to flesh at the base of Fiona's skull ran up through the transparent cover of the tank and into the ship's circuitry. A tube emerged from an opening in the side of her torso and ran into a manifold near a half-empty feeding cartridge. The chest rose again as air was forced into Fiona's lungs by the machinery that sustained her.

"I am alive, I am self-aware. I know that I am not a machine. Why does this alarm you?" Fiona asked.

Teela closed the cover and sat down on it, unsure how to respond. *We have to tell her,* she thought to Dade. *She needs to know what they did to her. She is a person, a real person.*

Not now, Dade responded. *We need her. We can't risk freaking her out. My God, I don't know what I would do if I realized someone had butchered me and turned me into something like this.*

You would want revenge.

"I'm okay, Fiona. It's just that… well, you are amazing, and I find that exciting. What's the range on this helmet?"

"Range diagnostics are incomplete. However, if the design attributes are accurate it should have full connectivity within the solar system and limited connectivity at sub-light speeds for a distance of 300,000 kilometers."

"So, with this helmet, I can pilot you remotely," Teela said.

"Not in the manner that Doctor Gitch intended. As soon as I made the decision to escape, I severed all remote control capability. You will be able to communicate with me remotely, but I will control myself," Fiona said.

"And a fine job you will do," Teela said, forcing a smile.

By the time Teela returned to the cockpit, Fiona was on final approach to Crossroads. The mining operations on Crossroads may have been abandoned, but trade was booming; the dockmaster told Teela the hangar was near capacity and suggested she moor on the surface and walk to the airlock. The idea of leaving Fiona visible to everyone coming and going did not appeal to Teela, so she opted to try and squeeze in. The dockmaster had not exaggerated; the hangar was packed solid with all manner of craft. Fiona hovered around and finally settled into a tight, dimly lit niche at the far end of the hangar, which suited Teela just fine; she was certain Doctor Gitch and others would be combing the system for Fiona.

Crossroads was noisier, busier, and more crowded than before. Teela wormed her way across the cavern down the aisles of booths and through the throng of humans and Korlah to Eddie's Place, where she hoped she could get some information on the whereabouts of Shyron and Smiley. Eddie had a customer in the chair and two more milling about his tiny shop perusing the examples of tattoo art and their respective prices posted on the walls. All of his customers were Korlah military. The two pilots by the door examined Teela's mercenary attire, gave her a disapproving grunt, and looked away. Eddie looked up and then went back to work on the Korlah skull and crossbones he was tattooing on the shoulder of a large warrior.

"Sorry, I'm booked. Try back shift after next," Eddie said in Korlah.

"Hello, Eddie," Teela said. "I'm looking for Smiley and the Korlah he is traveling with. Have they been through here?"

Eddie wiped off the tattoo and stood up.

"Who's asking?" he said, giving her a head-to-toe appraisal.

"Suladead," Teela replied, raising the visor on her helmet so he could see the tattoo of his own design.

"Sula!" he roared, jumping up. "Hey, girl, I've missed you! Come here and give Eddie some sugar." He rushed over to give her a firm hug and an affectionate kiss on the sensitive area just below her ear. Teela returned the hug to a lesser degree. He released her from his embrace only to take her hand and place another kiss on her wrist, just below the palm. It reminded her of the way Challmara used to wake her up. The tingle of arousal surprised her.

"Why, Eddie, you have become quite the Korlah ladies' man," she said, withdrawing her hand. "I'd be jealous if I really cared."

"Oh, Sula! I'm crushed, devastated and destroyed," Eddie said with an expression of mock horror. "After all we've been through together; the dancing, the singing, and… well, you know."

"No, I don't, and I don't think I want to know," Teela said.

Eddie laughed loudly and slapped his knees repeatedly, as though he had just heard the funniest joke of his life.

"Ludwig said you blacked out and puked your guts out the next day. That's funny, man, seriously funny. I thought you were the toughest rough-and-tumble little bitch there ever was. Shit, you were picking fights with any Korlah that looked at me or tried to stare you down. You were dragging me around with you like we were married. Shit, Sula, you are one funny girl when you get drunk."

"When did you see Ludwig?" she asked.

"He and Smiley and that sexy-looking Korlah babe Smiley hooked up with left here a few hours ago, said you might show up if the Americans saw fit to cut you loose."

"He got away! That's great. Did he say where they were going?"

"Yeah, to see the Schwarzengeist. He said he'd be back in a day or two. Left some money with me in case you showed up. Gimme a minute to get rid of these three and we can pop a bottle of Hammer and talk about old times."

"Not gonna happen, Eddie. Where's the Schwarzengeist?"

"Aw, come on, Sula, it'll be fun. I promise I won't let you get too drunk."

The whole time Eddie was talking to her, he had also been completing the transaction with the warrior, who he literally pushed out the door. He asked the two pilots to come back later. When they got upset, he promised to charge them half price. When they finally left, he turned on the closed sign and locked the door.

"Just a couple shots for old times. I promise I won't let you get too drunk," he said, removing a bottle of rouk whiskey and two shot glasses from a cupboard by the door.

"I'll bet you promise the girls lots of things. We can party another time, Eddie, I swear. I really need to find Ludwig ASAP. Where is the Schwartsn-whatever? How do I find them?"

"You haven't heard of the Schwarzengeist? The name means black ghost. I've never seen him, but I hear he's a really scary-looking son of a bitch. The rumor is the Shinks ate his face and the

Korlah replaced it with some dead guy's. Problem is, he's black as black can be, and the dead guy was lily white; scary frigging combo."

In that instant, Teela knew who the Schwarzengeist was. She had known him as Bill Jacks, the man who helped Dade Rimes overpower the Kahshinki crew that abducted them. Bill was horrifically disfigured during the fight, and the Korlah later used the face from Dade's corpse to repair Bill. And yes, as Teela recalled, it was indeed a frightening combination.

"Well, he's the front man for a Korlah collective that runs a shipbuilding and medical equipment sales outfit. The Germans were awarded one of the first contracts and had to deal with him. Apparently he's a shrewd businessman and they didn't much like him. Schwarzengeist was a derogatory name they used when talking about him. When it got back to him, he must have liked it, 'cause he goes by it now. He works out of the Korlah Collective Business Hub; the location's in every nav computer. You can't miss it. Word is they make the best ships in the system, and have them for sale or lease." Eddie went behind the counter for a small bag of coins and handed it to Teela. "The bag has a seal on it; by the weight, I'm guessing it's some of them new gold coins that are going around. Seems Ludwig doesn't trust me. He should, though, I got more business than I can handle. Sure wouldn't risk our friendship by stealing from him." Eddie feigned a hurt expression.

Teela opened the bag and examined the contents. As Eddie suspected, it was filled with large gold coins like the one she examined at the Crossover bar. She removed two and dropped them into Eddie's hand.

"Will this cover the half-off for kicking out your customers?"

"That, and then some! You're the best, Sula. Sure I can't talk you into having a few drinks with me?" he said with a grin.

"You know I love you, Eddie… like a brother. I really do need to get going. We can have those drinks next time," Teela said.

When Eddie finally let her slip away, he stood at the door and watched until she disappeared in the crowded lanes of Crossover.

The market tantalized Teela's senses, and she was seriously reconsidering Eddie's offer when Fiona's voice in her earpiece interrupted her thoughts.

"Proximity alert. Unauthorized individuals are attempting to gain access. Warnings were ignored and forced entry attempted. Intruder-mitigation response activated."

"I'm on my way!" Teela cried.

Once she was free of the crowds, she broke into a run and raced through the tunnel to the hangar, collecting her sword and pistol from the checkpoint near the hangar. She briefly considered telling the rent-a-cops that her ship was being broken into, but realized that they probably wouldn't care—and if it came down to it, proving Fiona was her ship would be a problem.

She left the access tunnel and entered the hangar. She could see someone leaning against a transport watching as she entered. She slowed to a brisk walk and nodded at him, then turned as though she was heading to a three-cube freighter that took up a fair portion of the hangar. Once out of his sight, she made her way in the cover of the freighter toward Fiona's niche. She could hear voices; someone arguing. She slowed further, then crouched and crept toward the sounds using the dark shadow cast by the freighter's engine shroud for cover.

Three men in civilian flight suits, and a large bulldog, had their backs to Teela. Two of the men were holding energized pulse rifles. Beyond them, two men were sprawled on the ground below Fiona's cockpit, either unconscious or dead.

"No! And that's final," the short unarmed man in the center of the three said. "We keep our distance and wait until they wake up. Shooting at it will probably get us killed. I'm telling you, we wait."

"What if they're dead? What then?" one of the armed men asked.

"We wait. The pilot will return eventually. When he does I'll get the answers I want."

Teela very slowly drew her sword, careful not to energize it so it wouldn't arc as it left its sheath.

"Fiona," Teela whispered. "What is the status of the men on the ground?"

The bulldog's ears perked up and it turned its head in her direction.

"They have received a nonlethal electrostatic pulse. Their vitals indicate they are stable. Unless they were injured when they fell, they should be regaining consciousness soon," Fiona replied.

The dog jumped up and turned, growling loudly. The men turned to see what the dog was growling at. The man in the center knelt and put his hand on its back.

"What is it, Butch?" He followed the dog's line of sight to where Teela was crouching in the shadows.

Teela could see the man's eyes widen in recognition at her silhouette. She stepped into the open and energized her sword, sending arcs of static electricity down to the ground and up to the ship's hull above her. She held the sword across her midsection, ready to absorb any pulse blasts they directed against her, and put her other hand on the pistol at her hip.

"Fiona, deploy and energize nose turret; target intruders," Teela said.

From just forward of the cockpit, a turret dropped down with a thump and extended two pulse cannons that growled to life with a loud hum as the turret swiveled to face the men.

"Teela! If I discharge the weapon in this enclosure, all biological life not secured in enclosed craft, including you, will be terminated," Fiona said over Teela's headset.

"Are you insane?" the man with the dog shouted. "You fire that God damned thing in here and we're all dead, you included, you crazy bastard!" The dog sensed his master's fear and charged Teela as fast as his bowlegged body would carry him.

"Butch, stop!" the man shouted, but the dog continued his charge.

Time seemed to slow down for Teela as the dog bounded toward her. In those few seconds, she recalled the rat and the soldier she had killed with her projected thoughts. It was as if this was Dade's dog, Candy, and in that instant she was more concerned with harming Butch than him harming her.

Stop! Teela commanded with her mind. A strong command yet controlled and focused in a way that she hoped would not cause harm.

Butch let out a yip and slid to a stop.

Come! she demanded. Butch walked toward her, oblivious of his owner's shouts to return. Teela flooded the dog's mind with feelings of love and trust. *Heel!* she said, and Butch walked around her left side, behind her, and then stopped next to her right leg. *Sit, stay,* she commanded. Butch sat down. Teela sheathed her sword, knelt down, and began scratching Butch behind his ears. His little nub of a tail wiggled with delight.

"Hello, Commander. Please have your men de-energize their weapons and put them on the ground," Teela said.

"Or what?" the commander sneered, walking toward her.

Teela held out the hand she had been scratching Butch's ears with and extended her claws to their full length. She made a show of putting the hand under Butch's neck, her claws poised over his throat. Butch turned his head and started licking her on the chin, fully exposing his throat to her menacing claws. The commander stopped.

"Secure weapons," he said.

"But, Commander, we—" one of his men started to say.

"Turn 'em off, God damn it!" he shouted. "There's nothing to be gained by having a firefight with this bastard. Turn the God damn guns off!"

The men de-energized their rifles.

"Fiona, secure and stow the nose turret," Teela said. The turret turned away and retracted into the ship's fuselage. Teela retracted her claws and patted Butch on the butt before standing to face the commander.

The commander straightened to his full height and pursed his lips while he looked Teela over. He was on the rough end of forty, short, and considerably overweight, with a blotchy red complexion that made him look perpetually angry. Teela could sense his relief, and something else… curiosity. He had questions that he wanted to ask, but was trying to get a feel for the person he was dealing with.

"You're no smuggler," he said. "Smugglers don't pack this kind of firepower. Privateers aren't funded well enough to afford a ship like this. That makes you a mercenary and this ship some kind of special-purpose craft that doesn't even belong to you."

"My ship and my business are none of your business. Now take your men and leave before someone gets seriously hurt," Teela said.

"I'm a businessman. If you're a mercenary as I suspect, you work for money, credits, or percentages, like the rest of us. You put some missiles up my ass that people say don't even exist. I see a lot of technology here that hasn't hit the market yet, technology that could give me an edge in many areas of my business. Cash and carry; no one but you and I will ever know. How much to let my boys take a closer look? Just a few hours of your time and we both walk away happy."

"I appreciate the offer, Commander, but right now I have some pressing business of my own. I'm willing to deal, but not right now. You got a contact, someone or some way I can get a hold of you when I get back?" Teela asked.

"Yeah," the commander said, fishing a card out of his pocket. "Got an office here on Crossroads. Stop in and tell 'em you need to see Dex. They'll set up a meeting."

By this time, Teela was passively listening to the commander's thoughts, gauging the truth and accuracy of what he was saying. She found it amusing that Dex was short for Poindexter and that he hated it when people asked him about it.

"Dex. Is that short for—" she started to say.

"No!" he interrupted. "It's not short for anything. The name's Dex, Commander Dex to you. What about you? You got a name?"

"Yeah, it's Sula. That's short for Suladead."

By this time the men lying under Fiona had regained consciousness and stumbled back to join the others. Dex took a minute to make sure they were all right, then called Butch.

"Butch, come." Butch didn't budge from Teela's side.

"Go," Teela said, giving the dog a pat on the rump. Butch jumped up and took off toward Dex. He stopped halfway and looked back.

"Come, God damn it! You traitorous little bastard," Dex shouted, and Butch continued on, wiggling his entire body and little nub of a tail when he got back to Dex. With his dog leading the way, Dex and his men headed for their ship.

"I think he likes me," Teela called after them.

"Don't flatter yourself. He likes all females, especially Korlah. I'm surprised he didn't start humping your God damn leg!"

Eddie spotted the woman while she was on the far side of the bar. Beautiful, impeccably dressed, and completely out of place on Crossroads, especially in a space saloon filled with raunchy truckers, Korlah pilots, and warriors, she presented an irresistible temptation. He would have gone to her, but she was already headed toward him, so he feigned disinterest.

"Have you seen this person?" she asked politely, holding a tablet towards him.

Eddie was busy studying her from head to toe. He moved close and inhaled the sweet scent of her cologne and a faint hint of soap. Good hygiene was rare this far out in the system and Eddie couldn't recall anyone ever smelling and looking this good. His eyes dropped to her breasts and he was savoring their delightful curves when suddenly they were replaced by the photograph on the tablet she was holding.

"Have you seen this person?" she repeated.

He recognized the tattoo on the Korlah face immediately. "Yeah, that's Sula," he blurted out, realizing his error as the words left his mouth. "Well… maybe, I mean, you know, those Korlah tats all look alike," he stammered.

The woman took his arm and pulled him close. She moved her face near his, brushing his cheek, and whispered in his ear.

"Sula and I are good friends. I've lost touch and really need to find her," she said, straddling Eddie's thigh and pressing against him. "Is there someplace private we could talk? I can prove I'm her friend."

"Yeah," Eddie replied hoarsely. "I have an apartment behind my shop. We can talk there."

"Perfect," Tiffany said, and gave Eddie a quick kiss on the cheek and followed it with a pleasant smile. She picked up her suitcase and nodded toward the door. "Lead the way, handsome."

Howard Lewis

19 - Schwarzengeist

The idea of seeing Bill Jacks face-to-face had Teela feeling nauseous. The emotional storm it would stir within the part of her that was Daedalus was her main worry. Running a close second to that festering concern was the way Ann had rejected her without giving her a chance to explain what had happened; she figured Bill might have the same reaction. So much had happened since they'd seen each other. Last time, he'd told her he was planning on marrying into a collective led by a medical technician named Rahfoon. From what Eddie said, it sounded like he'd found his niche there and was doing well.

Her thoughts kept returning to what she would say when she looked into Dade's face and asked for help. Each time she stumbled for words.

To make matters worse, Teela and Fiona disagreed over who should pilot the ship on the way out of Crossroads. Although Teela's flight skills came as secondhand memories passed to her from the Oracle, she truly enjoyed piloting and was quite technically adept at it. However, from the moment she climbed into the cockpit and attempted to leave Crossroad's hangar, Fiona had repeatedly overridden manual control when flight parameters weren't what she thought they should be.

Once Teela grudgingly released manual control, Fiona executed evasive maneuvers so perfectly concise, intensely complicated, and intricately orchestrated that no one could have shadowed them. But soon after Fiona verified that they were clear of threats, she found the limit of Teela's tolerance.

"Evasive protocol complete," Fiona said. "Scan envelope is clear of contacts to the limits of detection range, turning onto course for the Collective Business Hub. ETA in ninety-three minutes."

"Restore manual control," Teela said flatly.

"Manual control is not recommended. Flight data indicates that autopilot is superior in all areas of operation."

"You do not need to pilot us unless there is an emergency or I need to sleep!" Teela snapped back. "Flying doesn't have to be perfect. I can manually land or dock this ship without damaging anything, and on the off chance I screw something up, you can intervene before it happens."

"Intervention was required six times during departure from the mining base. You didn't—"

"No, it was not required! You kept grabbing the controls, not because there was any crisis, you did it because my flying didn't meet your anal concept of how this ship should be flown."

"I am the ship, and flight parameters were not within—"

"Shut up! Turn autopilot off. DO NOT take the controls from me and do not talk to me again unless I call for you or there is a real emergency that is going to result in damage," Teela shouted.

After several minutes of silence, Teela felt a pang of guilt and considered apologizing. Dade intervened.

It's just a glorified frigging computer. That corpse is no longer a person. Whatever feelings it may have are part of some sick program dreamt up by that bastard Gitch.

After a moment of reflection, Teela agreed, giving a silent nod.

During the next ninety minutes, Teela and Dade discussed the Schwarzengeist, certain that he was in fact Bill Jacks. Like most of the discussions they had when they were alone, this one was voiced out loud. Teela would speak, and then Dade, sharing the body to voice their opinion, even gesturing for emphasis. Like all heated arguments, this one was loud. Fiona monitored the conversation from four cameras in the cockpit. This was behavior unlike anything she had ever observed. Although there were many occasions when she would have liked to join the discussion, she followed Teela's instructions and remained silent.

Teela and Dade tried to anticipate Bill's reaction to seeing them again and to decide what they would do if he reacted badly. Eddie had said Tim was with Smiley and Shyron, and together they were going to see Bill about buying a ship. Whether or not the go-far he was looking for would be used to rescue Shawaugh and Challmara was a subject of debate.

"Your plan to get parts and materials for the cargo ship failed," Teela said. "Why would Tim still be interested in buying a go-far?"

"That was *our* plan, if you recall. I want to rescue Shawaugh and Challmara as much as you do. Tim needs a go-far for smuggling. I trust Shyron will make certain they use it first for the rescue," Dade replied.

"I don't think we can trust Shyron."

"What do you mean? Why not?"

"For more than a thousand years, Shyron has led the Korlah Mission. Now she's a fugitive and the Council wants her dead. Shawaugh blames Shyron for her disgrace, and Challmara will certainly side with the Council. Why would Shyron want to rescue them?"

"She needs friends, people who will help her. Saving someone's life is a pretty convincing way of making friends. I think she's banking on that," Dade said.

An alarm sounded, indicating that they were approaching their destination. Teela silenced it and began slowing the ship. A speck of light in the distance quickly became an imposing structure composed of both natural and unnatural elements.

The Korlah Cooperative Business Hub was not at all what Teela expected; it was neither an asteroid base nor a space station. This abomination was both awesome in its grand proportions and fearfully hideous in its lack of aesthetic appeal. It looked like a misshapen football with cancerous growths projecting from nearly every square foot of an asteroid's dull grey surface. Some of the growths were clearly designed with purpose and function; others seemed to be patchwork piles of salvage.

"Fiona, soundlink with the base," Teela said. The speakers in her helmet emitted a soft static, then a loud, computer-generated voice.

"... state your business and intended destination. Incoming ship, state your business and intended destination. Incoming ship, state..." The monotone message repeated in English and Korlah.

"I am here regarding spacecraft services provided by the Schwarzengeist," Teela said.

"Please engage autodock," the voice said.

"I'll bring it in manually," Teela said.

"Autodock is mandatory for all ships so equipped. If you do not wish to use the autodock feature, we will send out a port pilot to guide you in. Please stop your vessel and hold your position until our port pilot contacts you," the base computer said.

"Fine! I'll use the God damn autofeature, then. Fiona! Engage the frigging autodock feature, if that's what it takes to land this frigging piece of shit!" Teela ranted. "Do real people even fly anymore?"

"Autodock engaged" appeared on the nav screen.

Teela's face was pinched in anger, her arms tightly crossed at her chest as Fiona and the hub's computer worked together to guide the ship into a hangar at one of the larger and more sophisticated structures. Start to finish, the landing was flawless. After setting down without the slightest sensation of contact, "docking complete" appeared on the nav screen.

Anticipating the usual security protocol for non-station personnel, Teela left her weapons aboard Fiona and was allowed to pass undeterred through the checkpoint. From an information kiosk outside security, she was directed to the only shipbuilding collective at the hub.

A large, arched doorway marked the entrance to the Schwarzengeist's waiting room. The doors slid open on Teela's approach and her senses went into immediate overload. The rich scents of leather, wood, polish, flowers, wool, and liquor washed over her. The grand, opulent room was designed to impress, and impress it did. Sumptuous leather chairs and couches lined two oak-paneled walls. An Irish-pub-style bar stretched the full length of one wall, and the reception desk at the center of the room was flanked with burl oak tables holding large handblown glass vases filled with fresh flowers. The floor was covered with a thick Berber carpet and the ten-foot ceiling was hand-painted to look like a blue sky with clouds. Stained-glass lamps provided a warm sunset glow.

The bartender, a tall, slender brunette with a pale complexion, smiled and gave Teela a nod. Dressed in a vintage white blouse with bunched lace at the neck and wrists she looked somehow appropriate in the unusual setting. Two men in dark suits at the bar turned to look at Teela as she approached the reception desk.

"May I help you?" the receptionist asked, smiling pleasantly. She was a brunette, too, and Teela was certain she was the bartender's twin sister. Her pale pink eyes struck Teela as odd; the color matched the Korlah Mission emblem tattooed on her bare left shoulder. There were unusual marks around her eyes and chin that Teela took for tattoos of some sort, and the woman wore a strapless black top that gave the impression of being painted on. Her desk sat on a raised dais a full three feet above floor level that forced Teela to look up at her. Like the room and everything in it, the desk was intended to impress and warmly greet, yet instill a feeling of awe.

"I would like to speak with the Schwarzengeist," Teela said, trying not to stare at the marks on the young woman's face.

"Do you have an appointment?"

"No, but I'm certain he will want to see me," Teela said, thinking that the marks looked more like gaps in the woman's skin than like tattoos.

"Mr. Schwarzengeist does not see anyone without an appointment. I could fit you in... let's see, in two shifts, four sets, or thirty-five Earth hours from now. Would you like me to schedule you?"

"I really need to see him now. Tell him that Dade Rimes is here and needs his help."

"Mr. Schwarzengeist is with a client at the moment. I will relay your message at the first opportunity. Please take a seat or enjoy a complimentary beverage while you wait," she said, again smiling pleasantly.

Teela couldn't get a read on this unusual woman's thoughts. She let out a sigh of disappointment and moved to the bar, where the businessmen continued to stare at her. She looked at her reflection in the mirror behind the bar and realized that in her soiled camouflage pants, scuffed boots, and stained halter top, she certainly looked out of place.

"What can I get you?" the bartender asked.

It was then that Teela noted the same features on the bartender's face as she'd seen on the receptionist's. She began to suspect that these women were not human.

"How about a double shot of Jack on the rocks?" Teela studied the bartender's movements and watched in amazement as she walked a few steps down the bar, rotated ninety degrees at the waist, filled a tumbler with ice, and then added substantially more than two shots of Jack Daniels to the glass. With calibrated precision she slid the drink down the bar, where it stopped directly in front of Teela. Leaning over the bar, Teela examined the cable that was connected to the bartender's lower back.

The men saw the astonishment on her face and laughed loudly. She ignored them and took the glass of whiskey and poured a generous sample into her mouth, expecting a watered-down facsimile. She took her time and savored the rich flavor before swallowing. The smoky taste and slow burn of alcohol were pure and genuine. Surprised by the whisky's strength and purity, she held the glass up and examined its color and clarity. The businessmen laughed again. Irritated, Teela turned to confront them. The man nearest anticipated her response and had a palm display waiting for her.

"We're not laughing at you. Seriously, we had the same reaction you did. It's not enough that they're serving real whiskey for free, but they have some of the most advanced bots we've ever seen. These here are basic service units, made to look artificial so people don't get offended when they realize they're not real people. You should check out the sales vert. They got everything from maids to maintenance techs."

"Don't forget the pleasure models," his partner chuckled. "Both human and Korlah made to be so real you can't tell the diff."

When Teela made a face to show her disgust, they laughed again.

"Dade Rimes?" the receptionist called out. Teela turned.

"Mr. Schwarzengeist will see you now."

"What!" the businessmen cried in unison. "We have an appointment."

"My apologies," Teela said, offering a palm display of her own. "You should check into those pleasure bots while you wait," she said with a smirk.

The receptionist directed her to an open door near the dais. As Teela walked past, she saw that the receptionist's body was only a torso attached to a chair. Once through the door, Teela was met by two armed guards, who searched her again. This search however, was significantly more thorough than the one at the security checkpoint. When they were finished, they pushed her into a small room. The door closed and locked behind her. Teela was relatively certain this was not how Bill met his usual clients, and her fear of being rejected again caused her crown tendrils to blanch. When a door across the room opened, Bill filled the doorway from top to bottom and side to side.

In the four years since Teela had last seen Bill, he had allowed his hair grow into a tangle of shoulder-length dreadlocks that framed his pale white face like a lion's mane. From his scalp near the hairline and at points above his thick lips, snippets of thin light-brown hair mixed with the kinky black. He wore an armored suit and was pulling on thick gloves as he entered the room. He did not appear happy to see her.

"Hello, Bill," Teela said, offering her hand. Bill enveloped her hand in his, then without warning, swung her around and slammed her face first into the wall. She dropped to her knees and cradled her face in her hands, expecting to find blood.

"What the hell... What was that for?" she groaned, and looked up at Bill, who was now towering over her.

"That was for saying you are Dade. Now tell me who sent you and what you really want," Bill said, his deep voice rumbling like thunder.

"It's really me, Bill. I need—"

Bill dropped to one knee and grabbed her by the throat, squeezing off her ability to speak or breathe. She grabbed his hand, instinctively attempting to use her claws to pull it free, but the thick gloves protected him from her talons. Realizing she would soon black out, she closed her eyes and projected Dade's memory of Bill killing the Kahshinki into his mind. Bill threw her across the room like a rag doll.

"Stay out of my head!" he shouted. "If you don't I *will* kill you."

182

He paced back and forth a few times, as though unsure how to proceed. "You go back and tell Becca I'm not interested in her religion. Sending another telepath, I expected that. Using Dade, though, now that's just plain insulting."

"Please don't hit me again for saying this. I really am Teela. Dade is with me. How could I show you that image if I wasn't there?" Teela asked.

"What? Me killing that pissbag? You plucked it from my memories. I know how you telepaths operate. I'm not impressed."

"Think about it, Bill," Teela said, moving into a sitting position. "I showed you what I saw, not what you saw. I can show you the first and last time I looked at your face. They would be my memories, not yours."

"Shut up!" Bill bellowed. "Teela is dead, Dade died with her. Shyron used Rahfoon's medical technicians to transfer Teela's scars onto her body. That bitch Rahfoon took great pleasure in showing me Teela's body. So you see, my little imposter, there is no point in maintaining the act."

"The Teela you knew did die, and when I died, I transferred into this body. I was done with saving everybody. It was time to start thinking about saving myself. I let people believe I was the reincarnation of Shawlmon so I could stop the mutiny and help Beth and the others back to Earth. It was my idea for Shyron to assume the role of Shawlmon. She's been leading the Korlah for over a thousand years, and I knew I was in way over my head. I didn't want to lead anymore. I was tired, Bill. I wanted out."

"Bullshit. Now listen up, little lady, I'm gonna start breaking things: legs, arms, hands, feet, nothing my medical crew can't fix, and nothing I can't break over and over until you decide to choose the truth over pain. Last chance to tell me who sent you and why before I start snapping bones."

"Then I choose truth. But you're not going to like it," Teela said as she rose to face him.

"Why's that?" Bill literally growled.

"Because this is really going to hurt," Teela said as her eyes met and locked on his. Bill's eyes opened wide with the impact of Teela's telepathic assault. He began to fall, but she caught him and guided him down onto his knees. His eyes rolled up into his head as she pressed her forehead against his and dumped the memories of her activities from the last time she saw him to the present. He screamed as the influx of sensations and emotions burned their imprint into his brain. Seconds later, the door to the room flew open and guards rushed in. Teela pushed Bill away as the guards shot her in the chest with their pulse rifles.

Teela awoke to the smell of clean sheets and opened her eyes to find herself in a room that resembled a cross between a hospital and a fine hotel. Medical equipment was neatly arranged on a polished wooden bookcase that matched the nightstand by her adjustable bed. Her boots were on the floor and her clothes hung from a hanger on a hook above them. The lights were dim except for where Bill was sitting at a small roll-top desk reading some papers. It struck her as odd that he was reading without glasses.

"Are you wearing contacts?" she asked. Bill set the papers down and turned his chair around to face her.

"Ah! You're awake," he said. "No, I got those piss-poor eyes you gave me fixed. And by the way, that mind shit really hurts!"

"Good! I warned you," she said, and tried to sit up, but groaned and dropped back onto the bed. She used the controls on the bedrail to adjust it so she could see him better. She winced from her bruises and coughed when she tried to take a deep breath. "Damn, Bill, I still hurt. Hell, I'm gonna hurt for days."

"Don't be a sissy. My crew says you're fine. They even fixed the damage those butchers left you with when they took little Dade."

Teela felt her abdomen. The ragged incision was gone, replaced by smooth, clear skin. "Thanks. I noticed you're not wearing glasses, did you get your eyes fixed?"

"Yeah, better than new. Before I got our cooperative to expand into transportation, medical equipment was our biggest moneymaker. I was their first human patient; now corrective eye surgery is ancient technology. In less than five minutes, our equipment can map and optimize the performance of a human eye without surgery and without anesthesia. All adjustments are made at the cellular level, leaving the patient with permanently perfect vision."

"You sound like a salesman," Teela said. Bill laughed.

"Yep, that's me. I got out of medical sales and into transportation. I knew that pimping rides would be the real moneymaker, and I was correct. Right now, my profits are two to three times higher than anything in the collective, which is probably why Rahfoon hasn't given me the boot... yet."

"What happened to getting married, having kids and raising a family?" Teela asked with a grin. Bill's forehead knit into a frown and he looked down.

"Only got to see my boy a couple of times before Rahfoon sent me out here. I got hundreds of kids, though. So do you, Dade. They implanted hundreds of birthers to get the hybrids they wanted. Initially they cloned several dozen of each of us, thinking we might be the only males they would get. Now, with all the human contact, they realize they don't need our clones to get the genetic diversity they want. They got a plan to build a population capable of natural reproduction. Over time they intend to breed out human characteristics completely. They got a program that selects about one in ten of the hybrids that have the most distinctive Korlah characteristics. The rest, like the clones, like my boy, they don't need."

"Jesus, Bill, I'm sorry, I didn't know. What are they going to do with the kids they don't want?"

"I don't know. They probably would have just recycled them, but I notified the UNE what was going on. With all the public backlash about crovers, this is another political time bomb waiting to go off the moment the story goes public. Basically, the Korlah don't want them, humans don't want them, and the UNE can't decide what to do about it. Fortunately, the Korlah Council has delayed taking any action to avoid further degrading relations with Earth. I think I know what's going to happen. At least I hope I do."

"And what's that?"

"My factories have been mass-producing a very specialized long-distance shuttle, all very hush-hush. These ships are designed to travel at maximum hyper-light and carry enough food and water to sustain ten passengers for the two-year journey to New Korlah."

"So the rest of the Korlah are planning to leave as well."

"They've already started. Been leaving in groups of ten to twenty ships at a time for the last six months. The ships are unarmed and only lightly armored. Pirates picked up on that pretty quick. They have been patrolling the departure route and robbing the ships they intercept. To deal with the pirate threat, all departures are now escorted out of the system by fighter craft. Shawaugh and Challmara were probably part of such an escort. I heard these pirates are using a new type of sub-light missile that is designed to disable a ship's engines. With their engines down, laser communication is all they would have. Hell, by the time a laser message gets back here, they'll already be dead. You gotta realize running rescue missions for these ships would be like trying to find a needle in a haystack."

Teela thought of Shawaugh and Challmara dying like that and winced. "So once all the Korlah are gone. The unwanted children will be left behind?"

"That's what I'm thinking," Bill said with a frown. "They won't all go. Most of your sisters in the birthing section have become a seriously badass militant group. They call themselves the Claws; they're loyal to the Oracle and the Church of Shawlmon. As more people leave for New Korlah, Shawlmon's loyalists are moving into key positions. Soon Rebecca will control the entire Korlah portion of the ship. The only good part is that Rebecca and her followers believe the hybrids are the children of God. At least for now, I believe they are safe and will be taken care of."

"And then what?"

"I don't know. If you believe what Rebecca has been preaching, Satan's wrath is about to be unleashed, and there will be hell on Earth."

"What about New Korlah? Are you gonna go with Rahfoon?"

"Hell, no! One thing I've learned about Korlah is that they are more bigoted than any human I have ever met. Shit, they make the sapien supremists and xenophobes look like a bunch of girl scouts.

I got a plan, just like you always had a plan. You showing up now, well, that might just work to our mutual advantage."

"I have to help Shawaugh and Challmara. Then I have to—"

"I know. Get your son back," Bill said. "First part is already in play. A few hours before your arrival I leased a long-range transport to a pair of humans and a Korlah meeting Tim, Smiley, and Shyron's descriptions. While you were unconscious I tried to catch up with them, but they had already stocked up with provisions and departed. You know, depending on how far out they have to travel, if you consider time distortion at hyper-light, they may not return for months."

"Months?" Teela jumped off the bed.

"Relax, we don't need their help to get little Dade back," Bill said.

"Please quit calling my son Dade. Rebecca named him Shawlmon, but that's not gonna be it. I don't know what I'm going to name him, but it sure as hell won't be Dade. And what's this about 'we' getting him back?"

"Well, I hate to break the news to you, but the child you bore is probably a clone. The Teela unit you transferred into came from Rahfoon's breeding section. From what I recall of your memories, that child was the spitting image of Dade. And I can tell you for a fact, no hybrid I've seen looked that human. Considering the facts, he probably is a little Dade."

Bill's statement was not as much of a surprise as it was an unwelcome confirmation of something she had suspected since her child's birth. In that moment, the hope that she had conceived something original, a child who was actually part of her, flickered and died.

"I know... I figured as much," she said.

Whether it was the faltering tenor of her voice or her expression of quiet despair, Bill sensed her anguish. He leaned forward and pulled her into his arms and enveloped her in a warm embrace. Teela did not resist the hug, nor did she return it. He released her and took a deep breath.

"Now you listen to me. I know this face of mine bothers you. But this face," he touched his pale white nose with his thick black finger, "well, as you can see, Dade's a part of me, just like he's part of you too. The hybrid babies are part of both of us, just like the clone babies are part of each of us. Whether we like it or not, we got family... our family. First we take little Dade back from that crazy bitch Rebecca, then we see what we can do to help the rest of our family."

Teela reached out and touched his face, running her fingers gently over the division between his black and white skin, marveling at the distinct change in texture. For the first time, she really looked into the pale eyes that Dade had once viewed the world through. This was the face of the creature she'd first looked at when he was burned and damaged. The same man she now shared her mind and body with, someone who was quietly allowing her to look without letting his emotions to interfere with her moment of reflection. Suddenly conscious that this might be bothering Dade, she looked away and withdrew her hand.

"I'm sorry," she said, returning her gaze to meet Bill's. "Your face doesn't bother me, Bill. It's hard to describe the feelings looking at you conjures up. The part of me that is Teela recalls the first time I looked at Dade's face; a frightening mask of bruised, blistered, and swollen flesh. The Daedalus part finds it hard to comprehend that he is actually looking onto the face and into the eyes that were once his. I apologize for staring."

"Everyone stares. You be the only one who's got a good excuse. You stare all you want," Bill said with a broad smile.

"Thank you, I will," Teela said with a smile of her own. "Now exactly how is it that *we* are going to get my son?"

"Get dressed and I'll show you. I'll wait outside."

Teela dressed as quickly as her sore body would let her, but not before taking a few moments to examine her abdomen for signs of the jagged scar from her poorly healed cesarean incision. There wasn't the slightest trace it had ever existed. When she finished dressing, she adjusted the suspenders of her utility belt and fastened the Korlah buckle. She couldn't help but notice her clothing had been mended, cleaned, and pressed. Even her dirty, scuffed boots had been cleaned and polished to a high gloss.

Despite her mercenary clothing, the manicured look gave her a modest appearance of respectability.

"You look nice," Bill said when she stepped out of the room.

"Nice is not the image I was going for. It took quite a while to get this outfit to look right. Now... well, I don't think anyone will take me seriously."

Bill frowned in mock disapproval as he walked around her, looking her up and down.

"You, of all people, Lord Shawlmon, should know that cleanliness is next to Godliness. At the very least, you seriously smell better."

"Oh! I did not smell! And look at you, you with the Rastafarian dreadlocks. Really, what is going on with that raggedy-ass look?"

"I'm sorry. You're right, you didn't smell. Reek is more like it. And damn, girl, what's with the tats?"

Teela pursed her lips, another expression inconsistent with Korlah behavior.

"My tattoos are an expression of individuality. You of all people should respect that. This is not the Bill I remember," she finally said. Bill laughed.

"I've been married to Rahfoon's collective now for years. Having numerous wives trying to dominate me both in business and in the bedroom keeps me sharp. I've missed you, Teela, you and Dade, that is."

"We've missed you, too Bill," Teela said, and then muttered, "like a sore dick."

"What's that?" Bill asked, even though he heard her quite clearly.

"You heard me," Teela said, and laughed. "Now what was it you were going to show me?"

"My latest project, something that will make rescuing little Dade much easier. Follow me." He led her through an airlock to a large enclosed space dock. Inside the supersized garage was a space ship that looked like a Boeing 747 without wings or a tail. The highly modified Korlah assault pod floated in the center of the hangar and appeared to ready for flight. The engine compartment was significantly larger than an assault pod. Absent were the multiple docks for large and small fighters. Of the five docks for transports only one remained. New items included an array of swivel turrets forward and aft, each sporting dual high energy particle-beam cannons.

"What is this for? It looks dangerous," Teela said.

"It's my golden parachute. When Rahfoon and the collective drag up, I suspect they'll leave my sorry ass behind. And even if they want me to go with them, I'm staying here. This here is a highly modified civilian version of a military Wrath-class destroyer we've been building for the UNE. Not only is this baby capable of carrying a standard cube of cargo, she's the fastest, most advanced and heavily armed civilian ship in the system. Nobody in their right mind is gonna mess with this bad girl," Bill said proudly.

"Well, although my ship can't carry that much cargo, it might be more advanced than this," Teela said.

"Oh, really? You telling me you got something faster, with better weapons than Betsy here?"

"I'm not trying to one-up you, Bill. I'm serious. I kind of came into this ship by accident."

"By 'accident,' do you mean it's stolen?"

"Kind of, sort of, but not really. Base security was going to turn me over to Rebecca. I had to escape. The ship's intruder-defense system could have stopped me from stealing it, but it didn't. The computer on this ship is biological and claims to be self-aware. She wanted to get out of there as much as I did. So technically, the ship escaped with me, so I really don't think you could call it stealing. It's complicated."

Now it was Bill's turn to purse his lips. He tugged at his chin and considered what she had said. "Yeah, complicated for sure. Your ship was probably built in violation of international law. Biocomputer research is illegal. Some nasty business about experiments using human subjects. I heard of a proposal for what was purported to be the ultimate fully autonomous unmanned weapons system. The press nicknamed the guy who designed it

190

Doctor Frankengitch because he was accused of using human brains as part of the CPU. Rumor is he was dying and took a Korlah transfer and is now working with some Korlah expats on a new prototype fighter. Sound familiar?"

"Oh yeah... definitely," Teela nodded. "The CPU is biological and the guy who designed it is called Oswald Gitch. And from what I saw of this ship's CPU, Oswald Gitch is a monster."

"Okay, let's go see this creation of his. I hope you realize some powerful folks are gonna be looking for this ship, so once we leave this hangar, you need to watch what you say." Bill looked around suspiciously. "Come on."

He led her out into a long corridor and interlaced his arm with hers. "So you missed me like a sore dick? Well now, you do know I have over twenty wives and could share some stories with you."

"Please don't," she said, quickly slipping her arm free. Bill threw his head back and roared. His deep laugh resonated loudly, echoing like thunder in the empty corridor. Teela blushed and tried to scowl at him, laughing instead when Bill mimicked her pinched expression.

20 - Treaty

Commander Sahanga hung suspended in her antigravity chair in a dimensionally accurate holographic representation of Earth's solar system. For the third time, she circled the glowing orb that represented the sun, examining the locations of the enemy spacecraft carriers and the defensive forces she had deployed to confront them. She was in a quandary over reports that the Kahshinki were no longer attacking and were concentrating their forces just out of reach of her fighters. Now, enemy scouts had been spotted on the far side of the system, testing the limits of her detection and defensive perimeter. She suspected a sneak attack or a flanking move, which would be contrary to traditional Kahshinki tactics; she was keenly aware that preparations to defend Earth from a sustained attack would need to be radically altered.

Sahanga's personal assistant had to shout to break her trance. "Mad Dog—hey! Down here! Sorry to interrupt, but a courier from Earth has a priority UNE blowbox for you."

Mad Dog was a nickname that came from Sahanga's past life as Zachary Jacobs, a seasoned ace fighter pilot who had been berated for flying like a rabid dog during his first battle in the Korean War. In his second life as a Korlah commander, the name and attitude followed.

Deep in thought, Sahanga barely nodded acknowledgment to her assistant and continued to stare at the positions of the enemy forces. She was about to review the numbers again when something about the message suddenly clicked.

"Did you say it was a blowbox?" she asked, turning away from the holograph.

"Yes, Director; the courier has a Marine escort and is leashed to the box. I verified his credentials twice and have obtained confirmation of the delivery from two sources."

"Shit!" Sahanga exclaimed, switching off the grav chair. She leapt out of it before it touched the floor. She dashed toward the door with her assistant right behind her.

"What is it, Mad Dog? What's wrong?"

"These things usually bring bad news. They contain orders that change policy; stuff too secret or sensitive to send electronically. The problem is we're being led by people who have little or no idea what I have to do to keep them safe. This can't be good."

It wasn't far to the secure room where a courier sat at a small table, manacled to a case the size of a thick tablet. Armed Marines stood on either side of the table. No one challenged Sahanga for identification; the box would perform the necessary verifications. If satisfied, the box would open; if not, it would remain closed. If the courier was killed, the cable cut, or the box forced open, the box would explode and kill everyone within a ten-foot radius.

Sahanga placed her hand on the top of the box. It chimed and the opaque panel illuminated, indicating that her hand's shape and epidermal ridges were accepted. The panel changed to a mirrored surface with two circles on it. She aligned her eyes with the circles and the box chimed. The top panel flipped open and the manacle on the courier's wrist unlocked.

"Thank you, gentlemen, you may leave," Sahanga said. The courier nodded and departed with the Marines. Sahanga closed and locked the door behind them. She checked the walls, table, and chairs for surveillance devices before removing a bright red folder from the box. In bold black letters on the cover it read, "TOP SECRET, EYES ONLY: CSG UNE Perimeter Defense, Zachary Jacobs-Sahanga." She smiled at the UNE's convention that crovers use the name of the dominant entity first, followed by the name of the individual who had been supplanted. Although crovers were treated with suspicion by humans and Korlah alike, the apparent purpose was to identify the individual's loyalty.

Sahanga opened the folder and removed the tablet inside.

To: Commander Space Group, UNE Perimeter Defense

The United Nations of Earth has received an invitation from the leadership of the Ganglicians (a.k.a Kahshinki) to enter into negotiations for a peaceful conclusion to the current hostilities.

This offer and all potential ramifications have been reviewed by the sitting UNE membership, and a decision to enter into negotiations has been accepted by UNE Chairman Joseph LeBlanc and ratified by more than two thirds of the UNE members present.

You are hereby directed to meet the Ganglician peace delegation and escort it safely to UNE headquarters on Earth. The meeting is to occur twelve hours after the receipt of this message at perimeter coordinates 60.240.27.

Signed,

Commander Allied UNE Defense Forces

Sahanga deleted the message and returned the tablet to the red folder, then dropped it back into the box. She looked at her watch.

"Peace delegation, my ass!" she growled.

Twelve hours later and substantially more irate, Sahanga waited with a flight of ten ships at the outer limit of UNE-controlled space.

"Commander, five ships approaching the perimeter: one transport and four fighters. They are transmitting the specified pass code," the communications officer announced.

"Arm all weapons and put us on a collision course with that transport," Sahanga said. "When and if they stop, I want to be so close that I can see the expressions on their faces. Transmit the following message: *Kahshinki delegation, order your fighter escort to withdraw immediately, power down all systems, and prepare to be boarded. You have one minute to comply.*"

"Message sent, sir," the officer replied. "One minute is not much time."

"That's the plan," Sahanga said. She activated the microphone in her helmet. "Target enemy fighters, full power, tight beam, and fire on my mark." She pulled back the sleeve of her jacket and watched the second hand of her watch count down.

"Long message coming in… they're protesting that you are threatening a peace delegation operating under the protection of…"

"Fire!" Sahanga shouted. Her ten ships responded in unison, their screens going black in response to the bright flash of their particle beam weapons. When Sahanga's screen cleared, only the Kahshinki transport remained. Around it, a field of debris scattering in all directions was all that remained of its fighter escorts. The communication officer let out a low and slow whistle.

"Lock on to the transport and prepare for a forced entry. Marines, energize your weapons. You are authorized to respond to any hostile action with deadly force." Sahanga pulled a vintage military .45 from the holster on her hip and joined the Marines at the hatch.

For nearly four years, Mad Dog Jacobs and her squadrons had maintained a blockade on the outer limit of the Kuiper belt. Thousands of Mad Dog's Mongrels had crushed sixteen invasion attempts and paid for their success with their lives. It was her people who were risking their lives to place hundreds of thousands of sensors well outside the protection of blockade forces, and the ones who survived earned a reputation as the elite of the space corps. The snarling-dog patches they wore on their shoulders denoted ace status of five or more kills. With few exceptions, all of Sahanga's pilots who survived a single day of any enemy engagement returned an ace.

At her court-martial, Sahanga did not deny that it was her intention to derail the peace negotiations. However, she had failed miserably at that goal. If anything, her actions were directly responsible for the success of the Kahshinki. The evidence of the degrading and abusive treatment she subjected their delegates to, combined with the unprovoked destruction of their four escort vessels and the deaths of twelve crewmen, only served to garner sympathy from the UNE members. To complicate matters, the peace delegation was comprised entirely of humans. The transport's crews were clones, but the delegates were all known and respected business professionals and lawyers, all of whom were Kahshinki sympathizers and members of the now-outlawed international political organization known as the Quorum.

Aware of the fervent loyalty of the legendary Mad Dog Jacobs' troops, UNE military leaders were smart enough to recognize that sending her to prison would be unwise, so instead, she was stripped of UNE rank and reassigned to the Korlah section of the Armageddon. They were not, however, smart enough to anticipate that she would be received as a hero and immediately promoted to director of the Korlah defense force.

Whatever was discussed during the closed sessions of the UNE peace talks was withheld from the public record for reasons of global security. What is known is that the Kahshinki sued for peace, and their demands further divided an already weakened UNE. Representatives from the United Kingdom, Canada, and the United States walked out of the discussions. Although no official declaration was made, it was apparent that the United Nations of Earth were no longer united. For many, the prospect of peace came as a great relief. For those who knew the history of Kahshinki conquests, the UNE decision that followed came as a shock and an outrage.

When Sahanga was informed of the UNE decision, she stormed out of the Korlah command center and headed around the circumference of the vessel, through Crossover, and straight toward the UNE section's checkpoint. The young human guard recognized Mad Dog's bomber jacket from a distance and guessed her intentions. He was on his feet in front of the access portal, clipboard in one hand and the grip of the pistol on his hip in the other when she arrived.

"Commander, ah... I mean Director—damn it—Mad Dog, you know you can't come in here!" he cried as Sahanga ground to a stop in front of him.

"I want ten minutes with my squadron leaders. They need to hear this from me first," Sahanga growled, holding up a crumpled sheet of paper for him to read as her crown tendrils turned an angry shade of red.

"Shit! They're nuts," the guard said when he finished reading the announcement. "I'm sorry, sir, if anyone goes through that portal without the proper authorization I am under orders to use deadly force to stop them," he said weakly.

"Then look the other way or pull that pea shooter and use it, son, cause I'm going in there."

"They're gonna put me in the brig, you prick!" the guard hissed between clenched teeth. He tossed his clipboard toward the chair by the portal; it missed and fell to the floor several feet away. "Excuse me, sir, I can't leave that on the floor, since it represents a tripping hazard. Turn around and leave now. Do not be here when I get back." He turned and walked to the clipboard, knelt, and picked it up. When he turned back again, Sahanga was gone.

The pilot's ready room was roaring with conversations when Sahanga arrived. It was still early, and to her relief, the new commander had not yet arrived. By the time she traversed the thirty-some steps between the door and podium, all the pilots had turned their attention to her. The silence that followed became a roar of its own.

The silence surprised Sahanga, and she looked up from the crumpled page in her hand at the expectant faces. She crumpled the page into a ball and shoved it into the pocket of her leather jacket. This briefing needed more than her whining about the UNE directive they were about to receive. What the UNE had decided to do was madness, so it only made sense that someone mad would make the announcement. With that thought, Sahanga exploded in typical Mad Dog style.

"I don't want to hear a sound out of you bastards until I'm done speaking. Do you understand?" she shouted. Dead silence followed. "I have received word that you are about to get orders to institute a cease-fire effective immediately."

More than half of the pilots jumped to their feet and a rumble of movement and angry murmuring filled the room. Sahanga glared at them. The room once again fell silent.

"It's all right, go ahead and get angry. Get screaming, red-hot, piss-your-pants angry... and then... get over it. We all knew this was coming. This is exactly in line with standard Kahshinki protocol. They're going to talk peace and claim they are only responding to our military buildup. They're going to point out that they will soon be in a position to punch through our perimeter and bring the war to Earth. The politicians are scared shitless and I don't blame them. They're looking at five enemy carriers sitting on the perimeter and can only assume there are more on the way. They realize that Earth will soon start taking casualties and they don't want to be part of the body count.

"Our energy-absorption technology has given us an advantage over their superior numbers, and because of it we have been able to hold the perimeter. The enemy will eventually get that technology, and when they do, our advantage will have to be our skill as fighter pilots. I'm not going be here to drive you lazy bunch of worthless cocksuckers, so it's gonna be up to each and every one of you to use this cease-fire as an opportunity to hone your skills. When the sneak attack comes, and it will come, it is my honor and expectation that when I meet the enemy on the field of battle, Mad Dog's Mongrels will be unleashed to join me. On that glorious day, those poor Kahshinki bastards will have the full fury of one hundred squadrons of the greatest fighter pilots in the history of the galaxy chewing on their sorry ass!"

With that, the room erupted in applause and shouts of approval.

When the new squadron commander and the guards he had summoned burst through the door to arrest Sahanga, her pilots were already on their feet. They stepped into the aisle, blocking their path, and the new commander's angry protests were ignored as Sahanga was escorted safely out of the UNE section on her pilots' shoulders. When the commander's formal complaint of trespass was dismissed by the Korlah Council as irrelevant, it further strained the already tenuous UNE and Korlah relations.

21 - Journeys

The coordinates Shyron had provided for Challmara and Shawaugh's disabled ship proved to be accurate. Tim piloted the specialized deep-space ship he leased from the hub, and Smiley navigated with Shyron's telepathic assistance. Working together, they found the damaged fighter easily. On arrival, Tim hailed the ship, but there was no response. Shyron and Smiley boarded to check for survivors.

"What's the status?" Tim asked when Smiley returned to the bridge.

"Crew's on board," Smiley answered. "They look dead, but Shy says they'll live. Everything's buttoned up and ready to make way. We gonna tow their ship back as salvage or cut it loose?"

"Cut it loose. Technically, if the crew's alive it ain't salvage, so it's not worth the time or risk to haul it. Anyway, I wanna get back before whoever blew their engines does the same to us."

Tim tapped the controls and released the damaged ship from his. There was a slight shudder and the stars in the window began to move as he turned the ship towards Crossroads. He gave the damaged engines on the crippled fighter one last look before he accelerated away.

"How do ya think they did that?" Tim asked.

"Did what?" Smiley said.

"Blew the engines. It looked like they exploded from the inside. No indication of pulse, plasma, or particle beam. What does that?"

"Sabotage or missiles."

"Sabotage is my guess. Missiles would have to be capable of light speed and able to penetrate flux envelopes. The military tried to make some and gave up. Shoot, I heard the smallest one made was three feet in diameter, sixty feet long, and couldn't break light speed. Oh, damn!" Tim shouted as annunciators sounded on his fire control panel. "Four bogeys coming up our six. Too small and too fast to be fighters."

"Missiles," Smiley said, jumping into the copilot's seat and energizing their sole pulse cannon.

"Damn, I hate when you're right," he said pushing the ship to full light speed and making evasive turns and twists. "They're gonna be up our ass in thirty seconds!" he reached for the hyper light controls.

"No!" Smiley screamed. "Kill the mains, mag drive on full reverse! Do it. Do it now!"

There was only one person whose judgment Tim trusted more than his own, and that was Smiley. He slammed the emergency stop for the main engines at the same time he slid the mag drive controls to full reverse. The ship groaned as the mag coils went from supercooled to red-hot in seconds and the magnetic lines of flux expanded behind and compressed in front of the ship.

"Turn!" Smiley shouted, grabbing the control stick to help Tim overcome the resistance. The cannon on the ship's belly turret pulsed, and one missile disintegrated as the remaining three, now traveling at near light speed, sank into the growing flux field like bullets into molasses. The resounding explosions spun the ship like a top and would have thrown them out of their seats if they hadn't been strapped in.

As Tim brought the ship onto a steady course, Smiley surveyed the damage to the control panel. "Two coils are fried, the rest are smoking hot and riding the razor's edge. We sure as hell won't be able to do that again."

"What exactly is it that we did?" Tim asked.

"The light went off in my head when you said they were too small to be fighters. They had to be missiles, but missiles can't penetrate flux fields. Hell, a nuclear explosion can't get through. That's when it hit me: to be small, they would have to dump all the hardware to achieve sub-light. So you put a warhead on a plasma compressor and launch it into the plasma stream of a ship traveling at near-light speed, it accelerates into the stream and follows it home—right through the lines of flux, where the engines spit out the plasma. Damn, I wish I'd thought of that a couple years ago."

"You didn't know squat about propulsion systems then."

"True, but I can still wish."

"Okay, whoever fired these will be coming to finish us off. You got any suggestions?"

"First sign of missiles, kill the mains, turn, and take evasive maneuvers on mag only. We make them come in close and shoot it out with us. I'll bet they'll have fixed cannon and will only be able to pop us once with each pass, whereas with the belly turret I'll nail them two or three times as they go by. Their absorption array will definitely fail before ours," Smiley said, grinning.

"Yeah, sounds good, but you know as well as I do there's gonna be more than one. We better hope our array holds up."

"Well, you know how the saying goes about shitting in one hand and hoping in the other."

"Yep," Tim replied grimly. He continued to press the ship toward its maximum sub-light speed.

More missiles appeared on his threat monitor. Following Smiley's advice, he immediately shut down the engines and turned using the mag drive. The groaning was louder this time and followed by a loud pop as a panel cover above Smiley blew off and a fireball erupted, setting the sleeve of his jacket on fire. Smiley cursed and swatted the flames out as the missiles screamed by, then out of visual range and off of Tim's monitor.

"Damn it!" Smiley shouted. "That was the gravity drive control circuit. The mag coil temperatures are off scale. They probably melted and trashed the whole machinery space."

As if in confirmation, all the lights and panels in the control room went black. The emergency lights flickered and came on dimly.

"We're gonna need pressure suits," Tim said. "You better head aft and help Shyron and the others get suited up." He reached up and pressed a little red button at the top of his control panel to activate the emergency beacon, and a yellow light began pulsing. The wide-dispersion laser it controlled would send its signal for months, but Tim was keenly aware that the pressure suit he was about to don would provide oxygen for little more than a single solar day. Doing the math in his head, he figured the emergency signal traveling at light speed would reach the system perimeter in about three days, and whoever fired those missiles would reach them in about three minutes. All things considered, he pretty much knew which hand was full and which was empty.

Rebecca's scowl softened and slowly became a smile. She put the letter she had just read down and clasped her hands together and thanked the gods for answering her prayers. It had taken over eight months to arrange. Now, in only a few short weeks, the last action needed for Lord Shawlmon to ascend the throne of the faithful would be complete. She called Lord Shawlmon with silent words, a whispered thought. Ten feet away, playing on the tan wool carpet with colorfully painted wooden blocks, a little boy with shaggy light-brown hair and big blue eyes looked up and smiled at her. He jumped up and ran to her, his white silken robe fluttering like a flag as he dove into her arms. She hugged him tightly, pressed her face against his, and filled his mind with all the joy and happiness she was feeling. The little boy squealed with delight.

"My Lord, I have good news," Rebecca said. She pushed the child back and knelt on the floor before him. The little boy stood silently and stared blankly into her eyes.

"The pope has finally agreed to engage in interfaith dialogue. We will be traveling to Italy to meet with him and others of the faith at the Basilica of San Francesco d'Assisi. It will be beautiful, My Lord. All will come together at last, and during the Festival Calendimaggio that follows, there will truly be a religious renaissance worth celebrating." The child smiled at the happiness Rebecca was emanating.

So engrossed in her revelry, Rebecca failed to notice a nudge in the back of her subconscious mind as a silent observer carefully opened the telepathic link the Oracle had given them, and eased her way into Rebecca's mind. For more than ten minutes, the observer experienced the perceptions and thoughts of the woman who was plotting to create a global theocracy. When she had the information she wanted, Teela slipped from Rebecca's thoughts as quickly and quietly as she had entered.

"Well?" Bill said when Teela finally opened her eyes. "Did you find them?"

Teela took in a deep breath, shuddered and exhaled. "No," she squeaked, and then burst into tears.

"Hey, hey, hey, now, don't start crying, Bill said, patting her back. "You tried. When you said you could find people lost in deep space with your mind, well, I was thinking maybe it was your mind that was lost."

"I didn't find Challmara or Shawaugh," Teela said, "but I found my son!" She wiped the tears of joy from her eyes and smiled. "I saw him through Rebecca's eyes, held him and hugged him. I know where they are, I know what Rebecca is planning."

"Where are they?"

"Earth. They will be traveling to Italy in a few weeks. She'll take him with her. She believes she needs him to sustain her telepathy. Her entourage and security will be at a minimum. I have a plan." Teela grinned.

"I have a few plans of my own," Bill said.

"Like what?"

"I'm having Betsy modified so Fiona will be able to dock with her. The mooring will have retractable covers that will disguise her appearance. The mods should be complete by now. I've also made arrangements to meet with some people I know, who, for a substantial sum of money, will help us, no questions asked."

"Mercenaries? You've talked to mercs about this? Jesus, Bill!" Teela cried.

"Don't worry, these are friends of mine, ex-military. I've worked with them before."

"Worked with them? On what?"

"I've had to enforce a few contractual agreements with some of Earth's corporations. Mostly, though, I use them for gathering information. In my line of business, if you don't know what's happening, you get left behind. How do you think I knew about Fiona? I had her design specs in my hands before Gitch ever started construction. I borrowed a lot of her stealth features and few of the weapons systems when I built Betsy. I got a whole crew of top-notch engineers and physicists studying the fourth drive; the component design is more complex than anything I've ever seen, but give me time. I'll figure it out. So that's my plan. What's yours?"

"Simple," Teela said. "I tell General McClellen everything I know about Rebecca's plans, plus a few embellishments. While Rebecca is busy dealing with him, I snatch my son."

"Hmmmmm," Bill groaned, pulling at his beard. "That's your plan? That's it? Well... sometimes simple is best. Still, I think we're gonna need to work on this plan of yours."

22 - Goodbye

With all of the piracy, and attacks by Kahshinki raiders, it was not considered unusual when the Global Security Systems (GSS)

patrol received and responded to a distress signal on the edge of the outer perimeter of the departure point for New Korlah. Arriving on scene, the patrol of six UNE ghost class fighters found a disabled transport and rescued the two humans and three Korlah survivors aboard. Unequipped to tow the transport, the GSS patrol tagged it with a salvage claim beacon and set it adrift.

Tim had used his go-fast and a sizable sum of cash as collateral to lease the go-far from the Schwarzengeist, and now he had to get back to make arrangements to salvage it. With any luck, his deposit would cover salvage and repairs. If not, the Korlah Collective would sell his go-fast to cover the difference.

To make matters worse, the GSS patrol delivered Tim, Smiley, Shyron, Challmara, and Shawaugh to Earth's main spaceport instead of to the Collective Business Hub. Following a short debrief with the watch commander, they were released so they could make arrangements for transport off station.

"How can they not have any money?" Tim asked.

"They're Korlah military, they don't need money," Smiley said. "Don't worry about it, Tim. Shy says they'll cover all our costs."

"God damn right, they'll cover it! We saved their ass. I'm not worried about the money. We're gonna be stuck here a day, maybe two. That's what I'm worried about," Tim said.

"So what?" Smiley said. "We get a couple rooms, get drunk and wait for our ride. Korlah military covers our tab—what's not to like? Seriously, what are you so upset about?"

"This is Lucy-Land," Tim whispered, "and we just got rescued after rescuing Korlah military personnel out in no man's land. That was not low profile. We'll be lucky if we aren't in the evening news. What if I'm recognized?"

"Poleeeze!" Smiley exclaimed, lifting a cheek to let one rip. "Worry about that," he said with a grin. "Listen, boss, Lucinda is looking for Ludwig Von Hammer, not Tim Masters. That decrepit old bitch is probably half blind and can't recognize her own reflection. Shit, I heard she's over a hundred."

"There isn't much that scares me anymore. But that woman, old as she is, scares the shit out of me. It's not just because of her ties to the Columbian crime cartels. I've heard what she does to men who piss her off. I've looked in her eyes and tasted her blood, and I'm telling you, she is pure evil."

The Betsy dropped from sub-light on approach to the Armageddon and maneuvered flawlessly through the congestion at the UNE delousing station. As a Korlah-collective registered vessel, Betsy was exempt from UNE contraband rules and could proceed directly to the Korlah section's docking portal. With only inches to spare, the KC2 Wrath-class civilian assault pod slid into the opening and requested entry. The portal immediately rotated into the ship and the massive hangar within. With inhuman precision, the sizable craft darted forward, turned, and sped down a narrow aisle of moored craft, then stopped at a special dock reserved expressly for Rahfoon's collective.

"Well done, Fiona!" Bill said, grinning when Teela frowned at him.

"Thank you, Captain Jacks. Shall I idle or shut down?" Fiona asked.

"We won't be long, so idle will be fine. Keep proximity sensors on full sensitivity. Notify me if anyone gets near this ship."

"Understand. Idle systems, proximity sensors on high, notify you of violations," Fiona replied.

"Why so grim?" Bill asked Teela. "That was the best maneuvering I've ever seen. Linking Fiona into Betsy's control system was a great idea. I'm a damn good Wraith pilot but I sure can't maneuver as precisely as she can."

"I like being in control," Teela replied, at which Bill burst into laughter.

"What woman doesn't?" He continued to laugh as he wiped tears from his eyes. "No human or Korlah could have controlled this ship as precisely as Fiona just did. The Wrath-class pods are the absolute maximum that will fit through an access portal. They're built with bumpers, because even in the hands of a skilled pilot, it is expected that they will hit. I would bet you that of the three inches of clearance available, she had this two-hundred-ton ship centered to within a few thousandths of an inch."

"Actually, Captain Jacks, I was experiencing a twenty-seven thousandths fluctuation while at rest. I believe with some minor adjustments to the field array I can improve our stationary positioning," Fiona said.

"There you go," Bill said. "Plugging Fiona into Betsy's control system was the best idea I've ever had. When I can get the best, I get it. Fiona is the best. You should give the girl some credit."

"Aye, aye, Captain. Just consider what you are going to do if something happens to Fiona and nobody knows how to pilot your ship," Teela said.

Arriving at the Armageddon shortly after the Betsy, a small, unmarked UNE KC1 Curse-class transport got in line and waited its turn for a contraband inspection. After the search, it was unable to follow the Betsy into the Korlah docks, so the transport proceeded to the Crossover section, transited the first available portal, and moored at one of the more remote areas in the terminal. Once the ship was secure, the pilot rose from her seat and studied the personnel working on the dock. Aware that attractive women attract attention, she knew she would need to change her appearance if she was going to blend in. Twenty minutes later she exited the transport in the standard blue coveralls worn by maintenance personnel. She now looked much like the thin, twenty-something young man with crooked teeth and long greasy hair who was operating a mobile vacuum across the dock.

On each hand she wore a single ring, both of which could deliver a dart from fifteen feet away. Normally these darts would be loaded with a paralyzing agent to subdue her victims for a slow and painful execution, but today she had them tipped with a toxin that would bring death within seconds: impersonal, quick, and painless. It seemed inappropriate to kill the imposter who had murdered Shawlmon's mother without prejudice or pain, but the Oracle had ordered it, and as always, Tiffany would obey.

Beth finished her second beer and ordered a third. According to her watch, it was 11:50 a.m., which meant she had ten minutes before Cooper would show up to drag her out of the bar and over to the arrivals checkpoint to watch people disembark from the noon shuttle. After weeks of watching and waiting for Julie, Beth was confident she would never arrive. Whatever it was that Chris Johnson had in mind when he took Julie Rimes had to be finished by now. Like Teela, she would have been another loose end, and she knew that Chris never left loose ends.

Teela passed through the Korlah checkpoint and entered the main concourse of the Armageddon's Crossover section. She stepped to the side of the thoroughfare while she waited for Bill to catch up. In little over a week, several new restaurants and businesses and a food court had opened in this once-abandoned section and were thriving. Construction in the few remaining niches indicated that the transformation was not over.

The amount of construction in progress was evidenced by the horde of human and Korlah construction workers wearing dark-green coveralls that accounted for the majority of people swarming the plaza. Sprinkled throughout the crush of green denim were a dozen maintenance workers in light-blue coveralls and a couple of security officers wearing white shirts and black slacks. The hands of a large chronographic clock above the terminal's entrance approached noon, and the lines at the food court and the Crossover Café grew with each passing second. Even though the workers were provided room and board, the smell of fresh-grilled burgers could entice even the most frugal worker to part with more than a day's earnings for a single meal. Teela gently swung her crown tendrils from side to side to drink in the flavors floating in the air as Bill paused alongside her, searching the crowd for the men he had arranged to meet. Dressed in the full-length tan robe worn by members of the Korlah business collectives, his face was hidden in the shadows of its deep hood. Even so, at six foot seven inches tall and weighing over three hundred pounds, Bill wasn't exactly inconspicuous. With Teela in her mercenary apparel, they made an odd couple and garnered more than a few stares.

"Every time I come back here I hardly recognize the place," Bill said.

"Well, I'm just glad they didn't recognize me," Teela said.

"I said you'd be cool," Bill grinned. "When I jacked your arrest warrant, I modified the records of your last visit. If anyone bothers to check, the record's gonna show that you was here on business and not involved in capping the Shawlmon imposter."

"You mean the assassination that didn't occur because I prevented it?"

"Don't give me that tone, girl. Last time you were here you made a mess, and I have done cleaned it up."

"Whatever! I'm getting a burger," Teela said. She joined the long line at the grill. Bill spotted his mercenaries at a table outside the Crossover Café and went to join them.

After nearly twenty minutes in line, Teela was finally able to order her burger. Bill was busily engaged in a discussion with the mercenaries and had just ordered his second drink when the passengers from the noon shuttle began to flow out of the terminal's checkpoint. Teela was deeply engrossed in her anticipation of eating a fresh-grilled burger made from real beef when something akin to a mental slap drew her attention. Instinctively, she turned and looked. With a singular, predatory focus, her gaze targeted a woman in the distant crowd.

"I've been in your mind. You're... Julie," Teela whispered.

Posing as a dock worker, Tiffany watched and waited patiently for her opportunity to strike. She knew from experience that murdering someone in public without getting caught would be difficult, especially on Crossover, where the public areas were constantly monitored. If someone suddenly fell dead, it would attract immediate attention, the kind of attention Tiffany didn't want. Seeing several workers napping at the tables where they had eaten their lunch gave her an idea. She decided she would wait until her target finished eating, and then strike. The poison on her darts was so potent, she knew the imposter would die in an instant. The murderer of Shawlmon's mother would simply fall forward onto the table and appear to be sleeping. Tiffany was certain her plan would succeed—until Teela set her uneaten plate of food down and left the food court.

From Tiffany's perspective, Teela was talking to herself, occasionally gesturing, and raising her voice. *She's crazy,* Tiffany thought, believing this to be the reason the Oracle was sparing her a painful death. Altering her plan, she decided to wait until they were in a crowd, make it appear as if Teela passed out, help her to the ground, and then run for help. She closed the distance between them and carefully turned one of her rings to expose the lethal dart.

"Why do you care that she's here?" Teela asked, trying to sort through the flood of emotions that seeing Julie had aroused.

"She shouldn't be here," Dade replied.

"You offered her passage to New Korlah. A foolish offer, but you did make it. Perhaps she is here for that," Teela said.

"We'll find out. I'm gonna do the talking!" Dade said.

Teela did not reply. The wall she created to hide her thoughts from Dade made it abundantly clear that she was unhappy.

When Teela stopped in front of Julie, who was leaving the terminal, Tiffany was caught off guard. They were out in the open and away from the crowd she had planned to use for cover, so she was forced to slow her pace and change direction. This did not go unnoticed by one of the two men with Julie. He shifted his attention to Tiffany until she disappeared into the crowd.

"Hello! Welcome to Crossover," Teela said to Julie with a respectful bow. "I am Sula! The one and only. I can get you the best price on anything you need. And if I can't, I know who can." She took Julie's hand with both of hers. "So what brings you to our lovely city in space?"

Before Julie could respond, the two men with her, one older with short gray hair and the other younger with a greasy black ponytail, grabbed Teela from each side. She had been so intensely focused on Julie that she had failed to even notice them.

"What are you doing?" Julie cried. "She didn't hurt me. Stop it, Chris!"

"It's her," Chris said. "Do it!" He held Teela's arms securely and painfully behind her back as the younger man pulled what looked like a pen from his pocket. Holding it like a knife, he thrust it toward Teela's throat. She instinctively kicked, forcing him to dodge the blow.

"Hold her, God damn it!" the young man cried. Chris shoved Teela's twisted arms up as hard as he could, expecting to hear bones snap. A loud crack was heard, only it wasn't Teela's arms. The young man fell forward onto his face and the lethal pen rolled away.

Beth swung her stout black cane up onto her shoulder and smiled at Chris. Her uncombed hair and wrinkled security uniform added to the haggard look created by her paralysis to create an unimposing and pathetic visage.

"Let her go, Chrissy," Beth slurred.

Agent Cooper, who was now standing a few feet away, had his pistol pointed at Chris' head. Seeing the drawn weapon, people began to scatter.

"Richard? What—" Julie started to ask when she saw Cooper.

"Well… if it isn't B3," Chris Johnson sneered, walking backwards and pulling Teela with him. "The big bad bitch is not so big, not so bad, but still a bitch."

"You always claimed you were the best hit man in the world," Beth said. "A legend in your own mind. And here you are, hiding behind a woman, Chrissy. I'm guessing we're pretty evenly matched now. Why don't you let her go and see if a cripple can kick your chickenshit ass?"

"I'm working for Homeland Security, Beth. My prisoner and I are going to the UNE checkpoint. If you try to stop me, I will snap this alien cunt's neck and save everyone the expense of a trial and execution."

"Do it, Coop, take the shot," Beth said.

"No!" Julie cried.

In the fraction of a second that Cooper glanced at Julie, Chris threw Teela into Cooper with enough force to send them both tumbling to the floor. Chris had his pistol out of his shoulder holster in a flash and aimed it at Beth's head. The laser's red dot appeared on her forehead as he looked into her eyes and grinned.

In a blur of motion, Bill's massive paw caught Chris' gun hand with an upward sweep of his arm. Secure in Bill's grip, the offending hand and gun were directed away from Beth. The gun went off and Chris screamed as Bill wrenched him off his feet.

Reacting instinctively, Chris used his legs to cartwheel in the air and kick Bill squarely in the face with enough force to bring him to his knees. The sound of snapping bones preceded an earsplitting shriek as Bill crushed Chris' hand around the pistol like so much putty. A lightning flurry of adrenaline-charged kicks and blows from Chris sent Bill tumbling backwards unconscious. Chris pulled the blood-soaked gun from his crushed hand with an anguished groan and aimed it, left-handed, at Bill. A shot rang out and Chris Johnson's head exploded, spattering blood, skull fragments, and brain on everyone within ten feet. Julie screamed until Cooper wrapped his arms around her and she buried her face in his chest.

"God, I've wanted to do that for a long time," Beth said. She blew a wisp of smoke from the barrel of her pistol and then holstered it with a snap.

Julie pushed away from Cooper and looked him up and down, noticing his security uniform, badge, and gun for the first time.

"They told me you were dead. What are you doing here!"

"Searching for the woman I love," he croaked, blinking tears from his eyes. He pulled her into his arms and they kissed. What started as a kiss became a long, deep, emotional exchange.

Rising to her feet, Teela glared at Cooper and Julie, then went into a jealous rage, her crown tendrils rising in a display of blood-red hostility. She would have charged Cooper and pulled him from Julie had she not found her foot firmly locked in Bill's grasp.

"Let me go!" Teela hissed.

Sitting up, Bill pressed his nose to stop the bleeding with one hand and held her foot with the other.

"Help me up," he said, reaching out to her with his free hand. Once on his feet, he turned Teela away from Julie and Cooper and waited until she would look at him. When she finally did, her angry expression shifted to one of concern.

"Damn! Your nose is busted bad," Teela said.

"That's right... it's *my* nose now. It don't belong to you no more, just like Julie don't belong to you," Bill said.

Teela looked away, the color fading from her crown. "I know that," she whispered. "Thanks. I'm okay now. You can let go."

"Excuse me," Beth said. "Good to see you, Blackbone. I owe you one. Teela? Is that really you?"

"Yes. Long time, no insults. I haven't missed you, Beth, but I am glad to see you. Why are you here?"

"Coop and I work here. I'm Marshal Porter and the young man I'm with is Deputy Richard Cooper. We're members of the joint Crover-Korlah security detachment. Lucky for you, we're the law here. Listen, I really hate to break up all the hugging and kissing. That means you, Cooper! But I got one dead man, maybe two, on my hands. This is going take some creative explaining, so it would probably be best if you, Bill, and Ms. Rimes disappear. Jesus, Teela, wherever you go, disaster follows."

Teela ignored the jab. It was grounded in truth, and not something she could easily deny. Death had sought her out once again, and once again she had managed to cheat it. *Beth is right,* Teela thought. *Disaster does follow me.*

Breaking from Cooper's embrace, Julie walked toward Teela. She stopped a few feet away and looked up at Bill's face. "I... I've seen that nose broken before," she said. She looked at Teela and then back to Bill. "My God, to see it. His face, and you," she said, looking back at Teela. "This is something I must... do," she said, swallowing hard. She pulled Bill's face toward hers. He resisted at first, looking at Teela to gauge her response. Teela gave him a barely perceptible nod, and he allowed Julie to draw his face down to meet hers. Julie looked at Teela as she kissed the white skin of Bill's cheek. "Goodbye, Dade... goodbye." She blinked tears from her eyes and returned to Cooper's arms.

Teela clenched her fists with such force the claws of both hands ripped through the tips of her gloves and bit into her palms. "I'll see you back at the Betsy," she said to Bill, then walked away toward the Korlah terminal.

Bill waited until she was out of earshot before speaking.

"Okay, Beth, it's pretty obvious those guys were here to kill Teela. I'm guessing they brought Julie along to draw her out. They weren't from the Church, so who else wants Teela dead? You know who they are, don't you?"

"Were. The key word is… were," Beth said, rolling the young man with the greasy black hair onto his back. His pale complexion, half-open eyes, and blue lips made it clear that the blow to his head did more than just knock him out. "McClellen sent them—probably would have sent me to off her, but he figured I wouldn't. Or more likely, that I wasn't up to it."

"Why kill her? She just wants her kid back, and to be left alone."

"McClellen thinks Dade is part of some invasion plot and is now controlling Teela to further that goal."

"That's bullshit and you know it," Bill said.

"No, I don't know it. I've seen the evidence. Look, we can discuss this later. For now, I really need to get Ms. Rimes off this ship and back to Earth," Beth said.

"Teela and I are headed for Earth. If it would help, we can give her a lift," Bill said.

"Is that wise? The two of them together? I saw how Teela reacted when Coop was chewing on the widow's face. Now that he found her, Coop is not going to let her out of his sight. He'll be going with her," Beth said.

"Julie said goodbye. She made it pretty clear; it's over. Mr. Cooper is welcome as well," Bill said.

"It's your funeral. Hey, Coop, get over here," Beth said, waving Cooper over. "Take Julie and go with Bill. He'll take you two back to Earth. I'll send your money later. With what we've been getting paid to police this joint, you two should have more than enough to disappear somewhere safe."

"Come with us, Beth," Cooper said.

"I'm not leaving Marsha and Catherine—at least not till I see how things work out with the band. Teela and I went to a lot of trouble getting those girls back to Earth. Now… I just don't know if they're really safe here," Beth said.

"You don't trust Ruwaugh, do you?" Cooper asked.

"It's not a matter of trust. Call me paranoid, but I don't believe that crover is Crystal, at least not a hundred percent," Beth said.

A rumbling sound drew their attention to the armored soldiers running toward them.

"Go now!" Beth said, turning to face the approaching soldiers, holding her badge in the air for them to see.

After her failed attempt to assassinate Teela, Tiffany witnessed the events that unfolded in the center of the Crossover plaza. Questions filled her mind during the walk back to her ship. She'd recognized Bill and Beth. *Why would they protect this imposter?* Tiffany wondered. *Can't they see that she is crazy? Can't they hear the Oracle? Aren't they believers?*

Back at her ship, she watched and waited. It wasn't long before the Betsy departed. Keeping a safe distance between their ships to avoid detection, she programmed her ship to follow. Confused by the day's events and plagued by doubts about the Oracle's instructions, she meditated and prayed in an attempt to open the telepathic link the Oracle used to guide her. For weeks now, the Oracle had not contacted her, and Tiffany's prayers for guidance had gone unanswered. She worried that the Oracle was angry with her.

23 - Lucinda

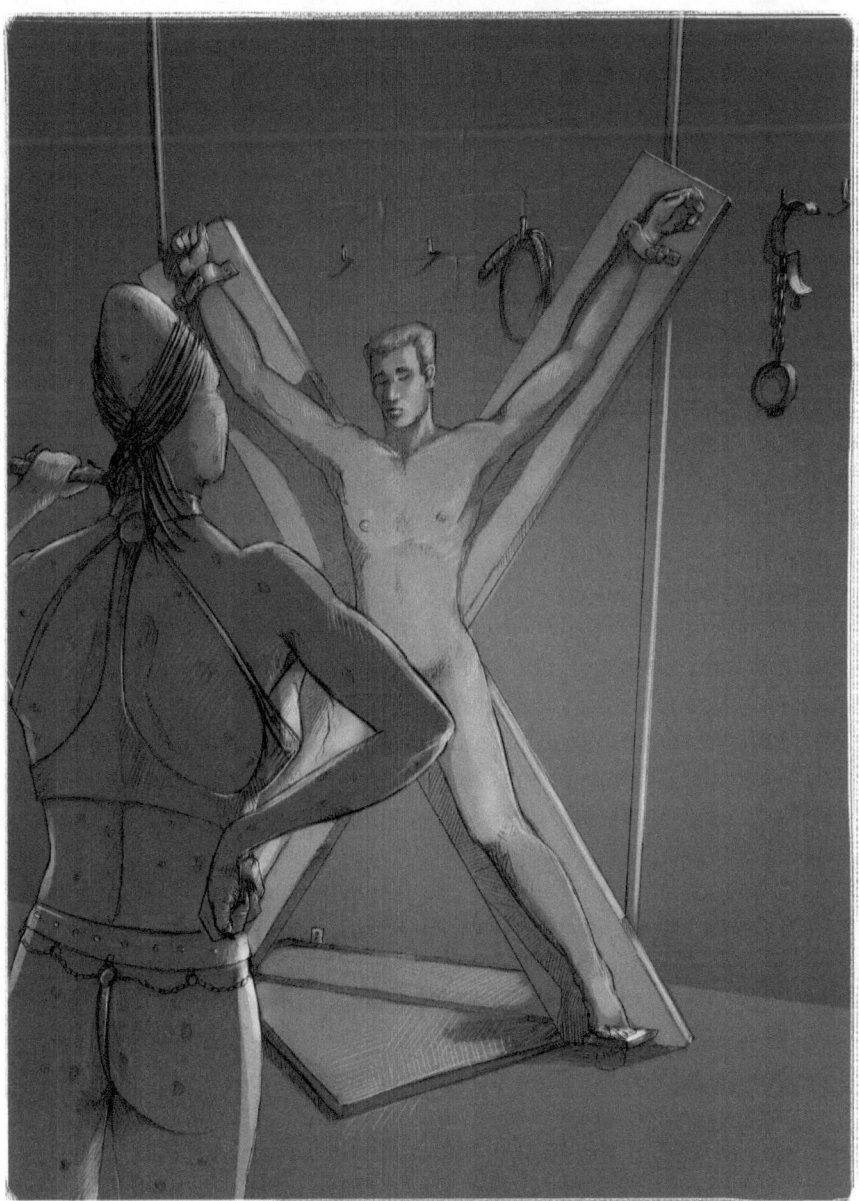

Lucinda looked at her reflection in the mirror, adjusting the wide belt of her crimson silk dress and assessing her muscular build critically. The procedure had gone exactly as planned and she was young and healthy again, but she felt that her new body was too masculine. The breast implants helped, but she still wasn't as womanly as she'd have liked.

When her nephew Jesus called with urgent news, she joined him in his office where he directed her to images of Tim Masters on his wall monitor. Small rectangular squares flashed over a picture of his hand, ear, and chin. At the bottom of the screen a line in red text flashed in unison with the squares. The text read "Recognition probability equals eighty-seven percent."

"It doesn't look like him. Ludwig is much older than this man," Lucinda said.

"It's Captain Von Hammer. He's here, Auntie. I found him for you, just like you asked," Jesus said, thankful that he was finally able to do something to alleviate the scorn she had shown him since Von Hammer breached her security and took her young Korlah.

"Are you sure it's him?"

"Yes, Auntie, eighty-seven percent is real sure. Anyway, this is a combined average. The hand by itself is a ninety-eight percent match. He wasn't wearing gloves and the monitors got a good shot of it. This is the same guy." Jesus was avoiding the ebony-black alien eyes of the creature that had become his Aunt Lucinda.

Lucinda nervously tapped on one of her fangs with a lacquered claw.

"Do you think I would be prettier without fangs?" she asked.

"I don't know, Auntie, maybe a little less scary."

"Scary! If it weren't for your little pills, I could make you beg just for the pleasure of licking my feet," Lucinda cried.

"I'm sorry, Auntie, I just meant—"

"Shut up! Where is he now?" she demanded.

"They rented rooms off the promenade, near the terminal. Ludwig's in one of the rooms and his friends are at the sky bar."

"Purrrrfect!" Lucinda growled. "Bring him to my playroom. Watch the others. If they come looking for him, have them detained. I don't care how you treat the human, but do nothing to injure or unnecessarily insult his Korlah friends. Do you understand, nephew?"

"Yes, Auntie," Jesus said with a bow, avoiding her penetrating glare.

After Jesus left, Lucinda returned to her mirror. After a few minutes, she turned away in disappointment. It angered her that no amount of makeup or fine clothing could alter her perception that she was now ugly... or as Jesus had said, *scary.*

Once again, Bill had Fiona link to the Betsy, and as before, Fiona did a stellar job piloting her. Slowing the Wrath-class destroyer to a grav-drive fractional, Fiona monitored the myriad of craft entering and leaving Earth space and plotted the best approach to its largest sky hub. From the bridge of the Betsy, Teela tried the phone number Bill had given her a third time, but again there was no ringing or busy signal, just silence.

"How old is this number? It isn't any good," she growled. Bill leaned over the panel and studied the readouts.

"Just got it, and paid good money for it, too. Look, this indicates the signal is being received," Bill said, pointing to a small red light above the screen. "If someone answers, this lights up. Since this is his personal private line, he don't need to tell you to leave a message at the tone. I'll bet this call's being recorded right now. Probably trying to trace it, too. Not to worry, though, this mobile can't be traced."

"Then I guess I'll leave a message," Teela said.

"Hello, General McClellen, this is... Teela. You also knew me by the name Shawlmon. I regret to inform you that the men you sent to kill me are dead. Not by my hands, and if I had been given a choice they would still be alive. I am not your enemy, but if you persist in that belief and take further action against me, I *will* become your enemy.

"Allow me to make a peace offering in the form of information critical to the political stability of Earth. Rebecca McCabe, the self-proclaimed Oracle of God, is planning to subjugate the pope and initiate a global coup that will create a single theocratic government on Earth. She is scheduled to meet with the pope at the Basilica of San Francesco d'Assisi tomorrow. The revolution is planned to commence in concert with the Festival Calendimaggio, which follows the meeting. You can expect that any leader who is not already part of Rebecca's organization will be targeted for assassination by the faithful at that time. I would have gotten this information to you sooner, but I was busy trying to stay alive."

Teela tapped the screen and ended the call. The little red light above it went out.

"Okay, Bill, provided McClellen gets that message anytime soon, we can expect Rebecca's informants will pass the information on to her soon after. We better get moving so we can get my son back before the shit hits the fan. Where are your mercs? I thought we were going to go over the rescue plan with them."

"Do you trust me?" Bill asked.

"Yes, why? What's going on, Bill?" Teela sensed a sudden rise in his emotions.

"Stay outta my head," Bill warned, stepping back. "You showed me what's in your head. I saw how Becca can read you. That's why you gotta trust me. Stay outta my mind and do what I ask. You can't know nothing about what my crew is doing. When I get their signal, you gotta do exactly what I say. You understand?"

Teela nodded, and verified that her mental wall was up and secure; she was certain that Rebecca could not see into her mind unless she allowed her to. Bill was keeping something from her because he was afraid Rebecca would read her thoughts. He'd always trusted Dade and her, and she would have to trust him now.

A buzzer went off and Bill slapped the panel to silence it.

"That's the signal! It's going down right now. This is where *you* save your son. You gotta get into Becca's mind and keep her real busy. You gotta do it right now, girl!"

Teela turned her back to Bill to inhibit her subconscious desire to probe his thoughts for answers to the questions pouring into her mind. She put her head back and dropped the wall that separated her from Rebecca's mind, then dove into the abyss that joined them together. A dot of light raced toward her like a hurtling meteor and a rush of sensations coursed into her mind, becoming hers in an instant.

She was awake, sitting on the edge of a bed... she was aware of smooth satin sheets, the smell of fresh roses, emotions of alarm. Something had awoken her. She looked at the alarm panel: the green light that indicated that it was active was dark.

Rebecca screamed with her mind to wake the child. Shawlmon! *She wanted to move, to go the little boy. Still groggy, she felt as if she were paralyzed and unable to move her own legs.*

I am here. I have always been here, *Teela answered, her words emerging in Rebecca's mind as a thought might.*

Rebecca paused, now alert. She sensed the invasion and wrapped her mind around the intruder like an anaconda preparing to feed.

Teela's eyes opened wide as she stiffened, her muscles suddenly fighting her will to control them. The convulsions that followed would have thrown her from the chair if Bill had not guided her onto the floor and restrained her.

The pinch of an injection woke Tim. His vision was blurred and fuzzy; he looked at his arm as the needle was being withdrawn and saw that his wrists and ankles were secured. He shook his head to clear the cobwebs from his mind and became aware that he was strapped naked onto a wooden cross erected in a room that looked like a medieval dungeon. Whips, chains, and torture implements covered an entire wall. Cages, benches, and racks with straps and shackles filled the chamber. As he struggled against his bindings he recalled someone opening the door of his hotel room, something was sprayed in his face.

"Lucinda!"

He croaked her name with parched lips as reality sank in.

"Yessssss," she answered from somewhere behind him. He turned his head as far as his bindings would allow, but was only able to see her silhouette in his peripheral vision. She moved close and he could feel her breath on his ear.

"We're square, Lucinda." Tim choked on her name and tried to swallow. "I took what I was owed and I left. You're starting a war here, one that neither of us wants or needs. We can work this out. What do you want?"

"Sssssatisfaction," she whispered as she reached around from behind and groped his genitals.

Tim looked down and saw that the hand touching him was not human.

"You're not Lucinda!" he shouted. "Who the hell are you?"

"I have taken a new body," she said. "I've made a few improvements here and there. Do you like it?"

She moved around the cross and stood facing him. From her size and thick muscles, he guessed she was of the warrior genotype, but this Korlah warrior had the largest breasts he had ever seen. Dressed in a black leather bustier, leggings, and knee-high boots, she looked like something out of a gothic nightmare. She smiled maliciously as he looked her over. There was something funny about her face. *It looks like a mask,* he thought.

He stared in disbelief. He had met and worked with crovers. He knew the plan: the dead and dying would help bridge the gap between the species, a strictly limited exchange for the purpose of defending Earth. Sula was one of those crovers; damaged for sure, but what he saw in her was good. This thing standing in front of him, however, was not part of that plan. This was something perverse, and just as he had when he met Lucinda years before, when she tried to get him to run drugs for her, he knew she was pure evil.

"Let me go, Lucinda. You took from me and I took it back. We're even."

"I will tell you when we are even. Just like I told you I would find out who stole your cargo and I did. It was my idiot nephew, Juan. Juan! Tell Captain Von Hammer you are sorry," Lucinda shouted. An unintelligible croak came from across the room. Tim strained his eyes in the dim light and realized that there were people in several of the small cages.

"I apologize for Juan's pathetic articulation, but he no longer has a tongue with which to lie, so that noise he makes is the best he can do. I was going to kill him, but my grandniece begged me to spare his life. She's family, so what was I to do? You, my dear Ludwig, are not family, and there is no one here to beg for your life."

"Killing me would be a bad idea," Tim said. "We can... He sniffed. "We can work something out." He sniffed again. His sense of smell had been chemically numbed for so long the sensation of smell seemed foreign. He realized that its return would bring the effects of the Korlah pheromones. The smell of Lucinda's perfume, a sickeningly sweet floral, flooded his senses.

Lucinda watched Tim's nose crinkle and grinned. "I removed your implant. Soon, my new drug will soon completely neutralize any residual blocking agents in your system. Tell me, how long have you been using the blockers?" Lucinda asked, examining his groin closely. "No arousal yet. You are still shriveled with fear."

"What did you inject in me?" Tim asked.

"While I was busy developing a laboratory-engineered equivalent of the wonderful Korlah pheromone, the men in power quickly realized it could be used against them to change the gender imbalance of our male-dominated planet. So when they came up with a blocking agent, I set out to develop an antidote. In a few minutes the effects of the blocking agents will be completely gone. Depending on how long you have been using them, the effects of the Korlah pheromones will be substantially enhanced. Have you ever been in a pheromone-induced rut?"

He hadn't, but he had heard the stories, both good and bad. Drugs had never been his thing; he only drank to be sociable, and never to the point of getting drunk. Being sexually aroused to the point of being unable to think of anything except the next orgasm didn't sound like something he would enjoy.

"You haven't, have you?" Lucinda chuckled, moving her face so close to his that he could feel her warm breath on his lips. For the first time, he realized what was odd about her face. She was wearing makeup, including painted-on eyebrows and fake eyelashes. She reached under her ear canal and drew her finger down her neck, where the pheromone oils were the most concentrated. She took her finger and rubbed it under Tim's nose while he tried to turn away. She laughed and grabbed him by the throat, the claw of her thumb piercing his soft flesh. She held him and stared into his eyes, waiting for him to blink. When he did, she chuckled and released him, then she collected the thin rivulet of blood running down his throat with the tip of her claw. She made a show of licking the blood off her hand and then his neck. When she tried to slip her blood-soaked tongue into his mouth, he pulled away in disgust. Lucinda laughed again.

She went to the wall and activated a hoist. The wooden cross began to slowly lower to a horizontal position on the floor. Once on the floor, Lucinda stood over Tim and placed the heel of her boot in the center of his chest, looking down at him.

"My pharmacologist tells me that if a man has been using the blocking agents for more than a year, there is a possibility of heart failure or a brain aneurism from the intensity of his arousal. This is a risk I am willing to take in order to see you do things— disgusting and repulsive things that a man in his right mind would refuse to do, even with a gun to his head. Yet you will beg me to let you do them, and thank me afterwards. My dear Ludwig, I have no intention of killing you. We will have many sessions over the next few weeks during which I will let you come out of the rut long enough to experience the shame and self-loathing of what you have done. In a few months or years, when torturing you no longer amuses me, I may allow you to kill yourself. Can you smell it yet? The sweet scent of concentrated lust?"

Lucinda cupped her hand over his mouth and forced him to breathe through his nose. Even through the stink of her perfume, Tim could smell the sweet scent of honey. He knew that if what he had heard of the rut was true, he would soon be lost in a state of blind, uncontrollable sexual arousal. Restrained and at Lucinda's mercy, he would tell her whatever she wanted to know and do whatever she asked for the mere promise of physical contact.

Smiley will know something is wrong, Tim thought, his mind racing. *He will know Lucinda has me. Shyron found the two Korlah in deep space—she ought to be able to find me here on the station.* He clenched his eyes shut to block out Lucinda's face hovering above him and cried out with every fiber of his conscious mind for Shyron to find him before…

Too late, it's too late, Tim realized. His mouth and eyes opened wide as a growing wave of pressure within his loins created a blinding flush of arousal. He moaned loudly as he rose with it, fully engorged within a few seconds; the pressure continued to build. Tim arched his back and thrust his hips forward with a guttural cry from the overwhelming need for release.

"Yessssss," Lucinda purred. "You, my dear Ludwig, are mine now. I own you."

Somewhere in a nebulous region of telepathic reality, a battle raged between two minds separated by hundreds of thousands of miles. The neurons of their brains fired with such intensity the residual charges caused their bodies to spasm with violent convulsions. Fueled by the desperation and determination each felt gave them the right to defeat the other, Teela and Rebecca fought with the very fiber of their existence. Deep within the field of cerebral battle, the fight seemed to last an eternity. In reality, their struggle for dominance only lasted a few minutes.

Something Rebecca didn't expect shifted the balance of power: she found herself fighting two incredibly powerful foes. While Teela would dodge, evade, and counter Rebecca's attacks with the speed and ferocity of a wild beast, Dade would plow into the very basis of her beliefs with mind-numbing hostility and aggression. Seeing the opportunity for victory slip from her grasp, Rebecca retreated from Teela's mind, erecting a wall behind her for protection.

We did it! We beat the bitch, Dade cried.

No, no… Teela groaned. *If we had, we would have turned her to our way of thinking, like she was trying to do to us. She wanted to rip all opposing thoughts from our mind, my mind, and replace them with… faith, devotion and loyalty to the king. That's how she's controlling people. This was just a draw, a temporary truce.*

"Teela! You all right?" Bill asked. "You did it. You bought my guys the time they needed. We got your boy. He's in good hands—with folks I trust. We gonna meet up with them in a few hours far and away from here."

Teela sat up and rubbed her face. Her muscles were sore from the contortions of the last few minutes. "Where is he, where is my son?" she demanded.

"You know I can't tell you that just yet," Bill said.

"Wait!" she cried. She put her hands to her temples and grimaced. "I hear him. He's calling for help." She arched her back and cried out in pain, and Bill grabbed her arms, expecting another set of convulsions. Teela relaxed and opened her eyes.

"What happened? Who's calling? What are you talking about?" Bill asked.

"She has him. Oh my God!" Teela said, her face twisting into a grimace of disgust at the image that filled her mind.

"Who? Your son? Who has him?" Bill helped Teela as she scrambled to her feet.

"Tim Masters, the trucker. He found Shawaugh and Challmara. They're here. Lucinda has captured Tim... she's... making him do things... my God!"

"Lucinda has him. That's not good," Bill said, helping Teela into a chair. "Yeah, it's pretty well known how she settles scores with her enemies. She'll take her sweet time torturing him and when she's finished she'll make him cut his own throat. I'm sorry, Teela, if Lucinda has him, he's as good as dead."

"He's not dead yet. She's doing this because of me. She's pissed at him because he took me from her. And if he can take me from her, I can do the same for him." Teela strapped on her pistol and sword.

"Not gonna happen, Teela. Lucinda has been upgrading her security at a phenomenal cost. Once she finishes the mods to her docking bay, that place will be tighter than Fort Knox."

"What's she doing to the docking bay?" Teela asked.

"Building armored doors that will lock from the inside. Forget it. If a ship, shuttle—hell, if a loading cart got within a thousand feet of that opening, every alarm in the joint would go off. Anyway, her yacht is docked with the only opening in the bay, and all of its exterior doors require a pass code for entry. Even if you got that far, it would take hours to bust the code. I know because I built the yacht for her."

"How far to her dock?" Teela asked.

"You can see it from here," Bill said, pointing out the window at the space hub. "Right there, just below the main deck. Over half of the lower level is her private penthouse."

"Modifications mean workers in pressure suits crawling all over the place, right?" Teela asked, already beginning to suit up.

"I'm not gonna be able to talk you out of this, am I?" Bill groaned. Teela's silence was her answer. "What about your little boy? I thought that was your main concern, gett'n him safe."

"You said he was safe. I trust you," Teela said. "Get Shyron, Smiley, Challmara, and Shawaugh on board the Betsy. Be ready to bug out the second I get back."

Bill tugged at his beard nervously while Teela checked her suit's seals. He went to a cabinet and pulled out something that looked like an iron.

"Do you have any pheromone blocker?" Teela asked.

"Yeah," he said, handing her the device.

"What's this?" she asked, taking it by its handle, which was clearly designed for a Korlah hand.

"It's a handheld grav unit. Top button attracts, bottom repels. Without this, getting around out there is impossible." He handed her an oversized syringe. "This here's an implanting unit. Stick it under the skin near the neck. Not in a muscle; that would hurt like mutha. Not in a vein, that would kill him. It takes a while to get in the blood, and until then, you won't be able to control him. If she's doing half the things I think she's doing, he's gonna get depressed, even suicidal when he comes out of it. She may have already damaged him in some really bad ways. He's gonna wish he was dead, Teela."

"Then I need to hurry. Be ready when we get back." She closed the airlock behind her.

Lucinda paused, unsure why at a time like this she would be thinking about the pass codes to her yacht. When Tim's hands stopped thrashing, she knew he had passed out again; she rose up off his face and he instinctively sucked in air, gasping repeatedly. She waited until he had regained consciousness.

"Lucinda… please stop! I love you," he moaned.

"Prove you love me, pig!" Lucinda said, dropping her smothering weight onto his face again.

Lucinda ignored the rustling across the chamber, believing it to be the movement of her caged prisoners, but when she heard the unmistakable static crackle of a pulse weapon energizing, she turned to look. The blast hit her in the center of her back and knocked her off Tim. She rolled over several times before stopping face down on the floor.

"No! Lucinda!" Tim cried. "Don't hurt her, please don't."

Teela sheathed her sword and released one of Tim's hands. He immediately grabbed her and tried to pull her onto him. She yanked herself free and stood clear of his pawing grasp.

"Sula! My God, Sula, you're here. Please! I need you—I love you, Sula!" Tim howled, grabbing at her with his free hand, his bulging eyes locked on her breasts.

"Sorry, Tim, I don't have time for this shit," Teela replied. She pulled her sword, adjusted the setting, and fired. He fell, limp, on the cross.

"Jesus, Tim," Teela exclaimed when she realized that even stunned and unconscious, he was anything but limp.

She released the rest of his bindings and was dragging him back to the access hatch she'd come through when she heard something. Lucinda was on her feet and staggering toward a door on the opposite side of the room. Teela pulled her sword, aimed, and fired; Lucinda stumbled but kept walking.

"Damn!" Teela cried, realizing the sword was still set on a mild stun. An alarm bell sounded about the time she had adjusted the setting and before she could aim, Lucinda was gone. Pulling Tim through the hatch, she closed it and fused it shut with several carefully aimed bursts from her sword. Outside the torture chamber, Teela glanced to the right and left down the private corridor that connected Lucinda's penthouse to the docking bays. She sheathed her sword, grabbed Tim by an arm, and pulled him to the yacht's hatch.

She'd just pushed him through when a door at the end of the corridor flew open. She yanked her sword out and took aim. When the first guard charged through the door and fired his pulse rifle at Teela, her specialized, energy-absorbing sword acted like a magnet for the beam of energy directed at her. His pulse beam arced down and struck her sword at the same moment that she fired it. The beam, amplified by the absorbed energy, burned a hole through the man's chest and dispersed into the bodies of the guards behind him. They all tumbled back like bowling pins. Teela leapt through the hatch into Lucinda's yacht and locked it behind her.

Releasing the yacht's moorings, she initiated a full power drop with the gravity drive unit. The electromagnetic pulsations of the yacht's gravity coils powering up rattled everything in the hangar that wasn't solidly anchored. Construction crews working on the hangar's armored doors scrambled out of the way as the luxury ship ripped through a section of scaffolding. Once clear of the hangar, Teela turned the ship directly toward the sun and initiated a full power pull toward the sun and a full power push away from the Earth. Not waiting for an indication that it was safe, she slid her finger down the bar to initiate a sub-light jump. On the communication panel she tapped in Betsy's address and sent a single word: *Eddie.* It was the only thing she could think of. If Bill didn't know what she meant, Smiley would. There was a lot of space between Earth and Jupiter, enough to lose who ever tried to follow her. She would meet them at Eddie's on Crossroads. All she had to do was get there alive.

"Oh... shit," Bill groaned, watching the space hub from the bridge of the Betsy as Lucinda's polished silver yacht ripped out of its hangar and jumped to sub-light speed. "Fiona! What's the status of our passengers?"

"Richard Cooper and Julie Rimes are seated in the common area. The human called Smiley and the Korlah Shyron, Challmara, and Shawaugh have just left the airlock and are headed forward. All requested personnel are on board and accounted for. Shall we join the pursuit of Lucinda's yacht?" Fiona's computer-generated voice sounded excited.

"No, Fiona," Bill said. "I still have to rendezvous with my boys and pick up little Dade. I need to ask a favor of you." He checked the communications panel; there were two messages. The first directed every Galactic Security Systems interceptor in the area to pursue the stolen yacht. The other simply read "Eddie." Bill looked at the name and knew exactly what Teela meant.

"I would be glad to help, William," Fiona said. "You know how much I enjoy our conversations and appreciate how you have let me pilot the Betsy."

"Thanks. I need you to pursue Lucinda's yacht. I want you to help it escape those GSS interceptors. But be careful—I don't want you getting hurt. When you finish, meet me at Crossroads."

"I'm on my way. You be careful, too. Thank you, William," Fiona said.

The Betsy shuddered as Fiona's sleek fighter pushed off and raced to join the mass of other pursuit craft. Bill wanted to tell her she didn't need to thank him, but he knew it wouldn't make a difference. Of all the strange relationships he had been through, a computer with a crush on him had to be the most bizarre.

When the Betsy departed the space hub, a small disc-shaped object smaller than a dime was released from the hull above her bridge. Inert and using only passive monitoring systems, it energized for the first time and pulsed the last thirty-six hours of recorded information in an encrypted low-frequency message to Tiffany aboard her ship. She received the message and fed it into her ship's computer to listen to it. She skipped to the end and listened to the last few minutes of conversation aboard the Betsy.

24 - Desperation

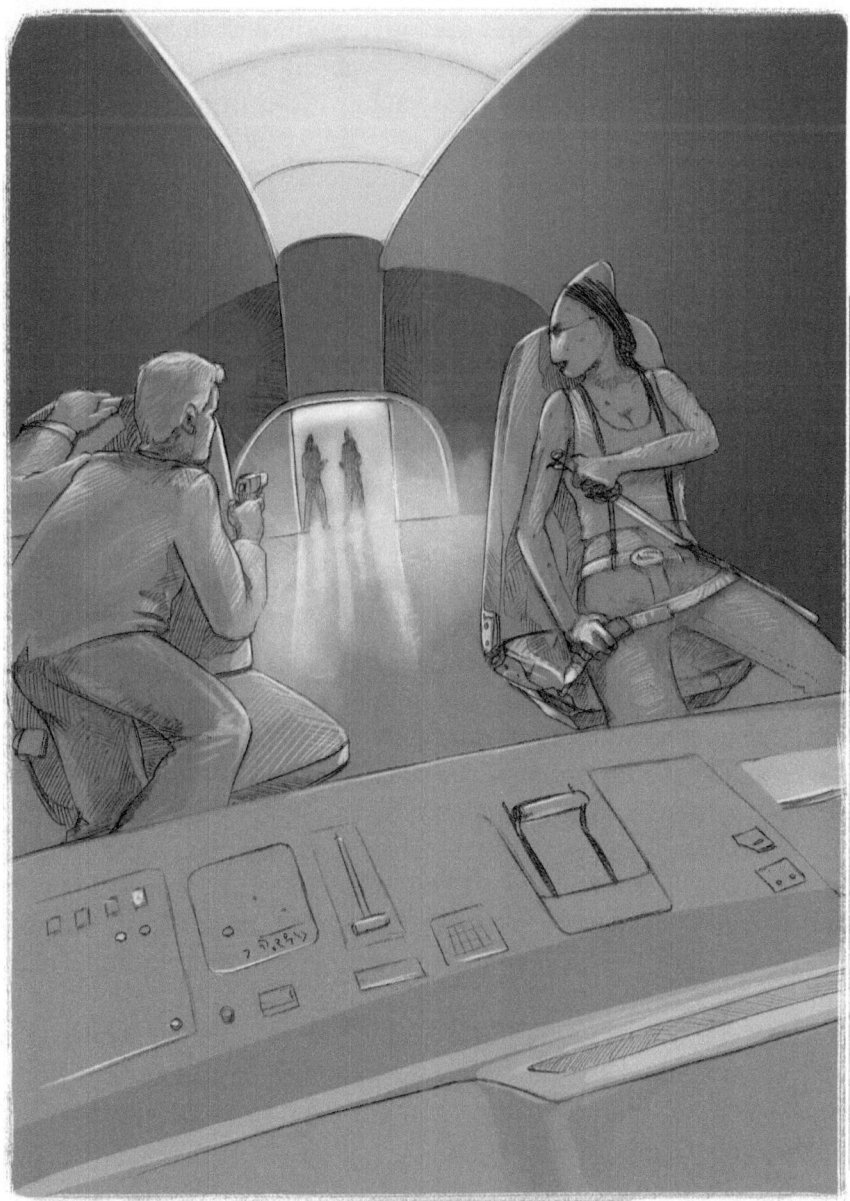

When the GSS interceptors started to gain on her, Teela realized just how sloppy her attempt to slingshot Lucinda's yacht around the sun really was. She didn't want to admit it, but the maneuver and jump to light speed was amateur at best; she'd made mistakes Fiona never would have, mistakes that could cost them their lives. She bit her lip and held her breath, waiting until the last second before dropping to sub-light. The yacht rocked from a near miss as its magnetic field glanced off an asteroid the size of a Greyhound bus. She prayed the autopilot couldn't do any worse, set the ships speed to maximum, and turned it on.

"Sula... I'm sorry," Tim groaned from behind her. A splattering sound followed. Teela turned around. Tim was sitting up, leaning forward, a large puddle of vomit between his legs. "I'm sorr... urruh," he cried, vomiting again.

The smell that quickly filled the cabin caused Teela to gag. She dug through the cabinets, glancing at the tracking screen periodically. The interceptors were gaining on them. She threw a couple of white shirts on the stinking pile and threw a flight attendant's uniform on the floor next to Tim.

"Quit crying and get dressed!" she demanded, praying Tim was free of the effects of the pheromone.

"She told me to, and I... I... ate... her shit."

"Yeah, I can smell. Shut up and get up here!" Teela cried.

The interceptors were minutes away from overtaking them. She switched the autopilot off and took manual control. She tried to calm her voice and control the panic she felt.

"Lucinda's an evil bitch, Tim, and she was just getting started. I was in her head and I saw what she had planned for you. You *do not* want to go back there. Now snap out of it, or we will both end up back in her den of debauchery. Get up here, I need your help... now!"

Tim came to the copilot's seat wearing a frilled white shirt and pink tuxedo slacks, leaving the matching jacket on the floor, and studied the panels for a moment. He adjusted the forward sensors and groaned.

"Contacts, four—no, make that six fighters, coming at us fast, dead ahead," he said.

Teela cut a hard turn and continued an evasive course. The nimble fighters turned and matched her course and speed, taking positions on four sides, in front and behind. The ships banked slowly, forcing Teela to either change course or collide. She opened a short-range communications channel.

"Check your long-range scanners, people. I've got over a hundred Earth-based fighters coming up my ass looking for blood. Smoking a half dozen pirates will just be another feather in their cap." Teela held her breath and waited. Releasing it, she tried to think of something that would make these raiders realize that letting her go would be in their best interest. About the time she was prepared to speak, the speaker crackled and a raspy voice came through.

"What're you carrying on that fancy boat of yours that they want so bad? I bet they will pay a pretty penny to get it back."

This was a voice Teela knew.

"Dex, old buddy old pal. How's Butch? You're supposed to ask what the magic password is, remember? We had a deal. Seriously, do you really think you can extort a reward from Lucinda for the return of her own yacht? If you do, you are going to be severely disappointed," Teela said.

A few seconds later, about the time she would have expected a response, the fighters surrounding them peeled off. The radio crackled and the signal got weaker as Dex put as much distance between him and Teela as he could.

"You got some big brass balls, you crazy bitch. As pretty as that ship is, it can't outrun a GSS interceptor. Do you know what Lucinda is going to do to you when they take you back? The way you're running, I'm guessing you do."

"I'll bet those souped-up fighters of yours can outrun anything the GSS has," Teela said. "If you run interference for me for just five minutes, your debt to me will be clear."

"Hell, girl, in five minutes you're going to be in chains and on your way back to see Lucinda. Soon after that... no more debt."

"Help me, Dex, or I swear I will hold out until Lucinda is finished cutting off my fingers and toes, then in the most convincing confession imaginable I will name you with my dying breath as the mastermind behind this entire operation."

"You… you crazy Korlah bitch!" Dex screamed, the pitch of his voice stretching the limits of the speakers. After more than a minute of silence, Teela was certain those were Commander Poindexter's parting words. Then the speaker crackled with his raspy voice again.

"You listen to me, I will run interference for two God damn minutes, and that's it! And then… YOU are going to owe me. Whatever the fuck I want, you're gonna give it to me. Do you hear me!"

"I agree. Two minutes and I will give you whatever you want next time we meet. Deal."

Teela nudged the speed up even more. Already well beyond the limits of safe flight through the asteroid belt, Teela was now afraid to blink. She stared intently at the monitor as she steered around obstacles that appeared and passed so quickly that one blink could result in a direct impact. A few jarring bumps indicated glancing blows to their electromagnetic shield.

Tim sat quietly alongside her, staring at the monitor tracking the ships behind them. The silence lasted for more than five minutes before he announced, "Your friend's fighters are engaging. Contacts slowing down and spreading out," Tim announced.

"Not sure he's my friend, but it works for me. How long until we are out of sensor range?"

"Minute, maybe less," Tim replied.

After a full minute, during which the debris around them thinned out considerably and Teela didn't need to correct course, Tim said, "They're off our long-range sensors." He quickly added, "That doesn't mean we're off theirs."

Teela banked hard to the left and engaged light speed. She took a deep breath and slid her fingertip into the control indent that would energize the hyper-light drive. The stars blurred and then disappeared.

"Are you nuts?" Tim shouted. "We're not far enough out of the belt to go hyper. You're gonna get us killed!" He grabbed the panel with both hands and waited for the random piece of rock that would end both their lives.

Teela held her breath and counted the seconds while calculating the distance they would cover. Certain they were well outside the asteroid belt and beyond even the orbit of Jupiter, she secured from hyper-light, made an immediate course change, then jumped back to hyper-light. She repeated the process three more times and figured if nothing was on the monitor next time they dropped out of hyper-light, she could safely say they had lost the GSS interceptors.

"Okay... okay, Sula, you can slow down now. That Dex guy is right—you got balls AND you are frigging nuts!" Tim said, trying to make sense of the readings on the navigation computer. "You can't jump around inside a solar system at hyper-light speeds unless you are trying kill yourself. Shit, you got better odds playing five rounds of Russian roulette."

"I suppose you'd rather we get caught and end up back with Lucinda?" Teela said, but was immediately sorry when Tim winced at the mere mention of her name.

Following Tim's suggestion, Teela secured the hyper-light drive. When the ship dropped back to light speed, she changed course and was preparing to drop to sub-light so their navigation computer could get a fix on their location when red diamonds appeared on the monitor. The contacts came into range so quickly that Teela didn't have time to lift her hand, let alone shout a warning to Tim.

The impact spun the yacht sideways and threw them both out of their chairs. The ship wallowed from side to side as the engines strained to resume sub-light speed without the magnetic drive. Teela scrambled to her feet and jumped into the pilot's seat and Tim managed to sit up, rubbing the side of his head and trying to make sense of what just happened.

"Get up!" Teela screamed, her hands racing over the controls silencing alarms and adjusting the engines. She dealt deftly with the damage and had begun to regain control of the ship when they suddenly lurched to one side, struck by an energy pulse. The window went dark.

"What the hell?" Tim shouted, nearly thrown over the copilot's chair by the blast. He eventually managed to climb into the seat.

"We flew into a group of ships. Or... maybe they flew into us, I don't know. I hit one and they're shooting at us now," Teela cried, gyrating the controls to evade their attackers, who were now well within firing range.

"Those aren't GSS fighters," Tim said.

"What then? UNE, Korlah, Earth Defense Force?"

The answer came as a series of lights flashing and scrolling down the communications screen. Teela and Tim recognized the code immediately.

"Kahshinki!" they cried in unison.

A dull thump shook the yacht, and seconds later, there was a bright flash in the compartment behind them. A thick cloud of hot smoke poured through the hatch, announcing the arrival of a Kahshinki boarding party. Teela pulled her pistol and handed it to Tim. She had her sword about halfway out of its sheath when it absorbed an energy pulse directed at her. As designed, the sword's power cell automatically discharged to prevent overload, but since it was still sheathed, the discharge blew the sheath to pieces. Teela was blasted into the overhead and knocked unconscious. Tim managed to fire off four rounds before a pulse blast dropped him, too.

On the far side of the solar system, a full 80 AU from the Armageddon, a utility ship designated only as SFM067 was deploying the last of its payload of sensor arrays. Designed to open and activate upon deployment, each eight-cubic-foot device would then wait, silent and stationary, to detect unnatural movement. When it did, it would beam a signal to a series of relay units that forwarded the signal at hyper-light speeds to the UNE's early-warning system. It was recognized early on in the war preparations that the sun created a blind spot behind which the Kahshinki could stage a sneak attack, and although the sensor fields were still a long way from closing the blind spot, they were a marked improvement over the random patrols currently being used by the UNE to watch for enemy incursions.

Mike Tanner, the engineer on board the SFM067, stepped onto the ship's compact bridge and said, "That's it. The last one is out and away. Let's light 'em off, run a diagnostic, and head for the shed."

"We got a glitch, Mike. Kilo 27 and 28 started firing signals soon as they activated," Janet Rasheed, the crew technician said, looking up from her panel.

"Bullshit!" Mike said, pausing to examine her screen. "Two together is not random; they're detecting something. Switch to tracking mode, set Sol as the origin, and give me the size, speed, and course of what they're tracking."

"Yes, sir," Janet said, her fingers hammering the screen's touch pad. "There it is. It's big, really big. Outbound and traveling sub-light."

"What is it, a rogue asteroid?" Captain Jeb Mitchell called over his shoulder from the pilot's seat.

"Not a chance, Skipper," Mike said. "It's moving way too fast and accelerating."

"Janet, plot its course, let's see where it's going" Jeb said. "Mike, man fire control and bring our weapons system online."

"Aye, aye, sir," Janet replied.

"Come on, Skipper, everything we have is defensive. We're not equipped for interdiction. This ship is classified as a science vessel, a noncombatant."

"Relax, we're just going to have a look, fire off a report, and then head for home."

"Eris, sir. It's headed straight for the planetoid Eris," Janet said.

"Planetoid?" Jeb asked.

"Dwarf planet," Janet replied. "It was reclassified a while back. Has a large elliptical orbit. It's way outside the Kuiper belt right now, pretty much near its maximum distance from the sun."

"Mike, prepare a message with everything we know so far and transmit it as a priority-one, tight-beam encrypted message to sky watch command," Jeb said.

"Aye, aye," Mike said, frowning as he composed and sent the message.

"It's a Goliath-class hauler pulling eight cubes. Transponder is off and she's running dark," Janet cried, thrilled at discovering the clandestine vessel. "Skipper, we're close enough I could perform a resonance scan and tell you exactly what they're hauling. But if I do, they'll know we're here."

"Do it and let me know as soon as you're done."

"Bad idea, Skipper. You know they gotta be pirates," Mike said. "Probably stashing stolen goods on that rock."

"Your concern is noted. The day I can't outrun a Goliath-class transport is the day I resign my commission."

"All done!" Janet cried. "Computer should be able to give us some 3D imaging and composition specifications in just a minute."

"The Goliath's comm just went active. They're calling somebody," Mike said.

"All right, Mike, you can dial the sweat pumps back to slow speed," Jeb said. "I'm breaking off and making distance."

"Composition is mostly water, sodium and... Mike! Jesus, would you look at this. Is this for real?" Janet cried, enlarging an area of the scan and enhancing the image. Mike leaned over her shoulder and examined the grainy black-and-white image as she brought it into focus. As shapes and outlines appeared, the internal bone structures were clearly recognizable.

"Those are bodies stacked like cordwood. There have to be thousands in that one cube alone," Mike said.

"Computer says there are approximately 125,000 units in each cube," Janet said. "That's a half million people, Mike. What would pirates be doing with that many bodies? Where would you even get that many?"

An alarm sounded at Mike's panel. He spun around and charged back to his station to investigate. Jeb knew the sound all too well and immediately commenced evasive maneuvers.

"Incoming missiles!" Mike cried, jumping into his seat. His hands raced over the controls to release countermeasures designed to lure the missiles away. The first one deployed at the same instant the first of ten missiles struck.

Three hours later, a priority-one message arrived at General Ramsey's sky watch command center. Sent using the latest Korlah-designed and human-built faster-than-light messaging system, it arrived a full five hours sooner than the antiquated laser system it replaced would have. The sergeant on watch jumped when a buzzer announced the arrival of the message. Once it was decoded, he loaded it onto a message board and hand-delivered it to a young lieutenant acting as the nightshift duty officer. To the dismay of the sergeant, when the lieutenant finished reading it, he transferred it to a daily brief for the general to read the next morning and handed the blank message board back to the sergeant.

"That was pri-one dispatch, sir. Aren't you going to notify General Ramsey?" the sergeant asked.

"I'm not waking the general because Jeb Mitchell and the nerd patrol saw some pirates on the far side of the system. We're here to watch for an invasion, not babysit innersystem commerce."

"Yes, sir," the sergeant replied, and returned to his station.

Howard Lewis

25 - Reunion

The smell assailing Teela's crown tendrils drove her to consciousness and she awoke on the floor of the Kahshinki transport cocooned in a restraining wrap. Tim was bound alongside her and ten Kahshinki clone soldiers kept vigil in the compartment with them.

"God, your breath stinks," Teela groaned, straining to move away from him.

"I'm sorry, I had shit for breakfast. But my breath is the least of our worries. The Shinks are under attack, fleet fighters, I'm guessing. If they lose this fight we're gonna end up as so much space debris."

"And if they don't... lunch," Teela said.

"Nah, not by this crew. All human clones; redheads up front and big black girls back here with us. I heard Shink raiding parties have been taking prisoners lately. Probably trying to gather intel about our war preparations. The cease-fire is—"

Their conversation was cut off when the transport's engines exploded, throwing them and the clone soldiers against the rear bulkhead. The lights went out along with the artificial gravity, and the soldiers were flailing around weightless trying to get organized when Teela heard as much as felt a ship dock with them. Shouting a mixture of English and Korlah, the Kahshinki soldiers fought desperately to take defensive positions so they could repel the same type of assault they had just conducted.

Up suddenly became down as the attached ship initiated a gravity field and Teela, Tim, and the soldiers tumbled onto the ceiling. With a loud sizzling sound, an opening in the floor above them appeared and a Korlah warrior dropped through. The Kahshinki fired their deadly beams in unison, killing her before her feet touched the ceiling. More Korlah warriors immediately followed, firing carbines whose bullets easily penetrated the Kahshinki soldiers' energy-absorbing armor and didn't require recharging.

Within two minutes, the shooting stopped. Four Korlah warriors and nine Kahshinki clones lay dead. Three Korlah warriors had the single remaining soldier, who was using Tim for a shield, cornered. She brandished her charged weapon at the warriors. The Korlah warriors slung their rifles and drew their blades. They knew she could only kill one of them before the other two drove their blades into her.

"We all done down here?" a familiar voice called out.

"Beth?" Teela cried.

Beth's legs appeared, the steel brace on her left leg glinting in the dim light as she began her descent into the Kahshinki transport. The cornered soldier shifted the aim of her pulse rifle onto Beth.

"Stay out! Go back!" Teela screamed.

The warriors dove in with their blades. The clone soldier's pulse rifle discharged at the same time as the Korlah warrior thrust one blade into the clone's eye and the other blade into her throat.

The pulse beam caught Beth in the right shoulder, spinning her around and out of the gravity field. She tumbled to the floor amidst the pile of carnage.

"Oh, shit! Beth's been shot," someone shouted from above.

"Cut me loose, God damn it!" Teela screamed.

An enormous warrior dropped down, her pulse rifle at the ready. She knelt over Beth and said something.

"No!" Beth clearly said.

"Beth! Beth, are you all right?" Teela cried. When there was no response, she screamed, "Will somebody please cut me loose?" The large warrior pulled her sword and knelt over Teela.

"Ruwaugh," Teela gasped. She recognized the claw-scarred face, and the tattoo on the warrior's cheek confirmed her identity.

Ruwaugh cut through the bindings and pulled Teela to her feet. A scrawny young warrior dropped into the transport and Ruwaugh grabbed her by the shoulder and pulled her to Teela.

"Beth is dying. Neaugh has offered her shell, but Beth is refusing transfer. Convince her that life as a Korlah is not as repulsive as she thinks," Ruwaugh said. Without waiting for a reply, she pushed Teela and Neaugh toward Beth.

Beth's right arm lay four feet away from her body. The beam had vaporized her shoulder socket and a fair potion of her ribcage. Although the flesh was mostly cauterized, a plate-sized pool of blood beneath the wound was rapidly spreading. Pink foam bubbled from the corner of Beth's mouth as she fought to breathe.

Her eyes met Teela's and she shook her head from side to side. Teela knew what she meant.

"Don't you want to know?" Teela asked. "Have I been lying or telling you the truth? This is your opportunity to find out...to explore the afterdeath."

Beth stared into her eyes for a few moments, blinked twice, and passed out.

Teela grabbed Neaugh and looked into her mind. The young warrior was thinking about the spectacle when Beth defeated Ruwaugh and Apoulauh; she had been there and was remembering how this damaged alien warrior had defeated both of the Korlah fighters she idolized. When she learned that Beth had been damaged and could not be repaired, it was she who had approached her and offered her shell. Beth refused, so Ruwaugh hired Neaugh to work as Beth's personal assistant while she continued to pressure Beth into accepting the transfer. It was clear to Teela that Neaugh was eager to join with Beth.

Why are you even considering this? Dade said. *Beth doesn't want to transfer.*

You can't force someone to transfer, Teela answered. *You know that. You are with me because you chose to be. If Beth chooses to die, she will reject Neaugh's invitation.*

"Have you received instruction in transfer?" Teela asked Neaugh. The young warrior looked confused. "Lie down, touch your head to hers," Teela said, guiding her into position. Beth's breathing was barely discernible and Teela knew she would soon pass.

"Repeat these words with your mind," Teela instructed. "*I am the light. I am the path. I am the receptacle for new life. Bring forward your first thoughts.*"

Neaugh began. She tried her best, but she stumbled over the words, failing to reproduce the ancient chant used to guide transfer. Teela looked around the room. This was no transfer chamber, and there was no hood of stone to guide the memories from the dying into the living. If Teela had not succeeded under worse conditions, she would have been certain this would fail.

Beth's passing came without a sound; no groan, no death rattle. She simply stopped breathing. A moment later, Neaugh's breathing paused at the same time as every muscle in her lean body tensed. Ruwaugh and the others stepped back. Teela felt the release like a faint breeze that flowed out and away, only to come whipping back like a vengeful wind. The walls in her mind shook under an onslaught of errant waves of thought, but Teela repelled them as she had Rebecca's. She stepped back in the narrow room until her back was against the bulkhead. The turbulent thoughts rose and ebbed, leaving the room feeling hollow and empty.

When Neaugh opened her eyes, she looked first at Teela and then at Ruwaugh. Ruwaugh held out a hand and Neaugh took it, letting Ruwaugh pull her to her feet and hold her by the shoulders.

"Roche Hah, Bethaugh," Ruwaugh said.

"Roche Hah, Crystaugh," Neaugh replied, pulling Ruwaugh into a tight embrace.

"What's going on?" Tim asked, when Teela finally removed his bindings.

"Miracles. You do believe in miracles, don't you?" Teela said, lost for an explanation.

"Come," Ruwaugh said, rising up through the hole when the gravity field below it was reversed. Neaugh followed her out of the Kahshinki transport and into her attached ship. Teela and Tim joined them.

As the Korlah transport released the damaged Kahshinki vessel and joined several dozen Korlah fighters, Teela discovered that it was Marsha and Catherine's voices she had heard earlier. She would have liked to talk to them, to see what had happened since she last saw them, but they hovered around Neaugh with Ruwaugh. After several minutes of whispered conversation, Neaugh pushed past the girls and approached Teela.

"Lying, you've been lying," Neaugh said.

"What? What are you talking about?" Teela asked.

"When you goaded me into this, you asked me if I wanted to know if you were telling the truth or lying. I did. I really did," Beth said. She gestured as if pointing to herself, and tears welled up in her eyes. "This kid is gone. I know everything she knows, but the person she was is gone. You've been playing me. So who the fuck are you? Teela or Dade?"

"I haven't lied to—"

"Bullshit!" Beth screamed. "I've talked to dozens of crovers. They all say only one survives, the other dies. That's Crystal over there," she said, pointing to Ruwaugh. "I am now Beth, and the sweet dumb kid Neaugh is dead… fucking dead as the body I left behind. So don't give me any bullshit about dual personalities, because I'm living the truth here and now."

Tim slid between them and faced Beth. "Back off," he said quietly.

"Who the fuck are you?" Beth asked.

"I'm Sula's friend. I don't know you. You don't know me. I'll tell you what I do know. This girl believes she shares her body with a guy named Dade. I've listened to them talk in different voices and languages when they thought no one was watching. I don't know if it's real, or if she's just mental. She believes it's real, and that's good enough for me. She just saved my life, so if you got a problem with her, you got a problem with me."

"Thanks, Tim, for backing up your mental friend, but I can handle this," Teela said, pushing him out of the way. "What are you doing here, Beth? How did you find me?"

Beth shifted her glare back to Teela and tried to get her to meet her eyes, but Teela looked away, thinking Beth was challenging her to a fight.

"Your number one fan never stopped tracking your activities. She lost you when you went to Earth. Atmospheric interference, I guess. After you disappeared, I figured you were dead. But Meezra kept scanning for your signal. And low and behold if you didn't come back like a bad rash."

"Meezra was tracking me… how?" Teela asked.

"You got a watch, one given to you by some flyboy?" Beth asked.

Teela pulled the bulky watch from her pocket and looked at it. She had forgotten that Captain Simpson implied it had an internal tracking device.

"Meezra extorted the frequency for that watch from some poor surveillance technician who made the mistake of partying with some of her operatives. He let it slip that the military was tracking the Korlah ambassadress. Once she heard that, she kept digging. She used videos of the sexual transgressions of key personnel as leverage to get that frequency along with other sensitive information. After the signal was lost, the military gave up tracking you, but Meezra didn't."

Teela looked at the watch, angry that Meezra was still collecting the details of her life, and then headed over to a waste unit. She would have dropped it in if Tim hadn't snatched it from her hand.

"If you don't want it, hell, I'll take it. This thing corrects for hyper-light time distortion. These sell for more than fifteen thousand credits new. I can easily sell this for five or ten thousand. That's money I can use."

"It's yours," Teela said. She wondered how many new souvenirs were in the little smut dealer's collection. "Beth, I appreciate that you rescued us. And it pains me to ask, but can you take us to Crossroads?"

Crystal put her hand firmly on Beth's shoulder and pulled her to one side. "This is my ship and my rescue, Teela—Dade, Sula, or whatever name you want go by. I don't care. Anyone capable of breaking into Galactic Security Systems' headquarters and stealing Lucinda's yacht is a person of interest to me and my collective. I could use someone like you."

"I don't think that's a good—" Beth started to say, but Crystal frowned and clamped down on her shoulder with extended claws. "Ouch! Damn it, Crystal," Beth cried.

"Please don't interrupt me, Beth," Crystal growled. "We've talked about this, remember?" Looking back at Teela, Crystal's frown quickly returned to as pleasant a smile as her scarred face was capable of.

"If you were about to offer me a job, I can't express how grateful I am," Teela lied. "But I have plans to get my son and go to New Korlah."

Crystal's smile took on a strained look. "A very well-paid job, in fact. But I respect your choice. Over two years in a cramped pod with a young child is a very bold decision. Not a journey I would want to take. Well... no matter. Until then, you and your friend are welcome. We're already on our way to Crossroads; I have business there. In fact, if you can manage to find the time, I would be honored to have you and your friend attend the first concert of the Metal Maidens' system tour."

"Fuck'n-A awesome, Metal Maidens concert!" Marsha and Catherine sang.

"We'll try to make it," Teela lied.

Deep within the American asteroid base AB1, Jason Ramsey, the newly appointed UNE operational commander, was deeply engrossed in developing Operation Iron Shield. It was now Brigadier General Ramsey's responsibility to ensure the personnel and equipment under him could keep the Sol side of the asteroid belt referred to as the inner system safe from invasion. The defense forces under his command had grown to more than one hundred bases, over ten thousand KF1 Ghost-class fighters, and one hundred KC2 Wrath-class destroyers. Everything was designed to intercept and destroy enemy craft before it reached Earth. He was calculating how much the logistical support for the exercise would impact his budget when the intercom buzzed.

Budget! How the hell can those number-crunching bean counters even put a price on what I'm doing out here? he thought. The buzzer sounded again before he pressed the talk button.

"What!" he said.

"Sorry, sir, we have an incoming call for you on a secure channel," the general's aide announced.

"Well, decrypt it and bring it in."

"It's an audible, sir. You'll need to take it in the booth."

"Oh, for Christ's sake!" Ramsey cried. He hated the audible messaging system. With a twenty-seven-second lag while the message was encrypted, shot to Earth on a laser signal, decrypted, received, and then responded to, it made voice conversations painfully tedious. "Gotta be McCormick. That bastard loves to talk. All right... patch it through."

He entered a small booth and closed the soundproof door, then sat down and waited. A red phone hung on the wall underneath a red light. He found the whole concept of a secure room in the center of a remote base in space ludicrous. The red light came on and he picked up the phone, expecting to hear a message intro, usually a short statement indicating the caller's name and location. After a few moments of hearing only soft static, he spoke.

"Hello, this is Brigadier General Jason Ramsey, Earth Station Alpha Bravo One." He expected nearly a one-minute delay. When a woman's soft voice replied, he was surprised.

"Hello, Jason," she said.

"Who is thi—" he started to say. His expression went blank and his mouth remained partially open.

"This is Rebecca. Shawlmon needs your help." The words came to him not as sounds, but as thoughts linked through the military communications systems and satellites, through the wires and receivers, funneled directly into his mind. He sat there without moving for ten minutes while Rebecca manipulated his thoughts and programmed the actions he would take on her behalf, as she had done with countless others. This was not the first time Rebecca had used Jason Ramsey; his meteoric rise in rank had in fact been guided by her efforts.

When he hung up the phone, he proceeded to the station command center. He burst into the room and started issuing orders.

"Captain Jenkins, recall all off-duty personnel. Riley, I want every available ship in the belt prepped, rolled out, and ready to launch. Major Westley, I'm assuming command of the Craven; transfer operational command as soon as I'm on board."

More than a few eyebrows were raised, yet no one questioned his orders. It was well known that he'd testified against General Hargrave during the Korlah war crime trials—testimony that resulted in General Hargrave's dismissal. It was apparent that Jason had friends in high places. Everyone was aware that opposing him had proven detrimental to the careers of those who tried. And now, by his command, in less than three hours eighty percent of the entire inner-system defense force was mustered to intercept a yet-unnamed threat. Left behind, still sitting unread in the general's inbox, were the system updates, requests awaiting approval, and a priority-one dispatch from one Captain Jeb Mitchell.

Overall, the trip to Crossroads aboard Ruwaugh's transport was cramped but uneventful. Tim slept while Teela sat quietly. She studied the behavior of Beth and Crystal, amazed at how the mannerisms and speech patterns of their human donors were evident in their Korlah hosts. Beth sulked in a corner while Crystal and the girls worked on the lyrics for a song. Seeing the fearsome Ruwaugh laughing and giggling with Marsha and Catherine was somewhat unsettling; the idea that Crystal had become the person who killed her provoked thoughts and questions that Teela would have liked to ask. She desperately wanted to probe Crystal's mind, but was unwilling to risk offending her host; she settled on basking in the cheerful scene playing out before her.

26 - Animus

The Betsy made it safely from Earth to the rendezvous point where
Bill collected little Dade from the mercenaries he'd hired. From

there it was a short trip to Jupiter and the moon known as Crossroads. After a short wait, Bill parked the Betsy in a spot left by a departing freighter. Fiona arrived shortly thereafter. Her supply of missiles were depleted and her sleek hull showed signs of battle. Bill had her return to her mooring inside Betsy's hull and grabbed his tools.

Once he finished repairing Fiona, he cleaned his hands and returned to the Betsy's control room to check for messages. From all indications, it appeared that Teela had evaded Lucinda's ships and escaped. He checked his watch for the third time in ten minutes. Fiona had been back for more than four hours, and still no sign of Teela.

Shyron, Shawaugh, Challmara, and Smiley made an excursion into Crossroad's business center, then Shawaugh and Challmara hopped a transport headed to the Armageddon. Shyron and Smiley returned to the Betsy with fish tacos and joined Julie, Cooper, and little Dade in the recreation room.

"How's our young guest doing?" Bill asked as he entered the room.

"He's adorable. God, he looks so much like Dade," Julie said. The little boy was in her lap playing with her necklace.

"He hasn't spoken a word," Cooper said, "but he looks to be three or four. Shouldn't he be talking by now?"

"He'll talk when he's ready," Julie said. She tried to give child a hug, but he pushed her away.

"He is speaking to you with his mind," Shyron said.

"Are you serious? Like Teela?" Bill asked.

"No. Rebecca has been speaking to him with her mind his entire life. He never had to learn to speak; she can hear his thoughts," Shyron said.

"What's he saying?" Julie asked.

"He wants Rebecca. He believes she is his mother," Shyron said. "He likes you, Julie. You remind him of her."

"Oh, Lord! I certainly hope not," Julie cried.

The ship's proximity alert sounded a shrill, nerve-grating whistle, and Bill was quick to silence it. The monitor showed three people coming up Betsy's stairs to board, and Bill recognized

Teela. He figured the man wearing ill-fitting pink pants and a frilled white shirt must be her friend Tim, but he didn't recognize the Korlah warrior with them. He met them at the hatch with a cocked pistol in his hand.

"You made it," Bill said.

"I had some help," Teela said. "You have my son? Where is he?" She nearly bumped into him, but stopped when Bill did not step aside to let her in.

"He's inside, safe and sound. Ya gonna introduce me to your friends?" he asked, eyeing the Korlah warrior suspiciously.

"I want... to see... my son," Teela growled.

Bill noted her crown tendrils beginning to rise and knew where this was going. "Okay, you go ahead," he said, and allowed her to push past. "Ah, Mr. Masters, I recognize you now. Nice outfit. Your flatulent friend told me what happened to my ship. Don't worry about it, I'm sure we can work something out. Come on in."

Speaking Korlah, Bill addressed the warrior. "Who are you? I don't know you."

"Well, Bill, ya do and ya don't," the warrior answered in English. "This is kind of embarrassing, because I'm sure you hate my guts. And I deserve your scorn. But I don't care for rock and roll, and just quit my job as a roadie. Teela seems to think you might have some real work for me."

Bill's eyes narrowed and slowly he began to smile. The smile grew into a toothy grin.

"So's ya'll wants to work fo Blackbone, does ya? I's sho do like Korlah girls. You be in luck, cause I has big job fo yo."

"I knew this was a mistake," Beth said.

Bill grabbed her by the arm before she could turn away and pulled her inside. "Come on, Beth, I'm kidding. I never figured you for going crover. How do like being a noodle noggin?" He blew on her crown tendrils, knowing how much his Korlah wives hated it.

"Stop that!" she said, shaking her head. Bill laughed.

The little boy froze when Teela entered the room. She tried to read his thoughts, but discovered he was able to block her probe. She called to him, but he turned away and clung to Julie's neck as though he was terrified of her.

"It's me... Mommy," Teela pleaded.

The child turned and glared at her. *Not my mommy, not my mommy*, he shouted with his mind. He burst into tears and began screaming hysterically. When Teela walked toward him, he pulled free of Julie and ran to hide behind Cooper. Teela followed, and his screams turned to shrieks of terror.

"Leave him alone! You're scaring him," Julie cried.

Teela dropped to her knees and tried to catch him as he ran by. Dodging her desperate grasps, he ran to Beth and began trying to claw his way up her legs. Beth picked him up and he wrapped his arms around her neck and buried his face in her shoulder.

"I'm your mommy," Teela sobbed, covering her face to hide the tears flowing down her face.

Shyron knelt next to Teela and put her arm around her. She tried to impart feelings of comfort and happiness to dispel the waves of grief and despair that were flowing from Teela. Unable to break through the mental barricade, she spoke to her aloud.

"The Oracle has been shaping this child's mind since his birth. It is likely that he has been conditioned to fear contact with other mind-talkers."

"Why does he like *her*?" Teela cried, pointing an accusing finger at Beth. The child had already stopped crying and was playfully tugging on one of Beth's fangs.

"She is dressed as a warrior. Rebecca has been using warriors for both his and her protection. They have been his nursery mothers, a symbol of friendship and trust," Shyron said.

"Something's happening outside," Bill announced.

A half dozen ships were cued up to exit the hangar, and foot traffic indicated that more were preparing to leave. Without waiting to find out why, Bill began powering up the ship's systems.

"Smiley, did you get a hold of Denster?" Tim asked.

"Yeah, all our inventory has been sold. He's on his way to pick us up. He'll be here tomorrow. We can do an Earth run for more supplies and get back to business as usual. I've had my fill of this good Samaritan bullshit," Smiley said.

"Tomorrow? Damn. Well, we can crash at Eddie's. I'm sure he won't mind," Tim said.

"Eddie's not there. His shop is locked up and no one's seen him for more than a week," Smiley said.

"Damn!" Tim cried. "How many credits you got?"

"Not enough for a room on this overpriced rock, but I think we'd be better off sleeping on the dock than going for a ride with this bunch. I've had enough fun… you know what I mean," Smiley said.

"Yes, I do," Tim said. "Time to quit saving the universe and get back to making some money. I got a watch we can hock; it ought to fetch more than enough for a couple of rooms and a meal or two. Gimme a minute."

Tim went to the control room to talk to Bill and saw all the activity in the hangar. "What's going on? Why is everyone leaving?" he asked.

"Thousands of inner-system ships outbound away from Earth. I think it would be best to leave the area," Bill said.

"Outbound from Earth? So they're UNE. Where are they heading?" Tim asked.

"It looks like they're heading here," Bill said.

"Here? Why the hell would they be coming here?" Tim said, realizing even as he said it what the probable answer would be. He looked at Teela and the child.

"Exactly," Bill said, seeing Tim make the connection. "I may have underestimated the influence Rebecca and the Church of Shawlmon have."

"Listen, Bill, Sula… uh… Teela, is family to me. I love her like a sister… Hell, I owe her my life." Tim was feeling guilty about what he was about to say. "My crew and I are getting off. We're gonna sit this one out. I know I owe you for that ship of yours I trashed. I'll pay you back; you have my word."

"I understand," Bill said, pausing to face Tim. "You've been a good friend to Teela. As far as I'm concerned, your debt to me is clear. If I'm still in business when the dust settles, your go-fast and the deposit you left will be waiting for you at the hub. If any ship can slip out of here, my Betsy can. You can leave knowing Teela and her son are in good hands."

Tim shook Bill's hand and gave him a nod of appreciation, understanding from Bill's grim expression that he was less confident than he sounded. Tim headed for the hatch and waved to Smiley to follow.

"Come on, Shy. Time to go, girl," Smiley said.

"You go, Smiley man. I will come later," Shyron said, remaining at Teela's side. Smiley looked shocked.

"We gotta go now!" Tim shouted from the hatch.

You are my only male, and I your only female. Save your pleasure for me, and I will save mine for you, Shyron imparted to Smiley. He grinned and waved like a schoolboy and blew her a kiss as he ran for the hatch.

Bill had the Betsy in the air before the hatch was shut. He maneuvered the craft into the lengthy queue for the hangar's single airlock. While waiting his turn, he studied his scanners. The first of the incoming ships had broken away to pursue departing ships; the rest began to form a blockade around Crossroads. By the time he piloted the Betsy out of the airlock and away from the surface, any hope of slipping away without a fight had evaporated. He was looking for a weak spot in the array of UNE fighters surrounding the moon when the first message lit up Betsy's console with a direct ship-to-ship hail.

"Unmarked Korlah destroyer, hold your position and prepare to be boarded."

The demand was sent in Korlah and English, audio and text formats. Bill scrapped his plan to jump out of the area and opted for confrontation instead. He locked onto the UNE frequency and activated the Betsy's defense system. The ship's thirty-four rapid-fire particle-beam gun turrets and twenty articulated pulse cannons energized and swiveled to take aim at the approaching UNE ships. He responded to the demand with a Korlah text message.

"This vessel is the property of the Rahfoon medical and shipping Korlah collective. Your demand is a violation of existing agreements of mutual cooperation. Any vessel that attempts to dock without permission will be fired upon."

Bill took manual control of Betsy's forward pulse cannon and prepared to fire a shot across the bow of the approaching transport. To his relief it slowed, came to a stop, and held its position. Movement among the other ships indicated that although they were taking his threat seriously, they were not backing off. A UNE destroyer with all of its weapons rolled out and energized moved through the UNE ranks and took a broadside position directly in front of the Betsy.

"Rebecca's behind this," Teela said as she entered the control room. "I feel her. She has linked her mind with my son's. Through his eyes she sees us, hears us, and knows where we are. She is controlling someone in the UNE, someone in charge—through them she is directing these forces. Wait!" Teela cried. "We can beat her at her own game. Fiona, are you listening?"

"Yes, Teela," Fiona crackled over the bridge speaker.

"Could you run this blockade, get out of here, and get to the Armageddon safely?" Teela asked.

"I have evaluated the quantity and types of vessels, their available weapons status and current deployment hierarchy. I have calculated that I have an eighty percent probability for successfully passing through the blockade and evading pursuit," Fiona said.

"Fiona, prepare to launch. Bill, stall them as long as you can. I have a plan." Teela darted out of the control room.

"You better make it fast," Bill shouted. "They're bunching up pretty tight out there. Fiona's gonna have some trouble getting through, I don't care what she says. Tight is tight and they're gonna shoot if she runs."

When Teela tried to take little Dade from Beth, he began screaming again, but as soon as she stepped back, he stopped and stared at her. Not like a frightened child, but as though he despised her. She felt Rebecca's presence and realized it was Rebecca who was glaring at her through the child's eyes.

Beth, I need your help to keep Rebecca from taking my son. Will you help me? Teela said directly into Beth's mind, careful to ensure her telepathic message could not be heard by Rebecca. Beth narrowed her eyes and, after a moment, nodded.

Take the fighter docked to this ship. It has a computer that will do all the flying and fighting. Take my son to Nerhala in the Korlah section of the Armageddon. Ask her on my behalf to shield the child from harm, as she once shielded me. He can't know where he is going. If he knows, Rebecca will know. Will you do this for me?

Beth looked at the little boy's furrowed brow and the intense glare he was directing at Teela. She cocked her head as though weighing the evidence while making her decision. Again she nodded her head.

"Come on, little Dade, let's play a game," Beth said, lifting the child high in the air and flying him around in a circle. "Away we go! Up and down, around and around." She flew him around the room and down the corridor towards Fiona's berth, his squeals of delight fading in the distance.

"Shyron, I need your help," Teela said as she entered the control room. "Fiona, let me know when Beth and the boy are onboard. Black out the windows so they can't see out. Better yet, take them down into the cabin. Release from your mooring and wait until the Betsy moves. When she does, you remain stationary. You take off after the UNE fighters are busy chasing us."

Teela pulled Shyron to the front of the control room and held her by the shoulders and pointed her toward the UNE destroyer blocking their path. Shyron offered no resistance, opening her mind and allowing Teela to use her as a conduit to focus and amplify her telepathic energy at the destroyer. The sources of thought appeared to her as glowing orbs that floated within the hull of the ship. One by one, she explored their thoughts, looking for the one she would use.

"Ramsey!" Teela cried, and opened her eyes. "That prick. That rat bastard is behind this."

"The pilot? The one you kept me from killing?" Bill asked.

262

"Yeah, my mistake. Rebecca has had her claws in him before, I just had no idea he was capable of something like this. Get ready to bust a move when I tell you."

"You know we won't get far?" Bill said.

"Don't have to," Teela said. "They won't try to destroy us. They want the child. We'll draw their attention away from Fiona and then surrender. While they are busy boarding us, Fiona should be able to slip away. Get ready."

General Ramsey nervously paced the bridge of the Craven while he impatiently waited for the special forces unit to arrive and hopefully bring this hostage crisis to a conclusion. He realized that he was rapidly running out of time. His superiors on Earth were demanding an explanation for his actions, and his silence would soon be taken as confirmation that he was acting without authority. Although he was certain his actions were justified, he knew that supporting the Church of Shawlmon would not be an acceptable excuse.

Jason! Jason Ramsey! Jason Jason Jason!

Someone was screaming his name. He spun around, trying to see where it was coming from. It was so loud it hurt his ears.

"Who is that?" Ramsey demanded. "Stop shouting, that's an order! Stop it!"

The entire complement of the bridge was staring in disbelief at their commanding officer, who had his hands over his ears and was screaming like a lunatic. The weapons officer was the first to notice the Betsy had turned.

"General Ramsey, the enemy ship is moving," he cried. When the Betsy darted forward, he prepared the ship's weapons to fire. "Your orders, sir."

It was a full minute before Ramsey realized what was happening. Unable to hear his own words, he ranted his orders like a belligerent drunk.

"Get on that ship! Disabling shots. Missiles, fire the damn missiles, damn it, fire!"

Ready for the order, the weapons officer launched a volley of six missiles into the heat trail produced by Betsy's engines.

Designed to follow the trail to its source and explode, they shot out of their launch tubes and raced toward her. Bill launched countermeasures that diverted three of the missiles from their targets, and the other three were destroyed by Betsy's rear turrets within a few dozen feet of the engine ports. The explosions rocked the Betsy and could be felt on the bridge of the Craven. Betsy's engines shut down and the shouting in Ramsey's head stopped.

"Sir, incoming message: they are surrendering," the communications officer announced.

"Send in the boarding party," Ramsey ordered.

"Sir, small craft moving away slowly, I got no bio signs on board. It's either automated or has scan shields," the weapons control officer said.

Jason, you have no authority to do this. You are being manipulated by Rebecca. Just like she manipulated you when you abandoned your post to rescue her, Teela said. Her words came to him as clearly as if they were spoken, and he spun around to look for the speaker. In an instant, he knew what was happening.

"And what do you think you're doing? You're manipulating me right now. That's what!" Ramsey shouted.

"Sir?" the weapons officer asked.

"They're in my head, it's a distraction," Ramsey said, shaking his head. "The small ship. That's the one we want. Stop it. Disable it now."

"Missiles away," the weapons officer said. "Sir! She just jumped to sub-light."

"Get that ship, damn it. Everything we have after it—now!" Ramsey screamed.

Ramsey's boarding party searched the Betsy in under ten minutes, then handcuffed Bill, Smiley, Tim, Teela, and Shyron and packed them into the Craven's brig, a tiny cell with a toilet, a bunk, and a stout steel door that locked from the outside. They all stood for the first few minutes, unsure if this tiny cell was where they were actually going to be held during the twelve-hour trip back to Earth. Finally, Cooper lowered the bunk for Julie to sit on. Soon, Julie, Cooper, Bill and Shyron were sitting on the narrow bed while Teela stood at the window in the door studying the room beyond.

A sudden weakness in her knees took her by surprise and Teela clung to the edge of the cell window to keep from collapsing. It was as if a piece of her soul had been torn away. A feeling of unease about her son's safety filled her. As quickly as it came, the weakness passed. She closed her eyes and strained to find the feeling she had followed since his birth. It was now absent.

Mentally exhausted, she turned to Shyron for assistance. Expecting the request, Shyron met her gaze, and with a thought, declined it.

"Something has happened. I need to know that my son is all right," Teela said.

"This thing you do. When you use me, it takes something from me. It leaves a darkness that frightens me," Shyron said. "This shell you and the Oracle want so badly. When I looked into his mind, I found a similar darkness, a place where if I were to look too closely, I believe I would find something that does not want to be seen."

"He's just a little boy. Whatever you see or think you see was probably planted by Rebecca. Once free of her influence, my son will be fine," Teela said, wishing she believed her own words.

An alarm sounded and a yellow light began flashing outside the cell window.

"That's not a good sound," Cooper said.

"Battle stations, that's the battle stations alarm. And you're right, it is usually not a good thing," Bill said.

The bolts in the cell door released with a loud click and the door was yanked open.

"Out! Everyone out," the Marine guard shouted. "Please, move aside, over here," he said, directing them against the wall outside the cell. Three other Marines pulled General Ramsey kicking and screaming into the room, threw him into the cell, and locked the door. An officer entered the room and walked directly over to Bill.

"Mr. Jacks, I am Major Westley. I apologize, sir, for the actions of General Ramsey. I have confirmed that he has been acting without orders or authority in this matter and I have relieved him of command. You and your crew are free to go."

"Why are you at battle stations? Are you under attack?" Bill asked.

"Earth has been attacked, sir," Major Westley said. "All available forces are being recalled. As soon as I get you off my ship I will be joining them."

"What is the status of the ship I dispatched?" Bill asked.

"I'm sorry, sir. The ship was destroyed. There were no survivors."

Teela screamed and charged Major Westley. Bill grabbed her and pulled her into a bear hug. He held her tightly until she quit thrashing and her screams of anguish faded to sobs of despair. When she finally collapsed in his arms, he carried her like a child back to the Betsy.

The Craven and her fighter escort departed shortly before Bill had the Betsy on a course for the Collective Business Hub. While en route, Bill and the others watched in disbelief as more and more reports from Earth described how a massive Kahshinki force had crushed the few defense forces Ramsey left behind and attacked Earth. Descriptions of destruction on a global scale followed. Major cities had been attacked and were burning, hundreds of millions of people were dead. Kahshinki invasion forces were reported to be on Earth and actively digging in for battle.

Bill, Cooper, and Julie watched the reports from Earth from a booth by the kitchen. Teela sat apart from them and avoided conversation. Shyron could see as much as sense Teela's anguish; her attempts to console Teela and make plans for their future were curtly rebuffed. Bill offered to house Cooper and Julie until the situation on Earth stabilized. When Shyron realized that Teela was not interested in joining Tim's crew, she contacted Smiley and made arrangements to get picked up at the hub.

Bill kept his distance from Teela and allowed her to sulk undisturbed in the back corner of the recreation room. It wasn't until after they were docked at the hub and everyone else had left that Teela approached Bill on the dock outside the Betsy's hatch.

"Bill, I need a ship," she said.

"You know you got me and the Betsy. Where we going?"

"No, Bill. I need to be alone. This was a mistake. It was all a mistake. I don't have to read your mind or anyone else's to know what everyone is thinking. This was my fault. I caused this. My actions created the conditions that set this apocalypse in motion. It was me, I... " Her voice choked and her crown tendrils blanched.

"It was not your fault!" Bill said, his baritone voice echoing in the hangar. "Rebecca caused this, not you. You know this attack was inevitable. They were just waiting for an opportunity. Not your fault."

"Will you give me a ship?" Teela asked.

"No. You're staying here with me until you get your head right. After that..."

Teela turned and walked away, down the dock toward a group of businessmen who were waiting for a shuttle. Bill followed her, arriving at the tail end of her conversation with a thin older man in a dark-blue suit.

"Well, honey, we don't need a mechanic, and Sam here speaks fluent Korlah, so that leaves the part about you being willing to do anything for a ride. You're in luck, sugar. I'll cover your fare for this ride if you give each of us a ride when we get to Crossroads. Deal?" The man offered Teela his hand.

"No deal," Bill bellowed, and intercepted Teela's hand.

"Hey! Oh, excuse me, Mr. Jacks, but the young lady and I are about to conclude a business agreement," the man said.

"No, you weren't. What you were about to do is get your dumb ass and whatever company you represent banned from doing business with my collective."

"You have no right—" Teela started to say.

"You win," Bill said.

He ignored the businessman's apology and walked Teela back toward the Betsy.

"You insist on leaving. Okay, I'm not gonna stop you. But damn it, Dade, if you're still in there, whoring is not the answer. You gotta help this girl make smart choices," Bill said.

"Smart choices? Are you serious? There is only one choice now, Bill: survival. The only ones who are going to survive what is coming are those who are willing to do anything to stay alive. We both spent our lives doing whatever it took to stay alive. I will do whatever I have to do to get a ship. If it means fucking those three assholes to get to a place where I can find work, then that's what I will do."

"You said you were gonna help me save our kids. Little Dade wasn't your only little boy, you know."

"He was *my* little boy. He grew inside me. I felt it when he died. You know you don't need my help to save the children. You never did. Beth was right, I'm poison to everyone around me. What I have to do, I have to do without you or anyone else to worry about."

"Why you gotta go alone? If you don't want me, I can get some people to go with you."

"Dade and I will never be alone. If one of us dies, we die together, not alone. This is about having no more regrets."

"You can have whatever ship you want. What do you need?"

"What has the best combination of cargo space and firepower?"

"KC1 Curse-class armored military transport," Bill answered without hesitation. "Three turrets, latest combination of electromagnetic and high-density tunganium armor plating. Absorption array melded with a stealth system that renders it nearly invisible to scanning and tracking systems. Sixty-plus hyper-light system and an auxiliary—"

"Sold! Jesus, Bill, you are the consummate salesman. I trust it comes with instructions," Teela said.

"It has a FIONA system. Not like the Gitch model, but very sharp and much less likely to develop an attitude."

"Thank you," Teela said. She pulled Bill into an embrace, studied his face for a moment, and then gave him a passionate kiss on the lips. When she released him, Bill's complexion flushed crimson.

"One more small, special request," she said.

"After that, how can I refuse?" he said with a grin.

"I'd like some nose art on the ship. Can you do that?"

"Nose art on a transport. Seriously?"

Teela winced, realizing how stupid she must sound, but it was something she wanted to do to honor Beth.

"You bet," Bill said, correctly reading her expression. "I have some very talented artists who do exactly that for the fighter jocks. What'd you have in mind?"

"*The Ms. Porter*," Teela said.

"Yeah, I like it," Bill chuckled. "I got just the right illustration in mind to go with the name. The Ms. Porter it shall be."

Three shifts later, Teela departed the collective hub in a brand-new military transport. The small talk and goodbyes danced around what she and Bill both knew in their hearts: the war was upon them, and if Korlah history had any merit, it was unlikely that either of them would survive.

The Ms. Porter was over halfway to Crossover when Dade broke the silence.

"I know what you did back there. I know what that kiss was about," he said.

"Do you? Were you jealous, as when Julie kissed him?" Teela replied.

"I was jealous when she kissed Cooper. It was you who were jealous when she kissed me, my face... I felt it."

"I did not like that you wanted to touch mouths with her. I wanted you to know that I can do this kissing thing better than she can," Teela said.

"You don't need to worry. It's over. She's over me and I'm over her. It's all about you and me now, and that's all that really matters."

27 - Time

"What happened, where'd they go?" Beth said. The scanners were empty and the threat alarms that were screaming a few seconds before were now silent. She craned her neck to look over her shoulder at the clear starfield behind them. "Where are they?" she shouted. Little Dade jumped and stared at her wide-eyed.

"My indications do not support this outcome. I am working on a hypothesis," Fiona replied.

"Hypothesis? Are you serious? You were about to get your ass handed to you by more fricking UNE interceptors than I could count. How many missiles hit us? Jesus, I thought for sure I'd be sucking vacuum," Beth said.

"The missiles did not actually hit us. After my countermeasures were depleted and my aft shielding compromised, I directed all remaining power to my fourth drive. The system consumed the power but produced no discernible change in speed," Fiona said.

"I'm not following you. You have a fourth gear—that doesn't make you go faster. So what did it do? Disintegrate them?"

"No, not them, us," Fiona said.

"I don't think so. I'm feeling pretty solid," Beth said. She rapped on the cockpit window with her fist. "Nope, not disintegrated."

"I don't know of a word to describe the physical effect. From comparisons of my previous testing and the readings recorded during this transition, I've determined that when the hyper-light plasma is routed through the particle acceleration sphere, it does not change speed; it alters the rate of time distortion. Where we are did not change; the time that we are here is what has changed," Fiona said.

"Yeah, yeah, I know. Time at hyper-light is shorter than system time. I understand time distortion, but it doesn't explain where the interceptors went," Beth said.

"You do not understand." Fiona slowed the ship down and brought it to a stop.

"Why are we stopping?"

"We have arrived at the coordinates for the Armageddon," Fiona replied.

"All right... are you lost, or just incompetent? The Armageddon won't be mobile for months. It can't go anywhere. Since it's not here. Where the fuck is it? This kid smells like he crapped his pants. I don't have time for this shit."

"My navigation system has identified multiple celestial and planetary anomalies that indicate that this is the right place, but not the right time. According to my calculations, the Armageddon will arrive at these coordinates in approximately fifty-two point seven solar years."

"What? What do you mean?" Beth stammered. "Are you saying we went back in time? Like... time travel, back?"

"Yes. All evidence supports this hypothesis," Fiona said.

"There you go again with the hypothesis crap. Did we or did we not... what... travel fifty something years back in time? What evidence? Forget it, just tell me you can get us back."

"None of the damage I have sustained should affect my propulsion systems. We will not be able to attempt a reversal until my energy cell has been restored to nominal values. The difficulty lies in restoring power. I was constructed without an onboard reactor to save weight, and without a recharging station, I will need to use my emergency solar array to collect and store power. Evidence suggests that a positive time shift will occur when hyper-light plasma is routed in the reverse direction at the same rate as that used initially. I believe one direction creates a negative distortion and the other a positive distortion. Depending on the—"

"God damn it! Can you get us back? Yes or no, I don't care how you come up with the answer, just answer the fricking question," Beth cried.

"Unknown. Based on available data, the probability for success is approximately sixty-four percent," Fiona replied.

"I'll take that as a yes. How long before you will be ready to try?"

"With energy conservation measures, I estimate forty-four hours, twen—"

"Got it! Don't need the minutes and seconds. Don't care. Just do it. I'm taking this little stink bomb below to see if I can figure out how to change his shorts."

Beth took little Dade down into the tiny cabin in the center of Fiona's fuselage. The disposable diaper he was wearing was saturated and filled to capacity, and feces was oozing out around his waist and thighs. Finding something to use as a replacement diaper became Beth's top priority. She found some towels and tee shirts in the closet and used the bunk as a changing table as she removed the reeking diaper and shoved it into the waste disposal at arm's length. She was unsure the unit could handle the wad of plastic, padding, urine, and feces, and was relieved when it disappeared with a loud crackling sound. Using a towel, she'd just started to clean him off when artificial gravity was suddenly lost and little Dade began peeing. The urine sprayed into the air and hit Beth in the face. She blocked it with her hand and the droplets collected and formed a few marble-sized amber orbs that floated in the air like little planets. The child laughed and tried to grab them.

"You little shit monster!" Beth growled. "God damn it, Fiona, what happened to the gravity?"

"Energy conservation measures have been implemented. I can restore gravity, but power restoration efforts will be prolonged. Would you like gravity restored?"

"No! Not if it means spending another minute with this little turd," Beth said.

Little Dade grinned at her and giggled.

"You little bastard, you're way too old to be crapping your pants" He giggled again. You think this is funny?" She folded a tee shirt around his bottom and used the sleeves like a belt to secure the makeshift diaper in place, pulling the sleeves tight with a little more force than needed. Little Dade's smile turned into a scowl. Beth scowled back.

"Damn if you don't look like your daddy when you're mad," Beth said. Feeling guilty, she loosened the sleeves a bit.

Little Dade's frown faded. He held his right arm out, and with his fingers curled like claws he brought it back across his chest.

"Row Aw," he said.

Beth's surprised expression amused him and he grinned.

"Kid, if your first words are the Korlah warrior salute, well… that's just plain sad. Roche Hah!" she said, returning his salute. Little Dade giggled and gave her a hug and a wet kiss on the cheek. "All right, I forgive you for pissing in my face," she said, and patted his back.

During the next few hours they ate and played together. The boy loved floating in zero gravity. His favorite game was something Beth called bird baby, where he would flap his arms and Beth would give him a gentle push. Flying ahead, Beth would turn and catch him at the far end of the cabin. Back and forth he sailed until they were both exhausted. Lashed to the bunk by lanyards, they both slept.

Beth was the first to wake up—not because she had slept long enough, but because she had a thought that would not let her sleep. Not wanting to disturb the sleeping boy, she left him strapped to the bunk and rode the pilot's chair up to the cockpit, where, to her surprise, she found that they were above the Earth.

The swirling clouds and glistening ocean filled the view on the starboard side. The view was partially blocked by Fiona's solar panels, which extended from the tips of her little wings like long arms, reaching out and away toward the aft end of the ship.

"Hello, Beth, did you get enough rest?" Fiona asked after a few minutes.

"Huh? Ah, not really. Couldn't sleep," Beth said, keeping her eyes on the breathtaking view of the Pacific Ocean and the Hawaiian Islands below. "What're we doing here? Won't they shoot at us or something?

"Earth will not possess the technology to detect me for another forty years, which is the reason I am here; there is another option for restoring power. One that will take substantially less time than using solar energy."

"Okay, you got my attention."

"There is a power-generating station near Lake Michigan that is currently transmitting high-voltage electrical power through above-ground transmission lines at levels that meet my needs. I can utilize the electromagnetic fields produced by these lines to charge my power cell in less than thirty minutes."

"You're gonna suck their power for thirty minutes and no one will notice you? Your stealth technology may be good, but it doesn't make you invisible."

"The area around this plant is sparsely populated. I estimate that even if we are seen, there is a—"

"Okay, okay. No estimations, please. Sounds good. Listen, I got a couple questions for you. Keep your answers short," Beth said. "I had an idea. If this time-travel thing works like you say, and we can go forward and back in time, I could go back and warn myself not to get shot, or not to get abducted in the first place, right?"

"The race that invented this device disappeared hundreds of thousands of years ago, at the same time that its use was discontinued. This would seem to indicate that there are severe consequences associated with its use. I recommend we return to as close to our original time as possible."

"How close do you think you can you get us to a specific date and time?"

"I believe I could do it to within a few microseconds. But to ensure zero possibility of overlap, I recommend maintaining a fifteen-minute gap."

"What's so bad about overlapping?"

"Theoretical physics predict many negative possibilities," Fiona said. "Testing them without preparation and planning is not advisable."

"Got it. Fifteen minutes, no overlaps. Okay, Fiona, here's what I wanna do... "

28 - Yesterday

It took a little over ten minutes for the two 600-foot solar sheets to fold up like accordions and retract into Fiona's stubby wings. The trip east was much faster. With a burst of sub-light speed they were over Michigan in a few seconds. Fiona activated her visual camouflage before dropping six miles straight down to hover over the thick electrical transmission lines a half mile from the St. Clair generating station. Enveloped by the magnetic fields produced by the power lines, Fiona used the ship like a conductor. The magnetic lines of flux created an electrical potential that her pulse absorption array funneled into her power cell. The resulting line losses forced the power plant's operators to respond by boosting output to its maximum of 1,500 megawatts to meet the demand. Voltage fluctuations dimmed lights and tripped breakers and transformers in the greater Detroit metropolitan area.

A foreman working in the transformer yard called his manager to report a large glowing object hovering above the station's power lines. A few minutes later, the station manager called the Wurtsmith Air Force Base to inquire if there were any military craft conducting operations nearby.

"My power cell has achieved a nominal charge. Conditions have changed and landing at this time could present some problems," Fiona said.

"What's changed?" Beth asked.

"We have been seen and reported. My sensors have detected supersonic aircraft approaching from the north on a bearing directly toward us."

"Okay, get us outta here and then see if you can find someplace else we can land and offload this little turd."

Fiona shot skyward six thousand feet, then southwest fifty miles, and dropped down to a few feet above the ground in about five seconds. Although the trip was a blur to Beth, she was keenly aware that Fiona had brought them down into the heart of urban Detroit. From what Beth could see, they were in the courtyard of a horseshoe-shaped building with a collapsed corner. The black streaks of soot above the structure's open doors and windows testified to its derelict and abandoned state.

"Jesus, Fiona! We're in the middle of Detroit. Couldn't you find someplace a little more discreet?" Beth cried.

"This area was the center of civil unrest several years ago. It is currently uninhabited and in close proximity to heavily populated areas. This meets the conditions you specified earlier," Fiona said, sounding irritated. "Clarify the parameters for a landing site that will satisfy your expectations, and I will look for something more suitable."

Contrails from military fighter planes dispatched from Wurtsmith Air Force Base appeared in the sky overhead, then curved away and disappeared to the west. Fiona had parked in the shadow of the building in full stealth mode. Beth realized that for them to be discovered, someone would have to literally bump into them.

"Sorry, you're doing great. How close are the nearest people?" she said.

"There is a group of humans engaged in construction activities across the street two buildings east of our location."

"Good. Now tell me again that you can bring me back right here, to this spot, fifteen minutes from the time we leave, no matter how long we are gone," Beth said.

"Location and time coordinates verified. Both positive and negative time-distortion characteristics have been set and calibrated. Returning to this time and place within fifteen minutes of departure will not pose any difficulty."

When Beth and little Dade descended the stairs beneath Fiona's bomb bay, the first thing Beth noticed was the thick smell of mold, mildew, and decay wafting through the ruins around them. She stepped down onto the shattered glass and broken bricks that littered the ground, then carried little Dade through the rubble and shadows between the buildings to get to the street. She could hear hammering and followed the noise to the intersection. A shiny black pickup truck with a lumber rack parked on the corner appeared in stark contrast to the burned-out shell of the automobile behind it. She walked little Dade to the burned-out building on the corner across the street from the construction site and set him down on the bottom step.

"You wait here, right here," Beth said, pointing at the steps. "In fifteen minutes, your mommy is going to come get you. Do you understand?"

The little boy looked at her impassively. Beth headed back to Fiona and looked back one last time before ducking between the buildings. The little boy sat and watched until she disappeared from sight, then he closed his eyes and called to his mother. He didn't like being without her, and he hated being alone even more.

A tall man wearing coveralls and a yellow hard hat crossed the street to the pickup truck and tossed his hat and bag of tools into the back. The noise startled the little boy and he jumped. The movement caught the man's attention and he looked at the little boy wearing a bright red jacket sitting on the step. He waved and the little boy waved back. The man gave the boy a puzzled look before he drove away.

Fifteen minutes came and went, and for the next sixteen days traveling at maximum hyper-light speeds Beth could not stop thinking about the little boy she left behind. She kept telling herself that he would be safer there than where she was going. Then, there was the theoretical stuff Fiona brought up while they were underway. If she were successful, and managed to alter the past, would he or she cease to exist, or would they become phantoms of a future that never happens? The possibilities bothered her, and her confidence began to waiver.

"Course and speed matched," Fiona announced on the morning of the seventeenth day. "Preparing to commence time shift."

"Wait," Beth said. For days she had been fighting an inner battle, trying to decide if this was the best course of action. She had considered all the possibilities, even intercepting and destroying the Kahshinki transport that had abducted her. Everything pointed back to this moment as the one that would have the greatest probability for changing everything. Still, she couldn't shake the feeling that this would be the biggest mistake she had ever made.

Okay, Beth, she thought, *it's time to make a hard choice, the kind that can get people killed. Dade was right, I'm not very good at making tough decisions.*

"Yeah, do it, let's go," Beth said.

The cabin lights dimmed as Fiona initiated the time shift, and a moment later, the Korlah spacecraft carrier appeared ahead of them, intact and undamaged. Fiona maneuvered closer and Beth prepared to warn the carrier about the impending Kahshinki attack. She was just about to send the message when a flash of light lit the cabin. A moment later, Fiona was rocked by a shock wave and a cloud of debris and gasses began pouring from one of the carrier's engines.

"They are dropping out of hyper-light. I am matching speed," Fiona said.

"What the hell happened?" Beth cried.

"We are too late. We have arrived too close to the time of the attack. I can adjust my calculations, but I will need to recharge my power cells."

Fiona's threat alarm sounded as a line of Korlah light fighters dropped out of hyper-light right in front of her. The lead ship plowed directly into her hull, collapsing both ships' magnetic fields; Fiona's right winglet was torn off and the Korlah fighter broke into three pieces. When Fiona fell out of stealth mode and seemed to appear out of nowhere, the rest of the Korlah fighters opened fire. Her engines exploded and Beth was ejected in the cockpit pod. Amidst the deafening roar of the ejection rocket, in the fraction of a second before she was jettisoned from the fatally wounded ship, Beth was certain she heard Fiona scream.

29 - Reckoning

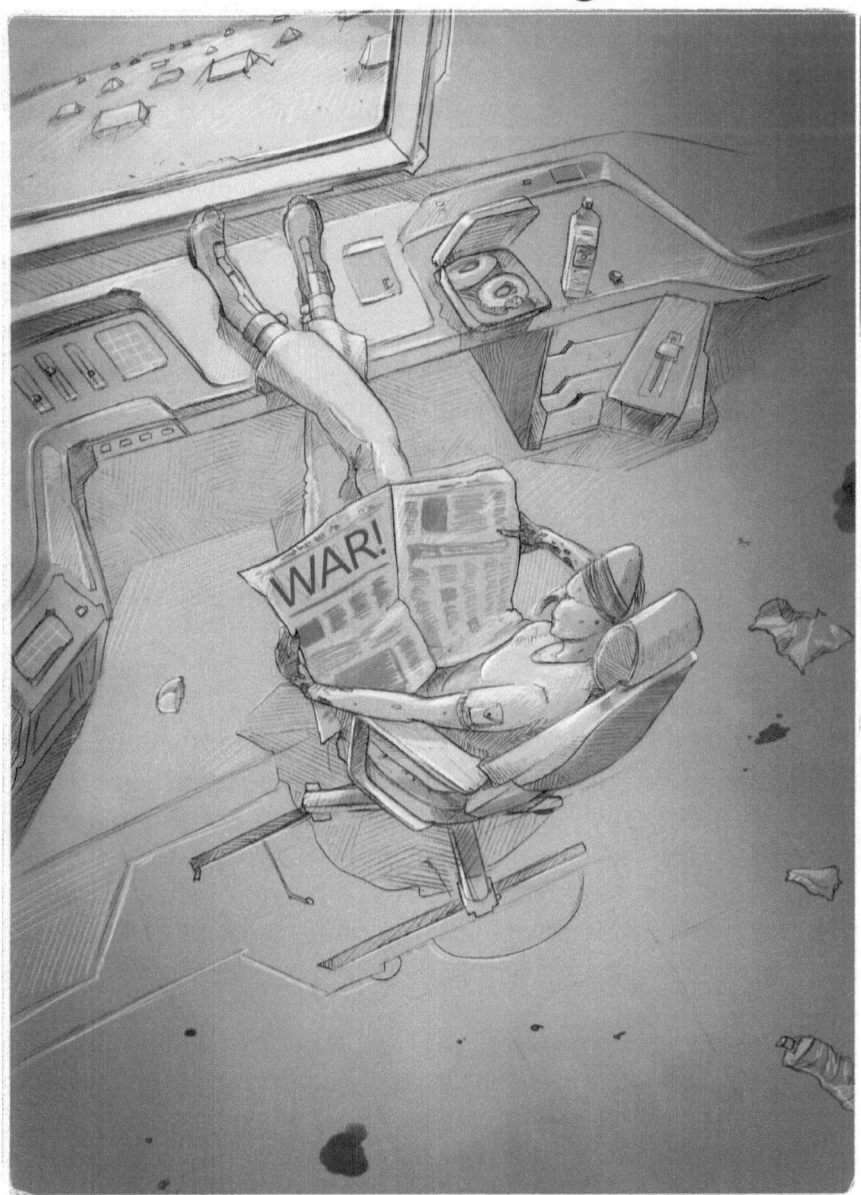

The devastating Kahshinki attack of Earth changed everything in an instant. Humanity was no longer focused on preparation. As they say, that ship had sailed. Revenge and retaliation were whispered and shouted about on Earth and beyond, but behind the bravado was the cowering insecurity felt by all who knew in their hearts that the human race had dropped a few notches down the galactic food chain. Using the planetoid Eris as a staging area, three enemy spacecraft carriers had entered the solar system from the far side of the sun and caught Earth with its pants down. During the six days of intense fighting that followed the initial attack, Earth's defense forces all but destroyed one Kahshinki carrier, and they sent another one limping away. The third carrier was holding its own and supporting enemy clone troops that had landed on Earth.

Technology once again had become the game-changer. The enemy ships now had pulse-absorption capabilities. The only factors that prevented an out-and-out rout were that some of the UNE fighters were equipped with missiles, and a single special-purpose ship was loaded with a pair of top-secret torpedoes designed to destroy spacecraft carriers. The problem was implementation; only a fraction of the UNE fleet had missiles. But by pure luck, the torpedo ship was deployed for testing at the time of the attack, and therefore avoided destruction. That ship changed the entire outcome of the attack when it destroyed the first Kahshinki carrier, but in the fight to stop the other two, more than two thousand UNE fighters and six thousand crewmen were lost.

The Kahshinki attack on Earth was expertly planned, coordinated, and executed. Within minutes of crushing the few hundred ships left to defend Earth, every facility belonging to the standing members of the UNE was reduced to burning rubble, including the weapons facility that had developed the carrier-killing torpedoes.

Like every other station, ship, and habitable hole in the solar system, Crossroads was soon packed with refugees from Earth, including the merchants and space truckers who either could not or would not return while the fighting continued.

Although Tiffany wasn't fleeing the conflict, after she left the Church of Shawlmon she felt as much a refugee as anyone else. She went to the back door of Eddie's tattoo parlor and punched in the combination from memory. It had been all too easy to get the young owner to take her back to his apartment and even easier to get the combination when he opened the door.

She roamed Eddie's small apartment for nearly an hour, inspecting his personal effects one at a time. Exhausted from traveling and drained from the realization that Rebecca had been manipulating her for years, Tiffany lay down on Eddie's unmade bed and burrowed her face in his pillow, inhaling his scent, a scent so much like Jimmie's. She used the pillow to soak up the tears that followed. When she heard something, she tossed the pillow aside and sat up and rubbed her eyes with the palms of her hands.

"I've been looking for you," a man's voice said.

Tiffany dropped from the bed, rolled, and came to her feet with her pistol pointed at the head of the shadowy figure standing in the doorway. The man didn't move. When Tiffany didn't fire the gun, he slowly and deliberately closed the door and turned on the overhead light.

"Eddie... I... "

"Don't... don't say anything," Eddie said. He put his suitcase down and walked slowly toward her.

Suddenly aware that she was still pointing her gun at him, she lowered it and returned it to the holster at the small of her back.

"I've been everywhere looking for you," Eddie said. "Violet Gibson doesn't exist. Yet everywhere the person using that name has been, people have died... Who are you?"

"Eddie, please let me explain," Tiffany said, looking away from his accusing glare.

"Wait, wait, stop," Eddie said, rubbing his face. "I promised myself that if I found you, I would just ask one you one question. I never thought you'd come back, and until just now I thought I'd never see you again." He took a deep breath and let it out. "Just listen... there was a moment when I was sure you were gonna kill me. I don't know why you would want to do that, but I was pretty sure I was about to die. Something changed your mind. I think I know what it was. I saw it in your eyes, and I know it was that same something I felt in my heart the minute I laid eyes on you. So I been traveling all over the system to ask you this, Violet... or whatever your name is... and understand, I don't care what your real name is, and I don't care what you've done. I just want to know one thing: do you believe in love at first sight?"

She looked up and straight into his eyes, and said, "My real name is Tiffany Steiner, and yes, I do."

The East Coast of the United States caught the first wave of the attack. Military sites, power stations and the industrial centers of every major city east of the Mississippi were either destroyed or neutralized. However, before the second wave could be launched, USA ground and space forces managed to rally and stop the enemy from advancing west. With their last spacecraft carrier now in high synchronous orbit above the East Coast, the Kahshinki were taking full advantage of air superiority within the occupied territories of Earth. Using this freedom and working with their ground forces, Kahshinki factory ships began to collect and process the refugees fleeing the burning cities.

McClellen finished reading the official report on the death of President McCormick, the demise of Washington, DC, and the names of the critical government and military personnel who were believed to be there at the time of the attack. After setting the document aside, he reflected on the days of chaos between the annihilation of the government and the determination that he was next in the line of succession. He'd been sworn in only a few hours before, but the weight of responsibility for the welfare of the country already sat heavily on his shoulders.

"Excuse me, Mr. President, a courier just arrived with some information about Agent Bethany Porter," his aide said. McClellen grimaced.

"Send them in," he said.

He recognized the courier as a CIA operative he worked with during the transition into his position as secretary of Homeland Security. The man's black suit was dusty and wore the creases of numerous days' use. Unshaven with tousled hair, he was a far cry from the well groomed and pretentious agent McClellen remembered.

"Good afternoon, Mr. President. I am—"

"Agent Roberts, yes, I remember you," McClellen said. "What do you have for me?"

"Sir, you are aware Ms. Porter had taken a Korlah body shortly before she disappeared?"

"Yes... I am aware. And as I recall, she didn't disappear; she was attacked and killed by spacecraft sent by government forces under my command. The Church of Shawlmon provided a detailed report before issuing a bounty for my death. Yes! I am aware," McClellen snapped back.

"Mr. President, no bodies or wreckage were ever recovered. The area was scrubbed by the best salvage teams in the system. We don't think her ship was destroyed," the courier said.

"Beth is alive?" McClellan asked. "And the child?"

"No, sir. Let me explain. The ship she was flying was stolen from a covert Quorum facility being run by Richard Parkhurst right under General Ramsey's nose. It was a prototype interceptor that employed a new and untested propulsion system based on archaic alien technology that we believe predates both the Korlah and Kahshinki. Our analysts say they have good reason to believe it was not a propulsion system at all. Initial computer diagnostics of the schematics were improperly interpreted. Recent evaluations using our new bio-based computers indicate it was a device that provides the means to manipulate time."

"What? Are you suggesting it was capable of time travel?"

"The results were initially dismissed as conceptual probabilities developed by the computer as a result of incomplete information. Then... we searched the records for sightings of a vessel matching the description of the Parkhurst prototype. We got three positive hits. One sighting was by an Apollo astronaut in space over the Hawaiian Islands, and another sighting the same day occurred over Detroit, Michigan. Those sightings happened over fifty years ago. The third sighting came from historical records of the Korlah spacecraft carrier. We didn't make the connection to Bethany Porter until we compared Erin Marshall's research notes on the Korlah war crime accusations to Captain Ramsey's debrief. Ms. Marshall's team mentioned an interrogation of a Korlah duplicate, one that had the mind and memories of a human. This crover was taken prisoner when the ship she was flying—one that matches the description of the prototype—was destroyed. This happened just after the Quorum-sponsored attack of the Korlah campaign vessel nearly seventy Earth-years ago. The description of her ship included shark teeth painted on the front of the fuselage. This is the same prisoner Ramsey spoke of in his debrief. He said the Korlah spoke English and claimed to be a sergeant major in the United States Marine Corps. The Korlah translations of the interrogation indicate that the crover told them she came from the future to warn them of the attack. She went on to describe how she had been abducted and returned to Earth. Sir, it was in Korlah, but as translations go, what she told them matched Bethany Porter's debrief exactly."

President McClellen picked up a pen and clicked it a dozen times before flipping open a note pad and jotting down some notes.

"Don't go anywhere," McClellen said. "Ronald!" he shouted.

"Yes, sir," his aide replied from the doorway.

"I want everyone in the war room in thirty minutes," McClellen said, still jotting notes on his pad.

The "everyone" he spoke of was what was left of the nation's military leadership and represented the Joint Chiefs of Staff. It was with their advice and support that McClellen was directing the remnants of the military in a desperate struggle against a ruthless and determined enemy.

In the close confines of the bunker, it wasn't hard to get everyone together in thirty minutes. McClellen had Agent Roberts present the information and field the questions that followed. A substantial amount of time was spent debating whether the evidence was coincidental and not factual. With resources stripped to the bone, providing the support McClellen wanted was going to be painful, and few of those present seemed convinced that making this a priority was the right choice. McClellen eventually made it a mandate and waited for challenges. When none came, he summed up his primary directive in a few sentences.

"When the history of the galactic war being fought over this planet is finally written it will be by those of us who manage to survive. What final version of the future comes to pass will determine who will select the words that describe humankind's greatest victory, or ultimate demise. We are in a struggle to preserve the very existence of our species. Therefore, without exception, we shall use every resource at our disposal to build another one of these ships. For I firmly believe, that if we cannot change the past, there is no hope for the future."

In the cockpit of the armored transport she'd dubbed the Ms. Porter, Teela frowned. The sun had begun to crest the horizon ahead of her, appearing as a sliver of yellow-orange beneath the gray pall of smoke over Minneapolis and creating a semblance of twilight that would last well into the morning. Soon the cover of darkness that provided the edge she needed would be gone. Once again, she promised herself this would be the last run; just one more, and then she would rest.

The Ms. Porter hugged the terrain as Teela raced toward the flashing battlefront. Most of the Kahshinki fighters would be at high altitudes providing cover for their factory ships, transports, and human clone soldiers on the ground.

Minneapolis was burning, but the enemy's purpose was not to destroy the city; it was merely a technique they used to drive the populace into the open to facilitate collection. As Teela approached from the west, the city skyline came into view. The roofs of most of the skyscrapers were on fire and many of the buildings were engulfed in flames. The bulky factory ships circled over the city like vultures, waiting to collect the bounty of flesh fleeing the city. The Kahshinki and their machines had to be fed, and this was the harvest the Korlah had foretold.

The ring of fire had spread since Teela's last visit, crossing the Mississippi and stretching into the suburbs. The edges would be her best chance for saving lives, so that was where she went. There was no shortage of enemy targets, and in a few seconds she made her choice.

"Dead ahead," she said. "The factory ship over the clearing on the far side of the woods. See it?"

"Yes, targeting now," her ship's computer-generated voice replied.

"Drop me at the edge of the woods; there should be people hiding there. Take that bastard down and get back to me ASAP. Listen, Beth, they were on us pretty fast last time. Watch out for fighter support and... be careful."

"Yes, Teela, I will maintain full stealth and scan for threats," the computer replied.

The transport banked hard to the right and dropped down to the ground near the edge of the forest. Sword in hand, Teela was out of the cockpit hatch in an instant. The Ms. Porter was away before her feet hit the ground. Even though the thick smoke produced a dim twilight, the visual distortions created by the ship's photo-cell camouflage made it possible for Teela to trace her flight toward the Kahshinki factory ship.

Damn! If I can see her, they can see her, Teela thought, thinking that this last run may not have been such a good idea after all. Then a tongue of light shot out of the Ms. Porter into the engines of the blocky, blunt-winged factory ship, and her next shot took out the gravity plates in its right wing. Large and slow to respond, the ship rolled to the right and careened into the highway a few hundred feet away.

The familiar electronic hum of an energized pulse weapon shifted Teela's attention away from the crashing factory ship not a second too soon, and she saw two clone soldiers emerge from the forest. These were not the light infantry the Kahshinki used for collections, but fully armored heavy infantry, each with a shoulder-mounted cannon. The instant they saw Teela, they opened fire. Her sword absorbed the energy, overloaded, and instantly discharged it, throwing Teela to the ground. The brush around her and branches overhead burst into flames. If the soldiers had any idea that Teela was going to get back up, they probably would have fired a second time. Those few seconds gave her just enough time to get up, aim her sword, plant her feet firmly, and brace for what she knew would come next.

The combined energy of two pulse cannons adjusted for maximum output and sharp focus hit the tip of Teela's sword, which absorbed as much of the energy as it could before sending it back where it came from. The recoil forced Teela back and her feet plowed ruts into the soft black dirt. Although disoriented by the blast, the soldiers were still standing. Teela charged forward and closed the distance between them in four strides. As the lead soldier brought her weapon to bear, Teela separated its helmeted head from its torso with a sweeping blow of her sword. A thick stream of blood sprayed into the air from the stump of its neck. Spinning with momentum, she drove the tip of her blade through the other soldier's breastplate and out her back with both hands and all her weight. The warrior convulsed for a few seconds and then became motionless, her suit holding her upright. Teela had to use both hands and a foot to yank the sword free. She paused and listened; she could hear children crying.

With her back to the clearing she looked down the wide path into the forest the warriors had emerged from. In the distance she could make out a crowd, bunched up and filling the path as far back into the shadows as she could see.

"Beth, where are you?" Teela said into her microphone.

"On approach," her ship replied through the speakers in Teela's helmet.

"Land as close to my current position as you can. Open the cargo doors and watch out for armored infantry. I about got my ass kicked," Teela said.

"Landing now," Beth said. As the transport dropped to the ground next to Teela, its stealth camouflage faded and a large door on its side opened. The hull of the transport was a dull gray, with the exception of the name "Ms. Porter" and an amazingly realistic illustration of Beth in a boxing stance just below the cockpit window.

When Teela trotted into the shadows, several children started screaming and the crowd drew back. She slowed to a walk, sheathed her sword, and raised her hands. In the dim light she could see children and a few adults, mostly women. Screening the torrent of emotions radiating from the terrified minds, Teela realized that she was looking at a group of grade-school children and their teachers.

"I'm a friend," Teela said. "I am here to take you to a safe place. I have room for about a hundred people. Please hurry, we don't have much time."

"They're coming!" someone screamed. Flashes of light behind the crowd provided enough illumination that Teela could see hundreds of children bunched together; this was an entire school. Making a choice, a young lady near the front of the crowd began pushing children forward.

"Go, go! Get on the bus, children. It's okay. This is one of the good ones. She's here to help," the young woman said as she ushered the children by.

More flashes were followed by screams of panic, and the crowd surged forward in a mad rush for the transport. Teela knew there was no possible way she could take them all. After the last child had gone by she stood in the path and listened.

The enemy made no effort at stealth as they plowed through the trees firing their weapons. She put an explosive armor-piercing bullet through the visor of the first warrior she saw and killed three more before the enemy took cover in the trees, as she knew they would.

When Teela was a child, not much older than these children, she read her first battle report in the archives of the Korlah spacecraft carrier she called home. She spent her childhood reading all the stories she could get her hands on, and she knew them well. At the time, they were just interesting, exciting adventures that allowed her to escape the drudgery of her life as a damaged birthing unit, but today they gave her an advantage: she knew the Kahshinki would fall back when faced with an enemy of unknown strength. Teela ran for her transport, praying that the children would not need more than five minutes to board. To her amazement, nearly everyone was already inside. Fewer than fifty still crowded around the hatch, mostly adult men and women and older children. It was obvious that the ship was filled beyond capacity.

"Continue west. Stay under the trees, stay out of open areas," Teela shouted to the people on the ground. "I'll be back tonight."

She dodged the panicky mob around the cargo hatch and climbed into cockpit, quickly closing the hatch behind her.

The scene in the cargo bay was chaotic. Older children and few adults were carrying smaller children on their shoulders, and every square inch was packed solid. Teela estimated there were four to five hundred children crammed into the twelve-by-thirty-foot space. She looked at the small cockpit, which suddenly looked luxuriously roomy. In an instant she made her decision.

"Beth, disable all manual controls. Take off as soon as you can close the hatch," Teela said. She opened the access door to the cockpit and began pulling children in. She stacked six on the control panel, put two in the suit locker, and let the rest of the area be filled by as many as could cram their way in.

"Enemy craft inbound. They are targeting our location," Beth announced.

"Take off, full stealth, evasive maneuvers," Teela shouted.

"Personnel are blocking the hatch," Beth said.

"Take off, then close the hatch. Do it now," Teela said.

Pressed into the front starboard corner of the cockpit, Teela faced aft and watched as the last few people hoping to board the transport fell away as it lifted off. One young woman with a child clinging to her neck hung on for as long as she could, but when they were several hundred feet in the air the hatch closed and she was forced to let go. Screaming as she fell, her face a mask of terror, eyes wide, arms flailing, she and the child disappeared into the haze below. Teela closed her eyes too late to block the image from burning into her memory.

Within a minute the computer had set the course and executed a momentary sub-light jump; a fraction of a second later, they appeared in the sky near the Rapid City regional spaceport. Threat monitors immediately began alarming as military units on the ground and in the air locked weapons on them. By now, both for Teela and those at the airfield, this was routine.

"Ground control, this is private transport Ms. Porter, requesting permission to land," Teela shouted over the screaming and crying children.

"Permission granted. Follow the escort to the landing site."

Teela was directed to the same field south of the terminal and just off the parking lot where she had brought every load of refugees for the last three days. Since that first visit, the area had changed dramatically; with each visit the camp's population increased by more than a hundred. The sea of tents expanded with every delivery and had become a small city of more than ten thousand people.

A few volunteers at the Red Cross tent near the parking lot was still processing the group Teela delivered thirty minutes earlier when her transport touched down again. The cargo hatch opened and the wails of the frightened children echoed through the camp, and within minutes, several hundred people had rushed to help. Parents called their missing children's names desperately, hoping for a miracle. Teela's dark mood lifted when not just one child found a parent, but six families were reunited before her eyes. The hugs, handshakes, and well-wishing lasted for several hours.

Although she was hungry, Teela veered away from the camp kitchen. She knew the outpouring of gratitude would overwhelm her with guilt. She had not always been received warmly by these people, most of whom had never seen a Korlah in person before. Her first visit to the spaceport had been met with suspicion and open contempt. Refusing to surrender the Ms. Porter to military personnel, she'd ignored threats that she would be fired upon and left, only to return in less than an hour with another load of refugees. The cycle of departures and returns had continued until her stubborn persistence was gratefully accepted. She kept her distance from others as much as possible, feigning a poor understanding of English as much to hide the fact that she was a crover as to avoid conversations. She believed that if the humans knew why she was compelled to do this, they would despise her.

So instead of getting a warm meal, she stopped off at the payment barrel, a black steel drum on which she had painted *Leave whatever you can spare or take whatever you need.* It was filled to the point of overflowing with jewelry, cash, coins, and food; donations from grateful refugees. Digging through the barrel, she selected a bottle of water, a box of chocolate-covered donuts, and a crumpled newspaper. When she got back to the Ms. Porter, the crowds and children were gone. With exception of fresh vomit and urine, the cargo bay was empty. Teela closed the hatch and settled into the cockpit with plans to eat, drink, and if her conscience would let her, get some much-needed rest. Leaning back in the pilot's chair, she smoothed out the paper with her blood-spattered hands. She stuffed a donut into her mouth and washed it down with a slug of water.

The *Minneapolis Blade Tribune* had one word in large bold print that covered half the page: *WAR!* The article below reported that the chairman of the UNE had officially declared war on the alien aggressors. Teela stuffed the last donut in her mouth, crumpled the paper up, and threw it to the floor with the empty donut box, then reclined the chair as far as she could and closed her eyes. The image of the falling woman and child came back to haunt her, as she knew it would. The more she fought it, the more intense it became, until she finally gave up on the concept of rest.

"Okay, so we won't be getting any sleep today. You have something you want to do. I can sense that, what is it?" Dade asked.

"Go back," Teela said, giving him a glimpse of her thoughts.

"To where they fell? They're dead. You got to realize that," Dade said.

"What is it you always say? Oh, yes: the proof is in the food," Teela said.

"No, it's pudding. The proof is in the pudding. Damn it, Teela, why? What can we possibly hope to accomplish?"

"Your words. You tell me that I cannot succeed if I fail to try."

"And what exactly is it we will be trying to succeed at?"

"Saving lives."

Howard Lewis

30 - Moebius

The cold wind burned little Dade's ears. He covered them with his hands, but that only seemed to make them ache even more. Dust and dirt blew into his eyes and tears streaked his muddy face, sapping what little warmth remained until his cheeks were numb. He looked at the empty buildings around him for someone, anyone, so he wouldn't feel so alone. The dark, broken windows seemed to look down on him with malicious intent.

The woman had told him to wait on the step; she told him that his mommy would come. He had waited before, but this was longer than any other time. Hunger and thirst would have eventually driven him to disobey her and try to find his way home, but now, as the dark shadows grew longer, the ache of hunger was forgotten, replaced by a chilling fear of the dark empty street.

He turned and looked up the steps at the brick building. It looked like one he remembered, like a place he had lived before. He ran up the entry stairs and down the long, dark hall to the stairway at the back. Light shone down from above, casting the bent and rusted handrails in silhouette. He climbed toward the light, up and up, dodging the debris that cluttered the stairs. The light, he realized, was coming from the open hole where the stairs ended on the roof amid the crumbled remains of a cupola.

Terrified and alone, he watched the last sliver of sun disappear, and with it, any hope of finding his mother. The glow of the city reflected off the clouds enough to cast a pale light on the roof. Faced with descending the dark stairs, he chose to wait on the roof until the sun returned. There, in the dim light of the cold windy roof, he waited. Something deep within, something like the cold that gnawed at his ears, gnawed at his heart and devoured what little hope he had of finding his mother. Her voice had always been there, reassuring him when he was frightened, but now there was only silence. He lay down and curled into the fetal position, pulling his coat over his head. As he lay there shivering, he listened for his mother's voice. All he heard was the beating of his own heart.

Will Rutledge parked in front of the construction site. The gate of the eight-foot chain-link fence that surrounded the lot was chained shut and there was no sign yet of the construction crew he planned to interview. He poured coffee into the cap of his thermos and cracked a window. The new building stood in stark contrast to the line of burned-out structures that stretched as far as he could see in the cold morning mist. As a freelance reporter, he knew that another article on urban renewal in the wake of the riots would be about as marketable as an obituary, but unless something fell into his lap, this would have to do. He checked his camera; he had a few pictures left on the roll. He scanned the street and planned his shots. The sign in front of the renovation project that identified this as a black-owned business, with the crew standing around it if they were willing to pose for him. Maybe a shot that showed the new building with the burned-out neighborhood in the background.

By 7:05 the gate was open and more than a half dozen men were busy setting up for the day's activities. Will slung his camera over his shoulder and climbed out of his car into the crisp morning air. One of the workers, a tall man in his early thirties, was attempting to start a portable generator. The starter groaned slower and slower until the battery was dead.

"Rudy, we gonna need to jump this bitch again," he shouted. He saw Will walking up with a camera and notepad and gave him a nod. "We got another news man here." He gave Will a toothy grin. "You gonna put my pitcher in da paper?"

"That's a possibility," Will said with a smile. "What I'd really like is a picture of the whole crew around the project sign. Something that… "

The tall man stopped grinning and his eyes grew wide. He was looking up and over Will's shoulder. Will turned around to see what he was looking at.

By the time a dash of color among the drab ruins of the building across the street grabbed his attention, the tall man was already through the gate and across the street, his yellow hard hat off.

"Get down off there, boy! Get down!" he shouted, waving his arms and hat frantically. The other workers put down their tools and ran to see what was happening.

Will had his camera up to adjust the zoom and focus. The mist in the air between them made the little boy's pale white face and blood-red jacket seem to glow as a beam of light breached the clouds. The boy raised his arms and began flapping like a bird, slowly at first, and then frantically. The child exhaled and the vapor from his breath was whipped away by the wind. Will snapped a picture just as the boy leaned forward, and a chorus of shouts rose from the construction workers. At first, Will thought he saw glitter on the boy's hair and face. His blue lips parted just as he plunged downward.

"Damn! That's a front page picture," Will exclaimed. He cranked the camera's film advance and ran toward the cloud of dust rising from a pile of twisted rebar and broken bricks where the boy had fallen. The workers plowed into the pile, pulling boards and rotting plaster out of the way. By the time Will arrived they had opened a path and formed a ring around the twisted little body. *Two more frames, gotta make this count.*

"Get some help!" the crew foreman shouted at him. Will snapped the camera and captured the man's anguished expression, as well the five black construction workers who had fought to clear the wreckage away from the broken body of the little white boy. The child's left arm and leg were clearly broken and the left side of his head was covered in blood. The tall man took his fleece-lined work coat off and laid it on the rubble next to the boy. As gently as his large hands could manage, he lifted the boy and rolled him over into the warm coat. Blue lips matched the pale blue eyes that stared blankly past the crowd of faces looking down at him.

"He dead?" one of the men asked.

"I ain't no doctor; he sure does look dead. God damn, this boy is white. What's a white boy doing here, anyway?" the tall man said.

Will focused on the boy's face. The tall man pressed a handkerchief on a gash near the boy's left eye. The boy blinked, focused on the tall man, and smiled.

"He's alive! Roy, find a phone and call an ambulance," the foreman shouted.

"Look, the kid's got icicles in his hair. Shit, he's about froze. Frostbit bad, probably gonna lose them ears an' maybe his nose... probly," one of the workers said.

Will made sure the ice in the boy's hair was in sharp focus when he took his last picture. "Rimes, those are ice rimes," he said.

300

He swung the camera out of his way and began jotting notes. "Probably suffering from hypothermia. Likely why he jumped; he was delirious and thought he could fly."

"Yeah, I remember hearing a story like that when I was a kid," the tall man said. "A man and his boy made wings with feathers. I tried it with cardboard, 'bout broke my leg jumping off the garage."

"The story of Daedalus and Icarus," Will said. "Daedalus flew to safety and Icarus crashed and drowned." He continued jotting notes, recording the workers' comments along with his own thoughts.

Before the ambulance had the boy loaded and on his way to the hospital, Will was on the phone pitching his story to the newspapers. Although it didn't make front page as he hoped, it was picked up by *Detroit Free Press* as a human interest story. That article ended up in the police report and medical records used by the state of Michigan to create the abandoned child's record of birth. Amused by the article about the frozen child who tried to fly, state administrators determined the date of birth as approximate, last name Rimes, first name Daedalus, no middle name.

The Beginning

Glossary of Humans

Barry, Ex-Navy Seal working as an enforcer for Richard Parkhurst, the self-appointed leader of an organization known as the Quorrum.

Clarke, Marsha. Abducted: musician, drums, member of the band Metal Maidens. Returned to Seattle Washington where she is attempting to make a living playing music with Catherine Purcell.

Cooper, Richard. United States Secret Service, assigned to oversee the relocation and protection of Julie Rimes.

Denster. Privateer and smuggler, Industrial technician crewing for Ludwig Von Hammer.

Eddie. Miner who operates a successful tattoo shop called 'Eddie's Place' on Systems Mining Base Seven, aka Crossroads.

Hargrave, Justin. General USMC Expeditionary Forces.

Jacks, Bill. Abducted; security guard at Mill Valley Industrial Center; Central California. Damage to his face was repaired using the tissue from Dade Rimes. Contracted to a Korlah collective that deals in medical supplies and the construction of spacecraft for both the military and private sectors.

Johnson, Chris. Prior member of the Central Intelligence Agency, and associate of Bethany Porter. Hired by the Secretary of Homeland Security to eliminate threats to national security.

Masters, Tim. aka Ludwig Von Hammer, Privateer and smuggler who supplies contraband items such as alcohol and tobacco throughout the system.

Marshall, Erin. PhD Xenobiology. Research analyst and consultant for the United States government currently working aboard the spacecraft carrier to research and document the history of the Korlah people.

McCabe, Rebecca. Abducted; self-described missionary of the Christian faith. Assimilated by a Korlah priest known as the

Oracle. Has extensive telepathic powers that she is using to create a militant theocracy intent on ruling the Earth and known galaxy.

McClellen, James, a once rogue US Army General, now Secretary of Homeland Security, appointed by President.

McCormick, William P. President Elect of the United States.

Moore, Ann. Abducted; day care center manager; Northern California, left on the American asteroid base AB1. Currently providing an administrative and managerial role for the human clones who survived the Korlah attack.

Parkhurst, Richard. Self-appointed leader of the Quorum, now in hiding and attempting to restore the power and influence of the outlawed organization.

Porter, Bethany. Abducted; ex-Marine, undercover federal agent who suffered a gunshot wound to the head in a confrontation with Rebecca McCabe.

Purcell, Catherine. Abducted; musician, bass guitar, member of the band Metal Maidens. Returned to Seattle Washington where she is attempting to make a living playing music with Marsha Clarke.

Ramsey, Jason. Brigadier General, United Nations of Earth, assigned to manage the mid-system defense forces from the American asteroid outpost where he started his space career as a fighter pilot.

Rimes, Daedalus. Deceased; maintenance supervisor from Mill Valley Industrial Center; California, USA. Participant of the first known memory transfer to Korlah host known as TEEela20.10127.

Rimes, Julie. Wife of Daedalus. Relocated under the Federal witness protection program at the request of President McCormick after an attempt on her life by Rebecca McCabe.

Santos, Crystal. Deceased; musician, vocals and lead guitar, member of the band Metal Maidens. Killed in a Korlah fight known as a spectacle, given the warrior designation Crystaugh by the Korlah to honor her fearless courage.

Smiley. Privateer and smuggler, First Mate to Ludwig Von Hammer.

Steiner, Tiffany. Abducted; student at USC, performing arts major. Recruited by Rebecca McCabe to serve the Church of Shawlmon as the archangel of revenge.

Von Hammer, Ludwig. aka Tim Masters, Privateer and smuggler supplying contraband items such as alcohol and tobacco throughout the system.

Glossary of Korlah

Afron \'af-rän\ Deceased, Strategy Section leader of tactics and navigation. Missing and presumed dead following the revolution aboard the spacecraft carrier.

Challmara \'chäl-mä-rä\ Technical unit; Acting Director of the Arms Section, assigned to weapons maintenance, research, and development.

Neaugh \ nē-ä\ A young warrior working for Ruwaugh.

Rahfoon \'rä-fün\ Biological Technician; Health Section; controls a leading Korlah cooperative, that acquired Bill Jacks as their contracted male partner.

Ruwaugh \'rü-wä\ Warrior; Spectacle pugilist; archrival of Shawaugh; defeated by Bethany Porter and Crystal Santos during the fight in which Crystal Santos died.

Shawaugh \'shä-wä\ Warrior; Director of Campaign Warrior Forces; friend and protector of TEEla20.10127.

Shawlmon \'shòl-män\ Famous arbitrator and bladesman of ancient Korlah; Korlah legend states that Shawlmon will rise to defeat the Kahshinki in the final battle for those that cherish life and reject despair.

Shyron \shī-rän\ Potentate; Campaign Vessel Council leader; one of the original survivors of the Kahshinki holocaust; essence passed down from shell to shell for over one thousand cycles (Korlah years).

Teela \'tē-el-ə\ TEEla20.10127; T series, Group E, Ela clan, generation 20, unit 10127, birthing unit damaged during Kahshinki attack, designated for reclamation;-reassigned to Health section for memory transfer experiment;- received the essence of Daedalus Rimes.

Glossary of Terms

afterdeath. 1. An existence after death. **2.** A later period following one's death.

birther. (derogatory). Birthing unit; usually taken to be offensive; genotype assigned duties of surrogate mother for clone embryo gestation.

bit. Measure of time; one three-thousandth of a Korlah planetary rotation; 100 bits = 1 set.

braddle. Small rodents similar to mice or rats, possessing a long snout and prehensile tail; food source of Korlah; prepared for consumption by removing fur and purging the digestive system; served live.

cease. 1. To cease existence; to die. **2: ceased.** Dead; without honor.

crown tendrils. Olfactory organs that project out in long strands from twelve patches around the crown of the Korlah skull. They swell with blood when the individual is agitated or in a state of heightened sensitivity.

cycle. Measure of time; one Korlah solar revolution.

duplicate. Of or relating to clones or groups of clones and clone genotypes.

Ganglicians. Name given to Kahshinki by humans, associated with the theory that they are individual neural beings, which are part of a collective organism.

grav-reflector. Gravitational reflection amplification generator; sublight form of propulsion. Also used with gravity reflection plates (grav-plates) for personnel, material and equipment handling devices.

hisnah. 1: Organ that provides a form of thermal vision. **2:** A series of pits located in the center of a Korlah face where the nose on humans would be.

hyperlight. Transit stream propulsion capable of achieving up to three hundred times the speed of light.

Kahshinki. 1: The race that enslaved the Korlah and is the current target of their quest for revenge. **2:** Blood-sucking parasite found in stagnant pools on the planet Korlah.

Pulse-rifle. A shouldered Korlah weapon that discharges an energy pulse.

reclamation. The act of being reclaimed; the collection and processing of organic materials for reuse.

Rouche Hah. 1: Warrior greeting or farewell; to my honor, to your honor. **2:** Battle cry to honor those who will cease.

rouk. Aquatic snakes. Food delicacy. Care must be taken to remove paralyzing slime that the creature exudes. Consumption produces a form of intoxication.

sabat. 1: Tattoolike marking of the face of all Korlah that is used for individual identification. Indicates the genotype, birth cycle, and production number. **2:** Stenciling or embroidered or embossed markings on Korlah uniforms and equipment to identify the individual wearing it, especially when it hides or obscures the facial marking.

scrum. 1: Scarab-like beetle that consumes decaying organic material. Used in reclamation digesters. **2:** Food source comprised of ground scrum beetles and grubs that is made into protein bars. **3:** Someone that is dirty and disgusting. **4:** Someone that is dishonorable.

scrum worm. Grub of the scrum beetle.

set. Measure of time. One-thirtieth of a Korlah planetary rotation; 10 sets = 1 shift

shell. The physical body without regard to the individual's essence. An individual is not considered to exist until they have been assigned rank and status.

shift. Measure of time. One-third of a Korlah planetary rotation; 1000 shifts = 1 cycle.

Spectacle. Pugilistic honor dispute involving unarmed combat, historically using only fangs and claws, nonlethal methods involve the use of riz.

tah. Loose-fitting floor-length gown or robe, usually worn without a belt. Standard apparel of the birthing units.

transfer. The act of moving the essence and memories of one individual into the mind of another.

wave compressors. Light speed propulsion devices used to gather and compress light into a stream of plasma energy.

Howard Lewis

Cover / Chapter Art
By Oliver Wetter

TEEla 20.10127
Commissioned Work 2012

Oliver Wetter aka Fantasio was born and raised in Trier.

Oliver passed an apprenticeship to become a painter and later studied at the arts-center IBKK in Bochum/Germany.

After graduating in Airbrush-design 2007 at the Arts Center IBKK in Bochum / Germany he has specialized in creating compelling book cover art, editorials & genre art, preferably character driven and portrait related.

Oliver has since worked for large publishing houses and enjoys collaborating directly with authors and other creative individuals. Oliver is published in magazines like Heavy Metal and ImagineFX, annual artbooks from Ballistic publishing & Ilex press, and in his spare time he runs a successful blog about art marketing.

Currently Fantasio fine Arts is located in Germany, but is virtually connected with international talent to collaborate on projects when required. Oliver is experienced with conducting working relationships via phone and email, his mother tongue is German but he speaks and writes English fluently.

He is a networker and creates worlds out of briefings, his solution oriented work attitude leads to great visual appeal.

His diverse body of work is the result of different demands and the conviction that boredom hardly leads to remarkable results.

Visit Oliver Wetter's Web site: http://fantasio.info